Legacy-The Eternal Forest
Child of the Heathen Book Two

Lucia Carter Keates

ISBN: 978-1-62420-410-4

Credits
Cover Design by Ms G
Editor: Sherry Derr-Wille

Dedication

To Elanie Keats, my fantastic mother whose love sustained me after I left home and went to live in Canada. She believed that God lived in everything.

To my friends and relatives who "couldn't wait" to read book two.

THE CREE

The male members of the tribe are of medium stature, well formed and
of pleasing countenance.
John Maclean—Native Tribes of Canada 1896

That is not dead, which can eternal lie and with strange eons, even death
may die.
H.P. Lovecraft

PREFACE

Shrouded in mystery, veiled in legend and mythology, the dark beauty of the Wapiti Hills harboured secrets beyond the imagination of most people. A world of depravity concealed in the blackest corners of the mind.

For one thousand years it had lain dormant, arising now and then to alert the good citizens of the town of Maskek that its raw and decadent power still rumbled beneath the beauty of mother Earth.

And now it was growing, pulsating and tired of waiting. Expanding and spreading its heinous tentacles ever upward. Soon it must spew out the gnawing bestial ache within its distended bowels and within its cold heart.

CHAPTER ONE

Previously in Book one:
Talulah Bearhead's village; Loon Lake, December, 1968

Inside the sweat lodge the entity within Deacon's body was stirring, the steaming heat beginning to loosen the grip Arcus held over the youth. It was becoming increasingly uncomfortable for the demon to remain encased in Deacon's form. It thrashed about, tossing the borrowed body from side to side, its hold weakening as the temperature began to climb.

Drawing strength from the medicine power contained within the beaded necklace, Deacon Spirit of the Wind asked the Great Spirit for courage and endurance to deliver him safely from his steaming tomb.

The energy force within the necklace was growing and expanding until it began to vibrate around him and around the lodge.

As eyes riveted on the sweat lodge, Doctor Jeremy Lodge quietly prayed.

~ * ~

Up on Bittern Creek, Damien Drew pulled the heavy robe around his shoulders, his blue eyes as icy as the waters below. He guided the apprehensive youth through a tunnel of grasping branches.

"Do not fear, my friend. Have I not promised you everything you desire?"

For a moment Damien paused, his thoughts on the young Cree Indian he'd first met over two hundred years ago. When he looked up his eyes were moist with tears.

~ * ~

Within the circle of death beneath the charred and upturned crosses a tortured lament fractured the frigid air.

CHAPTER TWO

1940 Cranmore Clinic, Edmonton Alberta Canada

"Your wife is still in labour, Mr. Brewster," Doctor Bradshaw was telling him, "She's quite a bit older than the usual women who come here. Pregnancy is hard on a woman of thirty-five. I'm astonished she made it this far. She's well under weight, has she been eating?"

"Yes, she says she's eating for two but I don't know where it goes, she just keeps getting thinner. Doc, how can she be in labour it's only been four months. I bought her here because she was having problems and I thought it'd be the safest thing to do. She can't be having it yet."

"Four months?" Doctor Bradshaw raised his eyebrows. "Your wife must have got the dates wrong, she's at least seven months along possibly eight."

"It can't be. It's not possible. She told me when it happened, it's definitely no more than four months."

"She told you? You say that as though you weren't there..."

"I..."

"I know this woman, Doctor Cranmore you need to come now."

The doctor turned toward Nurse Kathy Morgan, the young woman was agitated and flustered.

"Excuse me, Mr. Brewster."

Leaving Brewster sitting in the lounge of the private clinic, Doctor Cranmore followed Nurse Morgan into the patient's room. Rita Brewster had been struggling with her labour for thirty-nine exhausting hours. Her strength was depleted, her eyes deeply sunken, her body skin and bone.

Doctor Cranmore glanced anxiously at Nurse Morgan his expression troubled. "It's almost as if she's being attacked from inside, eaten alive so to speak..."

"How is that possible?"

Women and young girls were bought to Cranmore clinic when they had nowhere else to go or something to hide, something that could not be known or shared in their community.

Doctor Cranmore didn't differentiate between wealth and poverty. Based at his home the clinic was there to help anyone in need. And this poor emaciated woman desperately needed his help. She was screaming in agony, clawing at the sheets with hands so thin they appeared about to break.

"Push, Rita, push," Nurse Morgan was saying, "Not long now we're almost there. One more push, Rita."

Moving in front of her Doctor Cranmore waited to steady the child as the head presented.

In the stunned silence that followed, Nurse Kathy Morgan saw the colour leave the doctor's face his steady hands begin to tremble.

"Quickly nurse, get a blanket. You asked me how it's possible to be eaten from inside out, well I think we have the answer."

Out of earshot of her patient, holding the new born in her arms Kathy gasped, "This child is not just deformed it's an abomination. Let it die."

~ * ~

Abandoned in the cold the child cried out to its father.

CHAPTER THREE

Maskek, Alberta Canada; January, 1969

"I was so relieved when Jeremy told me that you and Talulah had managed to destroy the demon," Emily Simpson told the young Cree Indian, "When Steve and I saw the fire, the lights and the red mist over your house on Christmas Eve I panicked, it was like an electrical storm. All kinds of terrible thoughts were running through my head. I wanted to help you but I had no idea what to do." She leaned towards him, her voice a whisper, "Is he dead? Did you destroy the demon?"

"Yes, ma'am he's gone. Let's hope that's the end of it."

Deacon's thoughts returned to the night his Cree Indian grandmother medicine woman, Talulah Bearhead and his cousin Lone Wolf placed him in the sweat lodge, in the hope that Native magic and the heat from the stones would free him from the power the demon Arcus held over him and from his father's eternal and tortured legacy. A powerful, heinous force that began in 1750, after his father Jonathan's chance meeting with dispossessed Englishman Damien Drew.

When he didn't reply immediately, Emily asked, "Are you alright Deacon?"

"Yes ma'am. I couldn't have done it without my grandmother she's special. I'm proud to be her grandson."

"Then I would call her a wonder woman."

Deacon threw his high school teacher a disarming smile, "I guess you could say that."

His hands hooked into his hand tooled leather belt, he lounged against the bar of Maskek's one and only coffee house owned and run by Native Canadian Stanley Cut Hand.

To escape the bitter cold of Maskek's winter, Emily ducked into the coffee house hoping to thaw out. Delighted to find her most favourite student alive and well and passing the time with Stanley Cuthand she had asked him to join her at the table.

"Are you coming back to school?"

"Nope, I'm working now. Momma's struggled long enough, it's time I took over."

"That's very commendable, Deacon. What are you doing?"

"Clayton and I joined the Forest and Wild Life Rangers. Ever since he watched the junior rangers on the television Clayton has wanted to join up. And I figured it would be a good way to protect the wildlife in this area."

"Clayton's not going back to school either?"

"No point, we're both eighteen now don't need any more school. I never liked it anyhow you know that."

"Yes, I do," Emily replied her thoughts travelling back to Deacon and Clayton's last six months at Maskek High. She could recall the fighting with fellow classmate Ryan Hoffman, the blatant sexual interest Melissa Ragan, Leona Rangel and half the girls in class had for Deacon, and his regular clashes with Assistant Principal and Science teacher Peter Gibson. Remembering too the agonisingly painful episodes Deacon had suffered in his head, resulting in a frightening change in his behaviour that left Principal Emett no alternative but to keep him away from school. She remembered too how she had become unwittingly embroiled in his father's tortured legacy.

Country music was playing loudly in the background. Three couples wearing jeans, checked shirts and cowboy hats, two-stepped in front of the juke box. Merle Haggard was in fine voice. When the juke box wasn't belting out country singers, the local Swamp Radio could be heard blasting out the latest rock and pop tunes.

Emily smiled her amber eyes sparkling. "You do know that Mr. Emmet would like you to return to school now that you've conquered your demons? It was never his intention to keep you out indefinitely."

"No chance! It was kinda nice staying home."

"Clayton wasn't over thrilled about it."

"Yeah he did complain a lot...every morning and every night."

"He missed you dreadfully. He said it was as if half of him was missing. But then you are best friends."

"That's how it is when we're not together."

Stanley Cuthand meandered over as if he had all the time in the world. "You guys want coffee or are you gonna sit there all day?" A huge grin split his dark features.

Turning to Stanley, Deacon chuckled, "If it means you doing some work, cousin yeah we do."

"Mr. Cuthand is your cousin?" Emily asked in astonishment as Stanley shuffled away.

"Mr. Cuthand? Nobody ever calls him Mr. Cuthand."

A Cree Indian of thirty-six, Stanley Cuthand owned and ran the only coffee house in Maskek. Because of whom he was Stanley took a huge risk setting up a business amidst a town of white entrepreneurs; it had paid off almost immediately with the people of the town welcoming a fresh outlook on their main street. The times were a-changin' and the town's founding fathers were eager to progress towards the next decade.

Stanley wore his hair short in the style of the whites, lived in Levis and covered his feet with black, Cuban heeled boots. He was anxious to be known as a 'modern' Indian.

"He's my cousin, somehow," Deacon replied, "I just haven't figured out the 'how' bit yet. Native relatives are different to those of the white man. Anyhow, people here tend to forget that Maskek grew up around the French trappers and the trading posts. And at that time the only other people here were us Indians. Can't see why there should be a problem for Stanley."

"I still can't find any information relating to this sequestered town except how to reach it...if you can find the road. There was little documented history, it's as if it doesn't exist. I'm no further along than I was last year."

"That's because the people living here want it kept quiet. Someday I'll tell you all about the history of this town. Are you teaching the senior classes again?"

Shaking her head, Emily sighed despondently, "We're leaving Maskek and returning to Edmonton. I've caused enough heartache in the time I've been working here." Taking his hand, she peered earnestly into his face. "I never thanked you for not telling the Principal about my disgraceful conduct with you in the stockroom. I still feel terribly guilty about it...

(Told in Child of the Heathen)

"No, you don't," Deacon replied amiably, "it's what you wanted."

"I didn't exactly plan it, not quite like that. I don't know what came over me."

"It wasn't what Mrs. Simpson, it was who and it wasn't completely your fault," he winked at her, "was it?"

Emily smiled relieved that he hadn't taken offence. "Not completely mine." She sat up abruptly. "What do you mean it's what I wanted?"

Tilting his head to the left Deacon locked eyes with her, the answer plain on his face.

"Yes. I didn't realize at first how attracted I was to you. Were you aware of it before anything actually happened between us, was it that obvious?

"Yes ma'am."

"No wonder Clayton lost it with me sometimes."

Now it was Deacon's turn to be surprised. "He did?"

"Indeed. He warned me off but I wouldn't listen. If I'd known the first time I saw you, how things were going to turn out I would probably have run a mile, but I'd never met an American Indian before...."

"That's Canadian Indian, Mrs. Simpson," Deacon grinned, "The American Indians are over the border."

"I'll remember that in future. I was both fascinated and intrigued with you and I let it get away with me...with a little help from Arcus. Have you ever taken a good look at yourself Deacon, I mean really looked? You are a sight to behold. At my age that's a bad sign."

Deacon's high cheek boned native features were stunning, his black eyes warm and inviting. The vermillion shirt he wore unbuttoned almost to his waist emphasized his smooth, toned chest and the copper colour of his skin. His waist-long hair as black as the inside of a coal mine, hung loosely at his back. Black denim jeans snuggled against him in every place that counted, and a red and white beaded necklace, a gift from his great-great grandmother hung around his neck.

"What's age got to do with it?"

"In this back country town age has a lot to do with it. It's a matter of impropriety." Emily smiled as Deacon attempted to get his tongue around 'impropriety.' English being his second language he still struggled with some of the words.

"Not in my book," Stanley Cuthand announced, placing a tray on the table. "Coffee and blueberry pie for two. In my experience you're only as old as you feel and you most certainly are not old."

A warm flush spreading over her face, Emily said, "It's been a long time since I was paid a compliment like that." She glanced at the two mammoth slices of blueberry pie and then at a smiling Stanley, "We didn't order this."

"I know but you got it so eat it. No charge."

Emily eyed Deacon questioningly.

"Go ahead and eat it. Stanley does things like that."

Picking up the fork and spoon Stanley had bought with the pie Emily stuck it into the scrumptious dessert. "Stanley's quite a good looking man in a rugged kind of way."

"Yasmin thinks so. She's his woman."

"He's spoken for then, that's a shame. I'll miss you and Clayton. I've never enjoyed teaching a class so much. I shall treasure the memories of my time with all of you."

"We'll miss you too, Clayt and me."

"Where is Clayton by the way, he's usually glued to your side?"

"He's with his father."

"Where is his father? He never mentions him and I've never seen him."

"If it's up to Clayton you never will. They don't get along. He visits because it's expected of him. He'll be around later tonight. Is it good?" indicting the blueberry pie. "If Stanley can't find blueberries, he uses Saskatoon berries. He makes the pies himself."

"It's delicious."

"Have you found a position in Edmonton?"

"I'm not going back to teaching. In order to keep the peace between us my husband has decided that I should become a lady of leisure."

A broad grin splitting his handsome face, Deacon said, "A lady of leisure? I can't see it." He dug into Stanley's legendary pie. "You ever taste Saskatoon berries? One of the places they grow is along the North Saskatchewan River that runs through Edmonton. Maybe you'll get a chance to pick them."

"Perhaps I will. I'll have plenty of time to kill. I'm not convinced I'll enjoy being a lady of leisure but I promised I'd give it a shot. Steve has every right to divorce me after the way I behaved. I'm very lucky."

"Will you in stay in touch?"

Moved by Deacon's request she felt the tears start. "I'd like that Deacon. Would it be alright with your mother? We have had a few issues in the past. Like the time she found out that you came to my house unannounced and uninvited."

"Sure, it would. She doesn't dislike you she just got upset."

"I'll take your word for it."

Shifting her position, she glanced through the window overlooking Main Street and beyond. Serene and inviting Loon Lake glittered in the winter sun. The ice speckled water sparkled like a crystal chandelier, drawing her towards its frozen beauty. Even the sinister Wapiti Hills back dropping the lake filled her with awe. At thirty-five and widely travelled she had never experienced such untamed splendour as this country displayed before her. Wherever you looked in Maskek you could see Loon Lake. It was as if the town had grown out of the water.

"I'm going to miss this wonderful place. I've grown to love everything about it. It grabs you right in the heart and I don't want to leave. I'm going miss it almost as much as I'll miss you. You're so lucky to live out here. I'm really not looking forward to returning to the city."

"Why did you come to this town on the edge of civilization?"

Bemused she asked, "Edge of civilization why do you say that?"

Deacon gestured to the window. "Look around you. What do you see beyond here?"

"I see a very beautiful wilderness."

"Only to the white man is it a wilderness. Beyond Maskek there are deep forests, hills of grass, vast lakes and swift flowing rivers. There are no roads and no towns. Here, the people of Maskek say civilization ends. For my people there is plenty of life beyond Maskek. If it flies, crawls, runs or swims you will find it out there and some creatures you would rather not see."

Emily listened touched and intrigued by his spoken thoughts. Only now when it was too late was she beginning to realize that she did not know the real, true Deacon at all.

"You have not answered me. Why did you come here?" His accent peculiar to the Cree thickened when he spoke about the earth. Emily adored the sound of it.

"To escape the city like many other people and because Steve heard that real estate was rife in this part of the country. When I look at the view through this window, I can well believe it and now it has captured my heart."

"Does your husband know how you feel?"

"I tried telling him, but he's not listening. I can't blame him really. He's put the house on the market he'd like it sold as soon as possible. We're leaving tomorrow. I just hope that whoever buys the place won't have to contend with its sordid past. Do you think it's over?"

"The demon is dead and Damien has disappeared...I don't know whether it is over I hope it is. If you are leaving tomorrow can you come over to our house tonight?"

"I've already said my goodbyes."

"Please."

"How can I resist a plea like that? Should I come over about eight? Is that okay?"

"Yeah, that's cool. Do you need a ride home?"

"Thank you, I'd like that."

"Spirit of the Wind," Stanley Cuthand called from the back of the bar, "Your mom just phoned she's wants you home...."

Spirit of the Wind was Deacon's true name given to him by Lupin, his Cree Indian mother and Jonathan Sparkling Eyes his father.

"Wondered how long it would be before she called. I don't think she trusts me."

"Maybe if you didn't give her reason not to trust you, she'd let you alone," Stanley Cuthand cracked, "Anyhow I said I'd send you along in a little while."

At Emily's questioning glance Deacon grinned, "Don't ask."

"How long have you been using your Cree name?"

"My people have always called me Spirit of the Wind but it wouldn't have gone down to well with the teachers or the school board. Deacon Pierce was easier for them to accept. Now that I am no longer in school and when I become chief of my village I will be known by my true name."

"How did you come to be raised by Mrs. Pierce and your grandmother, what happened to your parents?"

"They were killed within six months of each other. Nonie Pierce was working for my father at the time. When he was dying, he asked her to take care of me. I was born in the village so she took me back there to my grandmother. When I was six years of age, she chose to adopt me and bought me to Maskek."

"Why not stay in the village with your people?"

"She wanted me to be educated in the local school rather than the residential schools."

In the 1960s, as well as the ongoing horrors of the residential schools, the Canadian government wanted to integrate Native children into white society by having white families adopt them, thereby removing them from their homes and culture. In 2008 the Canadian government realized its mistake and the Prime Minister issued an apology to all the families of the First Nations who had been affected.

"Perhaps that was the best thing for you. If she hadn't sent you here, I wouldn't have met you. How did you come to meet Clayton Rykker?"

"I've known him since we were six or seven. In the summer momma took me to Wilderness Park, Clayton was already there with his mother. I watched him struggling to make a bow, I showed him how. He didn't speak Cree I didn't speak English. No words were needed, we understood each other. Later I taught him sign language and that's how we got along. We've been friends ever since."

"That's thirteen years. That's a good friendship."

Emily pointed to Deacon's shirt, eyeing him suspiciously, "You didn't come dressed like that did you?"

Glancing at his shirt, he said, "You don't like it?"

"I meant did you come without a coat?" She was looking for his magnificent fur lined parka made from animal skin and beaded with intricate designs. Although traditionally worn by the Inuit and Aleut people in the Arctic conditions of Canada's far northern areas, Deacon chose to wear it throughout the long cold winter rather than any other garment. The beautiful beaded and porcupine quill designs representing his woodland home had been applied by his grandmother, Talulah Bearhead.

"It's hung at the back," indicating with his thumb to where a wooden rack stood behind and to the side of the bar. This was the coat he'd been wearing when he'd arrived unexpectedly and unannounced at Emily's home last year.

"Oh yes, I see it. I love that coat. It made such an impression on me the first time I saw you wearing it when you came to my house."

"Let's no go there," he said, his black eyes clouding over, "I still don't recall what happened that night but it caused far too much heartache."

"I know what happened..."

"Please, Mrs Simpson I don't wanna talk about it. That's the past, okay? I'd like it to stay that way."

"I'm sorry I didn't mean to bring it up. When did you learn you were to become the chief, you never mentioned it at school?"

"I suspected it, but I didn't know for sure until momma told me who my true parents were. Now it all makes sense. Nobody at school needed to know."

"You'll make a wonderful chief. How do you feel about it?"

"If I can be half as good a chief as my grandfather Eagle Hawk, that's all I ask."

"I'm sure you will be. Even at school you seemed to have natural leadership abilities. Tell me about the rangers. I remember you and

Clayton saying you wanted to join the rangers."

"A lot of folks would like to join the rangers. We got lucky I guess."

"You'll be enforcing the law, won't you?"

"Wild life laws mostly."

"That'll suit you. I shouldn't think there's much you don't know about protecting the Earth and its creatures, with your heritage."

"Ain't it about time you came home?"

Deacon glanced up to see his best friend and blood Brother Clayton Rykker, grinning at him from the other side of the bar.

"Hey Clay," his black eyes lighting up, "Thought you were with your father?"

"I was until I couldn't take it anymore."

"Why, what's up?"

Clayton shrugged and slid into the chair next to him, "Got another woman with him. This one he says he's gonna marry."

"Honest?"

"So, he says. She's kinda young though, about twenty-three I'd say. Pretty...but she isn't right for him. He'll ruin her life just as he did my mom's. Hi Mrs. Simpson it's good to see you."

"Nice to see you too, Clayton."

Emily watched her two most favourite ex-students discussing Clayton's father, Keel Rykker's dishonourable intentions. In his own way Clayton Rykker was as enchanting as his best friend Deacon. He had the most beautiful personality, but lacked the enigma shrouding his childhood friend. With his curly red hair and jade green eyes Clayton was as pale as Deacon was dark. At five feet ten inches, he stood a couple of inches shorter than Deacon. The two boys were inseparable. Clayton was wearing blue jeans, a fleece lined lumberjack style shirt, thick woolly green sweater and his parka. Despite the cold he refused to relinquish his tan cowboy boots.

Stanley Cuthand reappeared, cup and pie in hand. "While you're here, Clayton you may as well eat."

"Far out, thanks Stanley."

"You're welcome."

"Why are you here?" Deacon asked as Stanley moved away, "Did momma send you?

"That she did," Clayton told him, "You have been gone most of the day."

"I had things to do and some stuff to pick up for her. Besides I wanted to spend time with Cuthand."

"That ain't the only reason I came. Captain McNally called, he wants to see us on Monday, eight o clock sharp. Captain McNally's in charge of the rangers," he explained to Emily, "he's our boss."

"I'm really pleased for both of you. A Wild Life Ranger is certainly a worthwhile career. That will put a spoke in the wheel back at school for sure or do they already know?"

"They haven't seen Deke since November and I didn't tell 'em." Devouring the pie Clayton downed his coffee and turned to Deacon, "It's time we left, I promised your momma I'd bring you home."

"Better go then." He helped Emily with her heavy winter coat and reached for his parka. Pulling it over his head he adjusted his long hair over the fur lined hood. "Catch you later, Cuthand.

"Sure. Give your mom my love."

"I will."

"It's good of you to drop me off," Emily said climbing into the front of Deacon's red pickup truck, "it'll save me calling Steve. I feel quite privileged."

"Can't think why," Deacon chuckled.

"It's not every day I get to ride with an Indian chief."

"Fog's coming in!" somebody shouted frantically as Deacon was about to drive off. "Everybody get inside now!"

CHAPTER FOUR

The foul smelling grey-black fog rolled along Main Street, entombing the citizens in their homes, shrouding the town in semi-darkness.

Deacon and Clayton bundled Emily into the coffee shop and then set about helping Stanley to shutter the windows and tape up the front and back doors. Despite their best efforts, it did not shut out the odour of something long dead emanating from the poisonous cloud.

On the street a lone figure stumbled over the sidewalk, his collar hunched up around his face as he attempted to fight off the probing tentacles of mist that were forcing their way into his mouth and lungs. He stumbled a second time.

In a house on the corner of Main Street and Elk Avenue, a young woman screamed in terror, while her usually mild mannered husband pushed her to the floor. The rifle in his hand was pointed at her face.

Watching through the cracks in the shutters, Deacon said, "There's someone out there." Without thinking he ripped the tape off the front door and hurled it open, Clayton hot on his heels.

"Stay inside," Stanley ordered as Emily tried to follow the boys. Customers willing hands restrained her, pushing her gently back into the booth.

In a matter of seconds Deacon and Clayton were helping the struggling fellow through the door. Coughing and spluttering he allowed the boys to help him to a table. Stanley slammed the door shut and re-taped it.

"You okay, doc?" Clayton asked anxiously when the fellow could speak.

"My word, I've never seen anything like it. London smog has nothing on this."

Deacon grinned at Doctor Jeremy Lodge, the English writer and demonologist was the most understated person he'd ever met.

"Jeremy," Emily cried, "whatever were you doing out there?"

"I was trying to get in Emily." He glanced around at the patrons of the coffee house, their faces solemn and anxious and then at Deacon and Clayton. "Can you explain this phenomenon?"

"The Indians have a name for it," Clayton explained, "but it loses a lot in translation, they call it "The Unthinkable." It's been around for centuries, happens infrequently and without warning."

"Many of my people say it is caused by a bad spirit who is angered by the white man's treatment of his Native brothers. Others believe it is a warning from the souls of the dead."

"And what do you think it is, Deacon?"

"The Unthinkable is an accumulation of all that is wrong between our two nations. When the Unthinkable comes people will die."

"You seem to be familiar with it," Doctor Jeremy Lodge replied. Deacon did not answer. Doctor Lodge stroked his goatee, it had become characteristic of his deep thinking.

Listening nervously, Emily suddenly became aware of the rank odour filtering between the slats of the wooden shutters. "What is that awful smell?"

"It's the smell of death," Deacon told her, "When it has taken life it will pass over."

On the corner of Main Street and Elk the woman had ceased to scream and the house became still. The poisonous fog, now tinged with red drifted over the body of the man who had attacked her and crept stealthily away.

"It's moving," Emily said, peeping through the shutters.

"Then I guess it got what it came for," Clayton said quietly. "We can leave now."

"Shouldn't we find out if anyone was hurt?"

"The rangers have got it in hand," Stanley Cuthand said opening the door. "They'll deal with it. You should go now."

"Need a ride, doc?"

"No thanks Clayton I drove the jeep in."

"Catch you later then."

Deacon helped Emily into the pickup and drove away just seconds before rangers captain Virgil McNally and Tyrell McAllister removed two bodies from the silent and bloodied house on Main Street and Elk.

CHAPTER FIVE

"She's coming," Clayton said, his eyes on the window as they waited for their teacher to arrive. "Are you ready?"

Deacon Pierce and Clayton Rykker, the red headed one as Deacon affectionately called him, rounded up all their classmates and certain staff members, with the idea of giving Emily Simpson a first class send off. They had also invited English writer and demonologist Doctor Jeremy Lodge. He was a close friend of Emily and Steve Simpson. He'd also been instrumental in helping Deacon and Talulah establish a means of dealing with the demon Arcus.

Deacon's mother, Nonie Pierce, sought Rona Rykker's help in preparing the food for Emily's leaving party. Clayton's mother Rona and Nonie had been friends for thirteen years, since their first meeting in Maskek's Wilderness Park when the boys were children. Like their sons the two women had remained close friends.

The high school Principal, Barnstable Emmett, had kindly offered to supply the drinks. Although the students were under twenty-one, the legal age for drinking in the province of Alberta, this was a private party in a private house which was being supervised by their parents.

Melissa Ragan and Leona Rangel, previous classmates of Deacon and Clayton, were putting the last touches to the bunting inside the house as Emily's car crackled to a halt on the frozen snow outside the Pierce's front porch.

"Lights out," Clayton said.

Friends since they were children, Leona wore her wispy golden blonde hair in pigtails tied up with purple ribbons, and tonight they complimented her flowery cotton dress of multiple colours. Melissa painted her nails, applied false eyelashes and liked to wear clingy body hugging skirts. Her hair, the colour of burnt ochre was combed back into a beehive. Similar in height, around five feet three inches, the two girls were as different as night and day, their one common denominator being Deacon Pierce. They were overjoyed to see him again.

"That's odd," Emily mused climbing from her car, her stomach sinking into her snow boots, "Deacon said to come here at eight but it's all in darkness."

As a hesitant Emily was about to rap on the door Deacon opened it. "It's good to see you. Come on in."

Rona Rykker switched the lights back on and the room was filled with loud cheering. Hands flying to her mouth Emily felt tears welling up. "I'm really touched. I had no idea you all held me in such high esteem. Thank you."

"Sit down, have a drink," Nonie said, taking Emily's coat and hanging it on the front door. "There's plenty to eat so dig in. This is for you. For everything you've done for the boys and all the other students in your class."

Deacon stood to one side watching and admiring Emily. She had made an extra special effort tonight and she looked amazing. Her saffron coloured hair was back combed at the front and rolled at the back. The classy and elegant midnight blue dress she was wearing hugged her curves like a second skin. Black seamed stockings completed the look. She removed her boots and left them on the porch, replacing them with black stiletto heels.

"Pretty ain't she," Clayton whispered, sneaking up on Deacon's left side.

Turning to his freckle faced, curly haired companion, Deacon nodded, "Yeah, she's looking real good."

In their positions as hostesses Rona and Nonie watched them, observing the range of emotions flickering across the faces of the unruly teenagers in Emily's class. It was obvious that most of them regarded her with deep affection, the rapport between them easy and amicable.

"Those kids are going to miss her," Rona said. "I hope that whoever replaces her can handle them as well as Emily did. I don't think there's been such a popular teacher since Elaine Cartwright. Even Clayton listened and that is an accomplishment."

"Tell me about it. Now who's this?" Nonie wondered as a knock came at the door. Her question was answered when Deacon opened it and invited Doctor Jeremy Lodge inside.

"Good to see you Doc," Deacon said, hugging him.

"You too," Jeremy replied encompassing the youth in his arms, "and where's our honoured guest?"

"Under that bunch," he indicated a swarm of excited students under which Emily sat.

Nonie and Rona approached the doctor and Rona handed him a drink. "Glad you could make it, Jeremy. It's lovely to see you."

"May I say Nonie that you and Rona are looking stunning this evening."

Nonie smiled, her lavender blue eyes lighting up with pleasure. It had been many years since anyone other than Deacon and Clayton had complimented them. "Thank you, Jeremy."

At four feet ten inches, Nonie Pierce remained as slim as the day she'd first gone to work for Deacon's father, at the age of seventeen. Originally from England her family immigrated to Canada when Nonie was fifteen years old. Three years later her father's ill health had forced her mother and two younger sisters to return home. Working as a housekeeper for Jonathan and Lupin Sparkling Eyes at the time of her father's illness, Nonie had stayed in Canada, promising to visit as soon as possible. Nonie's hair the colour of ripened corn hung loosely to her shoulders, framing her pretty face and lavender blue eyes. The tight bodice and flared lilac dress she was wearing made her appear much younger than her forty-three years.

One year older than Nonie and born and bred in Maskek, Rona was swept off her feet by the dashing American cowboy Keel Rykker. After a whirl wind romance, she married him and went to live with him on his grandparents' ranch in Montana. Unhappy with the life she was leading there Rona begged Keel to bring her home. By the time Clayton was eight their marriage had begun to sour. On Clayton's twelfth birthday his parents divorced. Rona's wavy red hair and green eyes were set off perfectly by the low necked scarlet dress she wore.

"Hi Doc," Clayton said creeping up on Jeremy's right side, "Mrs.

Simpson's looking real nice ain't she? Don't seem right she's leaving."

"She belongs here," Jeremy said, "not hidden away in the city. So, how are you Clayton? I haven't really had a chance to talk to you both properly." Jeremy hugged him tightly.

"I'm fine doc, thanks. I'm glad you're here."

Jeremy stood for a moment watching the students with their teacher until eventually Melissa and Leona became aware of him.

Throwing him a welcoming smile, Melissa said, "Mrs. Simpson, there's somebody here to see you."

Emily looked up, her eyes bright with happiness. "Jeremy, I'm so glad you came. Isn't it fabulous, I had no idea they liked me so much."

"You're a very likeable lady, Emily," Jeremy replied, pecking her on the cheek.

~ * ~

As the night wore on and after all the speech making, Emily began to wish she wasn't going back to Edmonton. In spite of everything that had happened over the last eighteen months she had been shown nothing but kindness and welcomed into their hearts.

Edmonton could never compare with this.

Late in the evening when almost everyone had left, Emily sat with Jeremy Lodge, Rona and Nonie in the lounge. Melissa and Leona squatted on the floor on the hand woven Cree rug with Deacon between them. Clayton slouched by the window.

"I don't want this night to end," she said, leaning back against the ancient horsehair couch, with a cup of Earl Grey tea in her hand.

"What time is Steve expecting you back?" Jeremy enquired.

She shrugged, "Whenever. He said because it was our last night I could stay as long as I wanted and I want to stay forever. Oh, Jeremy, I really don't want to go."

"You should tell him. He's not a mind reader."

"Do you think he'd listen? Not Steve, he's set his heart on returning to Edmonton. I don't suppose you could persuade him otherwise?"

All eyes bore down expectantly on the English writer.

"I very much doubt it. Incidentally what has caused Steve's change of heart. I thought his real estate business was doing well."

"It isn't the business, Jeremy it's me. Steve thinks I'm having an affair. Just before Christmas we were getting closer again, starting over. Then out of the blue he changed. He accused me of continuing this imaginary affair. It isn't true."

"If that's the case you really need to talk."

"Doc's staying," Deacon told her.

Emily's face was a picture of undisguised shock. "You're staying here?"

"I certainly am. I have peace, solitude and bags of inspiration: everything I need to continue writing. I shall return to England only when absolutely necessary. More importantly I've grown extremely attached to Deacon and Clayton, they're the sons I never had and I'm not about to give them away."

"Steve and I will never see you."

"Of course you will, it's a good excuse for you to come back and visit us."

It was all too much, a marvellous evening wrought with emotion and happiness and suddenly it was over. Emily dissolved into tears. Deacon wanted to hold her and comfort her, but he knew it was not his place to do so. Jeremy Lodge took her awkwardly in his arms. A confirmed bachelor he was quite useless in situations such as this.

Deacon felt Melissa's painted nails digging into his hand. "She shouldn't have to go."

"It ain't up to us, Melissa."

"It's not up to her husband either. It should be Mrs. Simpson's choice, married or not," Leona butted in.

Turning his face away from Emily for a moment, Jeremy gestured helplessly to Deacon. "I'm hopeless at this."

With a quick glance in his mother's direction, Deacon took Emily into his arms, "You can come back anytime," he told her gently. "You'll always be welcome."

"I don't want to come back. I want to stay." Laying her head on

Deacon's chest, Emily gripped his waist squeezing him tightly, not ever wanting to let go.

Glancing anxiously at Nonie, Rona prayed there would be no trouble. In the past Deacon's mother's suspicions about Emily and her son had turned to anger. Fortunately, this time she seemed to be coping, either because she had reconsidered her previous verbal attack on the school teacher or because the contender for her son's affection was leaving town--or perhaps she really did like her. Deacon's presence and his arms around her, his magnetism and his sexuality were starting to arouse her. Emily couldn't allow the same thing to happen again. Sniffing she wiped her tears on her bare arm and raised her head. "I'll be alright now, Deacon, I've done my crying. It's been a lovely evening. Thank you, all of you, but it's time I went home."

Stepping forward Clayton said, "We'll drive you home Mrs. Simpson or at least Deacon will, he hasn't had anything to drink and I'll come along with you. I don't think it's a good idea for you to be driving right now, snow's pretty deep and it's black out there, hard to see."

"What about my car?"

"We'll bring it over tomorrow."

"If you think that's best." She was grateful for the opportunity to ride in the back of Clayton's mother's station wagon. "I don't really like night driving and there's far too much snow now. It seems so much denser out here."

Impulsively Nonie hugged Emily to her. "Take care."

"I will. Look after those boys they're the best."

Helping Emily into her coat Jeremy pecked her cheek. "Good night, Emily. I'll come by before you leave tomorrow. Tell Steve to hang on until I do."

Not trusting herself to say anything, the lump in her throat choking her Emily nodded.

Collecting his parka Deacon handed Clayton his jacket and opened the door. The frigid winter air hit him in the face stealing his breath away. Powered snow blew through the open door and melted on the bare wooden floor. The wicked, biting wind moaned hauntingly through the trees, whipping the heavy branches of the conifers against the window.

"Won't be long, momma," he said kissing her cheek, "we'll take the truck, Clayt."

"Snow's coming down pretty fast," Clayton remarked as they stepped into the bitter night, "temperature's dropping. There's a storm coming."

How true, Emily found herself thinking.

CHAPTER SIX

Deacon stepped out of the shower, his long hair glistening with droplets of water just as a furious knock came at the front door. Yanking on his jeans he'd left on the bathroom floor, his belt flapping loosely, he took the stairs two at a time. In blizzard conditions such as there were at the moment a late night visitor could mean someone in danger. Without stopping to ask who it might be he threw the bolt and opened the door, hearing Clayton clattering down the stairs behind him.

Melissa and Leona huddled on the doorstep, dishevelled and shivering. "Can we come in?". Both girls made a beeline for the wood fire still burning in the grate, holding their hands out to its welcoming warmth.

"Car's stuck. We skidded into the side of the trail where it's drifting. It's taken us this long to find our way back. Good thing you kept the light in the window. We could have gone on walking forever."

A light in the window was a beacon for anyone caught in a blizzard. Like a compass on a ship it saved many a life.

"You could have been in the lake. How long have you been out there?" Deacon asked, concerned.

"A couple of hours and we're freezing," Leona replied.

"I thought the lake was frozen," Melissa said.

"Some parts of it aren't. There's still a narrow channel open about the width of a canoe that never completely freezes."

Disturbed by the banging, Nonie and Rona appeared, both of them wrapped in warm dressing gowns.

"Pull the couch by the fire Deacon let them warm up. Take those wet things off girls. Rona will make you coffee."

"Thank you, Mrs. Pierce," Melissa said.

Deacon hauled the couch closer to the fire and with a sign of relief the girls sank into it. They removed their sodden shoes, of little use in the snow having left their warm winter boots in Melissa's car, handed wet coats to the boys and pushed their frozen feet against the fire.

"You're lucky you didn't get frost bite," Clayton said, "What possessed you to wander off in your shoes?"

"We put our boots in the trunk before we left here and when we got stuck, we couldn't open it. We didn't plan on walking through the snow."

"Would you like me to call your parents?" Nonie asked, "They'll be worried about you."

"Please, Mrs. Pierce," Leona replied.

Rona set about brewing coffee.

"Where'd you lose it?" Deacon asked, pulling up his zipper and fastening his belt.

"You don't have to do that on my account," Melissa purred, her eyes on his zipper.

"Oh yeah I do," Deacon grinned, "I don't trust you. Where'd you lose the car?"

Melissa's attention was definitely focused on Deacon and not so much her car. "Your hair looks so much longer when it's wet and it really shines."

"Where's the car, Melissa?"

"Along Loon Lake trail," Leona said, "towards Mrs. Simpson's house."

"What were you doing there that's completely the wrong direction?"

"We got confused when it started snowing badly. Then the car just conked out when we hit the drifts. Even if the engine had started again, we couldn't have got it out of the snow."

Nonie returned from speaking to Leona's parents. "I've let them know you're here, Leona. They were just about to send a search party after you. I told them the boys will try and fetch you home. But if the weather gets any worse you can both stay here. Deacon and Clayton will take a look at your car in the morning."

"That's very kind of you Mrs. Pierce."

"Did you manage to get hold of my folks?" Melissa asked.

"There was no reply Melissa. Leona's mother said she'll keep trying."

"They'll be out," she added bitterly, "they're always out."

"You wanna go take a look, Deacon?" Clayton asked. "Maybe we can tow it out if there's enough traction with the truck."

"Yeah, I guess we can do that."

"There you go girls," Rona said handing them each a mug of steaming coffee, "that'll warm you up."

"Thanks Mrs. Rykker," Leona said nudging her friend. Melissa still couldn't tear her eyes away from Deacon's hair.

"At least she's not looking below your belt for once," Clayton told him.

"Makes a change." He disappeared into the kitchen, returning a few seconds later rubbing his hair with a colourful towel.

"I can do that for you," Melissa offered.

"I can manage, thanks."

"I was just trying to be helpful. Do you need us to come with you to show you where the car is?"

"We'll find it," Clayton told her, "not too many people out here dumping cars by our lake."

"Please," Melissa pleaded.

"Not this time, Melissa," Deacon said, "We can do it faster on our own."

"But you might miss it," Melissa persisted, squeezing his arm tightly.

"No, Melissa."

"We can help..."

"I have spoken," Deacon said in a tone of authority even his mother dare not abuse.

Stunned into silence, the girls stared incredulously at a side of Deacon they hadn't seen before.

"You ready?" Clayton asked."

"Let's go."

"What was all that about?" Melissa asked when she'd recovered.

"Gets it from his father," Nonie answered with a smile.

"Does he talk to you like that?"

"Not very often, don't worry about it, he's not angry with you it's just his way."

As he closed the front door Clayton said, "Think you gave 'em a bit of a shock."

"Think I did."

"Won't do 'em any harm."

~ * ~

Ross Porter threw his clothes on the chair by the bed and standing naked scrutinised himself in the full length mirror on the inside of the wardrobe door. Bobby was staying overnight at his friend's home. From his bed he watched Ross with amusement. "No matter how hard you try you're never gonna look like Deke. Melissa is never gonna tell you she loves you."

"Who said I wanted her to?"

"You did. You told me she doesn't look at you the same way she looks at him. From the time Deke first came to school she set her heart on him, she's not gonna change now..."

"What's wrong with me, huh? I'm pretty good looking. I got a decent body on me. What's Deke, about six foot? Well I'm only a couple of inches shorter if that, a little thinner admittedly but I'm not skinny..."

"You don't have black hair, black eyes, or copper coloured skin and you're not an Indian. Let's face it Ross, Melissa is heavily into Native men, which we definitely are not."

"I got dark brown hair and brown eyes, doesn't that count for something?"

"Oh yeah that'll really do it. You ain't got what the girls say is a 'well filled crotch' either. Deke does."

"We can't all be built the same."

"Don't sweat it, man, doncha know it's not what you've got but what you do with it."

"Yeah, like I'm gonna get a chance to prove it."

Bobby chuckled, "Make a chance. Hell, it's not the end of the world. Anyhow, when Deke moves back to his village Melissa won't be going with him. You can always try again."

"Doesn't it bother you, Bobby?"

"Look at me my good friend; I'm a short arse, my hair is all over the place, mom keeps threatening to give me a basin cut and I'm heavier than the average beau. Not particularly bright either according to some of our teachers but I'm a nice guy. I look at it this way, it's not about how you look it's what you are inside that counts. Even Deke 'll tell you that."

"He can say that he's so damn handsome and sexy it wouldn't matter..."

"You think Deke's sexy?"

"Don't you?"

"Clayton does."

"See now he's another one. What chick can resist his green eyes and red hair?"

"Geez, Ross you've really got a problem here. Get over it. What's the matter you don't wanna be friends with Deke and Clayt anymore?"

"I didn't say that. You know I do. We're all friends and we love each other the way good friends should, it's just that...never mind. Let's get some sleep." He climbed into bed and pulled the covers tight around himself. "Neither Melissa nor Leona paid us any attention tonight."

"There's one thing you haven't considered and that is Deacon and Clayton ain't at school anymore. We are, and so are Melissa and Leona, that's in our favour."

Ross was about to fall asleep when Bobby disturbed him. "Know what you could do now Deke and Clayt aren't around as often?"

"What?" Ross mumbled, his head boggy with sleep.

"You could agree to take both girls on a moonlight stroll."

"In these temperatures, are you crazy?"

"They're both romantic, aren't they? Love hearing stories of gallant knights and fair maidens..."

Ross turned over and stared at his best friend in the opposite bed. "It ain't gallant knights its noble warriors they're interested in."

"Okay, so they're still gonna go for the idea. What's more

romantic than a walk by the river in the moonlight? Think about it."

Ross slept all night with dreams of gallant knights in which he was the knight, fighting fire breathing dragons and rescuing damsels in distress.

~ * ~

Following the trail from Deacon's home the boys turned right, around the lake.

"Geez, the weather's getting worse," Clayton grumbled.

The snow was spiralling out of control, slamming into the windshield, shrouding the slow moving vehicle in a white blanket. Despite its snow tires the pickup was sliding on the new snow covering the ice. The engine complained bitterly and the headlights were dim, almost useless against the pelting snow. Outside the truck the wind whistled and shrieked like souls from the graveyard, battering the heavy vehicle from side to side. Deacon struggled to hold it steady.

"Beginning to think this wasn't such a good idea," Clayton shouted, "Should have borrowed a land rover."

"Know anybody that's got one?"

"Nope..."

"I guess that's that then. Melissa's car's godda be here someplace," Deacon said, straining to see through the blinding snow. "I reckon we've covered six miles easy."

"Leona could've got it wrong."

"Hope not. Don't wanna be out here all night. Hey wait a minute I think I see something. Over there, see it?"

Swaddled in a blanket of white on the edge of the lake, was Melissa's car. He could just about make out the outline beneath the snow.

Clayton followed Deacon's pointed finger. "Looks mighty like a car."

Bringing the vehicle to an abrupt halt leaving the motor running and the lights on, Deacon reached for the flashlight in the glove compartment and climbed out, sinking up to his knees in freshly packed snow. He handed Clayton the flashlight. He shone it across the hood of the car and checked the windshield. "Looks okay no damage that I can see."

Moving round to the side of the car Clayton slipped as the ground dipped beneath him. His boots rapidly filled with freezing water.

"Jeez, I'm in the lake!"

Deacon was by his side instantly, hauling him upward.

"Jesus, it's so cold I damn near peed my pants!"

"Good thing you didn't," Deacon chuckled, "it's too cold for anything out here. Get back in the truck and take those boots off. I'm gonna try and tow it out."

"Wouldn't it be better to leave it until tomorrow when we can see what we're doing?" Clayton shouted above the howling wind as it gathered momentum. The wind stung their faces, pushing and shoving them against the car.

"Could be in the lake by tomorrow way the snow's shifting."

Clayton handed Deacon the tow rope and the flashlight. Careful to avoid stepping into the icy water where it lapped against the car under the fallen snow, Deacon searched for somewhere to attach the rope and decided to fasten it to the front axle. There wasn't anything else he could fix it to and the axle appeared to be strong enough.

"How're your feet?" he asked climbing into the driver's seat, intending to the move the pickup truck to the front of Melissa's car.

"They're thawing out."

Positioning the truck, the young Indian jumped out and attached the other end of the rope to the tow hitch at the back of the truck. By the time he'd done that he could hardly feel his fingers. Shaking his hands to restore some warmth to his fingers he climbed inside.

"Where're your gloves?" Clayton asked reproachfully.

"I left 'em at home."

"Not gonna do you much good there, are they?"

"I guess not. You ready?"

"Ready as I'll ever be."

Deacon slowly let out the clutch and started the truck moving until it lost traction on the soft snow. He tried again and again until the car began to slide away from the edge of the lake then stopped. Under normal conditions it wouldn't be a problem, the pickup was heavy, designed for hard work but tonight the vehicle was having none of it. He leaned back against the seat.

"What's the matter?" Clayton asked.

"Godda pee."

"The cold will do it every time. Bad?"

"Like yesterday..."

"Might have something to do with the fact that somebody didn't go before he left home?"

Deacon grinned at him, "You sound just like my mother."

"Someone's godda take care of you when she's not around, right?"

"Right," he chuckled.

"We'll get it shifted, we just godda be patient except if we leave it any longer, we're gonna be stranded out here. Try again."

"I should have put the snow chains on. Shall I try digging it out?"

"Hold on," Clayton said, "we're doing all this and we don't even know if it'll start."

"Got no intention of starting it, likely won't anyhow. Just gonna tow it home."

Outside again Deacon fastened the fur lined hood over his head, took the snow shovel out of the back and began to dig around the wheels. As fast as he cleared a space, the ever increasing velocity of the snow filled it in.

Breathing heavily in the freezing air he rested for a moment catching his breath, then started again. Despite the warm hood Deacon's long hair blew wildly around his face, the evil wind tearing his eyes. He brushed the tears away with the cuff of his parka.

Determined to help, Clayton pulled on his sodden socks and boots and jumped out of the cab.

"Get back in," Deacon told Clayton as his friend tried to help, "You got wet feet."

Reluctantly he retreated. Prolonged exposure to wet skin exacerbated the possibility of frostbite. In these temperatures it was asking for trouble.

"One more time," Deacon said throwing the shovel into the back and sliding behind the wheel. With the heavy pickup truck forcing it across the snow Melissa's car finally began to move.

"Yes!" Clayton yelled, "Hit it. Want me to drive being as you've done all the hard work?" He removed his footwear again and pushed his feet up against the heater vents.

"I'll drive, it'll take my mind off things, I'm busting and if we stop chances are we won't get moving again and I'd kinda like to get home in a hurry."

"It's not a time machine Deke, it don't go that fast."

With the weather rapidly deteriorating, his vision severely retarded by the pounding snow pelting the windshield and the whirling white mass ahead of them, Deacon pushed the pickup as fast as he dared.

"Not far now, my brother I can see the lights up ahead,"

Watching vigilantly through the front window Nonie saw the headlights looming up through the blinding snow. "They're back."

"Thank God for that," Rona said.

"Have they got my car?" Melissa asked excitedly, rushing to open the door.

"Stay inside, Melissa," Nonie told her, "Your car's going nowhere tonight."

Jumping out Deacon grimaced as the cold hit him with the force of a sledgehammer, aggravating his already urgent condition.

"Leave it for now, Clayton." With that he bounded into the house and up the stairs.

Melissa's eyes lit up, Leona pulled her away. "Leave him be he doesn't need you crowding him. Come on."

"So, how's my car?" Melissa demanded, reluctantly allowing Leona to pull her away.

"Looks fine," Clayton told her tossing his gloves on to the couch. Removing his parka Clayton hung it on the front door, "Don't know if it'll start, we didn't try it. Providing the storm let's up we'll check it out tomorrow."

"So, we can't go home tonight?"

"We could try and drive you in the pickup but it ain't safe out there and I'm not sure Deacon would want to right now."

"So, we get to stay," Leona said delighted at the prospect of spending all night at Deacon's house, "Where do we sleep?"

"It's all sorted," Rona told the girls as she appeared from the kitchen where she'd been washing the last of the coffee cups. "Deacon and Clayton will have one room and you and Melissa the other. Nonie and I will share."

"You don't have to do that, mom. Deke and me can bunk on the floor. It won't be the first time."

"I don't think so," Rona informed her son, "that's putting too much temptation in the way don't you think?"

"I guess it would." He looked directly at Melissa. "I was just trying to make things easier."

"I know, honey," she said, kissing him, "and it's appreciated. How bad is it out there?"

"If it doesn't let up, we'll be snowed in by morning." Dropping onto the couch he began to remove his sodden boots. At his mother's questioning glance Clayton told her, "I went in the lake."

"My car was in the lake?" Melissa was horrified.
"Not completely, just a part of the front wheel. If it'd been in the lake, Melissa it would've stayed there, it's too dangerous to be messing round in the water at this time of night under these conditions. It looks like you're stuck here for the time being and possibly tomorrow."

Throwing her hands together Melissa cried, "Won't that be great. We can stay here all day and all night."

"The bathroom is free," Nonie called from the top of the narrow staircase. "You girls want to use it while you can?"

"Where's Deacon," Melissa wanted to know "isn't he coming down?"

"He's gone to bed. So, unless Clayton is planning on staying up all night you'd better go too."

"He's not," his mother replied.

"Good night ladies," Clayton said offering his mother his arm.

"What?" Melissa gaped at the red-haired youth.

A broad grin splitting his face Clayton escorted his mother up the stairs.

"Better lock your door," she whispered.

"I intend to."

Whilst the girls wrangled about staying up or going to bed Clayton promptly slipped into the bathroom. When he came out ten minutes later, they were still arguing. He was about to slip the lock on the bedroom door when Deacon said, "Don't lock the door, Clayton."

"Sorry, I forgot you don't like to be shut in." For a moment it had slipped his mind that Deacon's childhood fear of locked doors still remained as powerful as ever. "Want me to leave it wide open? Okay. Move over, brother."

Roundabout five in the morning Melissa crept over to Deacon's bedroom, ecstatic to find the door ajar. Peeping inside she whispered to Leona, "Isn't that cute they're sleeping like a couple of babies." Both boys were naked. Clayton laid facing Deacon's back, his hand resting on best friend's waist.

"We shouldn't disturb them," Leona told her.

"Why not, we'll never get another chance like this. Can we come in? We can't sleep."

"Neither can we, now," Clayton grumbled, waking up and turning to face them, "Don't you pair ever rest?"

"Why would we want to do that when we can be with you?"

"Could give you a thousand reasons," Deacon muttered, instantly awake, "But I guess you wouldn't hear."

"We always hear," Melissa whispered glancing quickly at the other bedroom in case Nonie or Rona appeared.

"Yeah but you don't listen," Deacon told her quietly, "Go back to bed."

"We want to be with you. This chance won't come again."

"We or you, Melissa, somehow I don't think it's anything to do with Leona."

"It's not," Leona agreed. To her friend she said, "Will you come back to bed before Deacon's mom hears you.

"No, I will not! I am not a child."

"Then quit acting like one," Clayton told her, "Aunt Nonie was good enough to let you stay. Don't you think you ought to appreciate it?"

"Ross wouldn't have sent me back to bed...."

"Then go find him, Melissa we're tired and we'd like to get some sleep tonight."

"It's five in the morning," Deacon told him, "almost time to get up. Leave them be Clayton and maybe they'll go away."

"We will not go away. It's not normal the way you guys are..."

Exchanging amused glances, the boys pulled the blankets over themselves. Clayton dragged the pillow over his ears. "Whatever gave 'em that idea."

Leona tiptoed back to the guest room, glancing guiltily at Nonie's bedroom door. Melissa persisted. She wasn't going to miss this opportunity with Deacon if she could help it.

Eventually Deacon climbed out of bed and pulled on his jeans. "Keep it up and you'll wake momma and Aunt Rona, if you haven't already. Either you go back to bed or I'm gonna take you home right now."

"You wouldn't have said that to Mrs. Simpson," Melissa spat, angered by his refusal to oblige her.

Dark eyes flashing he took her to one side. "There's no call for that, Melissa."

"Maybe not, but I don't understand why you keep backing off. I really like you Deacon. I've liked you since the first day you came to school. We didn't plan this. It's not our fault the car slid into a snow drift."

"But you figured you'd take advantage of it anyhow, huh?" he grinned.

Now that Deacon was so close, so intense, strong feelings were stirring inside her. Despite her comment about Ross, she really did love Deacon. Breathless and wanting, Melissa rubbed herself against him fighting the desire to rip off his jeans and take his penis into her hands and into herself.

Locking eyes with her Deacon said, "It's not going to happen, Melissa."

Nonie provided both girls with warm cotton nightdresses. Melissa chose not to wear hers. Standing before him in mail order black lace underwear, she was mystified that he didn't appear to have noticed. "Why not, what's wrong with me?" Her hazel flecked eyes betrayed hurt and humiliation.

"Because you're in momma's house and she trusts us."

"That's it?" Melissa asked unbelievingly.

"No, that's not it, I just want us to be friends."

Devastated and speechless, Melissa stared at him. When she recovered, her voice was no more than a squeak. "I thought we were friends..."

"So, let's not ruin it...I'm sorry Melissa," his eyes were gentle and tender.

"That's not an answer, Deacon. I want you."

"Is there someone else?" Her heart was pounding against her ribs.

Clayton stepped outside Deacon's bedroom, "Yeah, there is."

"Who is it?" she asked cautiously.

"Me."

CHAPTER SEVEN

Stunned silence greeted his words. Leona was first to recover. "You guys are an item?"

"That's about the size of it."

"How long has this been going on?"

"Long enough..."

"Isn't that illegal?"

"It's not like that," Deacon told her.

"How can it not be 'like that' if you're together? Does your momma know, Deacon?"

"Sure, she does. They both do."

"And they don't have a problem with it?"

Clayton addressed Leona. "Why should they?"

Melissa was still in shock and unable to respond. "That's what most everyone in our class used to think isn't it, it shouldn't come as a surprise."

"So, are we still friends?" Deacon wanted to know.

"Of course we're still friends," Leona said, kissing his cheek. She helped Melissa up from the floor where her friend had collapsed on hearing Clayton's admission. "Aren't we?" she asked Melissa. Her mouth was working but no sound emerged. "She's in shock. She's not used to hearing things like that. I often wondered about your relationship Deacon. You and Clayton are so close you live in each other's pockets. What about Thorn Rose, I thought she was your girlfriend. Where does she fit in?"

"When we have more time, I will explain then you will understand about Thorn Rose." This wasn't the time to tell Leona about the ancient Cree prophesy.

Although Leona was disappointed that Melissa or herself were not going to get anywhere with either Deacon or Clayton it did mean that she would no longer have to listen to Melissa constantly nattering on about them. It also signalled an end to any petty jealousy that might have arisen had the boys responded to their wishes.

As Leona and a very distressed Melissa faded into the spare room, Clayton said "I think we sorted that. Let's get some sleep."

In the bedroom Nonie smiled and turned over.

~ * ~

There were no more disturbances from Melissa or Leona. At nine am Deacon climbed from the bed and glanced through the unshuttered window. The bright sunlight bouncing off a frozen world assaulted him, knocking him back. Shielding his eyes, he peered through the window into near blinding conditions. "Deep shit, there's a lot of snow out there." Deacon first heard Clayton use that expression when they were both children. When he had finally mastered a few words of the notoriously difficult English language, they had been his first two words.

"What's up," Clayton mumbled wiping sleep from his eyes.

"We better start digging."

Trundling over to the window Clayton glanced over Deacon's shoulder. "Man, I ain't seen snow like this in years."

Thrashed and battered over night by the remorseless wind, the snow had drifted up against the house, piling up until it was stacked as high as the second floor a fraction below the window ledges. It lay in mounds across the roof.

"There must be fifteen feet of snow out there. We don't need a shovel, we need a snow plow. Nobody's going any place today. Melissa'll love it."

"Not anymore she won't," Deacon reminded him.

"Oh yeah, I'd forgotten."

"They won't. Maybe we shouldn't have said anything."

"Now don't go getting soft on me it had to be done. I'm gonna hit the bathroom before the girls get in there."

Conspiratorial giggling across the landing put that idea to rest when Clayton peeked round the door just in time to see Leona and Melissa disappear into the bathroom.

"Guess I can knock that idea out of my head."

"Looks like it, hope they don't take too long."

Resigned to the fact that they might have a long wait the boys threw on their clothes and ambled downstairs. A steaming breakfast of pancakes and maple syrup awaited them.

"Sleep well?" Rona asked as Clayton and Deacon entered the lounge.

"Not really," Clayton replied kissing his mother's cheek, "Morning."

"We didn't either," Nonie answered as Deacon hugged her.

"You heard, then?"

"Yes, every word."

"Don't seem right though," Deacon said."

Sliding into a chair at the table, Clayton told them, "He's feeling guilty. I told him not to worry about it but he's not listening, are you?"

"I am listening."

The girls emerged a few minutes later enticed by the aroma of freshly made pancakes and freshly brewed coffee. With a quick glance at each other the boys left the table and rocketed upstairs.

"Something we said?" Leona asked.

Chuckling quietly Nonie smiled, "No, it's like this every morning. If you're staying here, you'll get used to it."

"There's nothing from your parents Melissa," Rona told her, "and no reply when I called this morning. I thought they might have tried to get in touch with you."

"They won't. I hardly ever see them. Mom's busy with her charities and my father is always working."

"Surely they should be concerned about their own daughter?"

"They're not, Mrs. Rykker," Leona said. "They hardly know she exists. Melissa spends most of her time with me. My folks have always made her welcome."

"Perhaps they don't worry because they know you're safe with Leona."

Nonie's eyes were troubled as she handed the two girls their breakfast. "It must upset you Melissa. If you want to talk about it, we're listening."

Shaking her head, she said, "I'm used to it." She glanced up at Deacon's mother, her eyes filled with sadness, "Will we have to go home?"

"Not today. Have you looked outside?"

The shutters were open and the huge picture window running the length of the front room filled the lounge with shining silver light.

"Don't you close the shutters at night, Mrs. Pierce?"

"Yes, but only when Deacon has gone to sleep. I open them before he gets up."

"Is that because of what happened at school when Mr. Reynolds locked him in the washroom?"

"It is."

Leona gasped, the area around and beyond the house was a complete whiteout. It was impossible to distinguish Loon Lake from the land because the trail around the lake was all but obliterated. Nothing stirred out there in the radiating brilliance of the morning sun or in the near luminous snow-capped countryside. The vista was breath taking.

"Beautiful isn't it." Leona hadn't heard Deacon come up behind her.

"Awesome," she replied, half turning to look up at him, "it also means we can't get out."

"We can—when we've finished digging."

"Even with all of us shovelling it'll take all day."

"We aren't expecting you to dig. Clayton and I'll do it."

"That's a whole heap of snow Deacon and it'll be frozen by now."

"Sooner we start digging then the better," he answered matter-of-factly.

Leona stared at him for a while. "You've done this before haven't you?"

"Just a few times," he grinned.

"It doesn't get quite this bad in town."

"It blows off the hills and across the lake. We're open to it here."

As Deacon continued to stare through the window Leona moved

behind him. Pushing his long hair to one side so that she could get a better outlook on the frozen landscape, she noticed two scars on the side of his neck. Fingering them gently she asked, "Are these the scars you got while you were trying to put out the fire in the school lab, last year?"

"Nope, momma says I got one of them when I was a baby. The Longhouse was burning and the flames in my bedroom caught my neck. The other one..."

Clayton entered tucking his shirt into his jeans. "The other is a birthmark passed down from his ancestors. All the male descendants of the Protector of the Wind carry this mark. It's to do with an ancient prophesy."

"You never told us that."

"You didn't ask. Anyhow, I guess we won't be seeing Captain McNally today the rangers will be out helping to clear the snow."

"Good thing too because today is still only Sunday," Deacon grinned. "If it's not, we're in trouble because we've overslept."

"If you've finished eating boys it's time to start digging."

"We're happy to do that just as long as you keep the coffee flowing, mom."

"I think we can manage coffee."

The telephone shrilled just as Deacon was about to pull on his parka. "Least the lines aren't down." He reached for the receiver, "It's your momma, Leona."

"Ooh, I loved the way you say Lay-oh-na." Taking the receiver, she moved away from the window. "Hi mom..."

"Just thought of something," Clayton mumbled while he and Deacon shovelled snow, "Mrs. Simpson said they were leaving today, didn't she?"

"Not much chance of that now."

"Do you reckon they'll be okay over there?"

"Depends on whether they were prepared for it. We can't get over there, the trail is blocked; the lake isn't completely frozen and we got our hands full here."

"Hope they'll be alright."

"They will be," Deacon said with more confidence than he felt.

Leona and Melissa watched in fascinated silence while Deacon and Clayton tackled the packed snow around the front door. First, they dug a kind of tunnel pushing the snow to each side clearing a path from the doorway and around the porch. When the entrance to the house was clear Deacon hauled himself onto the roof, the hard-packed snow acting as a makeshift ladder and helped Clayton up. Together they threw, pushed and scraped the snow off to each side until it was clear. Sitting on the hard, wet surface they took a breather.

"Gonna have to do this all over again when we get home," Clayton grumbled.

"I'll give you a hand. Maybe if you stay here long enough it will have melted."

"I wish." He stared ahead for a while then said, "Tell me again why we live out here?"

"You love it."

"Not when it snows like this. Maybe you could have a word with the Great Spirit, you are on speaking terms with him ain't you? Ask him to send something to take it all away."

"I'll do my best."

"Hey Hiawatha," Leona called from below, "Your momma says coffee's ready."

"Hiawatha?" Deacon mouthed.

"Well at least it proves she's read something," Clayton cackled. Deacon nearly threw him off the roof. "Let's go have coffee."

"We had a call from Captain McNally," Nonie said as the boys entered the house, knocking snow from their feet, "He says Mrs. Simpson's house is completely cut off and nobody can get out from town to help."

"And he'd like us to go over there?"

"Only if the trail is passable, is it passable?"

"Not by truck anyway," Deacon answered removing his parka and mukluks. "We could try the lake, it's not completely frozen. We can get across, it'll just take a while. There's still plenty needs doing here though. Roof's clear and so is the path to the front door, but there's still plenty snow at the back and sides of the house."

"That's okay isn't it? At least we can get out."

"I don't know, momma. I don't like the idea of leaving you both alone here whilst the snow's this bad. What if it starts again?"

"They have no one Deacon. I honestly don't think that Mr. Simpson is going to be much help in a situation like this."

Deacon looked to Clayton, "What do you think?"

"Not happy about the idea. Once we leave this house, we have no way of contacting anyone until we get over there. Come to think of it, Deacon what about Talulah? They're in tepees."

"Grandmother is used to it, there's plenty of help. The trees shelter the lodges. Once we get across the lake we'll go see if everything's alright with them."

"Where is Captain McNally?" Clayton wanted to know.

"In town coordinating rescue parties," Nonie replied. "All the rangers are out helping people to clear up. The snow plows are out, but it's going to take hours to get as far as the Simpson's house."

"How are you going to get across the lake if only half of it is frozen?" Melissa asked, handing them coffee. "It's dangerous, you could drown." This morning she was wearing her black, pointed framed glasses. These were her 'cat's eyes' and she thought them pretty cool.

"We'll take the canoe," Clayton replied, accepting his mug. "Thanks."

"But how..."

"We can do it," Deacon replied. "We just need to follow the open water. There is a way through. If we'd fetched the horses down from grandmother's village we could've ridden over there."

"Why didn't you?" Rona asked.

"Been pushing them pretty hard of late," Clayton said, "they needed rest."

Rona feed them both a hearty late lunch then waited with Nonie while they retrieved their grey and khaki uniforms and sorted themselves out, attaching snowshoes to their usual footwear.

"Is it easy to walk in those?" Melissa asked watching the boys strap the hand-crafted Cree snow shoes to Clayton's boots and Deacon's mukluks.

"When you get used to 'em it is," Clayton told her.

"You both look wonderful in your uniforms. I like a man in uniform."

Nonie and Rona smiled knowingly. "That brings back memories."

"Ooh yes," Rona replied her eyes glinting mischievously, "let's not go there."

"Be careful," Nonie said kissing both of them, "and call us when you arrive. Let us know you got there safely."

"Will do, momma," Deacon said.

Watching them make their way through the heavy snow Rona was beginning to have doubts. "I don't think we should have let them go."

"They'll be absolutely fine, Rona. They've been across the lake a thousand times," she squeezed her hand reassuringly, "stop worrying."

CHAPTER EIGHT

"It's gonna be dark soon," Clayton said, "and the sky's full of snow. We shouldn't have left them."

"I don't like it either. We didn't have to offer to help, we could have said no, but I guess there's gonna be plenty of other times we'll be working when we'd rather be at home." Locking eyes with his best friend, Deacon said, "We could go back to school."

"No way, Jose, we're outta there and we ain't going back," Clayton said with feeling.

Deacon's home was no longer visible behind the mountain of drifting snow. In front of them the lake stretched into infinity. Loon Lake trail, the lakeshore and the lake itself merged into one.

They made good progress on the snowshoes. When they eventually reached the shoreline, the boys unearthed the beached canoe where it lay in a silent grave under the white mantle.

The swiftly flowing currant running beneath the chilling waters of Bittern Creek flowed into Loon Lake from the Wapiti Hills; here a narrow channel remained open. Although it was too close for comfort to the notoriously dangerous Amisk inlet for Deacon's liking, it was this route they would have to follow to cross the half frozen lake. He was jumpy and unsettled.

"You okay?"

"I will be once we leave this place."

Hindered by the ice floating through the restricted channel their progress was slow.

"Getting mighty cold," Clayton said, "remind me again whose idea was to hit the lake in the middle of winter."

Deacon threw Clayton a broad grin. "Yours, I think. I only asked if we could make it."

Muttering incoherently the red head gave his attention to his paddle.

On the open lake the wind intensified, blowing the loose snow all around them dropping the temperature by five degrees. Further paddling bought them to the far shore as close as they could get to the Simpson's property. Instead of heading in that direction Deacon beached the canoe and led Clayton through the dense forest in the opposite direction, heading for his grandmother's village.

"Apart from checking on Talulah, what else are you thinking?" Clayton asked.

"We're gonna need help and I reckon Lone Wolf, Stands in Timber and Mule Deer can give us a hand. That's if everything's alright here."

Hidden amidst the rocky mountain and lodge pole pine conifers was Talulah Bearhead's village. It was here among these gentle people who refused the ways of the modern world choosing to live as their ancestors did, that Deacon Spirit of the Wind was born and later raised by his grandmother and Nonie Pierce. Between the evergreen trees Talulah Bearhead's encampment stood serene and beautiful, like a picture from the pages of history. Talulah dedicated her life to keeping it that way as much as possible. The birch bark dwellings, once the homes of the Woodland Cree, had long been cast aside in favour of the tipi. Everyone was welcome here, Native or white as long as the rules of the camp were upheld and respected. At the age of ten the boys had made a pact to remain together forever, cutting their wrists and sealing it with their own blood. They were now Blood Brothers for all eternity.

A reporter from the local newspaper the Northern Light, once dared to suggest that the village was also a refuge for hippies escaping the 'establishment' and draft dodgers from across the border. Chief Eagle Hawk, Deacon's grandfather had taken great delight in proving otherwise. The reporter had not written since.

The people living here loved and respected Talulah's vision. The village had stood in this same spot amidst the forest and overlooking the Wapiti Hills and the lake, long before the emergence of the lucrative fur trade. The people living within its sacred hoop were mostly descendants of the original inhabitants. Isolated within the closely woven pines they hoped to avoid many of the social problems such as alcohol and drug abuse that plagued the modern world of the 1960s and many Native American reserves.

"Looks like they've got things pretty much under control here, amigo," Clayton said. Everything was in order as it should be.

"Hey, Spirit of the Wind," Deacon's cousin Lone Wolf called out. At twenty-nine he was a strapping six-footer and a bit of a loner, "Glad you could make it. Talulah said you were coming." Lone Wolf hugged Deacon and then Clayton, "Good to see you."

"You have come to see me," a gentle voice asked as Talulah appeared, "or to help your teacher?"

"Grandmother," Deacon responded, his dark eyes lighting up with love and devotion the smile on his face as broad as the prairies of Saskatchewan. He hugged her tightly. "Why would I not come to see you?" Instantly, he was speaking the Cree tongue.

"You are working now, you have other commitments."

"There's no commitment more important than you, Talulah," Clayton answered before Deacon could reply.

"Thank you, Clayton," Talulah said, putting her arms around both the boys.

"That's because I mean it. When we saw the drifts this morning, we were a little concerned about y'all, but I guess you're used to it."

"Come inside." Talulah led them inside her tipi. The dwellings were warm in winter and cool in the summer.

"We can't stay long. Captain McNally wants us to go over to the Simpson's pl..." Deacon halted in mid-sentence. "How did you know?"

"I know everything you do. Stay long enough to warm up. Then Stands in Timber and Lone Wolf will go with you. There is someone wishing to see you, Spirit of the Wind."

Deacon looked into his grandmother's dark eyes, "Thorn Rose?"

"Yes. She has not seen you for some time."

Lone Wolf ducked into the lodge, bowing his head in respect to Talulah and Deacon, "Spirit of the Wind, Thorn Rose waits for you outside."

Excusing himself Deacon followed his cousin into the cold night. Thorn Rose waited by the lake, wrapped in a warm colourful blanket worn over the top of her Native parka.

"It is good to see you, Spirit of the Wind," she spoke her own tongue as Deacon responded in kind. Standing on tiptoe Thorn Rose pulled him close and kissed him. "I have missed you. I hoped you might come sooner."

Taking the girl in his arms Spirit of the Wind returned her kisses. "I'm sorry Thorn Rose. Because I am not here doesn't mean I don't want to see you. Captain McNally keeps us busy so I cannot always be here when you need me."

"Can't or won't?" Thorn Rose retorted sharply, returning to English. "I realize I come second in line to Clayton but you could make the effort once in a while. We're promised to each other. When will our hearts become one?"

A feisty and vivacious young woman of eighteen, not a drop of makeup ever touched Thorn Rose's face. Her dusky skin glowed with a natural healthy beauty that Deacon found irresistible and compelling.

"When I return here forever, we will be together."

"Then why are you here this day?"

"We came to see if grandmother and Nedipah were safe and if you needed our help. Captain McNally wants Clayton and me to head over to Mrs. Simpson's house now that everyone is ok here."

"Is she more important than me?"

"They're snowed in same as everyone else."

"We were snowed in, but we're fine now and we don't even have the protection of a wooden lodge. Surely, they can help themselves. She has a husband, doesn't she? A good husband would take care of her."

Clayton sat with Talulah, drinking coffee watching Deacon and Thorn Rose from the tipi. "It's not looking good, Talulah," he said shaking his head dolefully.

"I did not think it would be."

Deacon and Clayton had grown closer over the thirteen years they had known each other. Their friendship was blessed with a devotion and adoration so powerful and enduring that no marriage could ever match it.

Theirs was a love evolved from a distant past. It had become apparent last year over Deacon's six-month struggle with his father's demon and the sinister legacy left to him, that he and Clayton were meant to be together. The chance meeting in Wilderness Park when they were children was not chance, but a destiny prophesied by the ancient Cree ancestors. Their lives and those of their families depended on the boys staying together.

Deacon's love for Thorn Rose matched that of her own; passionate, strong and demanding. But always in the back of Deacon's mind lingered the love he bore Clayton. What the boys once believed was true friendship had escalated well beyond companionship stunning them both, climaxing when they reached sixteen. In his heart Deacon believed that the way he felt about Thorn Rose and his desire for her would not intrude upon his and Clayton's relationship. Clayton in complete agreement swore it to be the truth. And so it was until Deacon's father's legacy changed their lives forever, it became imperative that he and Clayton were never parted.

"I love you, Spirit of the Wind," Thorn Rose said, "Why can't we be together now. Is it because of your feelings for Clayton?" Rubbing up against him, she squeezed him tightly, afraid that if she let go, he would fly away.

"It is not because of Clayton, I have always loved you Thorn Rose. It's my father's legacy, you know that. If I cannot end it, we can never have anything more."

Squashing Thorn Rose to him he kissed her. Moving his body against her he felt himself stirring. The young Indian's love for Thorn Rose was never in doubt. If he had been old enough to know his blood mother Lupin before she died, he would have been shocked at how much Thorn Rose resembled her. His hands trembled as he held her.

Locking eyes with him Thorn Rose said, "Be honest with me. If it were not for your father Sparkling Eyes and Damian and their alliance with the unholy, would you be with me or would I still have to compete with Clayton?"

He held her gaze unwaveringly his black eyes burning into her, "You do not have to compete with my Brother, I love you."

"You did not answer my question. Will your blood brother always stand between us?"

"My brother does not stand between us."

"In your eyes and in your heart, I know it to be the truth. I want you for my husband, if it cannot be then I am not willing to share you with anyone..." Her heart was breaking as she held him close.

~ * ~

Staring through the window hoping to see the rangers riding up the snow encrusted driveway, Steve Simpson grumbled, "How long did Captain McNally say the rangers would be? It's already getting dark, what are they going to do without light?"

"We have lights. Switch on the perimeter light and the ones around the house that should be sufficient. Captain McNally didn't say they were definitely coming he said they'd try. They've still got to get across a half-frozen lake."

"That shouldn't pose a problem for an Indian," Steve said sarcastically.

Reserving comment Emily clenched her teeth and went in search of her dog, Wolf. For the first time since they moved into their new home eighteen months ago, Wolf had actually come out of hiding.

~ * ~

Talulah Bearhead stood up, wrapped a blanket around her shoulders and headed for the lake shore. Lone Wolf stood next to Stands in Timber, observing. Both young men were on guard duty for the evening. Talulah had always insisted that the Cree police patrolled the inner encampment from the lakeshore into the village and the outer perimeter of the encampment some distance away.

"If Thorn Rose were free I would have her," Stands in Timber said.

"Does she know your thoughts?"

"She does not."

"Then perhaps you should speak with her and tell her how you feel. If not, you will always wonder..."

"If I do that I would have to speak with Spirit of the Wind."

"He can be approached."

"He's the grandson of Chief Eagle Hawk and he's promised to Thorn Rose. I cannot ask this of him, he is my brother."

"If a man does not unburden his heart it will destroy him."

"How can you say this Lone Wolf? Spirit of the Wind is your cousin, you have chosen to serve him. He is soon to be our chief."

"I said speak to her I did not say steal her. He will not take her for his wife until the legacy is ended, therefore, she is technically a free woman. You heard her words, she's not prepared to share him. She may choose to wait for him or she may not."

"Would you speak with him over this matter?"

"I would not."

Her heart troubled, Talulah Bearhead approached Spirit of the Wind and Thorn Rose. She took their hands in hers. "Come, there is no more to be said tonight. You both need to think it over, sleep on it. We will speak about it later. Lone Wolf, please take Thorn Rose back to her father. Spirit of the Wind, come with me."

Nodding, not trusting herself to speak, Thorn Rose turned away. Stands-in-Timber was at her side instantly.

"I will walk you back," he told her. "Is that permitted, Talulah?"

"If Spirit of the Wind does not object it is allowed."

Glancing at Deacon, Stands-in-Timber waited for permission. Despite everything Lone Wolf had told him Thorn Rose was not his to have.

"You may take her."

Deacon followed his grandmother back to her tipi, his heart heavy. Clayton hugged him close. "I am here my Brother."

Deacon sat for a long time in silence. Finally, he spoke, "We godda go Clayton, we got things to do."

Taking his best friend's hand Clayton peered earnestly into Deacon's black eyes.

"Don't seem right you should lose her because of me. I love you man and I don't like to see you hurting."

"It matters, Clayton. It matters that you and I are together."

"You love Thorn Rose, you always have."

"What I feel for you will not change my thoughts for her."

CHAPTER NINE

"Jesus will you look at that snow," Clayton exclaimed, "how are we gonna shift that?"

Nestling below the Wapiti Hills, the Simpson's sprawling six bedroom home was rapidly taking on the appearance of an ice palace. Although the uppermost windows stared out through the white shroud enveloping the monstrous two storey building, the whole of the first floor and most of the second floor were hidden. The roof seemed about to collapse under the weight of the snow.

"Looks like Mr. Simpson hasn't attempted to clear any part of it," Deacon said.

"Yeah, well your momma said she didn't think he'd have much idea. She was right on that account. So where do you wanna start?"

"Better let them know we're here."

"I've found the door," Lone Wolf said with a chuckle. He'd been prowling around looking for access.

Scrambling over the near frozen snow to reach the front door, Deacon banged loudly "Mrs. Simpson, you okay in there? Mrs. Simpson?"

After what seemed like an eternity to the four young men shivering in the bitter cold, Emily dragged open the door. "Thank goodness you're here. We were beginning to wonder if something had happened to you." She stood back to observe and admire Deacon and Clayton in their green and khaki uniforms under their open coats "I'm impressed, you both look so different, so professional and dare I say, so grown up."

"Thank you, ma'am," Clayton said.

"We bought some help; my cousin Lone Wolf, you know him you met him outside school enough times and this is Stands-in-Timber."

"Please come in."

"We'd best get started ma'am," Lone Wolf told her. "Soon it will be too dark to see."

"Is Mr. Simpson home?" Deacon questioned.

"He's in the study."

"Can you ask him to grab a shovel and give us a hand?"

"That'll go down well," Clayton whispered, admiring Deacon's audacity.

"It's his place it's the least he can do."

Appearing in the doorway Steve Simpson turned his hands upward palms outward, "Where are the rest of the rangers?" his tone indicating that the whole force should have downed tools and come directly to his aid.

"They're out working. Yours isn't the only place needing help Mr. Simpson, so grab a shovel and give us a hand. We've been digging out since first light and we're getting tired."

Behind her husband, Emily snickered. The prospect of Steve actually getting down and doing some physical work was about as likely as roping the moon, so she was astounded when he reluctantly took up a shovel.

After two hours of digging and a heap of cursing from Steve, Emily called them all in for a hot drink and a hot meal.

"We can't do anymore tonight Mrs. Simpson," Clayton told her. "Even with your outside lights it's too dark to see and there looks to be another blizzard headed this way. To be honest we're shattered; not so much the snow as the cold that gets you. You got any candles or a fireplace. I can't remember seeing either when we were here last year."

"There is a fireplace but we've never used it. What do we need candles for?"

"You don't right now, but if it gets real bad and we lose power and it's been known to happen, you're gonna need light and some form of heat."

Emily looked from one to the other and all with the exception of her husband wore the same expression. "The only heat comes from the furnace. You don't think..."

"It's always a possibility out here."

Silenced, Emily flopped onto the chair.

"That'll never happen," Steve said. Excusing himself he faded into the office.

"Can I go to the bathroom, Mrs. Simpson?" Deacon asked.

"Yes of course you can. You know where it is."

Outside the bathroom Deacon hesitated. He'd entered this room in June of last year. The sudden inexplicable pain and sickness he'd experienced here heralding the beginning of his father's tortured and tormented past.

"How long do you think it will be before everything is back to normal?" Emily asked.

"Nothing is ever normal out here," Lone Wolf stated, "haven't you noticed that Maskek is the most 'unnormaliest' town you're ever likely to come across."

"Not likely to find that word in the Oxford English dictionary," Clayton grinned.

"Likely not, but it's the only one I can think of."

"Clayton," Deacon called from upstairs.

"Aw jeez, now what's he done?" Belting up the stairs Clayton met him by the bathroom door. "What's up?"

"It's still here."

"What do you mean 'it's still here'? Arcus is dead, Deacon."

"He might be, but whatever else was here is still around."

Clayton's heart sank into his boots. From the expression on his best friend's face something was seriously bothering him.

"I can't stay." His heart was hammering.

"We can't get home tonight. In case you hadn't noticed there's a blizzard out there."

"We'll go back to the village. I'm not staying here Clayton. I can't go through all that again."

"Okay, stay cool. I'll sort it."

As Deacon came into the room Lone Wolf was on his feet instantly, alarmed by the haunted look in his cousin's eyes. "Tell me."

"There's something here," Deacon said, "we must go."

"Best call your momma," Lone Wolf suggested, "tell her you won't be home tonight we're heading back to the village."

"You're welcome to use the phone, honey," Emily replied. She turned to face Clayton." There's been nothing since Deacon came here by himself that night. It's been quiet, even the basement has settled down."

"He's the catalyst," Clayton explained. "Every time he comes here, he awakens it."

Deacon heard his mother's sudden intake of breath. She knew immediately all was not well. "The weather's gonna get worse," he told her, "There's enough wood cut to last for a few days, you won't need to go outside..."

"Let me talk to her."

While Clayton relayed their predicament to Deacon's mother, Emily watched Deacon. He was agitated and his face was ashen.

"Clayton, I don't feel good." The rumbling in his head was beginning again and he was about to throw up his supper.

Taking one look at him, Clayton said, "Godda go now Aunt Nonie. Give mom my love and do like Deke says, stay inside. We'll see you in the morning."

Before he could reach the door, Deacon vomited up his supper. Lone Wolf grabbed the youth's long hair and held it off his face.

"I'll clean it up, Mrs. Simpson."

"There's no need Clayton, I'll tend to it you take him back to Talulah."

"You can come with us if you want. Take a look outside."

The night sky was already filling up with more snow and the shrieking wind was whipping up the snowflakes and swirling them around like bottomless whirlpools. The chain link fence surrounding their property and the cedar fence around the driveway were being buffeted like ships on the ocean. The lights anchored on the fence were popping and jumping, coming on and going off, blazing then dying, like an all night disco. All that was required to complete the picture was the music. Above their heads the conifers swayed and cracked tossing the snow onto everything around them. Even as they watched the top three feet of one of the trees sheared off landing heavily by the back door, splitting the wire from the house to the lights.

"I can't see anything," Emily cried momentarily panicked by the all-consuming darkness. Nothing beyond the room they stood in was visible outside. She clung tightly to Clayton's arm.

Glass shattered somewhere near the front of the house as a window imploded, bringing Steve running from his office to investigate. "What the hell is going on? Why are the perimeter lights off?"

"Told you it might happen," Clayton said.

"So, what do we do now?" Steve demanded, his face like thunder.

By the door Deacon shivered. It wasn't from the cold. "Clayton, can we go?" The pain in his head was intensifying, the churning in his stomach relentless.

"You have two choices Mr. Simpson," Deacon heard Clayton saying, "you can come with us to Talulah's village or you can stay here..." As Clayton spoke a second window ruptured spewing glass across the lounge, narrowly missing their heads. The screeching wind from the broken window whipped around them with a vengeance, almost snarling as it passed over Deacon's face leaving him breathless and fearful, "It is in this room. It's in the wind."

"Let's go, Clayton," Lone Wolf said impatiently, taking Deacon's arm and pulling him outside. Stands-in-Timber remained in the house waiting for Clayton.

There was a tremendous explosion, like a sawn-off shotgun fired in a confined space and the interior of the house was plunged into darkness. Still clinging to Clayton's arm Emily jumped, startled. "I'm coming with you. Are you coming Steve?"

"I'm not leaving this house," her husband replied seizing her arm, "and you aren't going anywhere, least of all over there."

"You won't stop me, Steve." Brushing his arm aside she picked her way through the blackness now that her eyes had partially adjusted to it and found her coat in the closet. She yanked it roughly from the hanger. "I'm ready."

"Emily, you seriously don't expect me to clean this up, do you?"

Ignoring Steve, she followed Clayton into the roaring night guided by the tail of his parka. Behind them the Simpson's house shook and shuddered fighting a losing battle with the raging wind.

"Will Steve be alright?"

"That depends on whether it's the wind...or something worse."

As Deacon glanced backwards towards the house a vision appeared in the corner of his eye, leaving him chilled.

CHAPTER TEN

Stands-in-Timber led the way from memory, the twisting blanket of snow making navigation by any other means virtually impossible. Lone Wolf followed behind helping Deacon along and Clayton with his arms around Emily steadying her against the wind bought up the rear. The closer they came to his grandmother's village the better Deacon began to feel. By the time they reached Talulah's encampment they were shaking with cold and Emily was near to collapse. Willing hands ushered them into the glowing warmth of Talulah's lodge. When Lone Wolf and Stands-in-Timber were certain that Deacon would be alright and Emily had fully recovered they took their leave.

Taking Emily's frozen hands Talulah sat her next to the fire. Talulah's younger sister, Nedipah, appeared with a cup of steaming, sweet colourless liquid and offered it to Emily. "Drink this it will warm you through."

"What is it?" Emily asked wearily.

"Don't ask," Deacon grinned, "just drink."

The boys removed their heavy parkas and snowshoes and sat cross legged by the fire, rubbing circulation back into their extremities. Talulah Bearhead peered earnestly into her grandson's face. Speaking in the Cree tongue she told him, "You have set if off again. In order to contain it you must stay away from Mrs. Simpson's home. When you leave here you must stay away from Mrs. Simpson."

"What does it have it to do with Mrs. Simpson?"

"More than you know, my child. The fact that the beast is dead does not guarantee safe passage, your father's legacy remains. You can avoid it but you cannot escape it. Soon you must return here and once that has taken place there will be no going back."

"This is for mine and Clayton's protection and that of our

families?"

"Yes. In the sacred hoop of the village no harm can come to you. Yet even now the evil grows."

"I saw something when we were leaving Mrs. Simpson's home. It was moving through the snow away from her house. It seemed to have the features of a man but it moved like an animal. Where there should be limbs it appeared to have protuberances. I didn't hang around to find out."

"Then it is closer than I thought. You must return here very soon."

"I can't leave momma alone, grandmother."

"I am aware of that. Nonie can come with you."

"I am not sure she will."

"She bought you back here when you were a baby. It will be again."

"This isn't just about my father is it, it's time for me to take my place by your side."

"I grow tired. I can no longer hold the people together as I once did. I need you with me. You are my only grandchild, it is your birth right. It is expected of you. From a child it was instilled in you...you will need to speak with Nonie."

"And whereas momma has a choice...I do not."

"She will choose you. You can refuse but I do not think you will."

Deacon smiled a warm and affectionate heart stopping smile. "I know my responsibilities grandmother, as I know my place. I will be at your side as much as I can."

~ * ~

Throughout the night the wind rumbled and squealed, shaking and battering the moose hide and canvas tepees, but protected by the forest they remained standing.

Somewhere in the distance or was it just outside, Emily couldn't be sure, the wolves howled incessantly their eerie mournful cries mingling with the bewailing wind. Strangely she didn't feel afraid as she would have had she remained in her home. Talulah's encampment felt safe and secure protected by the band of love abundant in the village and yes, perhaps even in the spirits of the forest. She lay on a bed of fur and blankets on the floor of the lodge, next to the fire. Earlier she'd removed her heavy winter coat and snuggling into the warmth of her makeshift bed dozed off to sleep. She'd awoken only when Deacon slipped outside for a moment. She didn't speak to him she didn't want to disturb Talulah or Clayton. Now she lay awake in the firelight watching Deacon and Clayton close up together under the blankets, listening to their even breathing. She couldn't make out much in the darkness and the glow from the fire but she knew they were there and it was comforting.

First thing when they bedded down for the night Deacon lay with his grandmother a protective arm around her. Emily couldn't understand what they were saying but evidently it was important. When Talulah was asleep he moved over and into Clayton's waiting blankets. It was hard to reconcile his sexual magnetism and hold over so many girls, with his love and devotion to Clayton Rykker. There was something about this young Native Canadian, something wild and untamed that inspired both excitement and fear, but he also had a sensitive, caring side Emily found attractive and appealing.

~ * ~

The morning sun sparkled across the snow and the wind had begun to purr. Last night's fierce storm was over. Emily remained alone in the tipi, everyone else having departed. Moments later Clayton Rykker appeared. "Mornin' Mrs. Simpson, how did you sleep?"

"Like a baby thank you, Clayton. Where is everybody?"

"They're having breakfast. As soon as you've eaten, we'll take you back and then Deacon and I godda go home and see that everything is okay there."

A delicious aroma wafted through the flaps of the tipi and Emily suddenly realised how ravenous she was. "I can smell food."

"It's ready when you are, ma'am."

"Oh, that's wonderful, I'm famished. Is Talulah about or any other women?"

"I can soon find you one."

"Thank you, Clayton. I do have a rather pressing need."

He returned five minutes later with a woman not dissimilar in appearance to Talulah. "This is Nedipah, she's Talulah's younger sister, you met her last night. Tell her what you want and when you're ready come and eat."

When Emily finally showed up with Nedipah, Deacon and Clayton had finished breakfast and were waiting patiently to take her back to Steve.

"Spirit of the Wind," Nedipah said bowing her head in respect.

"Why did she do that?" Emily asked as Nedipah took her leave.

"Because he's Talulah's grandson," Clayton said. "In the absence of the chief, Talulah as Medicine Woman takes his place. Therefore, she and her immediate family are to be given the respect due their status and bloodline. I can't say if it's the same in any other native village, this one is like nothing you'll ever come across again."

"So, you're a prince, Deacon."

"Wouldn't go that far," he grinned.

"I have heard the term 'Indian princess.' Wasn't Pocahontas and Indian princess?"

"Pocahontas was the daughter of a chief—she was not a princess."

"Yeah, maybe, but the Cree word for chief also means king, prince and leader, right?" Clayton responded.

"Now that I can believe," Emily said. "What happened to your grandfather, Deacon?"

"He died two years ago."

"I'm sorry."

"He gets upset so we don't talk about," Clayton responded, "they were really close."

To make it easier for Emily and to avoid struggling through the snow, Clayton saddled his buckskin mare, helped Emily onto the horse's back and sat in front of her. Deacon placed a blanket over the black stallion. He seldom used a saddle except when he was on duty with the rangers.

"You don't wanna be riding that mean ol' stallion," Clayton told Emily, "he's a devil."

Graciously thanking her hostess, Emily waved as they left the camp behind.

"That was an extraordinary experience. I'm beginning to understand what compels you to live in the forest."

"Glad to hear it Mrs. Simpson."

~ * ~

"Sounds like the snow plows out," Deacon said. "I guess Mr. Simpson won't need to do anymore digging."

Approaching what was left of Emily's home, Captain McNally waved them over. Emily looked on mortified. "What happened to my house?"

"Jesus on a dog sleigh," Clayton muttered, "What the hell hit it?"

The roof was partially caved in and most of the windows on both floors were shattered. Little remained of the wooden fence, all the cedar panels either lay on their side or had been uprooted. The ice palace was a complete shambles. The snow plow droned on clearing a wide space around the house, piling the snow into high drifts.

"The snow did this?" Emily asked, horrified by the damage and devastation wrought upon her home.

Heart thudding, Deacon backed away. "It wasn't just the snow."

The chief of the department of the Forest and Wildlife Rangers, Captain Virgil McNally strode over to Deacon, an expression of concern on his tanned and weathered countenance. "Tell me."

"I have to go."

Peering into Deacon's strained face, Captain McNally tried to read the expression in the youth's dark eyes. "You believe this is connected to your father or specifically to his legacy?"

"Both. This is where it started in June last year and again last night; the pain in my head and the sickness, just as he suffered with it. And it was where the demon Arcus first came to me. The demon is dead but we are not free of him. Last night grandmother told me that in order to contain it I need to stay away from Mrs. Simpson and this house."

"You defeated Arcus."

"But he's only one, that which bred him still lives and my presence awakens it."

With a feeling of trepidation Chief Ranger McNally pondered over Deacon's words. He'd been a good friend of Jonathan Sparkling Eyes for many years. The horror that had touched Jonathan as a young man lingered long into his life and it had finally destroyed him.

"Deke hasn't been here since Arcus wrecked the house last summer. We've avoided it. Now we know why, "Clayton explained.

"Alright Deacon go home and take Clayton with you. I dare say your mothers are probably worried about you. We can handle things at this end. Be at the ranger station tomorrow morning around eight am. We'll take it from there."

Relieved and grateful to be away from the house that had unleashed such fury on him the previous summer, he and Clayton left the canoe where it was and headed back overland.

CHAPTER ELEVEN

"Oh wow!" Clayton exclaimed as he and Deacon rode away from Loon Lake. "Snow plow's been around. No more digging out. Can't say I'm gonna miss it."

Dismounting they led both horses around the back of the house and into the barn. When the animals were settled, fed and watered the boys returned to the house.

Nonie Pierce and Rona Rykker appeared on the porch, relieved to have their sons back home. Hugging his mother, Deacon asked, "Are Melissa and Leona still here?"

"They wanted to stay until you got back. Melissa reminded us that you said you'd take a look at her car but the rangers fixed it and took them home."

"They'd have been real pleased about that then," Clayton drawled, "they'd have had another pair of pants to play in."

"Clayton!" his mother chastised, "even if it is true you could've kept it to yourself."

"Deacon thinks it's funny anyhow," Clayton mumbled, "sorry mom."

"Are you alright?" Nonie asked her son.

"I'm fine momma told you not to worry. Go inside and I'll tell you what grandmother said to me."

Nonie listened, her face grave. "Then perhaps it's the best thing for Mrs. Simpson to return to Edmonton."

Deacon faced his mother his gaze penetrating. "Even if she does go whoever buys their house will inherit the presence that lives there, that will never go away."

"Then you'll stay away. After your teacher leaves there's no reason for you to go back is there?"

"That's not what I meant momma. The only way to prevent it is to return to the village."

"And Talulah wants that immediately?"

"She didn't say when, but soon."

Nodding, Nonie took her son's hands in hers. "When it's time we'll go. You'll know when that time is."

"I wasn't sure if you wanted to after living here for thirteen years."

"We both know you can't stay here much longer. You must take your place among your people. Jonathan and Lupin would have been proud of you. He and Talulah had all this planned before you were born. It's your rightful place." While it was still unsettled Nonie was happy to go along with it. She placed her arms around her son's waist. He could feel her trembling.

Exchanging glances Clayton and Rona smiled. "Shall we go make some coffee," Rona tactfully suggested.

"I think that'd be a good idea mom."

~ * ~

After a leisurely lunch they sat in the lounge watching the snow tumbling gently from the trees in front of the house. Deacon turned to his mother locking his dark expressive eyes once more upon her pretty face. "Momma, when you hold me do you think of my father and wish I was he?" He had unconsciously lapsed into his native tongue.

"Why would you think that?" Nonie asked startled by his question.

"I watch you."

"How do you watch me?"

"The way you look at me sometimes, the things you say, the way you are."

Listening to their conversation Clayton was not surprised at Deacon's question it had been coming for a while.

"If I do," Nonie replied after struggling for an answer, "it's not my intention. You're my son, I love you. When I look at you, I see your father. How could you not have his face, but that doesn't mean I don't see

69

you or love you any less. What has brought this on? Does it disturb you?"

With his smile full of devotion, he said, "It does not disturb me. But there are times when I feel that you are afraid to let me out of your sight in case you lose me as you lost my father and my mother."

"Are you telling me that I smother you?"

"Sometimes you do. There are times when I want to be on my own for a little while, especially now."

"Is this to think about your future with Talulah?"

"To think about our future with grandmother it's not just about me."

"I didn't just lose your father I lost my best friend and I very nearly lost you. If I'm too clingy it's because whilst ever Jonathan's legacy lingers the fear will not go away. There's more to it isn't there? I believe it's because I sent Clayton to bring you home from the coffee house."

"I wanted to spend time with Cut Hand while I had chance. You knew where I was there wasn't any need to call him or send Clayton. I'd have come back pretty soon anyway."

"Did I embarrass you?" Nonie was feeling slightly uncomfortable under his penetrating gaze.

"No, you didn't," Deacon told her reverting back to English. "Captain McNally told us there'll be times when we need to be away for a couple of days and some nights too and I know that won't sit well with you."

Nonie's shocked expression revealed all that Deacon had suspected. "Why would that be necessary? The ranger station is just outside Maskek."

"That's headquarters, momma. We won't be working out of there we could be anywhere."

"Forearmed is forewarned...I think," Clayton said. "Deke's worried that you'll worry, Aunt Nonie. There's lot of land to cover out there and most of it on horseback. Most of the areas we'll be covering are inaccessible to vehicles. Cap'n was concerned about how you'd feel while we're away."

Nonie clasped Deacon's hands in hers. "You're growing up aren't you, you're not my baby anymore. You're a young man and it takes some getting used to. For the last eighteen years it's been the two of us. Now everyone wants a part of you, that's what I'm finding hard to accept, almost as hard as letting you go."

Tenderly Deacon took his mother into his arms. "I'm still gonna be here momma, you don't have to worry about that. Look at it this way, it gets me outta your hair for a while..."

"That's godda be a bonus," Clayton said dryly, "It won't be easy for my mom either, but at least you got each other."

Perched on the couch Rona said, "We can do it Nonie. We have to let them grow up. School's over, they're working, our lives are changing you and I can hold the fort. Don't forget that whilst ever you're missing Deacon, he's missing you. Am I correct Clayton?"

"Yeah, mom you are." He turned to Deacon, "I'm pleased you finally got that cleared up."

"What did your momma say when you told her?"

"Not a great deal. She got upset, cried a little and then wished me luck. I think she's just glad to be getting rid of me once in a while."

Deacon suddenly tensed, all senses alert.

"What's up?"

"Horses coming in."

"Who the hell be headed out here on horseback except maybe your cousin Lone Wolf?"

"It ain't Lone Wolf," Deacon replied shaking his head, "these horses are shod."

The fact that horses were approaching at all made him suspicious. The people from the village rode unshod horses. His friends wouldn't travel by horse and the rangers generally used vehicles, except when they were out in the forest. He reached for the rifle hung above the fireplace. Clayton swept up his own rifle, the weapon was leaning against the door. It was a few seconds before his ears registered the unmistakable clip clop of horses' hooves.

"Two ridden, one without a rider," Deacon said almost to himself.

Alarmed by Deacon's reaction Nonie and Rona moved closer to take a look.

"Stay away from the window, we don't know who's out there."

"Hello the house," a gruff male voice called out as the two strangers turned off Loon Lake Trail and converged on the front porch.

Clayton lifted the latch and he and Deacon strode onto the porch shutting the door behind them. "Can we help you?" Clayton enquired.

"Maybe you can."

Clayton studied the two, travel stained, unwashed men. Probably hadn't seen a bath or a razor in weeks.

The broader of the two the one who'd called out, elected himself spokesman. "I'm Darrell, this here's my partner Logan," indicating his weasel faced companion, "We've been up in the hills awhile, ain't eaten a decent meal in days. We were kinda hoping you might see fit to help us out a little."

"How'd you get through the swamp, it's dangerous enough when you can see it let alone when it's snowed over? "

"We didn't come that way, we know this area real good. We avoided the swamp because folks say its haunted. You ever hear of any ghosts up there?"

"Do tell. We figure it's something to do with the Indian burial ground, it's not far from there if you know where to look. Most folk don't."

While Clayton and Darrel talked, Deacon moved silently back into the house and out through the back door. Coming around the side of the house his attention was drawn towards the tarpaulin wrapped bundles fastened on the third horse. Their backs to him the two strangers were unaware of his presence. Deacon slid his hand under the tightly wrapped bundles on either side of the horse. Clayton watched him from corner of his eye, something was bothering him.

"What you got back there?" Clayton questioned inclining his head towards the rider less horse.

Both men shifted in their saddles, glancing backward. The one called Darrel said, "We got us a couple of pelts in the hills."

Under the animal's belly Deacon couldn't be seen. But he could hear and he could feel his anger churning.

"Pelts huh?" Clayton said giving no indication of his friend's presence or intentions, "What kind of pelts?"

The one called Darrel glanced nervously at his companion and back to Clayton.

"Why do you wanna know?" he asked suspiciously. "It's just a couple of wolves."

"I'd say it was a more than that," Deacon said quietly, slitting the strap and pushing the heavy bundles onto the ground. The scarred and bloody bodies of the wolves lay strewn across the glistening snow. Laying the wolves out, he ran his hand slowly over them, the pain in his heart overwhelming. His anguish quickly registered with Clayton. The haunted look in his friend's black eyes was nothing short of devastation. Deacon's affinity with wolves was well known to Clayton. Talulah told them both that his blood mother, Lupin Bearhead, understood the wolves as if she were one of them.

"What is it, Deke?" Clayton felt his bowels loosening but kept the rifle pointed on the two men, his finger on the trigger.

"These marks look like they've been made by strong claws drawn across their backs. What do you know of this?" he addressed Darrel. The vicious indentations made by the claws were so deep their bodies were practically torn apart.

Darrel shrugged matter-of-factly. "We found 'em like that, I figure they're good for a few bucks. This guy I know will take anything and sell it. He tells folks that don't know any better they're getting deer or elk meat or whatever, for a good price. The guy travels all over the country trading from his truck. He's makes a damn good living..."

"They were just lying there, huh?" Deacon said, "you godda do better than that Darrel. If it was meat this guy wanted why was their skin not removed, why were they scarred? In this condition they'd be no good to anyone, least of all your friend. How do you account for the claw marks, they weren't made by another animal?"

"No claws on my hands see." Darrel displayed his huge, filthy hams. His fingernails were thick with dirt and what appeared to be animal hair and dried blood. Deacon was about to reply when a sudden chill rode up his back and a feeling of disquiet stopped him. He stared at Darrel, his piercing gaze probing the hunter's mind.

"What's the matter Deke?" Clayton asked warily, his heart

thudding furiously.

"Something is not right with Darrel." He couldn't immediately identify what but it was bothering him. Ever since he was a child Deacon had possessed the ability to read another's thoughts. Usually he chose not to enter a person's mind believing it to be a private place. Darrel's mind however was different, a dark foreboding hole he could not penetrate.

"Honest," Logan said, "that's how we found 'em. Well that's how Darrel found 'em."

"Where were you?"

"Taking a dump. I thought it kinda strange when he showed up with 'em, but I didn't argue. Darrel and me have been partners a long time. You don't dispute your partner, do you?" He could see the young Indian wasn't buying it and the fierce look in his eyes was frightening. What he and his partner had done was wrong, very wrong and he'd tried to tell Darrel. Panicking, heeling his horse Logan tried to make a run for it. He was stopped instantly in his tracks as in a blur of movement eleven inches of cold steel whistled passed his head the knife embedding itself in a tree, very close to his weasel-like face.

"Deacon..." Clayton started to say.

Behind the lounge window Nonie was troubled. She'd seen that expression on her son's face before -it signalled danger. By her side Rona clasped her hands together nervously. "Should I call Captain McNally?"

"I thought about it. I'm hoping Clayton will be able to handle him. If it looks as though it's going to turn bad, we'll call. We may need him."

"He could've killed Logan," Darrel said.

"He wasn't aiming to," Clayton said chuckling at his own joke. He wasn't altogether certain Deacon meant only to scare the fellow. "If he wanted to kill him Logan would be dead right now. Climb down."

Wordlessly Deacon hauled Logan from his horse and pushed the unfortunate fellow towards the porch. Cutting a length from the rope draped over Logan's saddle horn he turned the two men back to back and tied their wrists together. Taking the remainder of the rope he hobbled Logan and Darrel around their ankles and attached the rope to the posts on the porch.

"Deke, what're you doing? We ought to be handing them over to

Captain McNally."

The barrel of the rifle pressed against Logan's face Deacon spoke his quiet words dripping venom. "I should kill you where you stand...rip you apart like the wolves."

"He's crazy," Darrel said.

"What would you have me do?" Clayton asked. "Shoot him?"

"Shooting's too good for him."

By the tone of Darrel's voice Clayton was of the sudden impression the fellow knew Deacon.

"Clayt let me have your neckerchief."

Clayton removed the neckerchief and handed it to Deacon "What do you want it for? What're we doing?"

Darrel opened his mouth to protest a second time and Deacon shoved the cloth into the fellow's teeth and tied it around his mouth, securing it in a knot at the back of his neck.

"Give me one good reason why I should not shoot you?"

Inside the house Nonie said, "Call Captain McNally, Rona."

Rona was connected almost immediately when she explained to the ranger on the other end of the line, the altercation taking place by the porch.

Clayton could only guess at the emotions raging through his best friend. He was appalled at the wanton destruction of these bold and beautiful creatures but that did not compare one iota to what Deacon must be feeling. He waited on egg shells, with no idea of the young Indian's next move.

Logan attempted to protest, Deacon cut him off with a swift blow to the jaw galvanising Clayton into action. Throwing down his rifle, there would be no trouble from the two captives, he grabbed Deacon's arm. "We don't know if they have done anything yet. Leave it, my brother. Maybe they did just find the wolves."

"You don't really believe that, do you? I saw blood and fur under Darrel's nails. His hands are bigger than most men, unnaturally big. His heart is as stone. His thoughts are unreadable and his mind is dark..."

"I'm not doubting what you're saying, but until we can prove it there's nothing we can do."

"The spirit of the wolf speaks to me. He asks that they be punished."

"They will be, but not this way, you can't take the law into your own hands." Releasing Deacon's arm Clayton locked eyes with his best friend. "Let it go Spirit of the Wind."

Rona came onto the porch, Nonie at her side just as Clayton told her son, "You're a ranger, we can't just do what we want. I can't put into words the things I'd like to do to these guys but out here we're the law. We protect and we serve and if that includes scum like Darrel and Logan, we have no choice but to obey."

"What choice did the wolves have?"

"I can't answer that, Deacon. All I can say is that if anything like this happens again, we'll be there for them."

The wolves in the area were protected by the rangers and by Deacon's people. To hunt them was against the code the Indians and McNally's rangers lived by. Deacon's uncanny ability to feel and communicate with the wolves helped enormously. The same ability could unleash a fury so terrifying that even Clayton steered clear until the anger began to subside.

"How long are you gonna keep us tied up like this?" Logan demanded, "We got rights and we got places to go."

Glaring at Logan Deacon said, "Did those wolves have rights? You're going nowhere until we say otherwise."

"I didn't do nothing," Logan protested, "Darrel, tell him I didn't do nothing."

Squirming under the scrutiny of Deacon's cold stare Darrel turned away. The bandana was chaffing his gums and hurting his yellowing teeth. This time Deacon's knife plunged into one of the posts on the porch, far too close for comfort. Darrel tried to jump away, but hobbled as he was and with his arms tied, he had no way of stopping himself and stumbled over his feet, taking Logan with him.

"Put it away, Deke, okay?" Clayton told him pulling the knife from the post and handing it to him. "Go inside."

"Can't do that yet the wolves need to be buried."

"Captain McNally will want to see them first."

Deacon turned to his mother. "You called the rangers?"

"No, Nonie didn't," Rona said, "I did. It'll save you a trip to headquarters."

Grinning at her he said, "Are you saying you don't trust me to get them there safely?"

"I am."

"We would have got them there, eventually."

"Mmm," Rona nodded, "it's the 'eventually' bit we're afraid of."

"So, what did you see when you touched the wolf?" Clayton asked. "I know you saw something, you've had visions since you were a kid."

Deacon's face darkened, the haunted look in his eyes replacing his smile. "You remember last year Stands-in-Timber and Mule Deer found those mutilated animals in the Wapiti Hills. We went to look?"

"Yeah and what we saw I never want to see again. Are you saying this is connected?"

"Maybe. Whatever mutilated those creatures was neither animal nor human. We never found it."

"You think it's still around."

"Closer than you think. Let's go inside."

Stepping onto the porch, Deacons sensed rather than saw a change in Darrel. His skin crawled with the touch of a million ants and his body went cold; he knew then what was bothering him. All senses on full alert he spun to see the hunter, his feet above the ground bearing down on him, ropes ripped apart and his eyes burning with an eerie red light. He'd seen the same light last year. He could shoot Darrel, cut him with the Bowie or try to physically tackle him. The former he'd have to explain to Captain McNally. The latter would only render Darrel harmless for a short time. It was a split second decision. Facing the hunter, Deacon closed his eyes shutting out everything and everyone around him. Clutching the red and white beaded necklace hanging at his throat and using the power of his mind and the spiritual power of the necklace he thrust Darrel backwards with such force the hunter hit the tree solidly, slid down the trunk and sprawled unconscious on the snow.

"Whoa," Clayton said, "was that a vampire? Whatever he is

remind me never to get on your bad side."

Nonie and Rona looked on in shock.

Dragging Darrel's unconscious form over to the porch Deacon laid him out and hobbled him once more to the wooden posts.

"Touched by a demon, I guess," Clayton said, recalling the red light he'd seen in the eyes of the demon Deacon had destroyed in December last year. "Might explain why he and Logan attacked the wolves." He said it as if it was common place, the pulsing in his veins and trembling in his hands said otherwise.

CHAPTER TWELVE

The boys had been in the house only a few minutes when Virgil McNally pulled up. Darrel remained dead to the world and Logan stood quaking with cold, both of them tethered to Deacon's home like a couple of bulldogged steers. Tyrell McAlister, the younger of the two rangers gawped, his mouth opening and closing soundlessly. Feeling a grin coming on Virgil McNally attempted to hide it but in the end he guffawed loudly. "That's my boy." Although he was suspicious of the man lying on his back, he made no immediate comment.

"That's godda be Deacon's doing. Is that procedure, Cap'n?"

"Nope, but when did that ever stop him?"

Virgil was well aware that the young Indian would not have got away with such unorthodox methods in any other ranger company but he was an asset his troop could not afford to be without. For the time being Virgil tolerated it.

"Guess we'd better go get some answers." Switching off the engine Virgil climbed from the land rover he considered to be the best all-terrain vehicle he'd ever driven.

Clayton met them at the door. "Come on in." He glanced at the green, short wheel base, four-wheel drive vehicle outside the porch. "We sure could've used that to tow Melissa's car out of the snow. How long you had it?"

"It's my own, but it sure comes in handy under conditions like this. I wouldn't drive anything else. Are you okay Deacon?"

"Yeah, I'm fine."

"Certain of that are you? Ladies." He touched his hat to Nonie and Rona and gave his attention to the boys. "Okay, sit down both of you. First off how long have those guys been out there?"

"Since mom called you," Clayton replied. "These guys say

they've been up in the hills for a while, which means they were out in the storm so it ain't gonna hurt 'em to stay out there a little longer, is it?"

A grinning Tyrell leaned by the window. "They're looking a little blue."

"Gee that's tough."

"Knock it off Clayton and tell me what happened word for word."

"Yes sir."

Clayton relayed the whole incident to Captain McNally and Deacon explained all that he had seen.

"When I touched the wolf, I had a vision. That thing out there, the one called Darrel, tore the bodies with his claws. I saw a shadow coming from the trees, I heard the wolves cry out. I couldn't see its face only its talons as it ripped into their bodies. When I looked into Darrel's mind, I could not hear his thoughts, the blackness within prevented me from entering further. A moment before he broke away it became clear."

"You think this guy is some kind of demon?"

"More like a goddamn vampire," Clayton responded, "you should've seen him jump."

"I find that hard to believe," Tyrell told him. "I know this town's got secrets but a vampire? You ever seen a vampire, Clayton?"

"Not in the flesh, but I wouldn't put anything past this town. Hell, we don't know what lives in the depths of the forest."

"I don't know what he is, a shape shifter maybe, a skin walker. He's not a demon," Deacon said. "I'm convinced it has something to do with the mutilation Stands-in-Timber and Mule Deer found last year. There may be more injured animals where Darrel says he found them. We should take a look. When he recovers, we'll need to tie him down."

"You think ropes will hold him?"

"I don't."

Tyrell threw Deacon a troubled glance. "If he is one of these shape shifting things what do you suggest?"

"Shoot him..."

"What, just like that? We can't go shooting the prisoners, Deke."

Tyrell was sceptical not altogether sure Deacon was serious. Deacon didn't reply.

"How many were killed?" Virgil asked.

"Four," Clayton answered.

Virgil was silent for a few moments, an expression of anger on his rugged, tanned face. "Show me."

Pulling on their parkas they followed Virgil and Tyrell outside.

"Looking mighty cold there," Clayton told the two shivering men.

Logan opened his mouth, Deacon flashed him a warning. He closed it quickly.

"Take a good look in those saddlebags Clayton, no telling what we might find."

Virgil dropped to one knee to examine the tortured animals. He shook his head slowly, his face grave, sickened by what he saw. "This is a goddamn crime. Tyrell get some pictures."

"Won't we be taking them with us?"

"They need burying that's the least we can do. It shouldn't have happened. How have we missed it? Someone should have been up there patrolling. This time of year, the wolves are near to starving and that makes them easy pickings for a couple of illegal hunters or whatever the hell this Darrel guy is. Found anything of interest, Clayton?"

"A couple of lethal hunting rifles wrapped in oil cloth under the saddlebags and one set of filthy drawers."

"Looks like you guys are in big trouble."

"Deep shit," Clayton agreed.

"That's a pretty good bruise you got on your jaw there," Virgil told Logan, "Mind telling me how you got it?"

Deacon averted his gaze, a hint of a smile on his lips.

Fearing a rapid reprisal from the young Cree, Logan said, "Caught the butt of my rifle on it. Yeah that's what I did."

"Uh huh," Virgil replied in a tone indicating he didn't believe a word. "Better be more careful next time. Tyrell cut them loose, get them in the land rover and sit with them. Sooner we get these great white hunters away from here the better."

"Or you could let Deke impart a few suggestions into his head, make the guy forget what he is long enough to get him in chains."

"And that'll work will it, Clayton?"

"Yeah I've seen him do it before—except the guy wasn't a demon."

"He's not a demon," Deacon repeated.

Virgil exhaled slowly. "Well, I guess we've godda start someplace. You want to try it, Deke?"

Virgil had witnessed Deacon's father, Jonathan Sparkling Eyes, alter a person's thoughts by pure suggestion once before. The fact that Deacon possessed the same ability didn't surprise him at all. The blood of his medicine woman grandmother also ran in his veins. Virgil didn't profess to understand, but he'd seen the startling results for himself.

Darrel began to stir, coming around slowly as if waking from a long sleep. When he opened his eyes, the red light had vanished. He was surrounded by Virgil McNally, Tyrell, Clayton and Deacon; four rifles pointed at various parts of his person.

"What the hell?" Darrel glanced from one to another and then at his partner in crime. He ripped apart the ropes for a second time.

Logan's weasel face wore a mask of shock and disbelief. He was colder than he'd ever been and it had nothing to do with the weather. Realization kicking him hard in his gut, Darrel snarled, leapt to his feet and hit out at Deacon. Deflecting his aim Deacon grabbed Darrel's arm and pushed it up behind his back. Darrel was strong and powerful. Deacon could feel the fellow's strength under his hands. Clayton was by Deacon's side in an instant ready to defend him if Darrel twisted out of his grip.

Turning the seething hunter to face him, Deacon said, "Look at me. You will hear my thoughts. Look at me."

Darrel attempted to pull away, but against his will he was compelled to stare into Deacon's black eyes; his gaze was intense, obtrusive, probing, the Cree youth was invading his personal head space. Unwanted images were filling his mind, stripping his defences and causing him to lose track of self, time and space. Holding out against Deacon, Darrel started to flag. The power of his mind did not match his physical strength. Deacon had expanded energy to thrust Darrel against the tree earlier and now he was beginning to tire. He released Darrel and Clayton caught the hunter as he stumbled. Virgil McNally and Tyrell hauled him to his feet.

"Did I really see that?" Tyrell asked incredulously.

Drained, Deacon swayed on his feet. This time the effort had taken its toll on him.

"Are you alright, my brother?"

"Just tired is all."

"Well, you will do these things. They can be energy draining."

"It was your idea."

Clayton grinned, "You didn't have to take me up on it."

"I saw your father do that and it still amazes me," Virgil said. "Don't know what it is you guys have or where it comes from but it's mighty useful..."

Deacon was staring at Darrel. "It didn't work."

"What do you mean it didn't work?"

"Darrel was not changed..."

Before he could say another word, the abomination had replaced the man. "There is another stronger than me whom you should fear, Spirit of The Wind. Look behind you for he is there." Doubled in height and weight, razor sharp talons replacing his hands the atrocity flew at them.

Shots rang out from the rifle Clayton found under Darrel's saddle bags. The huge monstrosity collapsed onto the frozen ground, blood oozing from the area around its shattered heart. Virgil McNally stood with the smoking barrel in both hands. The silence was deafening.

"Jesus!" Tyrell said, hanging on to the rail for support, "What the hell was that?"

"Good shot, Cap'n," Clayton said when he could speak, "Is he dead?"

"Most of his heart is missing," Deacon said "I guess he will be."

"First time I ever killed a man ..."

"I'd say that was a lot more than a man," Tyrell told him.

"Yeah, I'd say it was. Okay, we need to bury him and we need to bury these poor wolves. Deke, when is the next patrol from your village due up there? I want those wolves baby sat and guarded twenty-four hours a day. "

"Tomorrow."

"I'll send Tripp and Giovanni out there tonight, we're not losing any more of them."

"Bury him, Captain?" Tyrell asked, "Should we be doing that?"

"What would you suggest Tyrell that we take him into town? He's not human how would I explain it let alone keep him under lock and key. Whatever went on up there with Darrel must've happened in the few minutes Logan wasn't present..." he turned to the shocked, weasel faced Logan barely hanging onto his senses. "Got anything to tell me?"

"I ain't seen anything like it. I swear I didn't know Darrel was one of those shifting things. I've known him five years and I've never seen the like. You think I'd hang around him had I known what a freak he was. Take me away, lock me up, just get me outta here."

"Put him in the land rover Tyrell. I'll question him later."

"What do you suppose Darrel meant by there is one stronger than me you should fear?" Clayton asked Deacon. "He obviously knows you."

"I'd like an answer to that," Virgil McNally replied.

"I have no idea. I guess I'll find out soon enough."

"Well, you'd better keep all your senses about you from now on."

"I always do."

Still in shock Rona and Nonie watched while the four of them buried the dead wolves and disposed of Darrel's body.

"I'll expect both of you in my office first thing tomorrow morning and we're going to go over everything that's happened," he looked meaningfully at Deacon, "every little detail."

"Yes sir," Deacon replied knowing what was coming next.

"Now, I don't hold with what Logan has done and if I could put him away for life I would. But that's not going happen. He'll be punished, but I'll do it. And Deacon, no matter how angry you are or how much you're hurting, don't go roughing up the prisoners. Fortunately, you only hit Logan once and Darrel kinda fell asleep; as for hog tying them that's something else altogether."

"Kept them here, didn't it?"

"Indeed, it did," Virgil McNally slowly exhaled, "but that is definitely not the correct procedure. I'll overlook it this time, if it happens again don't let me find out."

"Would you like coffee Captain McNally?" Rona asked still

shaken by the incident. "We thought perhaps you might appreciate it after what you've all been through."

"Thank you kindly Mrs. Rykker but we need to get this great white hunter back to the ranger station. Can I leave you two to sort out their horses, they could use a good rubdown and by the look of them a good meal?"

"Yes sir, we'll tend to it." Attempting to ease the tension Clayton said, "Who did you send with the snow plow, because whoever it was fixed Melissa's car and took her and Leona home. That would have given Melissa another set of pants to play in."

"I sent Vince and Giovanni."

"She'd have been inside Giovanni's then."

"Why would it be Giovanni?"

"Because Melissa likes guys with black hair and brown skin and Giovanni's Italian."

"That how come you missed out, Clayton?" Tyrell cracked.

"I guess that's it, Melissa just ain't into red hair. Catch you guys later."

"Don't forget, my office first thing."

With a wave the rangers drove away.

"I wouldn't want to be in Logan's shoes when the Captain gets through with him. Deke you really had me going earlier I didn't know what the hell you were planning next. You were scary."

"I was, huh?"

~ * ~

In the early hours of the morning Deacon awoke disturbed by a presence outside. Climbing from his bed he went to the window and stared into the night. "The Spirit of the wolf is here. Do you see it?"

Struggling to come around, Clayton joined him and peered through the glass, straining to see whatever had caught Deacon's attention. Shaking his head, he saw only the blackness of the night. "I don't see anything."

Yanking a clean pair of jeans from the drawers beside the bed,

Deacon stepped into them and galloped downstairs and out to the porch.

"Get your goddamn parka on will ya, it's cold out there," Clayton shouted at him, shrugging into his own clothes. Taking Deacon's parka Clayton handed it to him and pursued him into the night.

"There she stands," Deacons said pointing directly in front of them. "I will speak with her."

Clayton watched, still unable to locate the phantom creature. Then suddenly it was there ahead of him, directly by Deacon's side. Regal and majestic its head held proudly the black wolf locked eyes with Spirit of the Wind.

From Clayton's vantage point human and ghost wolf appeared to be talking. Clayton didn't move concerned that any movement on his part might attract unwanted attention from the magnificent beast. It might have been a ghost but Clayton didn't want to find out. Behind him roused from their slumber he sensed his mother and Nonie watching from the doorway. They must have heard Deacon open the door. Clayton saw that the animal floating above the ground. It stopped and waited.

"She wishes us to follow her."

"Follow her where?"

"Their lives were taken in the Wapiti Hills, that is where we will go."

"Right this minute?" asked Clayton alarmed by the prospect of traversing those sinister hills in the middle of the night.

"Now," Deacon replied, returning to the house.

Nonie said nothing while her son collected his rifle and waited for Clayton to join him. She never questioned his visions. She took them in stride. Finally, she asked, "What did you see?"

"The spirit wolf spoke to me."

Clayton saddled up the little buckskin mare and Deacon jumped onto the stallion's back. The two women watched the boys vanish into the night following a ghost neither of them could see.

It would take time to traverse the lake following the lakeshore, which despite the plows remained buried under a mantle of freshly falling snow. The winding trail into Wapiti Hills was dangerous at the best of times. A new day was streaking across the sky by the time they reached the area Deacon believed to be the point of the animals' slaughter; the exact spot Stands-in-Timber had discovered the mutilation last year. In spite of the frozen conditions the putrid stench of death lingered heavily in the cold air. Clayton gagged as the odour hit him full in the stomach."

"You ok Clayt?"

"I'm fine."

These were not wolves but other animals and they had been hacked up. A headless elk lay next to a fully grown moose whose beautiful antlers had been removed, a grizzly bear stripped of its fur, the skin removed from a young doe. All of them shot with a high powered hunting rifle.

"Trophy hunters," Clayton said with disgust, "godda be. They'll pay hundreds of dollars for the privilege regardless of how they're taken. Better still if they don't have to do the dirty work themselves. You think Darrel and Logan had something to do with this?"

"You found the rifles. What I can't understand is, if they did this, why the need to torture the wolves. It doesn't make any sense." Deacon stared at the remains of these once wondrous creatures with tears in his eyes, his heart beating with such force that it threatened to splinter his ribs, he hadn't seen all this in his vision. "The ghost wolf led us here that we might see this."

Glancing up, Clayton could see the spirit wolf standing close by, observing them as if indicating that they were to carry this horror beyond the hills. That they were to make it known to other hunters that there would be a penance to pay.

"This is what we found last year except then we couldn't tell what was what. Think maybe we finally caught their killers? Given what Darrel was it's not surprising we couldn't track or trace him. Captain McNally needs to see this before we bury the remains. He needs to see it and take photographs so that we can prove what really happened."

"I'll stay whilst you go. I cannot leave it is not finished."

"You can't stay here alone, we're right above Bittern Creek. It's not safe for you. The thing that lives in these hills is too close, if I leave now it'll kill you. Heed your grandmother's warning, Spirit of the Wind." Clayton spoke the terrifying truth. Talulah had warned them last summer that if the two were ever parted the corruption and depravity of Deacon's father's legacy would destroy them both.

Deacon considered his friend's words. "I will speak with the wolf, I will tell her we will return." Satisfied he had appeased the animal he mounted and followed Clayton away from Bittern Creek. He was aware that something or someone was watching them. He saw nothing, yet the feeling of another's presence persisted.

It wasn't the ghost wolf.

CHAPTER THIRTEEN

In the trees above Bittern Creek, unmoving, barely breathing he watched Clayton and Deacon riding away. Right hand clenched around a twisted, flaming lance the man moved forward. his eyes dark and feral burrowing in to Deacon's back.

"You can never be the man your father was Spirit of the Wind. Sparkling Eyes was a leader among leaders. Only I can replace such a man. Your heart is filled with compassion. There is no room for compassion among us. I have tried to tell them this, yet still the women yearn for the son of Sparkling Eyes. Look behind you, the time will come when you are alone and, on that day, your white brother will grieve." Raising the burning spear, he thrust it towards the clouds. At the summit of the Wapiti Hills a bolt of light cleft the new day splitting the sky apart, a clap of thunder so forceful that it rocked the trees and shook the earth. "I shall make it happen!"

~ * ~

Huddled in a blanket on the couch in the study, one of the few areas of the house that retained enough of its roof to make it habitable, Emily observed the remains of their beautiful home; the cost of repairing it to its former glory more than she cared to think about. They had not long restored the damage previously done last year when the abomination known as Arcus, tried to destroy her as well. Steve insisted they did not leave their home, refusing to stay at either of the two motels.

"It's an omen. We were never meant to have this house. Deacon is right the evil still lives here. Even if Steve restores it again to sell, the thing dwelling here won't rest. If it follows us to Edmonton how many other lives will it destroy?" She shook her head. "No. I'm not prepared to live with it any longer and I'm not moving away. Whatever it is has to be contained in Maskek."

Her decision made and wondering how much it really had to do with leaving Deacon rather than the town, Emily prepared to face her husband. He would not be a happy man.

~ * ~

"You hear the thunder?" Clayton asked. "Kinda strange this time of year."

"I heard it."

~ * ~

"Couldn't you sleep?" Captain Virgil McNally asked, surprised to see Deacon and Clayton out and about so early. He'd burned the midnight oil and now he was ready to rest.

"You need to come with us," Deacon replied.

"What's up?"

"We've been in the hills," Clayton told him, "found where those hunters killed the wolves up near Bittern Creek. Same place Stands-in-Timber found the other animals last year."

"If it was Bittern Creek that explains a helluva lot," Virgil said, recalling that last year three young lives had mysteriously ended there. It was an area of the beautiful but inauspicious hills that the people of Maskek avoided at all cost. Bittern Creek was the place the legacy haunting Deacon's family, was evoked over two centuries ago.

"Spirit wolf led us there," Deacon said. "She waits for us. I told her we would return."

Swivelling his chair to face Tyrell McAllister, Virgil said, "Saddle up we've got places to go. Ask Giovanni and Lamar to join us. Bring the camera, we need to take more pictures."

"You guys were here all night?" Clayton questioned.

"Yep," Tyrell replied, "trying to fill out the paper work and figure out what to do with Logan. You've still got that to come."

"Lamar, huh, "Clayton grinned knowingly, "Better watch him, Deke."

~ * ~

Visible only to Deacon and occasionally Clayton, the ghost wolf stood guard over the devastation. Stunned into silence McNally and the three younger rangers stared in utter disbelief. Lamar threw up the contents of his stomach and turned away.

At last Tyrell spoke, his voice wavering, "Why would anyone do this? What pleasure is there in brutalising helpless animals? I'd sure like to know the answer."

Giovanni set up the camera, making every picture count. Their job was to protect wildlife, which they did with great affection. Devastation such as this was heart breaking and it affected each and every one of McNally's rangers.

After checking Lamar, Deacon moved towards the wolf. Clayton striding after him placed his arm around his friend's shoulders. "Captain McNally will see Logan gets what's coming to him you can count on it. Darrel may have done the damage but I don't believe he did it alone. I reckon Logan did his share. Five years with his partner he must've known what Darrel was."

Deacon reached out to the ghost wolf and his hand connected with solidity. Clayton saw only the trees.

"It is good," the young Indian stated. "She will not return."

"Then we have we appeased her."

"Indeed, my brother."

Giovanni finished with the camera and everyone else buried the remains of the slaughtered animals and covered the blood-stained earth with fresh snow. Deacon offered prayers to the Great Spirit and to the slaughtered creatures, Clayton as ever by his side.

When they had finished their prayers McNally spoke, "Thank you for leading us here Deacon the world needs to see this."

The rangers packed their photographic equipment onto their horses, mounted and turned the horses towards Loon Lake.

"What is it?" Clayton asked as Deacon hesitated.

"There..."

Clayton followed Deacon's outstretched arm.

"Do you see her?"

"I see another wolf," Clayton said, "I think she's staring at you."

True to his word the black wolf stood at a distance, her eyes focused on Deacon her gaze never faltering, she didn't blink but continued to watch him. The young Indian shuddered, a sense of belonging pulling at his heart strings. "She knows me..."

"Come again."

"She knows me."

~ * ~

When the small troop reached the house, Nonie and Rona appeared on the porch.

"You won't refuse coffee this time will you Captain McNally?" Rona asked, waiting until the rangers dismounted and inviting them in. She planted a kiss on Clayton's cheek.

"No ma'am, we'd sure appreciate it,"

While Rona served coffee, Deacon showed Lamar to the bathroom to clean himself up.

"Thanks Deke. You wouldn't wanna help me, would you?"

Grinning, Deacon told him, "Think maybe you can handle that all by yourself."

"It's such a waste," Lamar eyeing him up and down, "We could do so many things together..."

"There are some things better left alone," Deacon laughed, "especially if you wanna keep your scalp. Clayton's getting pretty good with a knife." Chuckling to himself Deacon left Lamar in the bathroom.

"What did you mean when you said the wolf knew you?"

"What's there to explain? Trust me Clayton she knew me."

CHAPTER FOURTEEN

"Captain McNally's here," Clayton mumbled through a mouthful of Stanley's Cuthand's legendary blueberry pie. He and Deacon were enjoying lunch in the Coffee House.

"By the expression on his face you'd better finish it quickly," Deacon chuckled.

"Captain," he acknowledged as Virgil reached their table, "time up already?"

"Reynard's dog escaped. It's running amok in the main street. I want you two to catch it."

"If it's a dog, Cap'n," Clayton stated, swallowing the last of his pie, "how come folks in town can't handle it?"

"They called us. Get to it. What's the matter, Deacon?" McNally inquired when the young Cree hesitated.

"Dogs and me don't get along. I'd sooner face a bear."

"It's a dog," Clayton repeated, "what do you want us to do when we've caught it Cap'n, arrest it?"

"Return it to Mr. Reynard. He's an old man, he can't chase after it. You're rangers, public servants. Go do your job. Let me know when it's sorted. And Deke..."

"Yes sir?"

"Don't forget your hat."

Glancing at Clayton, Deacon shoved the hat on his head and reluctantly followed his best friend from the coffee house. Untying their horses from the rail outside the coffee house the boys headed down Main Street.

"Whoa," Deacon said stopping abruptly, "that ain't a dog, it's a goddamn horse." He stared incredulously at Abe Reynard's Irish wolfhound standing almost three feet tall in its bare paws, although at that moment the dog was barking loudly and pounding around the main street upsetting the more genteel of Maskek's citizens. Standing on its hind legs the dog's paws would reach Deacon's shoulders. "You got your rope, Clayton?"

"Why for?"

"What d'you think?"

"It's a dog, Deke."

"Sure about that are you?"

The inquisitive crowd waited expectantly for the next move. Deacon untied the lariat from Clayton's horse, looped it and threw it out. It landed squarely over the dog's neck.

"Jesus, Deke."

The townsfolk on the boardwalk clapped and hooted appreciatively, bunching up around the startled animal.

"Hot dog!" Graph declared. He was the most senior of Maskek's senior citizens and owner of the only garage in town. "I ain't never seen anyone rope a dog afore."

"Whyn't you just hog tie and brand it as well," Clayton said, peering unbelievingly at his friend.

"It worked didn't it," Deacon grinned handing the rope and dog to Clayton. "I roped him and you can take him back to Mr. Reynard. I've never seen a dog that big before."

Bringing up the rear he led the horses, keeping well away from the dog. Graph tagged on behind watching Deacon watching the dog. A spindly man with bowed legs and a limp, Graph's hair was grey and white like salt and pepper, his skin the colour and texture of old leather, a man used to working outdoors in all weathers. His spindly frame belied his true strength.

"It sure is a soft thing," Clayton said stopping to pet it. "Could take to him myself. You wanna stroke it?"

"No way," Deacon responded backing off slightly.

For a split second Clayton thought he saw fear in his friend's eyes. He noticed Graph tense and relax.

"Mr. Reynard," Clayton called wrapping on the front door of the small, clapboard ranch style house. "We bought your dog back Mr.

Reynard?"

Sidestepping the dog, Deacon hitched the horses to Reynard's fence. He glanced around the yard house and outbuildings, all of them in a state of disrepair. "Fence is down," he pointed towards the backyard near the barn. "I guess his dog got out that way. It must've been tethered here." He indicated the meat plate sized paw marks and disturbed sandy gravel, "and for quite a while I'd say."

"You don't tether dogs, Deke."

"We tether the dogs in my village."

"Yeah but they're sled dogs that's different."

"Ol' Abe almost always keeps Alamo in the house," Graph replied.

"He's called Alamo?"

"That's the name Abe gave him. When Abe and his wife found the dog, it was barely alive he'd been mauled by a bear and left for dead. Guess the bear must've lost interest in it or found something more appetising. Anyhow, they bought the dog home and tended to its wounds. It was touch and go for a while. He sure was a fighter, he battled against overwhelming odds to survive; hence the name Alamo. He doesn't usually keep the dog outside though. Since Abe's wife died—God rest her soul—Alamo's been his constant companion. If he was in the yard there's a mighty good reason."

"Place looks rundown," Deacon commented.

"Don't seem to be any answer. Maybe we'd better take a look inside," Clayton suggested.

"The door'll be open, Clayton, Abe never locks it."

Pushing open the front door the boys were hit by the nauseating odour of unwashed bodies, grime and neglect. Clayton quickly opened the kitchen window to air the room out. Pulling free of Clayton's hands Alamo darted passed Deacon startling him, and into the kitchen. "Jesus."

Alerted by the fear in Deacon's voice Clayton rounded on him, "What's the matter?"

"Nothing's the matter. I'll go look for Mr. Reynard." He beat a hasty retreat in the opposite direction to that of the dog.

"This place hasn't been cleaned in a long time," Clayton said.

Alamo was hanging round his dish, making whimpering noises. Retrieving the dish from the filthy floor that hadn't kissed a mop in a long time, Clayton washed it out and filled it with fresh water. He checked the kitchen cupboards they were bare. "No food here."

"Or in here," Graph answered closing the refrigerator door.

Steering clear of Alamo, Deacon scouted most of the house inside and out and now stood in the doorway. "Mr. Reynard's gonna need help here Clayt, the whole place is coming down. I noticed the wood stove in the front room was cold it hasn't been used for some time. I checked the wood shed, none's been cut so how's he keeping warm?" His gaze lingered on the kitchen walls thick with grease, the windows looked as if they had been painted with dirt and long abandoned cobwebs. "Can we get him help? He's obviously finding it tough to manage. A couple of hands to fix up the outbuildings, maybe some help in the house. Can we do that?" Deacon asked earnestly his handsome face expressing concern.

"I reckon we can do that."

"I'll take another look upstairs," Deacon said just as Alamo chose that moment to terrorise the kitchen. "Clayton will you do something with that dog. Please."

Bemused, Clayton glanced quickly at Graph and grabbed hold of Alamo's collar. "What's the matter with him?" If Deacon was afraid there had to be a good reason.

"Clayton," Deacon called from upstairs, sounding alarmed, "come here. I'm in the bedroom."

Anxiously Clayton pounded up the stairs and halted abruptly in the doorway. Deacon knelt over the unconscious form of Abe Reynard. He was on the floor, his body cold, barely breathing.

"He's alive but only just. We need to take him over to the clinic."

"I'll call the ambulance. Might be why the dog is running all over town trying to bring attention to his master."

"Might not have the ambulance available we'll take him."

"We shouldn't move him until the he's been checked over."

"Nothing's broken I already checked. There are no other injuries that I can see..."

"He's skin and bone. There's no food in the house I don't think he's eaten for quite a while."

"This is hyperthermia. See if you can find a blanket, we need to keep him warm."

While Graph searched the house for warm blankets, Clayton called ranger headquarters over the handset looped on his belt.

"Cap'n says he'll meet us at the clinic."

Returning with two threadbare blankets Graph wrapped them around the old man.

"His pickup's out back we'll take that. Think you can drive it Deacon it's been around a while."

"I'll give it a try."

Alamo padded into the bedroom blocking the doorway, wanting to be near his master. Taking one look at Deacon's face Graph guided the dog downstairs and slipped a lead he'd found hanging on the kitchen door, over its head. When the boys emerged carrying the elderly man, Graph had the old '53 Ford pickup truck running and the dog in the back on the open bed. They laid Abe gently across the front seats. Clayton cradled the elderly man's upper body against his chest. Deacon took the driver's seat and Graph climbed into the back with Alamo. Meeting them at the clinic, Virgil McNally waited until the nursing staff came to take him off their hands. Mo-he-ya, a Certified Nursing Aide, (A certified Nursing Aide or CNA in Canada, a Licensed Practical Nurse or LPN in the USA was equivalent to a State Enrolled Nurse SEN in England at the time this story is set.) related to both Deacon and Stanley Cuthand, listened while the boys explained how they had found him and the conditions under which the elderly gentleman had been living.

"Will you let us know how he is?" Deacon asked.

"I will honey," Mo-he-ya kissed his cheek. "What are you doing about Alamo?"

Graph stepped forward. "I'll take him until Abe's well enough. Give him a good meal. You can tell him that Alamo's in good hands otherwise he's just gonna fret."

"Can you arrange help for him when he goes home, Mo-he-ya?" Deacon asked.

"I'm sure we can. I'll look in to it for you."

"Thank you."

Knowing Deacon was eager to be away from the clinic, it wasn't a place he entirely trusted, Virgil led the boys outside. Deacon didn't feel at ease in the modern white walled clinical atmosphere of the spacious one storey building.

Specifically designed and purpose built, partially funded by a generous donation from a business man who wished to remain anonymous, the clinic dealt with all the usual medical problems and the less serious accidents. It boasted an up to date maternity wing where Deacon's grandmother, Talulah Bearhead often presided in her capacity of midwife and medicine woman to the majority of the area's Native population and many of the white patients. Many of the women preferred to have another women looking after them when possible. Talulah worked alongside the doctors and the nursing staff. The money for the maternity wing had been donated by a wealthy family whose daughter's life had been saved by the clinic's staff. The facilities were used by everyone living in this secluded area.

During the 1960s and 1970s there were no trained midwives in Canada. In the city hospitals doctors generally delivered the babies. English midwives were abundant throughout the country but they were mostly employed as Registered Nurses. For most part in the isolated towns and villages the position of mid wife was filled by people like Talulah.

"Clayt and me thought we'd head on back to Mr. Reynard's place later, fix the fences and stuff. Is that okay?" Deacon asked Virgil.

"Sure, you boys go ahead. I'll send Lamar and Tyrell to give you a hand. This is Abe's dog, huh?" Virgil reached down to the pat the animal. "He sure is a big one."

"He's an Irish wolfhound," Clayton informed him, "One of the biggest domestic dogs you can get and docile enough to have around kids."

Unanticipated, Alamo vaulted from the open bed of the pickup, knocking an unsuspecting Deacon from his feet. Crying out, Deacon reached for his knife. Clayton was on him instantly taking the knife from his hand and pulling him into his arms.

"What is it Brother?"

"I can tell you," Graph said.

Both he and Virgil McNally listened while Graph expanded on his statement.

"I had a big dog like that one time. It wasn't an Irish wolfhound but it was a helluva size. I could do anything with it. Just like a big kid it was. When Deke was around six years old and not long out of his grandmother's village, be just before he met you Clayton, him and his mom came over to the garage, I forget what for. My dog Dandini was hanging around outside slouching on his blanket. He'd been chasing a ball. Deacon bent down to pick up the ball meaning to throw it for him. Dandini was on him in seconds snarling and biting. If Deacon hadn't turned onto his back Dandini would have had his throat. Had my rifle handy in the truck and I had to shoot him..." Graph's words met with stunned silence.

"Why didn't you tell me earlier, Deke?" Clayton asked when he found his voice. "We didn't have to go after the dog."

Deacon leaned against Clayton, his face ashen, his chest heaving. "Told you I'd sooner face a bear."

Virgil McNally placed his arm around the youth's shoulders. "If I'd known that I wouldn't have sent you to bring it in. In the future if you have any other problems like that make sure you tell me. Okay?"

"How badly was he hurt?" Clayton asked Graph.

"Back and shoulders. He was bleeding bad, needed stitches. I was gonna run him over to the clinic, not this one the old clinic. Nonie wouldn't let me. I patched him best I could and she took him home to Talulah."

Blowing air through his teeth Clayton shook his head. "That was risky, man. You generally need a tetanus shot if you've been bitten, doc should've taken a look at you. Are you alright?"

"I'm okay. Just keep it away from me." Deacon watched warily while Graph returned Alamo to the truck and shut him in the cab.

Perplexed, Clayton asked, "How come you're not afraid of the sled dogs?"

"Sled dogs are half wolf we don't keep them as pets. They need to be tethered all the time otherwise they'll bite and fight each other. I can handle them."

"Sorry about Dandini, Graph."

"I'm over it now Virgil, but I sure do miss him. I couldn't understand what came over him he'd never done anything like that before. Hell, I let my young nieces and nephews play with him all the time."

"Think I can," Clayton said, pondering over a similar incident a year ago. "While Deke and me were at Mrs. Simpson's house last June, her dog Wolf took flight the moment it saw Deacon. It didn't attack, just took off scared to death. As long as I've known him, he's had misunderstandings with dogs. I figure it's got a lot to do with whatever exists in those hills and Mrs. Simpson's house."

"Grandmother is right," Deacon stated, "It is time to return to my village, forever."

CHAPTER FIFTEEN

With very few places to socialise in a town the size of Maskek, the residents tended to congregate in Stanley Cuthand's coffee house. Living and working on 'Indian' time Stanley stayed open until the last of his customers left the building. He was in no rush to push people out and close up shop.

The church women and the quilting bee often came in for coffee. Workers on their lunch and mothers idling away the hours until their children came home from school, but mostly the town's young people gathered here. They had the made the coffee house their personal meeting place. Today was no exception. Deacon, Clayton, Ross and Bobby, Leona and Melissa, Stalking Moon and Stands-in-Timber were gathered around a table, putting the world to rights. Other students drifted in and out as they finished school for the day. The place was humming making it difficult to hear the music from the juke box over the noise of the vocal crowd.

Devoted church goer and the late Reverend Solomon's anchor woman, Rita Brewster stepped inside the coffee house. Rita was a buxom woman in her early sixties, stooped slightly due to the weight of her breasts. She wore her brown hair fastened in a bun at the back of her head. A stalwart campaigner for Native American causes she knew many of Deacon's people. Glancing swiftly around the crowded room her gaze came to rest on Deacon's back. Sensing her there he turned to face her.

"Something I can do for you Mrs. Brewster?"

"Join us Spirit of the Wind. Come; take your father's place. We have waited eighteen years for the son of Sparkling Eyes to stand before us, to become our new prince. Since your father Sparkling Eyes died none has been able to fulfil his exalted position. As his son you are required and expected to follow him, to lead us as he once did."

The room fell as quiet as a graveyard, ears perked up and all eyes beamed toward Deacon and Rita Brewster. Rita appeared to be in some kind of trance, staring directly but unfocused at the young chief.

"I am to inform you that if you choose not to join your fellow disciples your family will be in danger. This I have spoken."

Immediately suspicious, Deacon stood and approached Rita Brewster. "These are not the words of the one who stands before me but of another." Although nobody actually stood behind Rita, Deacon looked beyond her towards the door. "Does the great warrior hide behind a woman? Is the great warrior afraid to speak to me directly? Show your face, Thundercloud."

"Thundercloud is not afraid."

"Then why does Thundercloud speak through this woman?"

Rita Brewster suddenly reeled and collapsed in a faint. Placing his arms under her back and legs Deacon carried her to a chair. "Stay with her, Leona." Leona went to stand by Mrs. Brewster.

"Show me your face, Thundercloud that I may hear your thoughts."

Ross, Bobby and Melissa turned to Clayton. Bombarded with curious whispers from the three of them Clayton shrugged helplessly. "I don't know Thundercloud, Deacon hasn't mentioned him before."

They were all aware of Stalking Moon and Stands-in-Timber coming immediately to attention ready defend their new chief to be.

"Stand down," Deacon told them.

The room was filled with a sudden frigid cold. The gawping crowd gasped as the one known as Thundercloud stepped inside the coffee house. Skeletal in appearance his eyes were dark and fierce, almost feral. His face was painted with jagged black and white stripes and his hair hung in long braids. The wolverine head and skin he wore over black pants intensified his fearsome appearance. In his hand he carried a flaming lance.

"I do not fear you Spirit of the Wind. It was necessary to use the woman to gain your attention. Sparkling Eyes is gone. Damien has not returned. Our people grow tired of waiting. In order to continue the work of Arcus we require a leader. You are he yet you do not come to us. Now

I ask, is Spirit of the Wind afraid?"

"Spirit of the Wind is not afraid. I do not wish to become part of my father's past. I will not join you nor will I use the disciples as a reason to kill."

"Sparkling Eyes did not allow these thoughts to cloud his mind."

"I am not Sparkling Eyes I am Spirit of the Wind." His voice was filled with pride, his back straight, his head held high.

Spring loaded tension immediately added to the curiosity in Stanley Cuthand's coffee house. Many of Maskek's older population, middle aged and above, remembered the controversy surrounding the late Jonathan Sparkling Eyes. Not one of them could explain the devastating effect Jonathan had on the female population of the town and on the women who attended the lavish parties he held in the Longhouse. Awash with adulation a number of these women had ultimately forsaken their partners for Jonathan. Twenty-five, thirty years on and tension still simmered beneath the solitude of this small community. While loved and respected in the general community, there was some doubt about Jonathan's nocturnal activities; which were believed to involve the occult. The local newspaper, the Northern Light, had published unsubstantiated stories about nefarious gatherings in the basement of the Longhouse over which Emily Simpson's house now stood, and in the infamous Wapiti Hills.

Married to Lupin Bearhead, the daughter of Deacon's grandmother and the late chief Eagle Hawk, Jonathan had asked his father-in-law to squash the stories in the paper. Chief Eagle Hawk had acted promptly and no more was ever written. Even so the rumours persisted to this day. (Told in Child of the Heathen)

"Do you fear you cannot live up to your father? Are you aware of Sparkling Eyes' magnificence? He held the whole of Maskek in his embrace. He became a true leader of the disciples he once despised. Can you do the same?"

"My father is dead I did not know him. When he was taken from me, I was six months of age. My mother Lupin was taken when I was only six weeks of age."

"When the white woman Nonie took you from your home you

were but six years..."

Bobby shuddered. To Ross he whispered, "Six weeks, six months six years. 666, the mark of the beast."

CHAPTER SIXTEEN

Ross stared at him incredulously. "Are you outta your mind, Bobby? You've been watching too many horror movies."

"There was a beast," Clayton told him, "but not that one."

"How does Deacon know Thundercloud?" Ross asked. "Thought you two shared everything."

Clayton didn't reply. Instead he returned his attention to the man in the wolverine skin.

"I will take your place," Thundercloud continued, "I will instruct and lead the disciples of Damien. I will end your family. I will be prince!"

"Grandfather taught me all life is sacred, but if you harm my family, I will kill you."

The nervous, expectant crowd waited on tenterhooks. Neither Deacon nor Thundercloud moved, each defying the other. Even the air seemed hostile. After what seemed like an eternity to the people in the room, Thundercloud threw down the burning lance and reached for his knife.

"Take me, Spirit of the Wind. Would Sparkling Eyes be proud of his son? Show me. Show me your skill. Show me your power."

Raising his head to the skies Spirit of the Wind closed his eyes, he spoke in his own tongue.

"What's he saying?" Bobby asked.

"He calls upon his namesake, the spirit of the wind," Stalking Moon replied. Although asked to stand down the two members of the warrior elite did not relax their stance. Before Stalking Moon had finished speaking, the power of the wind blasted open the front door. The wind shrieked and swirled around and between the tables, harming no one, but as they watched the wind twirled and curled around Thundercloud, forcing the knife from his hands, forcing him to his knees. It whipped the wolverine's skin from his head.

"Your mother, your grandmother, all your relatives will suffer the same fate as Lupin," Thundercloud screamed above the roaring wind, "terrible deaths as those of your father's previous wives and all children born to them. You are finished!"

Reaching for the lance he held it to the sky. Thunder clapped and lightning struck the coffee house with such force that it sheered the wall. Stanley's customers screamed and dived for cover under the tables.

Mastering all his remaining strength Thundercloud pulled himself to his feet. Like a bolt from a crossbow the wind smacked him hard in his chest, toppling him. He lay winded and injured on the wooden floor. The wind whirled and rapidly dissipated. Nobody breathed, nobody moved and nobody spoke. The calm after the storm left them stunned.

Spirit of the Wind hauled Thundercloud to his feet, his black eyes almost as wild as those of his tormenter. "Don't threaten me or my family."

In obvious pain Thundercloud glared at him but his mouth remained firmly closed. The lance lay cold by his side, snuffed out by the wind.

Deacon retrieved Thundercloud's knife and handed it back to him. "Stay away from my family." His tone was deadly.

Packing his injured body and wounded pride Thundercloud left the coffee shop. Deacon threw the lance after him. Complete and utter silence followed Thundercloud's indignant departure.

"Couldn't you just have gone for him with your knife?" Clayton said when he pulled himself together.

"That would have been too easy. He has been humiliated and that hurts worse than any wound. I should know. My knife would have been useless against the power of the flaming lance."

Ross, Bobby and Clayton glanced quickly at each other and all spoke at once. "Whose Thundercloud?"

"A rat," Deacon answered.

"Never told me about him," Clayton said reproachfully.

"The ghost wolf led us to Bittern Creek ..."

"Yeah, what's that got to do with Thundercloud?"

"When we left there to see Captain McNally someone was watching us. That was Thundercloud."

"How'd you know it was him?"

"The thunder cracked and the sky split in two. Nobody but Thundercloud could do such a thing. How is Mrs. Brewster, Leona?"

"She's recovered now. She doesn't remember anything."

"It wouldn't surprise me if Darrel was acquainted with Thundercloud. He could be the one Darrel said you were to fear."

Deacon was silent for a moment pondering on Clayton's words. Turning to his brother he said, "Still want coffee?"

CHAPTER SEVENTEEN

"So, did you ask the girls about a walk in the moonlight?" Bobby questioned as he and Ross sat in the dining hall having lunch.

"Yep, they're up for it. All I godda do now is decide when we'll do it. Unfortunately they both wanted to know if Deke and Clayt were coming with us. I had to tell a little white lie and say that they were tied up with ranger stuff. When would be a good time?"

"The sooner the better, jeez Ross, get with it, man."

~ * ~

Captain Virgil McNally looked up from the rotor he'd just spent all morning doing, while Deacon straddling his chair backwards and Clayton balancing his on its two rear legs, waited patiently in their boss's office at the ranger station.

Situated at the far end of Main Street at the junction of Jack Pine Avenue and Loon Lake trail away from the centre of the town, the long, low wooden building backed onto open grassland. Loon Lake as always displaying it sparkling icy waters beyond.

A small garage where all the transport used by McNally's troop was regularly serviced or replaced stood at the rear of the office. One man with biceps like buffalo haunches and huge hands to match tended to everything, including the paperwork. There was nothing Bison Bailey as the easy-going rangers had daubed him, didn't know about jeeps trucks, even motor cycles. He was a first class mechanic and much appreciated by McNally's troop. To the right of the garage and further to the rear stood a corral holding a number of strong working horses chomping contentedly on the lush grass. Very much a rural area dotted with dense forests, raging rivers and tranquil streams, many of them running into the lake from meandering destinations; horseback was the safest, easiest and preferred mode of transport. And that suited Deacon and Clayton down to the ground. Raised with horses from the time he was old enough to sit bareback, there wasn't anything you could teach Deacon about horses. An avid rider from the first time he'd accompanied his father Keel Rykker on his hunting, camping and fishing trips, Clayton was perfectly at home in the saddle. Often, while still attending school the boys had ridden there preferring four legs to four wheels even after they were old enough and competent enough to drive.

Addressing the latest and youngest members of his troop McNally told them, "I want you both down at the High School. Seems there's a lot of interest in joining up, particularly among your ex classmate." Virgil winked, his face cutting a smile. "It could have something to do with you boys joining up. Makes sense to send you two since I figure you're better suited to it than the older guys."

"Does that mean we godda stand up and talk in front of the class?" Deacon asked in dismay.

"That's exactly what it means, it'll be good experience for you. As you progress through the troop you'll be dealing with a whole lot of different people, may as well begin there."

"Deke's never been much on talking in front of the class. He used to get out of it by sweet talking the teacher," Clayton grinned, "those big black eyes they'll do it every time."

"I did not," Deacon said jabbing Clayton in his ribs almost knocking his chair from under him.

"Yeah you did."

"I didn't."

"You did."

"That won't work with me. Get a move on and Deacon..."

"Yeah, I know don't forget the hat."

"What's the problem with the hat, anyhow it's part of your uniform. You should wear
 it with pride."

"I feel like a goddamn cowboy. I'm an Indian, I don't do cowboys."

"I've seen plenty of your people wearing cowboy hats, especially at the rodeo."

"It ain't the hat, Cap'n," Clayton responded, "he don't like to mess up his hair. He's totally vain when it comes to his long black locks."

"Get on over to the school," Virgil chuckled, "I'll come by later and see how you're doing."

"Yes sir."

~ * ~

Inside Maskek High School's senior class the students chatted loudly, impatiently awaiting the arrival of Maskek's finest. On a par with the Royal Canadian Mounted Police, namely one Sergeant Abel Cain Hibbett and his half Indian partner Constable Ira Haines, the local rangers were a well-respected, much admired troop of men and women whom many of the town's younger members aspired to.

School Principal Barnstable Emett had arranged with Captain McNally to send over two of his men to discuss a career with Parks Canada as it had been known since 1911, or more astutely with Captain McNally's troop after a number of the older students confessed to liking the idea of becoming a wildlife ranger. Now they waited, debating upon whom might turn up since most of the rangers were well known.

Elaine Cartwright taking over permanently from the class that Emily Simpson had taught for the last twelve months, entered the room, beaming. "The rangers are here now, so settle down and be quiet. I think you're going to be delighted with Captain McNally's choice..."

"Is that why you're smiling, Mrs. Cartwright?" Melissa wanted to know.

"It might just be. Deacon and Clayton are here to talk to you and answer your questions. I'm sure you'll have many."

Elaine Cartwright, married to a Native Canadian truck driver, taught Deacon and Clayton over the years from elementary school to high school, although last year Emily Simpson had laid claim to that pleasure. Extremely fond of both of the boys Elaine looked forward to seeing them again.

An attractive woman of fifty Elaine's mid length chestnut hair was slightly back combed, flicked up at the bottom and sprayed solidly with lacquer. She was wearing a purple blouse and skirt and a long hippy necklace of coloured beads. Childless through accident not by choice, she looked upon her students as her children. Through contact with her husband's family she understood and could relate to Deacon and the problems he encountered.

Good natured hooting followed their teacher's announcement. These teenagers grew up alongside Clayton and later Deacon when the young Native Canadian was first introduced to the school almost thirteen years ago. All were present last year when Deacon had been asked to leave school prior to Christmas until he'd conquered the demon in his head. Most of them hadn't seen him since late November.

Clayton strode through the classroom door and pulled up sharply, beaming, "Do all you guys wanna be rangers or do you just wanna see us?"

"Whoa, Deacon," Ross Porter said as the young Indian entered on Clayton's heels, "never thought we'd see you wearing a cowboy hat." They had never understood his aversion to Stetsons.

Knowing full well he'd be ribbed for it, Deacon said, "I've been ordered to."

"It isn't really a Stetson it's just similar," Clayton replied with broad grin "but I guess that's a little too close for Deacon's liking."

Elaine Cartwright came from behind the desk and kissed both boys on the cheek, "Nice to see you again boys, we've missed you."

Deacon threw her a devastating smile and returned her kiss, "Good to see you too Mrs. Cartwright."

"So what d'you guys wanna know?" Clayton enquired. "We haven't done this before so we can't guarantee you all the answers."

"And we don't have a clue what we're doing," Deacon admitted. Removing his hat, he hung it on the back of a chair and perched on one of the desks.

Leona gasped in amazement. "Who did your hair it's fabulous. You've never worn it that way before."

"Grandmother fixed it."

Throughout school there had always been contention with the length of Deacon's hair. He wore it long and loose, sometimes holding it back with a beaded leather band. The school authorities protested loudly and Deacon blatantly ignored them, believing it to be his right to wear his hair any way he wanted. In the end the powers-that-be had conceded. Refusing to fasten his hair at the back of his neck, braid it or cut it, Virgil McNally insisted that he 'do something with it' that would be acceptable to the ranger troop. Talulah had come to her grandson's rescue.

Leona gazed lovingly upon his midnight black locks. Talulah fashioned two thick braids binding them with soft leather leaving a length of the braid loose at the bottom and the remainder of his waist-long hair hung down his back. It was attractive, tidy and smart. He could even wear the hat without much disruption to his hair. He wouldn't have got away with it in any other ranger company.

"I've got a question," Ross Porter said, "when did you join up and what exactly do the rangers do? What are their duties? If I'm considering becoming a ranger, I'd like to know precisely what I'm letting myself in for."

"That's three questions, Ross," Clayton responded, "and Deacon will answer them for you."

"The hell I will."

Clayton threw him a look that made him reconsider that statement.

"Alright, I'll talk." When his best friend gave him that 'look' he knew better than to argue. "We went to see Captain McNally at the end of December. By mid January it was settled."

"That was quick, how come?"

"We just got lucky, I guess."

"Some folk have all the luck," Ross grumbled.

"It helps when the captain knows your father," Bobby added.

"I'd like to think that wasn't the only reason," Deacon grinned.

"You're forgetting that he knew Clayt's father as well, Bobby," Ross told him. "Go ahead Deacon, tell us what you guys do."

"We haven't been with them long enough to tell you much of anything. Don't know why Captain McNally asked us to speak to you."

"Try it anyway. He must have thought you were capable or he

wouldn't have sent you."

"The rangers enforce the local, federal and wild life laws. If folks make too much noise out on the campground the rangers will be there checking up on them..."

"What, no parties?" Billy Joel Kramer asked in dismay. "What kind of a vacation would that be?"

"If we catch anyone hunting or fishing out of season, I'll have their hides before the rangers get a chance to. But if a hunter kills more than he needs or allows a wounded animal to escape there'll be no need of the rangers because Pakakos will find him." Although Deacon had spoken amiably, they all knew that when it came to the killing of wild animals legally hunted or otherwise, he was deadly serious.

"Who's Pakakos?" Bobby asked.

"He's a spectre, a skeleton that lives in the forest and protects the animals. Even a Native hunter would be attacked if he took more meat than he needs."

"Jeez, that's kinda mean isn't it?"

"Any hunter that kills for pleasure or gain deserves it," Clayton said. "We'll also come down heavily on anyone hunting without a licence, even an out of date licence. And one law we've all been guilty of breaking now and then -underage drinking."

"Only now and then, are you sure?" Billy Joel Kramer responded, "I swear it's been more times than one."

"I'd keep that under your hat," Clayton chuckled. "Go ahead Deke, continue..." If looks could kill, Clayton would have been struck down then and there. The redhead grinned, unfazed by Deacon's reaction, "He ain't too happy about speaking up in front of you-all."

"Nothing's changed then," Bobby chortled, "and you ain't got no teacher to bat your big ol' black eyes at neither. That's too bad."

"Sit on it, Bobby."

Feeling compelled to support Deacon, Leona said, "He's shy, Bobby. He's always been shy about talking in front of the class or of meeting new people. It takes him a little while to accept them. We're not all as brazen as you."

"You're always sticking up for him, Leona."

"What's wrong with that? I care about him."

"In the summer when the outsiders come, much of the ranger's time is taken up with search and rescue."

"You mean the tourists?" Leona questioned.

"I mean anybody. Folks come down from the city, park up on the campground and wander away without leaving details of where they're going, which trails they're taking and when they plan to be back. You should always lodge the route with the proper authorities before taking off and here it's the ranger station. It's dangerous out there if you don't know what you're doing, you don't have to be a ranger to realise that."

"Including emergency response, giving first aid and arranging transport to the hospital or clinic," Clayton added.

"Protecting wildlife and plant life is also a big part of a ranger's work." Looking directly at Ross and Bobby, his black eyes twinkling, Deacon told them, "You get to count the blades of grass, talk to the flowers, hug a few trees..."

"You're kidding, right?" Bobby asked.

"I'm not."

"Oh, for goodness sake, Bobby use your head," Leona told him, "he means that rangers do have to work with the trees and the plants, especially if a tree should come down with a serious disease that could infect other trees, or maybe a plant native to Alberta is becoming extinct... stuff like that. He's having you on." She shared a surreptitious smile with Deacon.

"You could just have said that."

"Gee I didn't know trees got sick," Billy Joel responded.

"You also get to work with the cops."

"You mean McCready," Billy Joel said contemptuously.

The recently demoted Sergeant McCready had been a perpetual pain in the posterior of Maskek's youth for years, but his racial hatred of Deacon Pierce and other Native Canadians, was the reason for McCready's demotion, if not dismissal three months ago.

"Not McCready," Deacon told him, "not anymore, it's Abel Cain."

"He means Sergeant Abel Cain Hibbett formerly Constable

Hibbett," Clayton clarified.

Bobby gawped, "That's his name?"

"Well Deacon kinda likes it."

"So why do you work with the cops?" Ross asked.

"To keep peace with the Indians," Clayton grinned, "being as it's the Mounties we work with."

"Are you serious? We don't have problems with the Indians...do we?" Deacon chuckled at Billy Joel's startled expression.

"Not unless one of them is named Deacon," Melissa quipped. Deacon threw her a heart stopping smile. Seconds later he said quietly, "My name is Spirit of the Wind."

Instant silence descended over the entire class, something in the way he'd said Spirit of the Wind catching their attention and leaving a few hearts beating faster than a moment ago. Observing his former fellow students and friends, Clayton noticed a slight change in their demeanour.

"We've always called you Deacon," Billy Joel responded.

"Momma called me Deacon when we left grandmother's village. She figured it'd make it easier to live among you and attend school. My true name is Spirit of the Wind."

Billy Joel and most of the class turned questioningly to Clayton Rykker. The red headed youth nodded, his expression serious. "That's the name he was given by his blood mother Lupin. Better get used to it."

"We knew that anyway and Melissa and me love it," Leona said. "What's wrong with his name, it doesn't change the person he is."

Elaine Cartwright sat quietly behind her desk listening to the conversation, watching the changing expressions on the faces of her charges. Somewhere along the way the rangers had been forgotten and now, as then, when Deacon had been at school, his personal life had become the main topic of interest. Tapping on the window overlooking the corridor alerted Elaine to the school principal behind the glass, beckoning to her. Striding to the door she opened it and stuck her head out. After a quick discussion with Barnstable Emett she moved over to Deacon.

"Your grandmother is here with Lone Wolf and Grey Owl. They want to talk to you."

"Grey Owl? Why does Grey Owl come here?"

Clayton strolled over to stand beside him.

"Grey Owl never comes into town. I guess I'm in trouble."

The attention of the class was now riveted on Deacon's back. Talulah Bearhead and Grey Owl entered side by side and Lone Wolf bought up the rear.

Deacon stood and respectfully bowed his head. "Grandmother, Grey Owl."

Tribal elders such as Talulah Bearhead kept the memory, the history and the knowledge of the ancestors, and shared life experiences to help younger people understand their community and make better decisions. They helped to solve personal matters and family disputes as well as problems in the community. The elders also offered non-judgemental guidance.

Deacon kissed her cheek, his actions evoking a gentle and loving response from some of the girls in the classroom. Releasing Talulah he gave her his undivided attention. "Why are you here grandmother? Why does Grey Owl accompany you?"

"We are here because it is difficult to pin you down. We tried your home, the coffee house and the ranger station. Captain McNally told us we would find you here. He keeps you both very busy. We have come to a decision my child. It is time for you to return to the village forever, to take your place as the new chief. You can no longer remain in your home with Nonie."

"I am ready grandmother, but my mother still hesitates."

"Nonie has known this day would come since you were an infant. It is time to entrust you to your people."

Stepping forward Grey Owl planted his moccasins firmly in front of Deacon. He was a proud man of seventy-five years; short and squat, with piercing dark eyes that belied his true age. A man of few words Grey Owl expected and usually received respect.

"The woman Nonie who is your mother, must choose to come with you or remain in the wooden lodge beyond the lake."

"I will not leave my mother alone Grey Owl," Deacon spoke quietly, respectfully and with authority.

"Your mother has raised a good man. I did not expect it from a white woman but now she must allow you to return to your people."

"My father would not have given me to this woman if he did not believe in her."

Nodding slowly, Grey Owl glanced swiftly at Talulah Bearhead as she took the hand of Spirit of the Wind. "You speak well of your mother, Spirit of the Wind. Only she can make the decision to stay or come with you. When the sun stands high two times you will come to your home. This night when you return to the wooden lodge you must make her understand. This was the decision of your father Sparkling Eyes and your true mother Lupin." Grey Owl stepped back indicating the conversation was over.

While Spirit of the Wind was delighted to return to his home, he was disturbed by his mother's reluctance to leave the lakeside cabin. When they had first discussed the possibility of it happening soon, Nonie accepted the situation but as the time drew nearer, she began to have doubts. It wasn't just leaving Nonie alone that concerned him but that he did not want to be without her. Acutely aware that Grey Owl would probably object to the public show of affection, which he Grey Owl, believed should remain within the lodge, Spirit of the Wind pulled his grandmother into his arms. "I will speak with my mother again."

"When you come you will bring Clayton, for he cannot remain here without you and you cannot be without him."

Fully conversant with the Cree tongue, Clayton replied, "I will be with him Talulah."

"How will it be with your mother?"

"She's happy to follow me."

Long before Grey Owl ended his discussion with Deacon, the Cree tongue had replaced the English language annoying Leona and Melissa who were hoping to listen in.

Deacon responded to Clayton in English. "You spoke to your momma?"

"I did and she's willing to come with me."

Deacon beamed his smile lighting up his face. He'd waited eagerly for this moment, wanting more than anything to return to his grandmother's village where he was born and spent the first six years of his life. Looking back to last year, in June 1968 when Nonie finally revealed the truth about his parentage, he realised that his grandparents and other members of the people had been preparing him for this moment from the day of his birth. Never questioning what he always suspected he waited for Talulah to one day confirm it. Talulah's teaching stressed the values of; wisdom, love, respect, bravery, humility and truth, enabling the people to live in harmony with everyone and everything in creation. From the time he was a child he'd been taught to respect everything in the natural world. These beliefs were reflected in the songs, dances and ceremonies of his people.

Talulah believed that even in the modern world of the 1960s these traditional ways and customs should not be allowed to disappear. All the knowledge Deacon had amassed leading to the time when he would relieve his grandmother of the responsibility of the village and the people living in it and hoist it upon his shoulders. He was proud. It was a mammoth task. He was only eighteen, but willing and ready to apply all that he had learned.

"It is my place, grandmother," Deacon turned to Clayton, an expression of love and affection in his dark eyes, "and my brother will be by my side."

Clayton squeezed his friend's hand, "I will remain always at your side, brother."

Glancing over his shoulder as Talulah and Grey Owl departed, Lone Wolf took his cousin's arm. "Even if it were not time for you to take your place by Talulah's side, it is no longer safe for you to stay here. Talulah is having visions which disturb her."

"Are these visions related to my father?"

"Indeed. The fact that you destroyed the demon does not free you from the bad spirits that live within the hills, it is far reaching and it is growing. You must not delay." Lone Wolf looked toward the door. "I must go." Pressing his hand to Deacon's shoulder he followed the others from the room.

"So, what was all that about?" Ross enquired.

Clayton said, "You'll find out soon enough."

"I guess that means it's none of our business."

"So c'mon you guys, you must have more questions," Clayton prompted, "we haven't covered half of what the rangers do."

"I got one," Ross said. "What are you doing about bear baiting? Why don't you just tell us all about it, that's your job isn't it?"

Grinning all over his face Clayton pulled up a chair. "May as well get comfortable it's gonna be a long morning."

CHAPTER EIGHTEEN

"I'm not leaving Steve," Emily Simpson informed her husband.

"What do you mean you're not leaving?"

"Maskek it's our home now. We've got friends here and here is where I would like to stay. Your business is doing better than ever it did in the city, you've got everything you strived for. What is there in Edmonton we don't have in Maskek?"

Staring in astonishment at his wife, Steve Simpson's anger returned, what was she playing at? "If this is anything to do with that Indian kid..."

"Deacon doesn't know anything about it. He thought we were going the day the storm hit us."

"We damn well should have while you were still in your right mind. What's happened to change it?"

Arms outstretched encompassing the lounge she said, "This house. Look at it. The snow didn't cause all of this devastation, it's something to do with the malevolence still living in our basement and it is connected to Deacon and me. I'm afraid that if I move with you to Edmonton or anywhere else the thing will follow me and innocent people might die. It has to be contained. Not only that, but whoever buys the house will also have to contend with its sordid past. It's not right Steve. Last year we lost our friend Janine during our housewarming party and the day after it we lost Reverend Solomon. Hikers have died in the hills and one body was found in the lake, all of them under mysterious circumstances. These are a small minority of the inexplicable deaths this town has encountered over the last two hundred years. I won't be a party to anymore death."

"Surely that's all the more reason for moving..."

"Didn't you hear what I said? We could spread it."

"Oh, for Pete's sake Emily, this is ludicrous. Think about what you're saying."

"My mind is made up."

"Emily. We're not just talking houses here, what about our marriage?"

"Think about it, Steve."

Snatching her coat from the chair she took the keys to the car. Deacon and Clayton had returned it to her after the snow cleared. She headed toward the garage.

~ * ~

Taking his mother into his arms Deacon explained, "Grandmother and Grey Owl came to school today, it's time to return to the village. It is no longer safe for us to remain here. We go tomorrow."

Nonie stared at her son, stunned by his directness. "Go now? Why so soon? What about the house and..."

"The house will remain. We will not."

"We can't just leave like that."

"Momma I have no choice. I want you to come with me."

"This is my home..."

"And grandmother's village is mine. I will not leave you here alone nor will I stay here against grandmother's wishes."

Clayton slipped quietly into the room, Nonie in earnest conversation, did not hear. He knew Deacon was aware and grateful for his presence.

Peering intensely into his mother's lavender blue eyes Deacon took her hand. "My home, our home, is now within the sacred hoop of grandmother's village. It's time for us to leave."

Uncertain, hesitant Nonie said, "We've been happy here, haven't we?"

"You have, momma. I am here because of you, no other reason."

"It's been our home for thirteen years."

"It has been your home, mine is across the lake. This is house in which we have been allowed to live until now. That time is over."

"Our friends are here. Everything we know is here. Who will I have in the village?"

"You have me. You will always have me. You will also have grandmother as you did once before, you won't be alone. Momma my family is there they are also your family. When I spoke to you about leaving here you told me that I would know when it was time. Why have you changed your mind?"

All along she'd known at some point Deacon would have to return to the encampment. Accepting it was easy while it was still years away.

"Please, momma."

"I knew this day was coming I just didn't want it to..." Nonie shivered, had somebody touched her shoulder? Somebody had touched her, her shoulder felt warm and tingly. There came the feeling of another's presence. Was it Jonathan reminding her of her promise? A slight push such as she had experienced when Lupin brushed up close?

Deacon saw her flinch and turn slightly. He held out his left hand, "Momma, come to me." Smiling, Nonie came into his arms. He held her so close he could feel her trembling.

"Jonathan touched me. Lupin pushed me. It's time we'll go tomorrow."

"You're not gonna be alone," Clayton told her, "Mom and I are going with you. Only the house is changing. Home is where you make it and we'll make ours across the lake."

"Why didn't you tell me that in the first place?"

"I didn't think it would be necessary."

Nonie glanced around her small front room. It was sparse but cosy, everything in it a reminder of the last thirteen years she and Deacon had spent together away from his grandmother's encampment, although if she was honest, he spent more time in Talulah's encampment than ever he did in the cabin.

"Rona's ready, no qualms or concerns?" Nonie asked doubtfully.

"None that Clayton mentioned and the house will still be here. You can come back anytime. We will take only what we need, the rest will remain here for when you return, as I know you will."

"I'll be able to stay overnight sometimes and when my family visit?"

"If you wish to, I will bring you here. If I cannot Lone Wolf or any of warriors will do so."

"Then we shall go right away."

Deacon smiled, "Tomorrow is soon enough."

CHAPTER NINETEEN

"How's your mother settling in?" Virgil McNally asked Deacon.

"Good. She has Aunt Rona, grandmother, Nedipah and all the women in the village. She's content."

"I'm delighted to hear it. Because I figure if your mother wasn't happy you wouldn't be either and that's not a good feeling. Mrs. Rykker, has she taken to it?"

"Like the thunderbird to lightning," Clayton grinned, "she couldn't be happier."

Nodding slowly Virgil smiled, "So now I have contentment among my troops. What more could I ask?"

Throwing each other a sideways glance the boys eyed their Captain suspiciously. "But you are gonna ask, aren't you?"

"Uh-huh. You guys are working the weekend with Lamar and Giovanni."

"You mean this weekend?" Deacon asked, dismayed.

"The very same, why, you got a problem with that?"

"No sir, not usually, but this weekend Clayton will be made an honorary member of our nation."

"In the middle of winter, you still hold these ceremonies?"

"The weather is not important. It is time."

"That's it?" Virgil McNally stated incredulously, "It's time, nothing else? Why on the weekend what's wrong with the other five days?"

Deacon threw him a broad grin, "Because many of the people are working. Everyone in the encampment has to be present or it will not happen. Next time would be in the summer and that's too far ahead."

"And also, Spirit of the Wind is to be declared the new chief," Clayton added.

"I thought he already was."

"It has to be official."

Looking at Deacon to confirm Clayton's words, McNally pursed his lips, "Why do I get the feeling I'm about to have an even bigger headache than I had this morning." Exhaling noisily, he dropped his shift rotor into the bin at the side of his desk. "Go on. Get off to school and find me some more recruits."

"Does that mean we're off the hook?"

"Yes, Deacon, you're off the hook, but next weekend you'll be doing overtime. Now get going and don't forget your damn hat."

"Thank you."

Elbow on the desk, head resting on his left hand, Virgil McNally retrieved the crumpled paper and started all over again. "I knew I should've stayed in bed."

~ * ~

Glaring at the figures on his desk Steve Simpson threw up his hands in frustration. The cost of restoring the house for the second time in six months was astronomical. Hearing the side door slam he headed for the kitchen. "Emily is that you?"

"I've taken the house off the market."

"You've done what?"

"We're not selling. We'll auction everything and the bulldozers can do the rest."

"Are you out of your mind, woman?"

"Perhaps I am, Steve. But whatever is living in this house can be buried with it."

His mouth working soundlessly Steve glared at his wife.

"George Culver is coming tomorrow to take a look at our possessions. From what I've told him he says we should get a fair deal."

"And where do you propose we stay?"

"We're booked in to the Tamarack Motel. Don't look so horrified," noting his expression of extreme distaste. "You're moving back to Edmonton, anyway aren't you? It won't concern you for long."

"You're still determined to stay in Maskek?"

"I am. I'd like you to stay with me. I don't want to throw our marriage away, Steve. I'm convinced we can carry on as before. I still love you. When you told me we were selling and moving to a small town, you didn't consider my feelings or my job, you just assumed I'd come with you. Despite my misgivings this is the best thing we've ever done. I'm going to start packing. Are you going to help me?" It would be fatal to cave in now. She needed to stay in control of her emotions.

~ * ~

"So what's this about Clayton becoming a member of the Cree nation?" Ross enquired. He sat with Deacon, Clayton, Melissa, Leona, Billy Joel and Bobby in Stanley Cuthand's coffee house on Monday evening. Deacon and Clayton recently finished work for the day, the others hanging around after school.

"It is what it is," Deacon replied.

"Do we get to come and watch? Will we be allowed in the village?"

"If I say so, Ross," Deacon grinned. "Sure you wanna do that? You've never been much on hanging around in the cold."

"I could manage it this one time. I'll wear my red woolly long johns."

Leona touched Deacon's arm. "We'll hang around until we're frozen if it means we get to look at all those handsome warriors."

"So, what does it entail?" Melissa asked Clayton.

"A sweat that's not open to tourists I can't tell you anything about that. It's an important part of the ceremony I'm looking forward to it. As far as I know there'll be tournaments, tests of strength and endurance and courage and plenty of horse play..."

"Horse play?" Bobby butted in, "You mean you get to fool around with girls?"

"You could say that," Clayton remarked wryly, "plenty female ponies up there."

The others cackled at Bobby's look of dismay, "Jeez, you really had me going there guys."

"I suppose once upon a time a ceremony like this one would have been celebrated with lots of dancing, wouldn't it?" Leona said.

"What're these tests of courage?" Melissa asked mischievously, "Do they require you to remove your clothes?"

"At ten below, you godda be kidding."

"Yeah but Clayton that would be a real test of courage, don't you think?"

"Now don't go giving Deke any ideas I already got more'n I can handle."

"That's good my brother, you'll have so many things to think about you won't have time to be nervous."

"Oh, that makes me feel a whole lot better."

"You got nothing to worry about. If I didn't think you were ready you wouldn't be doing it."

"That's gospel huh."

"That's gospel."

~ * ~

"Our walk in the moonlight is all arranged for tomorrow night," Bobby told Ross, dancing around excitedly. "We're gonna meet by the holding corral at seven and take it from there; me, you, Billy Joel and Leona."

"It was supposed to be all about Melissa and me..."

"It was, but she won't come without Leona. Billy Joel said if he couldn't come, he'd tell everybody."

"In my opinion that's the least romantic thing I ever heard."

"Can't be helped Ross. Anyhow I figure we can lose Billy Joel somewhere along the route."

"Unbelievable. Bobby you're an idiot, you should've let me arrange it I'm the one who wants a chance with Melissa."

"It was my idea. Everything will be perfect. Trust me."

"That's what I'm afraid of," Ross said rolling his eyes.

CHAPTER TWENTY

Shrouded in mystery, veiled in legend and mythology, the dark beauty of the Wapiti Hills harboured secrets beyond the imagination of most people. A world of depravity concealed in the blackest corners of the mind. For one thousand years it had lain dormant, arising now and then to alert the good citizens of the town of Maskek that its raw and decadent power still rumbled beneath the beauty of mother earth. And now it was growing, pulsating and tired of waiting, expanding and spreading its heinous tentacles ever upward. Soon it must spew out the gnarling bestial ache within its distended bowls and within its cold heart.

~ * ~

Captain Virgil McNally stared out across the lake, he was touchy, edgy, nervous. On the opposite shore something wasn't right.

"The wolves have been howling nonstop for days," Tyrell McAlister said, joining his captain. "I can't figure out why. Did you send Spirit of the Wind to check it out? He understands them better than we do."

Virgil exhaled wearily, "I didn't."

"Maybe you should, it's not like the wolves to carry on."

"They were up there four days ago, neither of them said anything."

"Who's up there now?"

"It should have been Giovanni and Tripp. The wolves are restless, they didn't want to go. Got to be a reason for it, I just don't know what. It's bothering me."

"Yeah," Tyrell replied uneasily. "Something is gonna happen."

~ * ~

"Is everyone here?" Bobby asked, "Hope you guys are fitted out in warm clothing you're gonna need it."

"I thought we were walking by the river, Bobby why are we going this way?" Melissa asked. "It's very dark even with the moon."

"We could Melissa, but I figured you and Ross might like a little more privacy. Besides it's a beautiful night; clear, fresh and you can't see the sky for the stars. What more could you ask? It's a real winter wonderland. We'll hang back so's not to crowd you."

"Still don't know why we couldn't come alone," Ross grumbled.

"Because I felt safer having Leona close by."

"I wouldn't do anything to hurt you, I just wanted to have some time alone with you." The crest shaped moon hung in the sky as if painted on black canvas, the twinkling stars sparkled like a thousand city lights. The crisp snow crackled under their booted feet as they walked.

"Are you warm enough Melissa?" He placed an arm around her waist. "You can snuggle up to me if you want to."

Melissa leaned against him feeling his warmth, "This is kinda nice."

"Why'd you bring the rifle, Billy Joel?" Bobby wanted to know, "we're not likely to run into any trouble."

"We don't know who's out here do we, could be a mad man for all we know. You heard what Deke said, the are many things in the forest we know nothing about. Some things we'd rather not know about. I bought the rifle for protection can't you hear the wolves? Whose stupid idea was it to come on a moonlight walk in the first place?"

"You didn't have to come," Leona told him, "nobody forced you."

"We're nowhere near the river, Ross," Melissa said. "We probably shouldn't have ventured this far in the dark. The river is used as a landmark, so if we get lost, we can follow it. I've never been this way before, I don't have a clue where we are."

The further they walked from Maskek the louder the howling became.

"I'm not sure this is such a good idea," Billy Joel said.

"Deacon says they won't harm us as long as we don't harm them,"

Leona responded with more courage than she felt.

"Yeah, maybe they won't harm him, he's into wolves we're not."

"We could build a fire to keep us warm," Ross said, "it might help to keep them away. As far as I know wolves are afraid of fire."

"It's better if we just keep moving;" Melissa said nervously, "start walking back."

The river lay behind them like a silver serpent glistening in the light from the stars.

"As nice as this is, I think it's time we headed home," Bobby announced as he became aware of the distance they'd walked.

Up ahead a sudden movement in the trees caught Melissa's attention. "What's that?" Ross followed her outstretched hand, "It's probably just a rabbit foraging for food."

"It's bigger than a rabbit."

"I'll take a look." Warily he moved towards the area where Melissa had seen movement. He couldn't find anything. Relieved he returned to Melissa. "If it was a rabbit it's gone now."

"That was brave of you."

Swelling up with pride he pulled Melissa into his arms and kissed her. Surprisingly she didn't turn away. How'd you like them apples Deacon, she kissed me. His mind on his achievement with Melissa, Ross failed to see the dark shadows stalking the trees. All at once the incessant howling ceased. The night was still, deathly quiet. Bobby, Leona and Billy Joel glanced nervously at one another.

"What the hell?" Bobby called out softly to Ross and Melissa. "Hey you guys get over here."

"Why have they stopped?" Ross questioned.

"Look," Billy Joel said, "look at them, wolves, hundreds of them and they're circling us."

Bobby seriously doubted there were hundreds but there were too many for his liking. Growling, snarling, their yellow eyes piercing the night the pack advanced on the five young people shivering in the frosty air.

Aiming his rifle Billy Joel said, "They're gonna attack..."

~ * ~

Deacon and Clayton were about to take the trail around the lake when the world went quiet. Glancing quickly at his friend, Deacon set Diablero at a punishing pace. The area where the wolves gathered when they came out of the hills was well known to him, he knew exactly where to find them.

~ * ~

In the brightness of the moon and the twinkling stars, the five teenagers could plainly see the snarling animals. Instantly, and for no reason they could tell, the wolves stopped advancing and the growling quietened. His hands sweaty and shaking, Billy Joel squeezed the trigger and missed. Alarmed by the sound of the rifle the wolves turned tail and ran except for one defiant, angry grey wolf that came right for him.

~ * ~

Amidst furious pounding of horses Deacon and Clayton appeared. Swifter than Clayton could think, pumping adrenalin and with a magnificent leap Deacon landed on his feet directly in front of the grey wolf. Startled by the sudden intrusion the animal backed away slightly. Dropping to his knees Deacon locked eyes with the wolf neither one of them giving an inch.

Dropping his rifle Billy Joel collapsed onto the cold earth. The others stared in stunned disbelief, they'd never seen Deacon up close with wolves even though they were aware of his uncanny abilities. As they watched fearfully, Deacon spoke in his own tongue and the grey wolf suddenly adopted a subservient pose then turned heel and ran off into the trees. The rest of the pack returned, sat on their heels and waited.

Trembling shocked beyond belief Ross and Bobby didn't move a muscle. Leona and Melissa clung together hardly daring to breathe. Clayton watched as a female black wolf appeared. He recognised her he'd seen her twice before. In his mind he heard his friend saying 'She knows me.' Sure enough the female came to stand by Deacon's side, nuzzling him with what appeared to be affection.

Nobody spoke, their minds buzzing with unanswered questions. Finally, Bobby blurted out, "Did I just see what I think I saw?" No one responded to his question, each of them afraid to mention what had transpired between the wolves on this starry, majestic night, easier to ignore it and put it down to the spell weaved upon them by the amazing light show in the sky.

Billy Joel groaning on the frozen earth as he came to aroused Ross from his dreamlike state. "You okay, man?"

Confused, Billy Joel attempted to stand, his legs like sponges kept bringing him down. "What happened?"

"I'm not actually sure. And if I was, you wouldn't believe me."

Aghast, Ross stared at Deacon, "I know you can talk to wolves but do you make a habit of coming between them, he could've killed you."

"He would not have. You guys alright?"

"Yeah, thanks to you. That took some courage."

When Billy Joel's legs could finally support him, he marched over to Deacon, his eyes accusing. "You told us wolves are harmless they don't usually attack unless threatened."

Deacon glanced at the rifle in Billy Joel's hands. "What are you holding?"

"It's my rifle you can plainly see it's a rifle."

"Then so could the wolves. Anyone with a rifle is a threat to their lives. They have been unjustly hunted for years for no other reason than they are wolves. If you were one of them what would you have done?"

"I didn't threaten them until I thought they were about to attack." He carefully avoided the wolf around Deacon's legs.

"They see a gun as a threat. How are they to know you wouldn't hurt them?"

"The grey wolf jumped at me..."

"He is young, trying to impress the female just as humans do."

"So, you kicked his ass. Why didn't you finish him off?"

"There was no need. Humiliation was enough. Now he will know his place in the order. Why did you come tonight, didn't you wonder why the wolves are so restless? It was a stupid thing to do. You're a long way from town this area is a hunting ground for the wolves and best avoided."

"Why are they so restless?" Bobby questioned.

Deacon gazed up at the sparkling stars. "Something is going to happen that will affect us all." Eventually the black wolf left Deacon's side and faded into the night.

A silent procession of teenagers made their way back to Maskek. Deacon and Clayton saw their friends home safely and returned to the village.

CHAPTER TWENTY-ONE

Talulah Bearhead's village was generally off limits unless you had a specific reason to be there, but on Saturday it would be open to the public.

Under normal circumstances only the Indians would be present at the ceremony but this was Clayton Rykker's adoption and he was white (except in his heart) therefore with permission from Spirit of the Wind, the chief of the village, Clayton was given the choice of throwing it open or keeping it secret.

Since the ever curious population of the town of Maskek had learned that Deacon was actually the grandson of the late chief Eagle Hawk and Talulah Bearhead and next in line to become the new chief, they had shown a considerable interest in the proceedings and of anything relating to their 'very own' Native village. Now they were yearning to learn more about their mysterious neighbours across the lake.

Acutely aware of the townsfolk's curiosity and genuine desire to learn about his people, Spirit of the Wind was eager for Maskek's citizens to experience one of the biggest ceremonial events in the village calendar. After debating at length with the village elders and the tribal council, Red Crow allowed the new chief to have his way.

"I hope we do not live to regret this," Red Crow mouthed to Joseph Long Knife at his side.

"You will not," Spirit of the Wind grinned, having witnessed Red Crow's thoughts, "you have my word."

So it was one chilly Saturday in February 1969, Talulah Bearhead's village lay open to the citizens of Maskek on a scale not seen since Sparkling Eyes and Lupin proudly introduced their newly born son.

On the agenda were archery contests, open to Native and visitors alike rifle shooting and horse racing and a show of knife fighting restricted to the village residents. While these events sounded like fun, they were designed to test the skills of all the young men in the village; the modern day warriors and hunters, they were not to be taken lightly.

. The days of war and fighting between the whites and the Native Americans, (the First Nations) were long over, but the skills used in these battles and skirmishes were as important to Talulah's people now as they were a century ago. It was at Spirit of the Wind's insistence and enthusiasm that these skills never be lost.

Among the tests of endurance often undertaken in the summer were the ones that involved leading a wild horse into a raging torrent, diving in after it and coming out astride the animal. Swimming against strong fast currents was designed to tone and strengthen the upper body. Clayton would be expected to hold his own among the many and varied tasks with the other young men in the village, all of whom had grown up within a warrior/hunter society in theory if not always in practise.

Away from the thronging visitors there was to be a sweat in the designated lodge to welcome Clayton into the tribe. Spirit of the Wind, Clayton, Red Crow, Black Elk, Lone Wolf, Grey Owl, Talulah Bearhead and other members of the tribal council would be present. The day would end with traditional singing and dancing. Along with Clayton's adoption and naming ceremony the tribal council designated that, although Spirit of the Wind had already taken his place as the new chief, there would be an official ceremony to finalise it before Clayton's integration.

CHAPTER TWENTY-TWO

Saturday was cold and sunny, a perfect day for the forthcoming ceremonies. The women of the village were up early stoking the cooking fires, preparing a repast the people and their visitors would remember for time to come.

Before this day the young women had prepared their new dresses, leggings and warm mukluks of moose or deerskin. Today was special so they combed their hair until it shone and entwined coloured beads and feathers within it, a custom made easier by a continuous supply of pretty glass, wooden and sparkling beads available from Lola's Trading post and general store in the heart of Maskek's main street. When a new chief such as the handsome and charismatic Spirit of the Wind was to be presented to the people, the women, young and mature, wanted to look their best perchance he caught their eye. Clayton Rykker with his red hair and jade green eyes was well worthy of a second look. He would be the young chief's right hand. Thoughts such as these could turn a mere girl's head.

Inside his grandmother's large lodge Spirit of the Wind waited patiently while his mother, grandmother and her younger sister Nedipah clothed him in the stunning trappings of ceremonial regalia, which Talulah and Nedipah had painstakingly made and prepared in the traditional manner and sewn them with love. Talulah's exquisite beading and quill work dominated the fringed moose hide shirt and leggings over which he wore a breechcloth. The art of decorative quillwork was once widespread among Canadian Indians, only certain women were permitted to do this work however, and they first had to undergo certain religious ceremonies and training.

A blue sheen hovered over Spirit of the Wind's thick and lustrous hair where his mother had combed and arranged it. An eagle feather was fastened on the left side of his head. A war bonnet was not handed down from father to son and the eagle feathers in it had to be earned. With an abundance of birds in the woodland other feathers such as those from the crow or the hawk were also used in the making of it. War bonnets were not worn by every nation and in the past the Cree sometimes wore a headdress known as a roach or porcupine headdress. These headdresses comprised of stiff moose hair, porcupine guard hair, and a deer's tail hooked on a bone or leather base that could stand up like a crest. It would be a proud moment for Spirit of the Wind when the war bonnet was placed upon his head.

When Talulah fitted the newly made moose hide mukluks to his feet he arose. He stood tall and proud and as regal as any Aztec, Mayan or Inca prince. Devastating, wicked and wonderful he was a sight to behold. In similar accoutrements Clayton emerged from behind his mother. His curly red hair, now grown to collar length was held from his face by a finger woven deerskin strip with tribal designs on it and a hawk feather fastened at the side of his head. Rona's face was a picture of pride and happiness. "Look at my son, isn't he magnificent?"

"I wouldn't go that far, mom but I kinda like it."

A wide smile split Spirit of the Wind's face "Now you are truly my brother."

"Go now," Talulah said ushering her grandson and his best friend from the lodge. "Go annoy somebody while we women compose ourselves."

"Lame Deer," Spirit of the Wind greeted as a young man of thirty strolled over to them.

"Where is your woman, Spirit of the Wind?" he asked bowing briefly to show his respect, "Should she not be by your side this eventful day?"

"Thorn Rose is with Shell Woman, making ready in Black Elk's lodge."

"Getting all prettied up, I'd say," Clayton remarked with a wicked gleam in his eye, "for her young chief she must be perfection."

Returning his brother's smile, Spirit of the Wind told him, "How will you make better that which is already perfection?"

Stunned, Clayton stared at his best friend. That was the first time he'd ever heard him speak about Thorn Rose in such a manner.

"Do not fear, my brother for nothing has changed between us." He took his closest friend's wrist, his grip firm and strong.

Lowering his gaze Lame Deer smiled knowingly, "So she is not completely your woman. It is a strange relationship you have with this girl. In the cold night do you not long too feel her warm body against yours?"

"When I long to feel the warmth of her body I will go to her."

"More likely she'll come to you," Clayton said.

"As Shell Woman shall come to you my brother."

"Black Elk allows his daughter to come to you?" The older Cree spoke in awe.

"You've been gone awhile Lame Deer," Clayton responded. "Black Elk came to Spirit of the Wind requesting that his daughter be allowed to continue seeing him."

Like a startled rabbit, Lame Deer's eyes widened in surprise. "Black Elk came to you?"

"Why wouldn't he come?" Clayton said, "Spirit of the Wind is the chief. Only a foolish father would refuse his daughter the chance to be the chief's woman. They are promised, after all."

"I had not considered that."

"Why do you ask so many questions, my friend do you desire Thorn Rose?"

"I think she is beautiful but I do not desire her," Lame Deer answered quickly fearful of reprisal from his young chief.

From somewhere among the circled tipis a woman's voice called to him. "My sister calls I will take my leave." Bowing, Lame Deer retreated in search of his sister.

Alternating easily between the Cree tongue and English, Clayton said, "Sounded real suspicious to me."

"Lame Deer is not alone in his thoughts. Thorn Rose has many suitors."

"You'd better hang onto her then."

Alone with his blood brother, Clayton Rykker pondered nervously on the impending ceremony. "What will be expected of me?"

"Many things my brother, but you should have no need of these for you have proved yourself many times. Your heart is true and strong. Your place is here with us."

In all his dreams Clayton had never imagined this day. Now he stood with his brother and good friend, his spine straight and shoulders back, his heart swelling with pride, "This is a great day."

Resplendent in a quill encrusted dress of the softest doeskin Nonie stepped out of Talulah's lodge. Long fringes hung from the sleeves and around the bottom of the dress. Her shoulder length hair the colour of ripened corn was braided and dressed with brightly coloured beads. Her lavender blue eyes shining with adoration she reached for her son. "Will I do, am I suitably attired for the mother of the new chief?"

"Wow!" Deacon enthused, "you're breath taking, momma, and you are definitely suitably attired. I thank grandmother and Nedipah for dressing you so well."

"I'll second that," Clayton agreed.

A moment later Rona appeared and although her dress was not quite as flamboyant as that of her friend it was an exquisite garment. Clayton's eyes opened wide with admiration. "Way to go mom. I love it."

"Looking good," Spirit of the Wind replied with a smile, kissing Rona's cheek. He turned as Grey Owl, Red Crow and Black Elk approached.

Stopping in front of the young chief, Grey Owl touched his shoulder, "Spirit of the Wind we must speak with you."

Glancing quickly at Clayton he followed them to the council lodge. At his mother's questioning look Clayton shook his head. His eyes troubled, Spirit of the Wind faced Grey Owl and three of the tribal elders. His grandmother was not among them.

"Why is there need of this Grey Owl, my brother has proved himself many times? He has learned well. Two weeks ago we spoke about these things and it was agreed. I have told him he will not need to participate and now the council say different. Not only is this unfair it also means I have broken my word."

"You know it is a requirement before he can be adopted into the tribe."

"This is the truth, but only if he has not shown himself to be a true warrior."

"It is the decision of the council. It has been said."

"It is a decision that has been reached without grandmother's knowledge. She is still a member among you. She too should have been consulted," he replied in a tone of authority.

"It would have been one against many, therefore the result would have been the same. Now that you are the chief you have taken that responsibility from her."

"She is an elder and remains a member of the council. You will include her in all of your decisions. I have spoken." Bowing respectfully, he left the lodge.

"What's up?" Clayton asked.

"Grey Owl and the elders have agreed that you must show the people the skills you have learned and participate in the trials. You must fight."

"Who am I to fight against?"

"You are to fight against me."

CHAPTER TWENTY-THREE

"Will there be anything to drink?" Billy Joel wanted to know, before the five of them made their way towards Loon Lake to be taken along the trail hidden among the dense woods that led to the encampment.

"No," Leona informed him, "it's a dry village. If Deacon finds anyone trying to smuggle alcohol in there'll be all hell to pay. And he'll probably deal out the punishment."

"But there is food," Ross assured him, "and plenty of it, so I'm told. But if you're expecting burgers and fries, you're gonna be disappointed."

"So, what am I gonna drink?"

Throwing Billy Joel a look of irritation, Melissa told him, "Use your head, Billy."

"Well then how about one for the trail, so to speak."

"If that's what you want then you'd better go your own way, you're not old enough to drink," Bobby told him.

With that, Melissa, Leona, Ross and Bobby left him and headed for the lake via the ranger station.

"How come we've got to go this way?" Ross grumbled pulling his scarf even tighter around his face. Even with his long johns and extra layers of clothing under his sheepskin lined checked jacket, he was feeling the cold.

"Because Ross, the other trail in the direction of Deacon's home is roped off and you can bet his cute cousin Lone Wolf will be standing guard," Leona explained.

"Well why? Isn't it closer that way?"

"Think about it, Ross, would you want the world and its population parading past your home and parking all over your lawn?"

"Deke doesn't have a lawn."

"No, but they have gardens stretching down to the lake and the last thing they'll want is everyone and his car trampling over it. Honestly Ross sometimes you don't use the brains God gave you."

Suitably reprimanded Ross strolled in silence until they reached ranger headquarters, where Tyrell and Trip held sway with rifles.

"Expecting trouble?" Ross queried of Tyrell, a former pupil of Maskek High.

"Just making sure there ain't any."

"Are you going?" Leona asked.

"In the capacity of law enforcement," he smiled, "Captain McNally is working in conjunction with the RCMP and the encampment's police."

"Then you are expecting trouble," Bobby said. He was beginning to wish he'd worn something warmer than his leather jacket, even with a sweater underneath it wasn't very practical in the searing cold. Despite the thick woolly hat and scarf his ears burned with the cold. Frostbite might be his companion before the day was over.

"It's a big crowd Bobby swelled by outsiders who've heard about the ceremony. Anything could happen."

"Who's meeting us at the lake?"

"Mule Deer I think, maybe Stands-Alone too. Better get moving there's a whole heap of folks behind you. Have a good day."

Looking over her shoulder Melissa said, "That's a lot of people."

The citizens of Maskek were bundled up and on the march toting bags, back packs, and babies in buggies swaddled in snow suits and covered with blankets. Children were an important part of Native culture and always welcome in the encampment although social problems on some of the reserves had resulted in the loss of the strong family ties that once bound the people together. But today all children were welcome.

"I'm getting really excited now," Melissa said her eyes aglow with anticipation.

"Could've picked a warmer day," Ross moaned just as Deacon said he would.

~ * ~

True to Leona's prediction, by ten o clock Lone Wolf was leaning nonchalantly against his horse, turning people back. "Not this way folks. Take the trail via Jack Pine Avenue."

"But that's miles away," one gentleman protested.

"You got cars, don't you? Turn 'em round and head back. No access this way."

"That wasn't made clear to us," another argued his head through the side window.

"Yeah it was, you just didn't read it. Back there just as you're leaving town there's a big notice been put up by the town council. Sorry folks," Lone Wolf said bringing up his rifle, "this way's off limits."

"That's a fine way to greet your neighbours."

The caravan of cars and campers reversed and headed back in the direction of town.

~ * ~

Clayton's mouth fell open, his jaw sagging like a broken bed. "If it is a requirement, I'm prepared to fight whoever the council chooses, but I will not fight my brother. Even if I wanted to, there's no way I can compete with you."

"It's not about who wins, it's the skill they're looking for."

"Compared with you?" Clayton asked doubtfully.

"You godda believe in yourself Clayton, you have the ability. You just need the confidence."

"No. I can't and won't fight my Brother."

With barely a perceptible nod Spirit of the Wind ducked into the tipi. "Grandmother I must speak with you urgently."

Outside Talulah's lodge Clayton waited. Events had taken a turn neither had expected.

"You are troubled good friend," Lone Wolf said creeping up on Clayton's right side, startling him.

"Holy Moses, Lone Wolf will you stop doing that."

"Speak, Brother to Spirit of the Wind."

While Clayton explained his fears Lone Wolf's expression never altered. "This troubles you very much. My cousin speaks the truth, only your ability will be evaluated. It is not a contest. Has Grey Owl said which weapons you will be using?"

"He has not. I believe it will be the knife a skill I have not yet mastered. What experience I do have is negligible. I don't like knives Lone Wolf, they creep me out."

Talulah gestured to her grandson to sit. "In this instance you cannot undo the decision of the council, but you can request it to be fair. Which weapons have been chosen?"

"The knife has been chosen. I have not told him."

"How are Clayton's skills with the knife?"

"It's not his favourite weapon. He needs more practise."

"Since I am a member of the council and I was not informed of this change of plan it is not a true decision, therefore he may choose the weapon with which he is most acquainted that will show his true ability. This I have spoken."

"How goes it, my cousin?" Lone Wolf enquired when Deacon returned.

"I think we've fixed it."

Grinning all over his handsome face Lone Wolf winked at Clayton, "Good luck, Clayton I'll be rooting for you. Now I godda go stop the good citizens of Maskek from trampling all over your homes. Catch you later."

~ * ~

Mule Deer, Stands in Timber and Stalking Moon ranging around the perimeter of the encampment near the lake, were alerted by the sound of heavy footsteps and laboured breathing. They came instantly to attention, rifles at the ready. Minutes later Melissa, Ross, Leona and Bobby panting and tired emerged from the thickets.

Mule Deer lowered his rifle. "Have you walked far?"

"From the ranger station at the far end of town," Leona replied. "Even following the markers, I didn't realise how far it is on two feet."

"Walk slowly," Mule Deer replied wryly, "you've got plenty of time. The trail into the encampment is marked by the men from the village. You've still got a ways to go."

"That's not what we wanted to hear, Mule Deer," Ross grumbled.

The curious and excitable townsfolk reached the perimeter of the village, escorted by other men from the village; Mule Deer, Stands-in-Timber and Stalking Moon began the time consuming task of checking the motley assortment of bags and backpacks and even the baby strollers, looking for alcohol or any other illegal substances that could be smuggled into the encampment. Satisfied, Stands-in-Timber waved them on. They would be checked again by Captain McNally's rangers when they reached the entrance to the village.

~ * ~

"I have spoken with grandmother," Spirit of the Wind told Clayton, "Grey Owl made a grave error by not including her in the judgement of the council, therefore, although you will still have to fight you may choose your own weapon."

Clayton's eyes lit up, his face beaming, "Then I choose the bow. Thank you."

~ * ~

People were streaming between the tepees, with Leona, Melissa, Ross and Bobby in the lead, some in excited anticipation others curious but wary.

Pakito Running Deer the offspring of the strange coupling of a Yaqui Indian mother and Cree father, and Reno Brissaud, a Métis of Cree and French blood scoured the bags of the citizens as they entered the settlement. Rangers Giovanni, Tripp and Lamar were helping them as most of the able bodied population of Maskek crossed the threshold between the forest and the encampment in the clearing. The hills above the Native village were hung with visitors and tourists waiting to set foot in the previously unseen encampment. Nobody knew for sure what they'd find there. Rumours abounded. What they actually saw was certain to remain in their minds for a long time.

~ * ~

"There he walks, the son of Sparkling Eyes," Thundercloud told the four disciples watching the camp from above. Hidden in the rocks the five men waited patiently.

"Our brother Darrel failed to take him. Now it is my turn. When darkness comes there will be no escape. Spirit of the Wind will be no more, I shall be prince and Sparkling Eyes will be forgotten forever." Thundercloud raised the burning lance above his head and cried out to the heavens. A ferocious lightning bolt lit up the sky shattering the rocks around the five men. A thunderclap louder than any cannon split the air around the hills.

~ * ~

"What the hell was that?" Clayton asked.
"Thundercloud," Deacon told him, "He's close."
"Should we be concerned?"
"Not today, this is our day."
"What if..."
"He won't."

CHAPTER TWENTY-FOUR

By eleven in the morning the majority of Maskek's curiosity seekers and the outsiders were perched on waterproof tarpaulins, bundled up against the cold. As the temperature rose warmed by the winter sun, they began to strip off their outer layers.

Twelve noon the drummers and singers started up the hauntingly beautiful chanting. The ceremony had begun.

When Talulah Bearhead held up her hand the surging crowd had to be restrained by the men of the village and Captain McNally's rangers.

Gesturing to the excited audience Virgil McNally bade them sit. "The inauguration and naming ceremony will not commence until everyone is sitting down, this is for your own protection and that of the people of the village. I must ask you to keep all the children by your side. Do not allow them to wander through the encampment alone or into the forest. They are your responsibility. Anyone not respecting my orders will be asked to leave and escorted back to town."

"Ta'wow—Welcome. It is good to see so many of you here," Talulah declared addressing the crowd. "We have not seen so many present since the birth of my grandson, Spirit of the Wind, eighteen years ago. This is the first time any of our ceremonies have been open to the public. It is our hope that after the ceremony is completed you will come away with a clearer understanding of that which is a part of our diverse culture. We are gathered here for an important occasion—the inauguration of our young chief, my grandson, Spirit of the Wind. This will be followed by the naming ceremony and adoption of Clayton Rykker blood brother to Spirit of the Wind, into our nation. With no further delay we shall proceed."

"Are you nervous?" Clayton asked his brother.

"Yeah," Deacon replied, "are you?"

"Scared to death."

"It's a good day to feel afraid."

Appearing by their side, Lone Wolf returned from his assignment, guarding their homes, touched his cousin's shoulder. "It is time Spirit of the Wind. The council awaits you."

Winking at Clayton, Spirit of the Wind followed his cousin over to the council fire. A huge cheer went up as the young Indian took his place by the side of his grandmother.

"He's absolutely breath taking," Leona cried jumping up and down, her heart booming inside her breast.

"I see him," Melissa shouted, "Wow, if he'd come to school dressed like that the girls would've been all over him...or he'd have been shot on sight. Whoever made his ceremonial regalia and I bet it was Talulah, dressed him to kill. It must've taken months to prepare. He looks splendid..."

"Awesome," Bobby interjected, "look at the detail that's gone into the making of it. And I'll bet he loves every minute of wearing it. It's definitely Deacon's style."

"Spirit of the Wind," Leona corrected. "He's no longer Deacon, is he?"

"Jeez, no he's not, that's gonna take some getting used to."

Addressing her grandson in the Cree tongue Talulah took the exalted war bonnet of eagle feathers from Red Crow. Spirit of the Wind had earned every one of them. She spoke to the people of the village and turned again to her grandson.

Kneeling on the frozen ground he allowed his grandmother to place the majestic and treasured war bonnet upon his head. He stood and faced her. "I will wear the war bonnet in honour of my grandfather, Eagle Hawk, a great warrior and a fine chief and in honour of my grandmother, Talulah, without whom our village and our people would not be. I shall wear it with pride."

Not one to make long speeches or any speeches at all, Spirit of the Wind stepped away his head held high, his heart bursting with pride. What greater glory could his people bestow upon him? Eagle Hawk had entered the world beyond the stars when Spirit of the Wind was sixteen. Though unaware at the time that the gentle and dignified chief was his true grandfather, he felt his loss deeply.

Taking the boy under his wing Eagle Hawk had taught him the way of the Cree, the way of the warrior, taught him to walk with his head high and to be proud of his Native heritage. Following the premature death of his grandfather from tuberculosis, a common illness to which the Native people had little resistance, even in the 1960s, Grey Owl had taken over the continuing task of teaching and training him. Talulah Bearhead embraced her only grandchild, her dark eyes shining with devotion.

The roaring crowd slowly quietened as the newly inaugurated chief faced his people and their visitors. "Come forward my brother," Spirit of the Wind called holding out his arm to Clayton.

Probably for the first time in his life, a shy Clayton moved towards his blood brother and best friend. Stalking Moon walked by his side.

"My Brother has been my eyes, my ears and my voice throughout the school of the white man and always by my side. From this day forward and forever he shall be named White Hawk. For him this is a suitable name. White Hawk is to be adopted into our nation. Soon he will begin the first of many feats of courage, for such a position does not come about without much training and skill." Reaching for the necklace of large wampum beads Talulah was holding out to him on which hung a beautifully beaded white hawk, he placed it around Clayton's neck.

"It is an honour to serve you and my newly acquired people and I will remain forever at your side," Clayton said bowing in respect. "I am proud to accept these tests of courage which you have prepared for me. I will not let you down." The booming crowd applauded and cheered.

Spirit of the Wind respectfully took leave of his grandmother and the tribal council.

The young women of the village followed him with their eyes, the braver ones ventured after him.

"When do we begin?" Clayton asked.

"We shall begin soon."

When the two young men emerged from the throng of fluttering women, Leona, Melissa, Ross and Bobby pounced on them.

"So now you're called White Hawk how does it feel?"

"Like it always belonged, Ross."

"What happens now?" Leona asked.

"When Lone Wolf and Stalking Moon approach it is time to begin the trials. Stalking Moon will accompany White Hawk and Lone Wolf will accompany me."

Leona placed her arms around Deacon's waist pulling him close. "You look absolutely stunning in that war bonnet. May I kiss you?" Without waiting for an answer, she kissed him full on his lips lingering there until Ross took her arm.

"Leona, I don't think it's appropriate for you to be kissing the Chief in public view of everyone in the village."

"I don't hear him complaining and you're just jealous."

"I'm not jealous but Thorn Rose might be."

Turning abruptly Leona spotted Thorn Rose with Shell Woman in tow, bearing down on her. "I'm not frightened of Thorn Rose..."

"Be wiser if you were," Deacon chuckled, "Beautiful is she to me," he said cutting off Thorn Rose's intended tirade before she let rip. "You are dressed well."

"As your intended I have to be. I have prepared myself for you anyway. Do you like what you see?"

"I like it very much."

Pushing in front of Leona and the girls from the village, Thorn Rose embraced him with open adoration. She ordered the women of the village away. "Go! There are many suitable young men out there. This one is mine."

"And Clayton White Hawk belongs to me," Shell Woman announced to all and sundry, "I am promised to him."

"Who has given permission for this, surely not Grey Owl?" Clayton asked looking enquiringly at Shell Woman

"My grandmother and I," Deacon told him his black eyes twinkling. "It's nothing to do with Grey Owl."

"I'm glad about that," Clayton responded enthusiastically. He was about to enquire further when they saw Lone Wolf and Stalking Moon approaching.

Untangling himself from Thorn Rose's clutching arms Deacon

touched Clayton's shoulder. "My Brother, the time is here."

From the day Deacon had first made Clayton a long bow when both boys were but six years of age, he had thrown his heart into mastering the skill of using it. Deacon had spent countless patient hours teaching him how to shoot, handle and create a masterpiece. His own skills learned from his grandfather the late Chief Eagle Hawk had been severely tested and the result could be seen in Clayton's ability to use the weapon effectively and safely. He was fast and accurate.

Watching the two youths follow Stalking Moon and Lone Wolf, Ross said, "When Deke first told us about Thorn Rose, I expected her to be tall, slim and beautiful, with him being so good looking 'n all. But she's nothing like that. She can't be more than five feet and she's real curvy..."

"By curvy you mean she's too big?"

"That's not what I said, Leona."

"Sounded like it to me. What about Shell Woman? Is she more your type or is she too big as well. These are real women with shape and curves they look like women..."

"I'm not getting into an argument with you. Sorry I spoke."

At the far side of the village overlooking the river known as Snake River because of its meandering, twisting shallows, wooden targets had been set up at intervals along the bank. The river's name had lost much in translation over the years. Some folk believed it was formerly called The Snake in the Water, or msikinepikwa meaning Horned Water Serpent. Even the Indians who originally named it were no longer sure. The young chief removed the war bonnet and handed it to Lone Wolf.

Tall Hills Elk waited at one end of the riverbank with two ponies. He gave both the boys a bow and a quiver. "Grey Owl has instructed me to give you these."

Clayton took his weapon and mounted one of the ponies. When both young men were seated, Grey Owl, and Red Crow, the eldest and wisest of the tribal elders, approached them. Their instructions were simple and straight to the point. Shoot the targets from a moving horse at the swiftest pace, making each arrow count. If either of them missed one of the ten targets he would be disqualified.

"This is not a contest," Red Crow explained, "it is to show your skill and ability. When confronted by the enemy you need to be ready and confident. Your lives may one day depend upon it."

The excited crowd surged towards the river, angling for a front row seat determined not to miss anything. Their way was immediately blocked by the rangers and the men from the village who were concerned for the safety of the crowd. Reno Brissaud and Pakito Running Deer were despatched to direct the agitated audience to a safe place where they could watch the action without getting in the way.

"Sorry folks," Virgil McNally told them, "this is the way it has to be. Safety first; yours and the riders. A spooked horse can unseat the rider causing the arrows to go wide of their mark and possibly hitting someone or possibly causing commotion among the other animals." Virgil indicated the horses tethered loosely to a rope away from the centre of the village. "Set them off and we'll have a stampede. Not a good idea with the huge crowd here today."

"Who's winning?" Leona eventually asked.

"It's not a contest," Bobby and Melissa chorused together.

"Okay it's not a contest, jeez!"

Every arrow hit the targets head on. Deacon and Clayton were well matched and enjoying every minute of it. The pace was fast and furious, Deacon riding from the left of the riverbank and Clayton from the right.

"It's a well known fact that Indians like to show off," Stands-in-Timber quipped, appearing from nowhere and sitting by Leona's side, "Spirit of the Wind is no exception."

"Thought you were on guard duty?"

"I am but I didn't want to miss this. Clayton White Hawk is doing well."

"He's impressive, I'll give you that," Ross said, "had a good teacher though didn't he."

"He had the best. Spirit of the Wind has to the best because he's the chief. He has to be able to climb the highest tree, scale the highest cliff and hunt the largest moose so to speak. There was none better with the use of weapons than his grandfather Eagle Hawk. He imparted to his grandson all his knowledge and skill. When Chief Eagle Hawk left us, Grey Owl took over his training. Grey Owl was second only to his brother Eagle Hawk."

Mouth falling open in astonishment Ross said, "Grey Owl is Spirit of the Wind's uncle? He never told us that."

"He'd have got around to it."

With every arrow counted and no misses the stationary wooden targets were removed and quickly replaced by six men on horseback, each of them carrying a shield in their hands.

"Now they will aim at moving targets carried by the warriors on horseback. All will be moving. Much skill and courage is required, for this task they must pierce the shields without injuring the riders."

"Isn't that dangerous?"

"Indeed. One slip and a life could be endangered."

Once again starting at opposite ends of the riverbank the boys faced their targets. The roaring crowd was on its feet jostling and shouting, placing bets and passing money over each other's head. Stands-Alone and Stalking Moon's betting did not go unnoticed to Captain McNally's trained eye where he stood with Tyrell, watching the crowd.

"They're betting on who can stay astride those ponies the longest, not on who will win," Tyrell informed him, "Clayton's damn near as good as him on horseback. I guess that's because he was bought up with horses. When your father's a cowboy the first thing you learn is to ride."

"Clayton's father was a cowboy?" Lone Wolf asked in astonishment.

"Clayton never told you?"

"Probably 'cos you're an Indian," Ross chuckled

His face breaking into a wide smile Lone Wolf said, "Tell me more about the cowboy."

"Keel Rykker was born on a ranch somewhere along the Montana border. His folks owned a big spread out there. He lived and worked on the ranch until he met Clayton's mom. Seems he was wrangling horses over the rodeo season and Mrs. Rykker just happened to be present at the Red Deer Rodeo when he was there. She was born in Maskek and didn't want to live on the ranch. Seems Clayton's grand folks were kind of old fashioned. She told my mother the women were tied to the kitchen and the men folk spent all their time out on the range or hell raisin' with the Cattleman's Association. His mom wanted to come home. Clayton was born midway between the borders."

"Clayton's American?" a very shocked Ross asked.

"Technically he's also Canadian."

"How'd you know all this?" Bobby asked. "You would have only been about five years ahead of us at school."

"Seven years. My folks were friends of theirs, they used to go hunting together. But that all petered out after a while. Seems Keel and my dad had some kind of falling out."

"Did you ever go with them?"

"Not often. I do know that as soon as Clayt was old enough to sit a horse his father taught him to ride. He was a real macho cowboy, kinda like John Wayne. A man's godda do what a man's godda do kinda thing. To show pain is to show weakness and God forbid if you shed a tear. Stuff like that. Hell, he took Clayt hunting and fishing most weekends and every vacation. There's no way you can do that without learning to ride. They never really bonded."

"He sure kept that quiet," Lone Wolf replied.

"Well he doesn't talk much about his Pa, they didn't get along too well." Tyrell directed his attention to the 'not a contest' contest going on behind them, "Man, will you look at that?"

Spirit of the Wind was hanging under the belly of his horse, his knees barely in contact with the animal's flanks, firing his arrows each one of them making contact with the moving target.

"Now that's really showing off," Ross said disgustedly.

"Yeah but isn't he fabulous," Leona responded her grey eyes shining with affection.

"One of these days you and Melissa are gonna grow up and realise that there are other guys in the world besides Deacon and Clayton."

Leona glared at Ross, "Where did that come from?

CHAPTER TWENTY-FIVE

No contest no winners, but both young men had shown true skill and ability and thoroughly enjoyed it, which pleased Red Crow and appeased Grey Owl. Spirit of the Wind with Clayton White Hawk at his side approached the two prominent tribal members. He said nothing awaiting their response.

Red Crow spoke first, "That was indeed a magnificent performance. I need no further proof of your expertise Clayton White Hawk. I have seen you in action on many occasions and I am satisfied with the results. Spirit of the Wind, you have chosen correctly and taught your brother well. Your grandfather would be proud of you. That is all I have to say." Red Crow returned to the tipi to watch the remainder of the contests from the warmth of his lodge.

"Quite a performance indeed," Grey Owl replied, "but we are not yet finished. Come with me..."

"Grey Owl!"

Halted by the authority in Talulah's voice Spirit of the Wind and Clayton stopped in their tracks.

"Grandmother means business," the young Cree laughed, "when she uses that tone no one dare speak against her."

Planting her feet firmly in front of her brother-in-law, the Medicine Woman glared at Grey Owl. She stood no more than chest high to the council 'leader' but her demeanour was forceful. "There will be no more tests for Clayton White Hawk. This day he has proved himself well beyond the capability of some of our own warriors, as he always has in the past. This is enough. Spirit of the Wind has chosen him for his other traits not only his weapon skills. You have observed him in many forms of battle, however contrived, and he has met them all with honour. Therefore, these trials are over."

Bowing his head, Clayton responded with gratitude and affection. "As you wish, Talulah," Grey Owl said, humbled.

Watching her brother-in-law depart she put her arms around her grandson and Clayton. "Go, enjoy the rest of the festivities."

Spirit of the Wind led Clayton aside. "Today you were inspired. It is the best I have ever seen you perform. Well done, my Brother."

"I had to make it right for you so that you'd know your faith in me wasn't misplaced."

Watching Grey Owl walk away, Spirit of the Wind said, "There is much fighting spirit still within my uncle..." Hearing Lone Wolf call his name the young chief paused in mid-sentence. When his older cousin caught up to them, he peered into Lone Wolf's anxious face, "You are troubled, Lone Wolf."

"Grey Owl has issued a challenge, which as chief you must accept."

"Why does he challenge me?"

"To save face because your grandmother pulled him up over Clayton."

"How will this be?"

"With knives."

The young chief's face lit up excited by the idea of challenging his uncle.

"Didn't he teach you to handle a knife?" Clayton asked.

"Grandfather first taught me. Grey Owl took over later. I welcome the chance to show my own skill against his. I will be ready for him."

"Only to disarmament," Lone Wolf pointed out, "nothing more. He comes now."

Word spread quickly throughout the village and among the spectators as the thronging mass just a few steps behind Grey Owl, encroached upon the young chief.

"No sooner done than said," Clayton mumbled.

Not only had this event sparked the interest of the visitors but also that of the other men eager to observe their young chief in action against Grey Owl, a legend within the encampment for many years.

"Lone Wolf has spoken with you, Spirit of the Wind?"

"He has uncle and I accept your challenge."

Within seconds a wide circle had formed around the fighters. The event had not been planned and the tense, expectant crowd awaited the coming challenge with inquisitive excitement.

Having heard of the intended and forthcoming fight Nonie sprang forward, her face anxious. Laying a hand on her son's arm she pulled him round to face her. "Are you sure about this, Grey Owl is an accomplished fighter."

"I'm sure. Both grandfather and Grey Owl taught me to use the knife, I wish to show my uncle how much I have learned." He smiled at her, "He will decide whether their teachings were worth it." His black eyes twinkled with disarming wickedness.

"Well it'll be exciting if nothing else," Ross said.

"It's a bonus," Stands in Timber agreed.

Spirit of the Wind clasped the knife, crouching and ready, confident and totally focused on his opponent. Just as focused and determined was Grey Owl.

Spirit of the Wind effortlessly blocked every movement of Grey Owl's knife with his own. In the beginning they were well matched but within minutes the young chief had the upper hand. He was fast, nimble and light on his feet, his reactions swift and accurate.

Grey Owl was well into his seventies, although his piercing eyes belied his true age but he remained a master of the art. Ordinarily a force to be reckoned with, today he was losing ground to his brother's grandson. Spirit of the Wind was young and fit and thoroughly enjoying the chance to showcase his skill. It didn't take long to put the older man to the ground and disarm him. As if of one voice the frantic crowd was silenced while they waited for Red Crow to amble over to the contestants. The new chief held out his hand to his uncle and helped him to his feet.

"You have learned well and remembered all you were taught," the older man told him, "Eagle Hawk would be proud of you. The time your grandfather and I invested in you has not been wasted."

"Am I worthy of your teachings, uncle?"

"Indeed, you are. I wish your father Sparkling Eyes could have seen your performance. He too was a skilled fighter. You and he are well matched."

Red Crow, now in his one hundred and one year at least, addressed Grey Owl. "Are you satisfied or do you require more evidence of Spirit of the Wind and Clayton White Hawk's abilities?"

"I am satisfied. There is no need of further feats or contests. We shall leave that to our warriors and the visitors." Patting Spirit of the Wind's arm he took up his knife and retreated.

"Well done," Red Crow said. "The day is young go with your friends and enjoy yourself there is much to see. It is your day, make it a good one."

"So, what do you wanna do?" Clayton asked.

"How about you spend some time with us," Ross suggested, "we've hardly had a chance to talk to you guys."

Spirit of the Wind turned to Ross, beaming, "How good are you at riding?"

"I can sit a horse."

"But can you stay on it?" Clayton quipped.

"Why?"

"Because they're about to start the horse racing," the young chief informed him. "I don't want to miss it."

"Well if it means we get to spend more time together, then yeah I'm up for it, where do we start?"

"Across the river I will show you. Get up the tree..."

Ross stared at him, "Up the tree?"

Deacon shinnied up the tree as far as the heavy branches would allow and waited patiently for Ross to follow.

"Don't ask," Clayton chuckled, "just do."

Ross joined him at the top of the tree.

"Look beyond the river, Ross." His arm outstretched Spirit of the Wind pointed to an area of grass slinking between the trees, roped off on the opposite side of Snake River.

"There we will race. Three times round and back. It's an easy route you just godda stay on the horse."

Thrice round meant through and under the dense treed canopy and from this height the trail looked alarmingly narrow, barely wide enough for a horse to pass. "We're riding through there?"

"Sure, it's good practice for losing our enemies... if we get any," he grinned "You can change your mind..."

"Hell no, I said I was gonna do it and I will."

Squeezing Ross's shoulder, he was about to climb down when his attention was diverted by something slowly ascending the Wapiti Hills in the vicinity of Bittern Creek. A sudden angry wind rattled the branches and arrows of ice pierced his flesh with such intensity that he almost lost his footing. Shaken, he rapidly descended the tree.

CHAPTER TWENTY-SIX

A dark mass of cloud was moving crablike toward the summit of the Wapiti Hills, breaking off at intervals, almost like the tactical manoeuvres of a platoon of soldiers. The swaying, sideways gait of the bizarre formation ranged up and across the hills and toward the tiny island in the middle of the lake. The formation appeared to have limbs, which vanished then reappeared. Sometimes floating, sometimes walking, but always with a strange crablike movement. It was a macabre spectacle. Spirit of the Wind had witnessed the disturbing phenomenon from the top of the tree.

"You sure you ain't any kin to the bear, Deke?" Ross grumbled, joining him at the bottom of the tree. He'd noticed nothing out of the ordinary but Clayton had seen his brother's eyes. "What's up?"

"I don't know what is was Clayton, but it scared the hell outta me. I think it's begun..."

Clayton experienced a sudden pressure crushing his heart, "Your father's legacy."

The youth nodded, "Grandmother said it was closing in we could no longer remain safe in our house. Now it is here."

"It has chosen a bad day to manifest its presence." Not wishing to alarm the people around them they spoke in the Cree tongue.

Stalking Moon called out cutting into their thoughts, "Hey, Spirit of the Wind we're waiting. Let's go."

"Nothing we can do right now," Clayton whispered, "just godda get on with things."

On silent feet Talulah Bearhead glided over to Nonie and Rona. They sat around a huge fire with the women from the village, chattering and laughing. "Nonie, look to your son."

Alarmed by the anxiety in Talulah's voice Nonie knew

immediately what was inducing her fear. "It's here?"

"The unthinkable is manifesting there can be no turning back. We must keep him within the sacred hoop."

"That will be impossible Talulah. Whatever is threatening our lives, the people of this village and the town he has no choice other than to fight it. Does this prophesy speak of his death?" Her hands clenched as tightly as the pain in her heart Nonie looked to the sky. "The Great Spirit will not allow this to happen to my son." Nonie felt Rona's arms encircling her. She gripped her friend's hand and tried to remain calm.

Moon Woman, perhaps in her one century and fourth year of age, struggled to her feet from amongst the group of women who were now silent. Shuffling over to Nonie she reached for her hand. "Truly now you have now become one of us. In the beginning when you first bought the child home, we were unsure of you. Although you loved the boy as any native mother would, we were concerned that perhaps the ways of your people would intrude upon the raising of Spirit of the Wind after the manner of his ancestors. Even with the strict and gentle guidance of his grandmother we feared the worst. In the first six years of his life not once did you speak your own tongue or attempt to explain to him of the world beyond this encampment. Against your better judgement you allowed him the freedom, which all our children are given. You proved to be a devoted mother."

While Moon Woman spoke of the past years, Nonie sent out her thoughts. When they returned, every moment of those years was played out in her mind's eye. Nonie had struggled to follow Talulah's guidance, denying herself all memories of her life before that time and forsaking the memories of her own childhood in the world of the whites beneath the hills and beyond Loon Lake. It had been as if that world had ceased to exist.

"Did you know true happiness, Nonie?"

"How could I not know true happiness when the son of Sparkling Eyes, the child of my best friend Lupin, lay in my arms? I love him dearly."

"Then why did you take him from us, from his family, his home and his people. You allowed the evil ones to manifest themselves upon his person, leaving him open and unprotected and away from the sacred hoop?"

With the unthinkable closing in Nonie questioned her reasons for ever removing Sprit of the Wind from the safety of his village. Jonathan had begged her to 'keep him always within the sacred hoop.' By removing him she had betrayed his parents' trust and inadvertently exposed him to the terror of his father's troubled and tortured past. She had almost lost him. (Told in Child of the Heathen)

"You have asked the Great Spirit to protect your son. I will pray with you."

The young chief tried to shake off his fears. Perhaps within this race he could put aside the inevitable. Today was his and Clayton's special day he would not allow anyone or anything to destroy it. The hell with what was out there.

Lined up and impatient the braves and the visitors sat astride their horses, waiting for Red Crow's signal. Ross seated proudly on a patchwork pony waited intently. They were gone in an instant. He'd missed the signal. Kicking the animal's flanks, he lit out after them.

Again, the insatiable crowd lined the river bank, yowling and yelping and heaping encouragement on their chosen rider. Huddled to one side leaning against the trees, a small group of older Cree laid bets on their favourite to win. It was not uncommon to find the young men betting on everything they could lay claim to, especially their horses. Today was no exception.

Where they had dug out the course from under the frozen snow the ground oozed with mud churned up by the hooves of the horses. Even the sure footed ponies were slipping as they turned abruptly on to the narrow trail between the pines, their whooping, hollering riders relishing every moment.

"Sounds like a goddamn war party," Tyrell remarked to Virgil McNally.

Chuckling, the ranger captain wandered over to Lone Wolf. "Not entering the race?"

"Been there, done that, fallen off, got trampled, figured I'd leave that to the others. Placed your bet?"

"You bet."

For a time, Ross felt he was gaining on the leading riders until those riding drag overtook him. Clayton and Spirit of the Wind were long gone riding neck to neck way ahead of anyone else. He hadn't seen them since the start of the race.

"Well at least I'm still mounted," he told the pony, "that's godda be worth something."

"Can girls enter the race?" Leona asked, "not that I'd want to I'm just curious." The four girls stood together Leona, Melissa, Thorn Rose and Shell Woman, watching the riders.

"Would you choose to?" Thorn Rose said gathering the heavy fur robe about her shoulders. It was one thing to look attractive for her young chief. It was another to stand shivering in the cold. The sun's powers had dwindled since the ceremony first began and the spectators were starting to feel the effects.

"No. I just wanted to know if it was just a 'man' thing."

Thorn Rose laughed, "They like to think it is and we let them. It's good for their ego."

Wandering over to the girls, Nedipah, Talulah's younger sister by twelve years gave her attention to the pretty girl watching for Spirit of the Wind's return. "Thorn Rose, when did you decide he was worth waiting for? Not so long ago you stood by the lake and told him you would not wait for him."

"Since my sister Red Leaf announced that if I did not want him, she would have him."

"Red Leaf is not the only one to show a keen interest. What of the other girls?"

"There are too many. He is my warrior, my chief, my man. Why should I allow other women to lay claim to him? They only want him because he's the chief."

Leona glanced at Melissa, "Do you think she means us?"

"Probably, except we wanted him before he became chief."

Nedipah continued, "You know that is not so, except perhaps for Wind Song. But the main reason is because..."

"I love him."

"As he loves you Thorn Rose. No matter how he cares for Clayton White Hawk, his first love will always be yours. Does he not satisfy you under the blanket?"

"Oh, indeed he does," a dreamy look in her eyes, "I only need to catch a glimpse of him and nothing else matters..."

Melissa and Leona shuddered and tried to push the image of Thorn Rose entwined around Deacon, from their minds.

First back were Deacon and Clayton riding neck to neck, with Stalking Moon, Pakito and Mule Deer in hot pursuit. When all the competitors had returned the jostling crowd rushed over anxious to claim their winnings.

"Where's Ross?" Deacon asked, scanning the crowd.

"Haven't seen him since we started, do you think we should got look for him?"

"Think we'd better." They were gone instantly disappearing into the forest.

"This is cool, man I love it," Ross shouted as he swung between the trees, amazed he was still seated, "Helluva race, don't have a clue where everyone is but I feel great. Melissa should see me now."

The sure-footed pony knew exactly where to go, needing no direction from its exhilarated rider. Probably would have made it too if it hadn't been for the sudden dense bank of gray fog spiralling around the trees directly ahead of him, like some ephemeral shadow. Faced by the dark mass blocking its path the horse reared up, unseating the unsuspecting rider. Ross slid over the animal's rump landing awkwardly on his back, stunned and winded. The dreadful stench of decay emanating from the banked mass made him retch. The darkness was so deep that for a moment it became night. Somewhere beyond the fog he heard the horse take off, its hooves pounding frantically on the frozen ground. Flying passed Clayton and Deacon the piebald kept on running as if all the devils in hell were upon his hooves.

"Ross."

"Boy! Am I glad to see you guys," Ross said, struggling to his feet as the boys rounded the trees. "Something spooked my horse..."

"Yeah, we've just seen him, "Clayton replied, "Must've given him a helluva shock."

"What did you see, Ross?" Deacon asked apprehensively.

"I don't know. One minute it was there and then it was gone. Looked kinda like grey fog. You know how the mist hangs around the lake at the bottom of the Wapiti Hills? It was kinda like that. The smell coming from it was like something dead. I puked."

"Look anything like that thing that came into town a while ago?" Clayton wanted to know.

"Yeah it did."

"Let's go," the young chief said taking Ross's arm and pulling him up behind him.

CHAPTER TWENTY-SEVEN

While the contests and competitions between the villagers and their visitors continued unabated, Clayton and Spirit of the Wind, Nonie, Rona and Nedipah gathered in his grandmother's lodge.

"It will not happen this day," Moon Woman told them. "Enjoy the moment, for there is time enough to contemplate what we are to do tomorrow. Go now Spirit of the Wind your mother is safe with us. Embrace the company of your people and your friends because once it has begun it will require your full attention, the extent of your courage and your indomitable spirit."

Outside the tipi, Melissa, Leona, Bobby and Ross waited patiently. Melissa was first to spring a question on Deacon. "You promised to tell us about Thorn Rose. You said we'd be able to understand how it is with her. You obviously love her and she can certainly arouse you. So, what was all that about you and Clayton being an item? Was that a kind way of saying you don't like me?"

The young Indian stared at her stung by her words. "I never said I didn't like you Melissa. How can you think that? We've been friends since school."

"That's the impression you gave me when we were staying at your house. Why else would you say those things about you and Clayton?

"Because they're true."

"If it was true, Thorn Rose couldn't have turned you on like she did. I didn't miss your reaction when she kissed you."

"Thorn Rose and I were promised to each other when we were small. It was planned for us to marry. But now, because of my father's past, if Thorn Rose becomes my wife she will die just as my father's wives died including my mother. Until I can destroy the thing that haunts our lives, we can't be together..."

"That's not all of it," Clayton said, "not by a long shot. You all know that Deke and me have been friends since we were kids. Over the years our relationship has grown far beyond friendship. It wasn't until we were around sixteen that we really understood our feelings for one another. Love is no respecter of age or sex. I need to be with him, he needs to be with me..."

"Whoa," Bobby butted in, "am I hearing this right, you guys wanna be together?"

"Yeah, but that don't mean we ain't interested in girls. You've seen me with Shell Woman you've seen Spirit of the Wind with Thorn Rose."

"It is for us as it was for my father and Damien. Yet he had five wives and Lupin, his fifth wife, was my mother."

"Now it's all beginning to make sense," Melissa said, "why didn't you tell us before."

"It wasn't time."

"Just clarify this for me," Bobby added, "you still wanna have sex with girls, right?"

"Right, "Clayton said.

"Glad we got that sorted."

"Feeling better than she had in weeks Melissa jumped up and swung her legs around Deacon, kissing him full on the lips. "This means I still get to hang out with you."

Throwing the knife at an object was a sport with which the majority of Indians were particularly expert, and Ross, Bobby and Clayton were determined not to miss the action. With Melissa and Leona in tow, they headed over to join the circle of spectators gathered around the men waiting to perform.

Taking the knife in the palm of their hands with the handle towards the end of the fingers, standing ten to thirty feet from the target, the men threw their knives at the wooden target no larger than a saucer and with such precision that the weapon struck within the small circle at almost every throw. They were able to use both hands equally. At twenty-five feet from a target they could hit it twenty-five to thirty times consecutively. A roar went up from the delighted crowd.

"How come you're not taking part Clayton?"

"You how I feel about knives Ross, they aren't my most favourite weapon I leave that to Deacon. His father was heavy into knives I guess he takes after him."

"Well Melissa and I don't want to watch you boys playing with knives you're like big kids. We're going to watch the jingle dance." Leona took her friend's arm and marched her away.

~ * ~

Inside the sweat lodge amid the presence of Spirit of the Wind, Red Crow, Black Elk and Grey Owl Talulah welcomed Clayton into the tribe. For Clayton it was a magical and spiritual journey he would remember always. The visions he experienced there would remain with him as long as he lived

~ * ~

Darkness falling over the land ended the contests sooner than any direct result from competitors. After everyone had satisfied themselves with food and non-alcoholic drinks the drummers and singers returned.

Talulah came forward holding her arm up for silence. "Now that you are all refreshed and the night is still young, I hope you will join us in the circle dance. Some of you may know it as a friendship dance."

"All those who can stand get up and join in," Captain McNally said ushering people to their feet. "Talulah and her people have made a wonderful effort here today. Everyone has been made welcome. Most of you seemed to have enjoyed it. So, to show our appreciation we're all going to join in the circle dance. Hold hands and make the circle as wide as possible. The new chief and his grandmother will be leading the dance tonight."

Spirit of the Wind took his grandmother's hand and led the dancers in a shuffling side step, circling the blazing fire until everyone who could possibly stand or walk was carried along with the pounding of the drum and the chanting of the singers. Those who were slightly lame but could manage with help were given a helping hand from the warriors. The first song ending he led them in a second dance. With their hands still clasped together the new chief began to weave in and out, to the left and to the right.

"I guess that's called a snake dance," Ross said to Leona.

The drumming ended with them all back in a circle. Warmed and invigorated the cheering, clapping crowd returned to their roost.

"I was just thinking..." Bobby said out of the blue.

"Gee, that's dangerous," Spirit of the Wind responded.

"Sit on it, Deke. I was gonna say, Elvis was inducted into the Los Angeles tribal council by Chief Wha-Nee-Ota, for his portrayal of a Kiowa Indian in the movie Flaming Star. See, I'm a mind of useless information. Did you guys know that?"

"We know you're a mind of useless information," Ross said wryly. "But hey, Clayt you're in good company with Elvis."

"Spirit of the Wind," Thorn Rose called heading over to them, "do we have time to be together before the next dance?"

His friends wandered off to watch and take part in other events so the young chief seized the opportunity to be alone with Thorn Rose. Crushing the girl to him he kissed her, "There's time." Lifting her in his arms he took her to his grandmother's empty lodge, laid her gently on the bearskin and covered her with his body. "We have plenty time." Hearing Clayton and Shell Woman enter after him and close the flap he smiled.

Whichever dance was planned next he and his blood brother would definitely not be taking part.

CHAPTER TWENTY-EIGHT

Approaching the lodge a little later, Leona and Ross peeped around the entrance and came away quickly, shaking their heads. "This is not a good time," Ross told Bobby, ushering Melissa away. "We'd best make ourselves scarce."

"Why isn't it a good time?" Melissa asked.

"Not right now. Let's go."

Unfazed by Ross's warning Melissa pushed the flap aside and was instantly confronted by the sight of Spirit of the Wind lying on his back completely naked while Thorn Rose also undressed, sat astride him. Clayton and Shell Woman lay in a similar position. Absorbed in each other they did not hear Melissa's sudden intake of breath. Gasping in shock she quickly let the flap fall back and ran off in tears.

"Should I go after her?" Ross asked.

Leona shook her head, "Let her be, she'll get over it. I don't know why she's making such a fuss, Deacon never said he loved her. Besides, Melissa isn't the only one who's disappointed I wanted him too. In fact, I would have liked both of them just once and once is better than none at all. But it's not to be. Let's go find Mule Deer and Stalking Moon."

Ross and Bobby shared a troubled glance, "That wasn't nice," Ross said, "what's wrong with her? Melissa is supposed to be her best friend, thought she'd have shown a little sympathy."

"Maybe it's because Leona's upset too and doesn't want to show it. She did have her heart set on him." Bobby gave a long drawn out sigh, "I don't know, man. It's crazy."

"All my efforts with Melissa were wasted," Ross said sadly, "sometimes you just can't win. I told you guys to let me arrange things, didn't I?"

"Thought you didn't want me," Spirit of the Wind said playing

170

with Thorn Rose's long hair. He lay on his side facing her, both of them spent and content.

Running her fingers over his smooth, copper chest she told him, "I would wait forever for you. When I said those things by the lake, I was angry and hurt. But I could not give you up I love you too much for that...and my sister wanted you." Thorn Rose was quiet for a moment she seemed to be in a quandary.

"What troubles you Thorn Rose?"

"Stands-in-Timber expressed an interest in me. He has spoken with my father Black Elk."

"Why did Stands-in-Timber not approach me first?"

"He was afraid to come to you. He feared you would be angered by his interest in your woman. He thought because my father is an elder it would be better to approach him instead."

"I am aware of how Stands-in-Timber feels about you..."

Pausing, Thorn Rose looked at him questioningly, "How do you know of this if he has not spoken to you?"

"Ever since we were children Stands-in-Timber has looked upon you. As we have grown so has his desire for you. When Clayton and I came here before going to help Mrs. Simpson he asked to walk you to your father's lodge. He would not do that if he did not desire you."

"I do not want Stands-in-Timber," she told him snuggling against him, "I want only you."

"What has your father said?" He held her tightly, her body soft against his.

"Only that he wishes to speak with you."

"Then tomorrow I will see him."

Rousing Clayton who'd been listening to the conversation between his blood brother and Thorn Rose, Shell Woman said, "You must make ready. Red Crow will excuse you missing two of the dances, but if you do not appear at the third, he won't be very pleased."

"Deep shit," Spirit of the Wind grinned.

"Amen to that, brother."

From out of nowhere Nonie and Rona ducked inside the tipi, both of them holding a clay bowl and a cloth. It was Rona who addressed their wayward sons. "Quickly now you need to be washed and dressed. Red Crow is waiting and even his patience is limited. Go make yourselves ready, girls."

Thorn Rose and Shell Woman dressed and returned to their own lodges, Spirit of the Wind asked, "Where is grandmother?"

"Placating Red Crow," Nonie told her son, "We must hurry."

~ * ~

"Aw come on Melissa," Ross said, "don't let it spoil the rest of the day. You've known how he feels about Thorn Rose for a long time. You've got to accept his heart is with her."

"And with Clayton," Bobby said hoping to make her feel better so he didn't feel that Ross cuffing him on the back of his head was warranted.

"I didn't realise they were that close I thought they were just friends not lovers."

"It doesn't mean they actually did anything..."

"Then why was she on top of him?"

"Maybe they were just cuddling. You don't actually have to have intercourse to satisfy each other there are other ways of doing it. I always believed the girls in this village couldn't go that far without being married anyhow. Don't know if that's true or not but I'd think it was."

"The next dance is starting," Leona called, running after them, "Spirit of the Wind is in full regalia you should see him. Wow! Let's go watch it. Melissa, are you coming?"

Touched by a crest fallen Melissa, Leona suddenly felt guilty for dismissing her obvious distress. Placing an arm around her childhood friend she led her towards the dance area.

"How come you're not taking part?" Ross asked Clayton.

"I'd sooner watch, I haven't mastered the steps yet. Maybe next time I'll give it a try."

"Melissa's devastated. She came by the tipi and saw you guys with Thorn Rose and Shell Woman."

"She saw? Oh man."

Ross nodded. "Everything. She took it personally seeing him and

Thorn Rose together she's head over heels in love with him. Nothing in the world is gonna change that."

"She wasn't supposed to see it at all. If he'd known she was gonna come by and look inside, they'd have been more careful. I thought you'd made some inroads with Melissa, Ross."

"Figured I had, she let me kiss her and put my arm around her. She even told me I was brave. The next day it was like nothing happened between us. I can't figure her out."

The fire burned hot and bright, crackling and spitting in the darkness. The drummers clustered together around a huge hide tom-tom were completely absorbed in their music. With one hand clasped over one of their ears they attacked the drum with gusto, their voices carrying around the village. The sound of the drum would have carried as far as the town of Maskek. The dancers appeared in stunning regalia. The brightly coloured feather bushels, arm bands and headdresses of the dancers bobbed up and down as they moved. Bells on their ankles jingled with every step their cries splitting the night. It was wild, primeval and breath taking, hauntingly beautiful and very moving. The sound filled the forest and echoed around the Wapiti Hills. Silhouetted against the blackness of the night their faces and regalia hi-lighted by the light from the fire, it was truly a sight to behold. The spectators sat entranced some of them moved to tears, others excited and encouraging, mesmerised by the sheer, raw beauty of the pounding drum and the chanting of the singers. It was awe inspiring.

"It's like going back in time," one woman was heard to say, "it makes me heart swell. I'm so glad I came."

"Yes, it does. I consider it a privilege to be here today."

"I'm mighty pleased to hear that Mrs. Crandell, I wish more people felt that way."

"Virgil McNally, how lovely to see you, it's been such a wonderful day I hardly noticed the cold, but now my aged and weary bones are beginning to ache. You've got that to look forward to in the years to come. Aren't the dancer's costumes amazing..."

Spirit of the Wind returned to his friends, accompanied by the warrior elite. Taking him to one side Clayton told him about Melissa.

Striding over to her, his heart pounding he took her hand in his. "I'm sorry you had to see that, Melissa."

"Are you?" She refused to meet his eyes, "I thought we'd sorted things out."

"We have. We did, didn't we?"

"You know how I feel about you Deacon, I thought you cared about me. We've always been close ever since we were kids." She looked up at him her eyes wet with tears. "I thought there might still be a chance for us to be together after what you told us earlier. But when I saw you with her it made me realise the truth."

Melissa's honesty and anguish cruelly piercing his heart he struggled to find words to eliminate her pain, to express his sorrow for hurting her. Even if he could find them it wouldn't help her.

"What would you have me say, Melissa?"

"Is it because I'm white?"

"It's not because you're white, it's because I'm chief. It's expected that the woman I choose will be from my own nation."

"Doesn't love count for anything. Surely, it's more important to marry someone who loves you rather than simply because she's Cree? Night Horse was allowed to take Yellow Hair for his wife and she's white. Why aren't you allowed the same privilege?"

Night Horse worked in Stanley Cuthand's coffee house in Maskek.

"Yellow Hair has been raised by Night Horse's family since she was five. Her white name was Abby May. My grandfather found her and her mother hiding in the forest. They were running from the woman's husband. She told grandfather that her husband beat both of them all the time. They'd been in the forest three days when grandfather came across them. They were lucky to be alive. The woman had too many internal injuries she didn't survive. Yellow Hair was taken in by Wind Woman, the mother of Night Horse. She grew up among our people."

"And that makes it acceptable, does it?" Melissa asked bitterly.

"That makes it easier for her. She's more Cree than white."

"And what about Clayton and Shell Woman what's their excuse?"

The young chief glanced away then turned again to face her, his dark eyes deep and penetrating. Even in her bitterness Melissa had never seen them so full of affection and understanding or so beautiful. "If I did love you the way you wish me to, I still could not make you my wife." Gently he stroked her cheek. "I am truly sorry."

For a long time, they were silent Melissa resting in his arms. Refusing to accept his explanation she tried again. "Your mother is white doesn't that count for anything?"

Clayton came forward. "He's adopted, Melissa, you know that. His blood mother and his father are both Cree."

"I know that Clayton, but his father had four other wives and from what Mrs. Pierce told us they were either white or Spanish not Indian. Only Deacon's mother was Indian. So, explain it to me."

"The father of Jonathan Sparkling Eyes was Chief Many Moons of the Blackfoot nation and his mother Shadow of the Moon was the daughter of Cuthand, a Cree chief. You know that Lupin was the daughter of Talulah and Chief Eagle Hawk they're Deacon's grandparents and he's their only grandchild. Thorn Rose is the daughter of tribal elder Black Elk..."

"What you're saying it that neither my face nor my bloodline fit."

Clayton stared at her in amazement. "That's not what I'm saying, Melissa. You're reading it all wrong."

"It seems pretty clear to me."

"Clayton didn't mean it like that," Deacon told her, "he's trying to explain the way of my people in this village. Very few villages are like this one."

"You haven't answered my question about Clayton and Shell Woman."

"As long as Shell Woman's parents agree to her seeing him it's permitted."

"Come, child," Talulah said, placing her arm around the girl, "I will speak with you."

Clayton watched Talulah take Melissa into her lodge. "What're we gonna do, Deke?"

"Grandmother will make her better understand. I don't know what else I can say."

"Deke..." Bobby began before he was cuffed a third time on the back of his head, this time by Lone Wolf. "Hey, what was that for?"

Deke?" Lone wolf raised his eyebrows.

"Sorry. I meant Spirit of the Wind. How come you still get to call him Deke and we don't?" he addressed Clayton.

"He's my brother," Clayton grinned, "When you become his brother you can call him Deke. Okay?"

"If Thorn Rose and you didn't have this bloodline thing hanging over your heads would you marry a white girl if you loved her?"

"I would not."

"I guess that answers Melissa's question then."

"That's not the way it is, Bobby. Would a white girl want to live in a tipi in the forest unless she was raised here as Yellow Hair has been? There's no plumbing or electricity, no place to wash except the river or the lake...none of the things she's used to. I would not ask it of anyone who has not known this way of life." He looked directly at Leona, "Could you live here with us, with me?"

"I could live with you anywhere. I'm enchanted by this village, I would dearly love to share it. But I don't think I'll ever be enough of an Indian for you. Living in a tipi in the middle of winter is quite intimidating; there's no heat except for a campfire, no hot baths, and I don't believe in hunting. And no matter how strong love is would it be strong enough to survive the cultural differences? Melissa loves you with all her heart but that doesn't mean it would work. How your mother copes Clayton is astounding. Does she ever regret leaving her home?"

"No way is mom going back, she says she's found her place here. Everyone needs to find that spot that special place, where your heart is settled and you feel you belong. Not too many people ever find it."

"Can I say something?" Ross asked, "and I'm gonna say it even while you're here, Spirit of the Wind. It's not my attention to offend you we've been good friends for almost thirteen years. While you were at school and we went to your home you were the same as us. You've been bought up among us white folk since you were six or seven but you've never wanted to or been allowed to forget your roots, your blood or your culture. Since you left school and returned to your real home, you've changed. Not in a bad way I'm saying but you've become more 'Indian' more 'native'... if you know what I mean. This is where you belong no one can deny that. I've been observing you today and the difference between your culture and ours is becoming more and more apparent. Maybe the fact that this village is so steeped in tradition makes it more obvious. I'm sure there aren't any more villages like this one. I honestly believe that Melissa wouldn't be happy here either no matter how much she cares for you. It's great coming here, but to live here you've got to be a special type of person or an Indian. Clayton's obviously got what it takes so has is mother. The rest of us can only dream about it."

Stunned silence flooded the air thick enough to cut with a knife. Bobby with his mouth gaping and Leona turned warily to Spirit of the Wind. Contrary to the reaction they expected he smiled. "I have heard your thoughts, I'm pleased you have chosen to voice them. I may have been living among you for thirteen years but I've spent more time in grandmother's village than I have in momma's house. I've been raised in the ways of my people not yours. "

"You're not offended?" Bobby asked.

"Why should I be it's the truth. I've never denied my heritage. Just hope it doesn't affect our friendship."

"No way, man," they said in unison clustering around him.

"We'd miss out on all of this," Ross told him displaying his hand to encompass everything around them. "We're not about to lose you...that is unless you want us to?"

"That'd be too much, I'd miss you moaning about standing around in the cold and a million and one other things." He looked directly into their faces his eyes moist his expression sincere. "I'd miss you all too much. Just so you know, I'm not easy to live with either ask momma."

"You got that right," Clayton responded.

"Group hug," Leona said bringing them all together.

"All for one and one for all, huh," Lone Wolf said his black eyes twinkling.

When they separated, Deacon suddenly asked Leona, "What do you mean you're not Indian enough for me?"

"You messed that up didn't you," Bobby grinned.

"Exactly what I said, I couldn't do half the things Thorn Rose does. I can't tan hides or create exquisite handicrafts. I can't even bead a moccasin. As for cooking over a fire I don't think I could handle that. I don't even like camping, I'd make a very poor wife. Besides I like shopping too much I like to have everything to hand."

"Is that what you think it's all about? There's more to living here than cooking and beadwork." He smiled at her, "You could learn."

"Is that a proposal?"

"It wasn't."

By the time Melissa and Talulah returned, Deacon was dancing again and Clayton joined in. Ross, Bobby and Leona watched them closely.

"Melissa and I have spoken. I think we have reached an understanding. There will be no more tears or unhappiness. You are always welcome here. If your friendship were to be broken over affairs of the heart it would destroy all of you. Your friendship is important to Spirit of the Wind and to each other, keep it that way."

"Thank you Mrs. Bearhead," Leona said. "We all love him to pieces."

Whatever Talulah had said to Melissa it seemed to be having the right effect because she was smiling. When the apple of her eye reappeared with Clayton, she reached up and kissed his cheek.

"Everything is okay?" Deacon asked.

"Absolutely fine, but don't count on us leaving you alone for a long time yet."

Bemused, Clayton asked, "What did Talulah say 'cos it sure seems to have worked."

By ten pm the people of Maskek and the out-of-towners were beginning to make their way home, escorted by Captain Virgil McNally and his rangers, who in turn were guided by three members of the warrior elite. The fires still burned and the drummers kept on drumming until the last of the guests were gone from the village.

"Nice to have it to ourselves again," Spirit of the Wind said, "way too many people."

"Amen to that, brother," Clayton replied, "Let's hit the blankets."

"Alone?"

"We're not exactly alone we have each other, right?"

"I can go for that."

CHAPTER TWENTY-NINE

"What are your intentions with my daughter, Spirit of the Wind?" Black Elk enquired, "Stands-in-Timber offers marriage. Do you?"

"My thoughts have not changed, Black Elk. There can be no wife for me until my father's legacy is ended. I love Thorn Rose but I will not risk her life. Will you?"

Black Elk pondered on Deacon's words. "I lost my first born daughter Lighting Swan, to the residential school. She did not return. I fear she may have lost her life. My second daughter, Red Leaf comes with the beginning of spring and vanishes with the coming of winter. One moment she is here and in an instant she is gone. Thorn Rose remains with me, a reminder of her mother. No, I will not risk her life. She is in love with you, yet Stands-in Timber asks to take her. When you have destroyed that which took away your father and mother, will you make her your wife?"

"She is my woman Black Elk, wife is just a word. My feelings for her will always be whether she is my wife or not. I have no more to say on this matter. I will make it right with Stands-in-Timber."

"Stands-in-Timber is your friend and a fine addition to the warrior elite. Be careful that the two of you do not lose your friendship over a woman. It has happened many times in the past. It is a sad thing when two such friends part in sorrow."

Deacon was about to go, changed him mind and sat down again. "I have been unfair with you. I do have more to say on this matter, Black Elk. I'm eighteen and not long out of school. I have today been made chief and I still have much to learn in these matters. White Hawk and myself are now rangers and new to the work. I don't want any more responsibilities right now. To make Thorn Rose my wife at this time, even if she were not in danger, is more than I can handle." His black eyes twinkling he threw Black Elk a smile. "We got plenty years yet."

Taking leave of the elder, the young chief strode over to the lodge of Stands-in Timber's mother, Black Shawl. She was waiting for him outside. Bowing in respect she pulled his face down and planted a kiss on his cheek.

"How are you, mother?" he asked, showing her the same respect she had shown him.

"I will be better when my son chases these foolish notions from his head. He is waiting for you." Black Shawl stood to one side allowing him to enter.

The young man in question stood and lowered his head. "Spirit of the Wind," gesturing for him to sit.

Seated cross legged on the ground the new chief asked, "Why did you not speak to me before approaching Black Elk?"

Stands-in-Timber hung his head, a guilty look upon his copper face. "I was afraid you would be angry with me. She is your woman and I wanted her. When you both stood by the lake and Thorn Rose told you she would not wait for you I saw my chance. I sent out my thoughts, she did not reply..."

"Did you think that Black Elk would help her to choose?" There was no bitterness in his voice only a question.

"I no longer know my thoughts they are scrambled."

"Stands-in-Timber you are my brother and my friend, it has been so for many winters I do not wish to endanger that. If Thorn Rose truly desired you, I would not stand in her way. Last night she opened her heart to me and it is me whom she wants. You are free to look upon another. There are many women here who would look upon your face. Are we clear, brother?"

Nodding vigorously Stands-in-Timber took his chief's hand and placed it on his heart, "We are clear, brother."

Upon Deacon's mother's death, when he was only six weeks old, his father Sparkling Eyes approached Black Shawl, asking if she would suckle the baby. Having recently lost her youngest child who was still born, her breasts heavy with milk Black Shawl had agreed. "I would be honoured, Sparkling Eyes." In the eyes of Black Shawl and her two older sons, Spirit of the Wind was their brother.

Black Shawl, listening by the side of the tipi jumped as Spirit of the Wind ducked outside.

Winking at her he said, "It is good."

Throwing up her hands in jubilation Black Shawl turned he eyes to the sky, "Thank you."

CHAPTER THIRTY

"Emily, have you reconsidered your decision to stay here?" Steve Simpson asked, retrieving his bathrobe from their hastily unpacked cases. While the contents of their house were being evaluated by men in suits clambering all over the furnishings, Emily and Steve booked into the Tamarack Motel for an indefinite period, much to Steve's displeasure. A motel room always seemed to say to him seedy, needy and not particularly pleasant.

"I haven't. I wish you would change your mind about staying. Real estate is still rife that's what bought us here in the first place. Last year we were getting along better than we have in months. What's changed between us?"

"You have Emily. Ever since that Indian kid bought you back from his grandmother's village."

"You mean Spirit of the Wind?"

Steve was staring at her as if she'd lost all sense of reason. Perhaps she had taken leave of her senses. "I thought his name was Deacon?"

"It is. It was. Spirit of the Wind is his Cree name."

"Give me strength." Steve pressed the heel of his hand to his forehead. "Are you in love with this kid?"

"Don't be ridiculous he's just a boy."

"He's eighteen, he's an adult. That boy hasn't been a boy for months. I don't know much about Native culture but I do believe they grow up much sooner than our kids. I think I'm right in saying that a century ago he would have been a man at the age of fourteen. Don't kid yourself Emily, that boy is all man in every department and in every way that counts. And you are besotted." He stared at her suspiciously, "Or maybe you've already found out? You were alone with him when he rescued you from whatever abomination was stalking you last summer weren't you?"

"He took me straight to his mother's house she was present all the time."

"How do I know he didn't try anything with you in that Indian camp last month?"

"Steve, please. Nothing happened. We could make a new start here in a smaller house without a past. There is a beautiful log cabin... well it's more of a lodge than a cabin, on the edge of town close to the ranger station. We'll start over. Have a second honeymoon..."

Despite his suspicions Steve took her hand. "No, honey it wouldn't matter where we were living be it here in Maskek, Edmonton, Fort McMurray or Tuktoyaktuk that boy will always be in your heart. I don't compare with him and I most certainly cannot compete with him. You've always harboured a dream of a young lover and now you have one."

"He's not my lover, he never was. He has a girlfriend her name is Thorn Rose and he's head over heels in love with her. He's not interested in me."

"But you're infatuated with him. To say otherwise would be foolish."

"Steve..." Gliding over to her husband, Emily slid her hands inside the bathrobe and pulled him closer until she could feel every contour of his body. She fitted herself in there like a glove. Rubbing gently against him she was delighted to find him hardening. Slipping her hand down between his thighs she cupped his erection. Pulling away, Steve lifted her onto the bed and covered her with his body. Beneath him Emily shuddered, his actions had a frightening finality about them.

~ * ~

"You guys were due at the ranger station two hours ago," Virgil McNally told Clayton, on Monday morning. "Where's Spirit of the Wind?" He glanced around the village.

"On a vision quest he left yesterday. He's seeking help to deal with his father's legacy. Whatever it is, cap'n, it's on the move."

Virgil listened in silence while Clayton explained all that Deacon had seen from the tops of the trees.

"It's not human," Lone Wolf said, coming up behind them, "it lives beneath the circle of death, the accumulation of all that was wrong between our two races since the beginning."

~ * ~

Clad in warm moose hide clothing, the skin of the bear over his shoulders and the bowie knife for a companion, Spirit of the Wind entered the gloomy interior of the forest, the home of his ancestors its location known only to his people. No white man ever set foot here. Hidden in the boreal forest this sacred place had stood for hundreds of years.

The young chief knelt and looked up at the trees. "Oh, you people who are always standing, the protectors of the winged, I come to ask for your knowledge and wisdom, for there is nothing you tree people cannot tell me." Bowing his head, he offered a prayer of thanks to the tree people who had lived longer than civilisation. Calling out to the spirits of the forest he made known his desires.

As the day wore on, he took no sustenance of any kind. In order to obtain a vision, he must fast, his thoughts and mind open to knowledge and visitations from the spirits, his head clear, his path defined.

His prayers ended he lay upon the bear skin on the snow covered earth, his body calm and serene, his mind clear of any thoughts other than that which was part of his destiny. In his mind's eye Spirit of the Wind saw himself in the lodge of his grandmother. The Medicine woman held him in her arms telling him of his ancient past, of the legend prophesied in the annuals of time.

"The Great Mysterious created this beautiful land for the use of the Indians, the animals to hunt, the fish to swim and the trees for our protection. For a time, all was well and we were happy. Then a great darkness descended upon the earth. It changed the hearts and minds of the people. Some ran willingly welcoming the darkness, which stole upon their hearts turning them against their families, the people and all that is good. The ancient ones were so disturbed by this change that they feared for the future of their children. A leader was called to protect and care for the people, a true warrior with a heart of courage and the skill and ability to succeed against this dangerous foe. All the clans gathered together in the heart of the forest to choose this wondrous leader. But amongst all our fearless warriors none could be found. The elders called upon Kiche Manitou to find this special chief. 'Is there no one to lead our people? Then I will create one. Seek out the greatest of the warriors, the greatest of the chiefs and bring me a woman of the Medicine clan, the most dynamic and beautiful of her kind: a child of nature to whom our world is sacred."

Talulah spoke so softly that at times Deacon thought he was dreaming the images unfolding in his mind as she talked.

"For many years the people searched for their deliverer. Then one summer morning the elders bought from the plains the most magnificent war chief. In true Cree style he stood tall and proud, his handsome face a pleasure to behold. His hair was so long that he could sit upon it. The people looked to him to shelter the women. He carried with him a knife of the finest and sharpest bone, a weapon of extraordinary power. The war chief was called Protector of the Wind. With this wondrous knife he fought and won many great battles.

Later that night the ancient ones returning from searching the woodland, bought with them Sun Dancer, the daughter of the most famous medicine woman among the people. Her beauty was staggering, her presence intoxicating and Protector of the Wind fell instantly in love with her. Within days they were promised to each other and many beautiful children were born to them."

"The great mysterious took Protector of the Wind aside and said to him, 'In days to come a descendent of your children will lead our people out of the darkness. He will be strong and powerful. He will instil fear into the hearts of our enemies.' Those special people were the ancestors of your father, Sparkling Eyes, and your mother, Lupin. You are the one decreed in the ancient prophesy to end the legacy of darkness. The mark of the Protector of the Wind is drawn upon your neck. All that has happened to you since your father died, all the trials he went through have made you strong, preparing you for this the most spectacular of destinies."

Stunned by these revelations Deacon left his grandmother's lodge. She called out to him, "Once you have found the power knife of bone it will protect you. Do not forget that Spirit of the Wind."

The night had sealed the forest when his eyes finally closed, his soul at peace. He should have been cold, shivering in the freezing temperatures yet he felt warm and comfortable cradled in his fur blanket on the forest floor. Much later something shook his blanket. It was the wolf. He locked eyes with the majestic and fearless beast and their minds began to touch, their thoughts to coalesce. In the eyes of the wolf he saw a vision of what was to come. The animal turned her head beckoning him to follow and Spirit of the Wind saw she walked above the ground.

CHAPTER THIRTY-ONE

Spirit of the Wind returned to the encampment leaner, light headed and dizzy with hunger and fatigue. Exhausted but delirious with eagerness he started to explain to his mother what he had seen.

"You will eat," Nonie said taking her son protectively into her arms, "and then you will sleep." She led him into the lodge where his grandmother, Nedipah, Clayton and Rona waited.

"How was it?" Clayton asked. "You've been gone for days."

"Shush now, Clayton," Nonie told him, "you may speak with him when he's rested."

Clayton was keen to hear the full story but he knew the young chief needed rest. Until he was renewed the women of the lodge would not allow him near.

Nonie covered her son with a blanket of elk skin and sleep crept upon him. In the heat from the fire and the warmth and security of the blanket he drifted into oblivion.

~ * ~

When he awoke many hours later the village was silent. The usual every day sounds were missing. He shivered with the sudden coldness filling his body, tightening his chest and creeping stealthily along his neck and spine. It was here waiting beyond the hoop of the village. The time had come to end his father's terrible legacy.

Nonie appeared with a nourishing meal. When he'd eaten she helped him to dress, handed him his knife, bow and quiver and accompanied him to the heart of the encampment. The men of the village waited with their horses to follow him. Ross Porter and Bobby Blaine stood a suitable distance away watching the proceedings. They had arrived earlier in the day with Captain McNally and Tyrell and now waited in anticipation of what was to come.

Red Crow, Black Elk, Grey Owl, Talulah Bearhead and Moon Woman, sat in a circle around the fire. They were deep in earnest conversation when Spirit of the Wind approached them.

Turning to face him Red Crow asked, "Are you well rested Spirit of the Wind?"

"I am, Red Crow."

"What did the spirits reveal to you, have they shown you the way?"

"The black wolf appeared to me. She seemed to know me."

Clayton flinched jolted by his best friend's comment. Hadn't Deacon said that once before? Was this the wolf who'd come to him after Billy Joel's disastrous encounter with the grey wolf.

"Our enemy is not human; our weapons may be defenceless against it."

"Look for the knife of fine bone, for there you will find a way to destroy it," Talulah told him quietly.

~ * ~

Resplendent in warm traditional regalia, the warrior elite of the Cree police, fanned out behind Spirit of the Wind, Clayton White Hawk and Lone Wolf. They were joined almost immediately by Stanley Cuthand's nineteen-year-old nephew Lucan and other men from the village who chose to ride with the young chief into the heart of the vaporous enemy. Parents and family looked on anxiously their hearts heavy with fear. Not one person truly knew or understood the extent or the power of this adversary.

Nonie and Rona stood with Talulah and Nedipah among the women, observing quietly. This was not a time for words each knew the others' thoughts. Spirit of the Wind threw his mother a wicked smile and with a loud war cry waved the warriors forward.

"Think he's been waiting for this chance all his life," Ross whispered to Bobby, "sure wish I was going with him."

"You would choose to ride with them, to fight an enemy of which you have no knowledge?" Red Crow asked, having heard his quietly spoken words.

Turning to face the tribal elder Ross bowed his head, "We would consider it an honour to ride with our friend..."

Nodding slowly the old man said, "It is good that you have stayed so loyal to our young chief. If you truly wish to follow, then go with our blessing." Red Crow called to a youth of eleven. "Little Wise One, bring horses for these men they wish to follow Spirit of the Wind."

"Riding with the warriors makes us men, huh?" Bobby said. "Far out!"

Within minutes the two youths were fitted out in suitable clothing and mounted on fast ponies, Bobby hoping against hope that he could stay seated.

Nonie and Rona waved as Ross and Bobby shot after the vanishing, whooping war party. Talulah smiled with pride. "My grandson has outstanding friends."

Bringing up the rear, Pakito called to Spirit of the Wind as the two young men advanced at a furious gallop with Bobby perched precariously in the saddle. The new chief acknowledged them with a wave and a beaming smile.

"Well I'll be damned," Clayton said, "that's what you call loyalty."

The young chief led them to an area deep in the forest where Ross had fallen from his horse during Saturday's race. There the 'fog' had stopped. Now it had returned. The seething, gyrating mass of grey rolled towards them, its tentacles reaching out and festooning themselves over the trees like Christmas garlands, draping the frozen earth with a thick carpet of vapour. Pulsating, rumbling, ever changing, decreasing and increasing in shape and size it seemed to coat everything around it with its foul odour and fetid breath. Nothing tangible was present in the surreal mass, only the deepening greyness as dark as midnight. It was moving fast over land like some alien being.

Stalking Moon pointed to the west, "Look, see from whence it comes. Not only is it here but it straddles Amisk inlet covering the island with its poisonous venom."

"It is the essence of the departed souls whose deaths were violent and unnatural that will wander forever between two worlds. Among them are our own people who strayed from the true path and whose greed led them to their deaths," Spirit of the Wind replied.

"Souls in hell," Clayton said, "and now they're set to drag us down there with 'em."

CHAPTER THIRTY-TWO

"It covers the hills of grass as far as Bittern Creek," Stalking Moon said.

The warriors turned to look at the Wapiti Hills. Sure enough the rolling mass was spreading up and across the hills until they were hidden within its heaving, revolting magnitude.

Assaulted by an alarming vision Spirit of the Wind swayed on Diablero's back. Clayton and Lone Wolf each put out a hand to steady him.

"What did you see?" Clayton asked.

"I saw my father kneeling above a man. My father's hand was curled into a claw and he was tearing out the man's heart. He was wearing the black hooded robe of Damien's disciples."

Six months previously Spirit of the Wind had been taken captive by Damien Drew in an attempt to persuade him to join the followers of the demon Arcus... a result of his father's desire for immortality, which came at a deadly price.

"The disciples were gathered around him as my father ripped out the man's heart and raised it up in triumph. Thundercloud spoke the truth and I did not believe." He was quiet for a moment. "I guess my father only told momma what she needed to know. The rest he kept to himself. For over two hundred he has been a part of that which began many centuries before when the darkness descended upon the land."

"Your mom said he left that life behind when he married Lupin. He gave his life for you, she wouldn't say that if she didn't mean it. Maybe he changed. Maybe meeting Lupin was the key..."

"Perhaps it was. Whatever happened, his legacy still remains. It is time. Let's go."

Enveloped in the choking, stinking greyness the war party rode on, the maleficent presence reeking of death, debauchery and destruction drawing them inwards. The silence was shattering and oppressive. The area on which the voluminous cloud had settled previously was burned black despite the icy conditions. The trees were gnarled, twisted and charred like firewood, as were the upturned crosses in the circle of death on the island in the middle of Loon Lake known as Amisk Inlet. Even as they rode the tendrils of the fetid cloud closed in behind them.

"Go now," Spirit of the Wind commanded, "before we are cut off." Men and horses moved as one skirting around the expanding mass of depravity into a clearing where they re-grouped.

"How will we fight this enemy, my brother?" Clayton asked in the Cree tongue. "There is nothing at which to aim our arrows."

While Clayton was speaking the cloud began to thicken, plunging them into darkness so dense they could not see their hands in front of their faces. "Be still," the young chief told them, his gently quietly spoken words a calming influence.

As if on cue there came movement among the clinging vines of tentacles and the forest was filled with the sound of anguished wailing and despair so utterly lost and broken the hearts of the warriors were pierced with barbs of deepest sorrow.

"The souls of the dead," Spirit of the Wind said. "We must show no fear, they will feed on our fear. They are greed and depravity, the bringers of the demons."

"The beginning of hell," Clayton said.

The forest rapidly swarmed with the faces of the dead floating unfettered in the blackness. Sensing his way Spirit of the Wind urged the black stallion forward, his eyes slowly adjusting to the lack of light. Clayton came next, the flanks of his buckskin mare Moonshine rubbing against his blood brother's legs. At his cousin's left side Lone Wolf whispered, "Remember what your grandfather told you, in battle you must use all of your senses; ears to hear, your eyes to see..."

Removing the knife from its beaded sheath, Spirit of the Wind clasped it tightly and in a movement so swift it would have been almost invisible to the naked eye even in broad daylight, cut into the face closest to him feeling resistance against the blade. "It lives!" he cried in jubilation.

He attacked a second and a third time, the grinning faces of evil falling under his blows. Instantly, as if someone had thrown a switch, the darkness cleared leaving only the veined and interwoven heart of the grey seething mass of miscreants. These abominations were neither animal nor human merely fleshless beings of indescribable inhumanity. When had the vapour become a solid substance? Perhaps in the blinding darkness when no man could see.

Again the mass descended, its putrid breath choking them, its tentacles reaching out to form around the legs of the warriors paralysing them where they sat. They cried out in pain. Spirit of the Wind slashed mercilessly at the clinging vines of membranes. With no thought for his own safety he weaved in and out of the breathing, heaving cloud, his war cry loud and distinct. Behind him Clayton, Stands-in-Timber and Stands Alone unleashed a hail of arrows. They hissed as they cut through the air, sharp projectiles striking hard against the tendrils of the animate substance imprisoning the warriors. Released from their paralysis Stalking Moon, Pakito, Reno and Mule Deer took up the fight. Mule Deer produced a tomahawk, a sharpened axe that tore through the sinews of the entity. Within the grasping suffocating tangle of undead flesh, the young chief heard his name.

"Spirit of the Wind you are the last remaining descendent of Protector of the Wind and the exquisite Sun Dancer, you cannot end this nightmare. Your father Sparkling Eyes bought it upon his family when he gave his soul to this heinous power two hundred years ago, the evil that lived before time evolved."

The perverse avenging vapour-like mass shifted to move in and protect the heart of tendons and veins from which the voice seemed to emulate. As it shifted to protect, it opened a void and from it arose spectre after spectre of whirling entities, the ugliness of their wretched souls manifesting in acts of unspeakable violence and terror.

Among these spiralling dregs of barbarity, Spirit of the Wind recognised the black robes of demonic possession and worship, a frightening reminder of the time last year when the disciples of Damien had taken him and spread-eagled him across the altar right here in the hills where his father's lover Damien had sought to end his life.

Bobby Blaine and Ross Porter looked on in horror. All around them were scenes of war, tribe attacking tribe, nation fighting nation. The ever lingering threat of pestilence heaped upon the indigenous peoples as the rolling tide of Europeans covered the land, destroyed their homes and livelihood and transmitted disease after disease. As dead as the buffalo that once roamed the plains.

And now Spirit of the Wind saw them; the pitted faces of smallpox, the ravaged and wasted bodies of consumption and tuberculosis, and the emaciated bodies of starving women and children. The baptism of fire as their homes were raised to the ground, the buffalo slaughtered and other animals hunted to the point of extinction; a decimated people with nowhere to run nowhere to hide and no hope for the future. Clayton touched his brother's arm. There before them stood a circle of stone and strangely dressed people in a land they did not recognise. The language was indistinct and unfamiliar. These ancient people appeared to be worshipping the sun. Again, the young chief reeled, Clayton and Lone Wolf ready to steady him should he fall, his vision strong and powerful.

"From where he must've taken his power before he left England," Clayton responded, "and from where he drew the words to evoke the demon."

As Clayton was speaking complete and utter blackness enfolded its wings around them, an impenetrable fortress of obscurity. Clayton felt Deacon's hand tighten around his wrist seeking reassurance from the other's presence. In the midst of the dense forest the air was heavy with the prayers of the warriors, their fear almost a living thing. Never before had they encountered an enemy such as this, nor darkness so fathomless.

His breathing accelerating in the claustrophobic blackness Spirit of the Wind cried out, his heart pounding mercilessly against his ribcage. A child of the forest, the earth and the open sky, he had always feared enclosed spaces and at this moment he felt the darkness as if it were a solid wall. In his mother's house beside the lake, apart from the front door the other doors in the house were never closed, the windows unshuttered. If he couldn't see he couldn't breathe, his senses distorted. Night in the forest was profound, yet he could smell, hear, sense and feel. But this oppressive fog was closing in, pushing him down, weighing heavily against his chest, crushing him. He struggled to breathe as terror washed over him. He wanted to scream, to run to escape its malignant presence. He had never known such dread.

Even as a child when he was locked in the dark, dank windowless school washroom, by one of the teachers who sought to 'teach him a lesson' had he been so afraid. Well he'd been taught alright, taught to fear anything and everything that had walls and a lockable door. Clayton and Lone Wolf felt him tensing, heard his breathing change to short, sharp inhalations. They could almost taste his fear.

He tried to slow his breathing, tried to overcome the near hysterical surge of fear, felt the tears start. Clayton and Lone Wolf well acquainted with his paralysing fear remembered seeing his eyes wild and panicked, his body bathed in perspiration as he fought to gain control. Speaking quietly and soothingly they placed a reassuring hand on each of his shoulders.

"Breathe brother, it cannot harm you. It will pass over."

"Spirit of the Wind, give in. You cannot hope to win." The same voice that had taunted him earlier resounded around him, seeming to dissect his fear. Something inside him snapped, jolting him back to the present and the dangerous and unenviable task awaiting him. To fail now would be disastrous and bring shame upon his family and himself. To be dishonoured was unimaginable.

Taking a deep breath, he said, "I came to end my father's legacy. I will destroy it. There can be no other ending. Upon my birth the spirit of the wind entered the lodge with great happiness. Upon the death of my mother the spirit of the wind returned in anger to mourn her. I now call upon the spirit of the wind to help me destroy that which is corrupt and harmful to my people."

A man learns from what he sees when his eyes are closed. How many times had his grandfather, the late Chief Eagle Hawk, uttered those words.

Closing his eyes, he recalled the pulsating heart of the enemy. He spurred the stallion forward in the direction of the voice he'd heard. For a split second the darkness peeled back and then he saw it, the fine boned knife of extraordinary power, imbedded within the tallest and widest of the trees, guarded by the flaying tentacles of putrid flesh. It was the most magnificent weapon he'd ever seen. It was as if the weapon had been sculptured by the hand of the Great Mysterious.

Spirit of the Wind flashed by the creeping tentacles, as he reached for the knife its unearthly force shook the tree. Curling his fingers around its smooth, carved handle, he attempted to remove the bone knife from its place of rest but the weapon would not be dislodged. The groping tentacles of flaying flesh curled around Diablero's hooves, snaking upwards and reaching for the rider's throat. Slashing the membranous vines with the Bowie he retraced his steps and charged once again. This time the sacred knife came away in his hand, the power building and pulsating within it. Too late he realised he'd turned his back on the enemy and stinging, burning tentacles whipped the knife from his hand and sent it slithering across the frozen earth.

Surging through the trees as though in agony the ferocious wind lashed the tendrils of undead flesh forcing them downwards and backwards away from the sacred knife of power. Leaning from his horse, Deacon reached for the precious weapon. With his eyes closed he took his bearings and hurled the knife into the veined and sinewy pulsating heart. A bellowing scream of startled rage emitted from the throbbing and offensive organ. Thrashing and gyrating wildly, the crumbling structure of miscreants within the dying heart collapsed onto the frozen earth, pulling the groping tentacles with it. Retrieving the knife of power from the centre of the failing heart Spirit of the Wind slashed the last of the obscene vines. Jumping from his horse he touched the heart of the enemy. Unravelling from the branches of the trees they fell away with little resistance, squealing with almost human terror in the throes of death. The darkness began to lift, fading from black to grey to white until the forest was enriched with the light of day. In its place stood the figure of a man, his long raven hair falling around his shoulders like a long black veil.

"Spirit of the Wind, look at me."

Deacon recoiled, stunned, "Father?"

Jonathan came towards them reaching out for the young chief,

"My son."

Spirit of the Wind had no recollection of dismounting or striding over to Jonathan, only the warmth and love in his father's eyes as Jonathan's arms encircled him.

CHAPTER THIRTY-THREE

Emily Simpson stood by as her husband piled his cases into the trunk of the car and climbed into the driving seat.

"Couldn't you wait until the weather improves Steve? This is no time to be driving, they've given out further blizzards your car isn't equipped for it. You need a jeep or an all-terrain vehicle."

"Goodbye Emily. If you change your mind you know where to find me. Good luck with your new single life."

"Goodbye Steve, I love you."

"Not enough to come with me?"

The two of them had talked long into the night, many nights in fact, trying to find a solution which would suit them both; a reason to continue their marriage, a reason to stay together. Between Emily's heartfelt insistence on staying in Maskek and Steve's determination to move on taking her with him they failed to reach a compromise. In the end neither of them could agree on any one thing.

"Then we should agree to disagree," Steve told her. "This is not the way I imagined our relationship would go. I don't know what else I can say to make you change your mind. After twelve years it looks as though it's goodbye."

Steve turned the car toward the main street that would take him out of Maskek and out of her life. Engulfed by a sudden heart breaking sadness and a feeling of total emptiness, Emily sank to the ground and let the tear falls. She had not anticipated this reaction, hoping he'd change his mind, the fact that he didn't left her stunned. Experiencing a sudden urge to go after him she started to run. "Steve, Steve come back..."

Overhead the sky darkened as if filling up before a storm, the air turned colder and the temperature dropped. Daylight vanished as quickly as an eclipse. Alarmed, Emily stopped in her tracks. She stared at the charred sky and then at her surroundings, except that she could no longer see the trees, the lake or any of the motel buildings across from where she stood. Feeling her way, she managed to locate and enter the room in which she'd spent her last night with Steve. Locking the door to shut out whatever lingered beyond the wall she went to the window, straining to see through the creeping fog...if that's what it was. The bizarre and frightening phenomenon was much worse than when she had experienced it the first time. She felt safe locked in the coffee shop with Deacon, Clayton and Stanley. Out here she was cut off from Maskek and other guests at the Tamarack Motel, completely isolated.

The stomach churning odour emanating from the putrid mass filtered through the glass and under the door. The cloud was changing shape becoming less of a fog and more of a solid substance. It was moving as if on legs. Emily could clearly see appendages forming and the whole assemblage appeared to be breathing. The magnitude of it was staggering. Blinking back the tears, trying to hold herself together she called the ranger station. Perhaps Deacon or Clayton might be there. Her hopes were dashed when after a long interval a young man by the name of Tyrell answered her call. "Stay inside ma'am. Keep all the doors and windows closed. That stuff out there is lethal. It's poison. You don't wanna be anywhere near. Just let it pass over."

"I know that. I know it's dangerous, but it's nothing like I saw before when I was in the coffee house. What if it gets in?"

"Pray it doesn't. We're stretched to the limit here, we'll get to you as soon as we can."

"My husband just drove away he'll be caught in it."

"Which way did he go ma'am?"

"He headed out of town from the Tamarack Motel about twenty minutes ago."

"Who am I speaking to?"

"Emily Simpson. I used to teach at the high school. My husband's name is Steve, you have to help him."

"We'll send someone to look for him as soon as we can. Are we able to contact you at the motel if we need to?"

"Yes. Thank you very much. Please hurry."

Beyond the walls of the Tamarack Motel the haunting spectre travelled along the main street toward the centre of the town. Somewhere out there her husband was trapped...

CHAPTER THIRTY-FOUR

When Sparkling Eyes released him Spirit of the Wind said, "You did not die. Last year when I heard you speak my name, when you asked me to look to Mrs. Simpson and when I thought I saw you before I entered her home I wondered if you were still alive."

"I saw you too," Clayton told him. "Although we couldn't be certain dared not hope, it's good you're here." Their conversation was carried in the Cree tongue and all but Ross and Bobby understood the words.

Taking Clayton's arm Jonathan Sparkling Eyes pulled the youth into his embrace. "I can now thank you for your devotion toward my son."

"No more than his devotion to me," Clayton responded, "wouldn't have it any other way."

Leaving his horse with Stands-in-Timber, Lone Wolf advanced on them. He touched Jonathan's shoulder. "I hoped it wouldn't be much longer before you made yourself known to your son. I have never believed the story about the fire Sparkling Eyes. Somebody died in there but it wasn't you."

Deacon's head shot up, his eyes flashing, "Why did you not tell me, Lone Wolf?"

"I could not. We were forbidden to speak about your father. None but I believed he had survived. Your mother Nonie did not know."

Before his fiery offspring could reply, Sparkling Eyes told Deacon, "It was as I requested. There was no reason for you to be aware of me until you could understand what happened. Do not question your cousin further on this matter." It was spoken softly but there was no mistaking the authority in his father's voice.

"Then why now do you choose to come to me?"

"You have destroyed all that was bad. The legacy is ended, you are safe and you are free. All that matters to me is that you are no longer in any danger. The ancient prophesy has come full circle. It was your destiny long before you were born." Gesturing to the warriors to dismount and gather round, Jonathan said, "Sit. There is much to tell."

Bobby and Ross moved closer, warily, unsure of the fellow's reaction. They hadn't heard Lone Wolf's spoken surprise nor understood the conversation between their friends and the man who stood by his side. Seeing him only from the back, they were stunned into silence when he turned round.

"My father," Deacon told them.

Gawping and mouthing words that would not come, Bobby and Ross stared in astonishment at this total stranger who could have been Deacon's twin, for their faces were identical and he looked no older than his son. Eventually strangled sounds emerged from Ross's gaping mouth while his addled brain tried to make sense of it. "Jesus Christ on a dog sleigh."

"He was dead and now he lives," the young chief told them matter-of-factly as if this kind of thing happened every day.

"You are Ross and Bobby," Jonathan smiled, "Ta'wow, welcome."

"How'd you know us?" Bobby asked suspiciously, not entirely convinced this man was who he said he was.

"I have watched, until now I have been unable to approach you. My presence would have placed my son in danger, therefore I could only observe from a distance."

Totally confused, Bobby turned to Spirit of the Wind, "Anymore skeletons in your closet or spectres in the tipi you haven't told us about?"

The young chief smiled, "Too many." Motioning to the circle in which the warriors sat, he said, "Join us." Spirit of the Wind glanced at his father, his black eyes twinkling. "For a guy who's two hundred forty years old you're looking pretty good."

"You must have read that the Cree are of pleasing countenance," he replied his eyes sparkling with merriment, "hope you look this good when you reach my age."

"I have read those words, father."

"Two hundred forty years!" Bobby scoffed, "That's immortality it doesn't exist."

"Then I am a living example of that which does not exist."

"Not only am I confounded I'm also deranged. None of this makes sense. It's not happening, man."

"So what happened in the forest wasn't real, huh," Deacon told him. "You imagined it all?"

"No, I didn't imagine it. I saw it with my own eyes."

"Then believe in my father, it's not like I have a twin brother or anything."

Bobby opened his mouth to protest and closed it again. He was without explanation, bereft of words.

Cross legged by his father's side he and Sparkling Eyes almost indistinguishable except for their clothing, Spirit of the Wind pointed to the repugnant remains of the membranous heart, "Will it live again?"

"We will burn it to be sure it is destroyed."

"Me and Bobby'll be real pleased to do that for you," Ross said. "I've never been so scared in my life. If there's any chance that thing could strike again, I want to know it's completely dead. Not undead but real dead!" Delighted to be of some use the two white youths sought out pine needles and resin and anything that would burn, to create a fire hot enough to annihilate the appallingly foul remains. Excusing himself Spirit of the Wind joined them.

"What do we call your father?

"He's Jonathan Sparkling Eyes Hare."

"Jonathan Hare? Thought your mom's name was Pierce," Ross said. "Where's Hare come into it?

"It is Pierce. She wasn't married to my father."

"Of course not," Ross said throwing up his arms, "why would she be."

"It'd be polite to refer to him as Mr. Hare, then?"

"As you wish Bobby, I don't think it'll bother him either way."

"Aren't you just a little bit shocked? I mean it's not every day your dead father turns up." Leaning forward, he whispered in Deacon's ear, "He is alive, isn't he?"

"He seems to be."

"How come you're taking it so easily?"

"He's not," Clayton replied striding over to them.

"Just because I don't always show my feelings doesn't mean I'm not as shocked as you are."

"You've godda mighty strange way of showing it."

Holding out his left hand the young chief said, "Feel me." Catching on to his meaning Ross took hold of Deacon's wrist and felt his pulse racing, his hands trembling. Ross placed his hand on the young chief's chest feeling his heart pounding mercilessly. "Say no more. I believe you."

Locating a packet of matches in the pocket of his over trousers Bobby struck four times before the fire blazed. Despite the rank odour from the burning miscreants, the flames provided pleasant warmth welcomed by everyone huddled on the frigid, unforgiving earth.

"Good riddance," Clayton muttered over his shoulder as he rejoined the war party.

By his father's side, Deacon asked, "Why aren't you dead?"

"It's a long story, my son."

"Then tell me," he said obstinately.

Jonathan smiled. "Just like Lupin. She always wanted answers instantly."

"Momma said you died in the fire in the basement over which Mrs. Simpson's house now stands."

"She had no reason to believe any differently. Previously I had asked her to take care of you because the demon was set to kill me. When the fire began, I called to her to get you out of the house. The last thing I heard was Nonie telling me she'd take you. Did your momma tell you of Eliza?"

"I know Eliza. Momma said Eliza was your cook and her friend."

"She was. She didn't live in, she came every day except on her day off. Eliza and her husband Lyle owned a house in Maskek. On that day Eliza and her husband came to collect something she'd forgotten, they saw the fire and dragged me out just before the house exploded. Lyle knew of the door hidden at the back of the house. Nonie would not have seen them."

His son was staring at him with a look of total bemusement on his face. "You became an old man now you are young again. Explain it to me. I will believe most things, father but this...how were you restored?"

"While Eliza tended me, Lyle brought a wise man to see me. His name was Buffalo Bear a Great Medicine man of the Blackfoot and also one of Damien's most trusted disciples. He had the power to restore life, but he could not give me back immortality. I will live out a normal life and then I will die just as any other mortal soul will die. In order to conceal my existence Lyle and Buffalo Bear replaced me with an old man who had recently passed away. The flames did the rest. When I was stronger, I returned to the home of the descendants of my true father, Many Moons. Now you have ended the legacy by destroying the unthinkable I will begin to age as any other human would."

"Will you stay with us?" It was a question laced with hope. "I'd kinda like to get to know my father."

Sparkling Eyes peered intently into his son's face and read the need there. "It will depend upon Nonie, she is now your mother she may not welcome my intrusion."

Deacon thought of his mother, how her eyes shone when she spoke about his father, and could not see any reason why she would not welcome him with open arms. To be reunited with him had lived in her heart and her dreams for nearly twenty years. "I think it will make her happy."

Clayton Rykker frowned, perturbed by what he was hearing. "Spirit of the Wind may I speak with you?"

"You are concerned, my brother. What worries you?"

Clayton stood and beckoned the young chief to follow him. With a quick glance at his father, Spirit of the Wind joined his best friend. Out of earshot Clayton said, "Deke, I know you'd like to see your momma and Sparkling Eyes together again but you need to stop and think about it. Since Lupin died you have been your momma's whole world. No mother could be more devoted than she is. You've had her constant undivided attention since you were a baby. You rely on her more than you think; she tends to your every need..."

A nervous sensation forming in his stomach Deacon read the expression in his blood brother's eyes.

"What I'm trying to say is, if your father comes back, you'll no longer have her fullest attention because it will be focused on him. That's gonna be hard to take."

"Are you saying I'll be jealous?"

"Not jealous, but resentful of his presence and the attention she gives him, believe me I know what that feels like. Now that my folks are divorced, mom and I have a much closer relationship. We never could when they were together because my father was always demanding her attention. He kept coming between us. Because I was a boy, I was expected to take it like a man. Boys didn't need kisses and hugs and little things like that, it was a sign of weakness as far as he was concerned. When he visits, I hate him being there. I feel angry and resentful. You've always had your mom's attention. Think carefully before you pursue it."

Deacon was silent digesting his friend's words. Eventually he spoke, "You do not think my mother deserves the chance to try?"

"Yeah, she does, but I'm thinking about you and your mother's relationship with a man affecting your relationship with her. I've known you for thirteen years we're closer than true brothers and when it comes to emotions, I can read you like a book."

Grinning, the young chief said, "Indians aren't supposed to show emotion it's in all the books and movies..."

"I'm serious. Think about it."

In spite of his comments about the books and the movies, Deacon chewed his thumb nail a sign of his anxiety. "I will speak with my father."

"There is no need," Jonathan said materialising at his son's side. They hadn't heard him approach. "Every word Clayton says is the truth."

"Guess you haven't lost your touch, sneaking up on us like that."

"Hope I never do. Come my son, we will go to your mother."

"Que pasa?" Pakito Running Fox piped up, "What's happening?"

"Beginning of a storm I'd say," Reno Brissard told him. "We are to return home. Will we return in triumph?"

"Perhaps we will, perhaps we will not, Quien sabe my friend, who knows?"

Delighted to be returning to the village, the warmth of their women's lodges far more appealing than the stark cold of the forest, the older men went to their horses and waited patiently for the warrior elite and their young chief and his father to join them.

Ross and Bobby kicked out the fire after first making sure the abomination was totally devoured by the flames. "Hope we never encounter anything like that again," was Bobby's parting shot.

What should have been a victory for Spirit of the Wind was diminished in the light of Clayton's concern. It was a solemn procession that wended its way back through the forest. Observing Deacon's body language Clayton said, "I'm sorry, I didn't mean to upset you."

"You didn't. It's what you said that did and the fact that my father agrees with you. I hadn't given it any thought. Now that I am it troubles me."

Nothing more was said until the group of shivering warriors reached the encampment. Jonathan hung back with the older men, this was his son's victory and he would not infringe upon on it.

Pushing his thoughts to the back of his mind, Spirit of the Wind entered the village in triumph holding up the knife of fine bone, in jubilation. "See, I have it the bone knife of power. It is over. The legacy is ended we are free!"

Whooping and hollering the people clustered around the young chief touching and congratulating him. A few adoring women surged forward pushing their way through the crowds to see him.

"It was not I alone who killed the unthinkable but all of us."

"The truth is that our chief struck the fatal blow," Lone wolf told the assembled audience. "Tonight, there will be much celebrating, we will tell the tale of victory around the night fires."

Casting his eyes around the encampment Spirit of the Wind searched for his mother. Locating her he heeled the black stallion in her direction, vaulted from the horse's back and pulled her into his arms. Talulah looked on with pride.

"It is done, momma," he whispered, "we are victorious."

CHAPTER THIRTY-FIVE

Hunted by the expanding cloud of evolving fog, Steve Simpson pulled up abruptly no longer able to see through it or around it. The odious vapour formed around the car plunging him into darkness as deep as midnight. He waited with trepidation. Did the offensive odour seem to be growing stronger? Something was growing even as he watched. The slithering mass was moulding itself into limb-like structures that pierced the body of the mustang and ruptured the windows. The limbs penetrated the car, probing and groping, locking onto anything they could reach.

Steve's throat began to tighten as one of the limbs entered his mouth and slid across his tongue, working its way down his gullet, choking him. Feeling for the door he could no longer see he found the handle and forced it open falling onto the frozen road. He tried to pull the appendage from his mouth. Attempting to stand he lost traction on the ice and his feet slid from beneath him dislodging the thing in his throat. He cried out in fear, the vapour entered his lungs instantly ending his cry. Disorientated by the darkness he reached out blindly searching for something on which to anchor himself. Dazed and confused, unable to breathe properly, he missed his mark and landed face down on the snow covered earth.

~ * ~

Inside Stanley Cuthand's coffee house the patrons waited on tenterhooks, watching the voluminous mist slithering down from the Wapiti Hills, stealing across the lake and into their town. Outside the building Captain McNally's rangers, their mouths covered with masks and neckerchiefs, coordinated the rescue of many stranded citizens. Graph the eldest of the seniors in town, taking time out from his garage held court over the imprisoned patrons. Stanley ventured into the mist to help.

"Ain't no one going anyplace until this mess lets up," Graph told them, "so sit down and drink your coffee. The rangers have it all under control."

All the air vents were shut and any other openings to the outside were sealed off for the second time. Windows were closed and shuttered and doors locked tight to prevent any chance the poisonous cloud might try to enter the building.

The 'Unthinkable' so named because its effects could be deadly, especially to the elderly and children, was presumed to be a bizarre weather phenomenon that happened rarely but with great intensity and loss of life. For the poison they had no answer. Stanley had experienced its blood curdling terror once before, years ago when he and his grandparents had been caught out as they checked their trap lines in the Wapiti Hills. Both of his grandparents had choked to death as the poisonous cloud attacked their aging lungs. Stanley had survived purely because he had youth on his side. Now it was happening again but he knew differently. This was no extraordinary weather pattern, it was the result of all the atrocities committed in the turbulent past which had haunted his people and the town of Maskek and their ancestors for centuries. Today his cousin, Chief Spirit of the Wind, would end it along with his father's ancient and terrible legacy.

"Stanley, we just had a call from Emily Simpson," Captain Virgil McNally called out as Stanley entered his limited field of vision. "Seems her husband is missing. She thinks he's trapped in the car. He was heading away from the Tamarack Motel, leaving town. Take Giovanni and Tripp and go look for him. Where's your nephew Lucan?"

"Up in the village, he wanted to ride with Spirit of the Wind. Cloud Walker, the man spirit, says it will be a victory."

"Hope to god he's right."

Faces covered Stanley Cuthand, Tripp, and Giovanni the son of the owner of Maskek's one and only Italian Ristorante, began a foot search of the main street leading to the Tamarack Motel. There was only one trail in and out of the town and Steve would have to come this way.

"We'll find him," Stanley said, "just hope we're not too late."

Under the frozen snow Main Street was no more than a dusty trail in the summer, muddy in the spring rains, and an ice road in the winter. The town council had debated for years whether or not to add tarmac. It was still ongoing with no likely prospect of ending in the foreseeable future.

"Did you hear that?" Stanley asked, "thought I heard a cry."

"Go for it, Stanley, I trust your hearing more than my own," Giovanni replied.

A second cry was not forthcoming but as the three men made their way slowly toward the direction from whence it came Stanley managed to pick out Steve's car. The fog seemed to be shimmering around it hovering like a predator. It wasn't that which attracted Stanley and Giovanni's attention but the body of a man lying face down at an odd angle by the driver's side of the car. The door hung open. Stanley gently rolled him onto his back feeling for a pulse in his neck. He listened for sounds of breathing, watching for the rise and fall of his chest. The pulse was absent as were the air sounds. Stanley tipped Steve's head back and opened his mouth looking for a foreign object that might have become lodged in there. He saw a slender, tentacle-like substance filling the fellow's mouth and protruding from his throat. Glancing at Giovanni he shook his head. The younger ranger knelt by Stanley's side. "Maybe we can dislodge it. Sometimes when objects are removed a person can breathe again. It's worth a try isn't it, Stanley?" Hope hung in Giovanni's eyes, "We've got to try at least. Tripp, what do you say?"

"Do it."

Stanley wasn't holding out much hope but the expectation in the eyes of the rangers spurred him on. Gently he pulled on the tentacle in Steve's mouth easing it past the fellow's lips until it hung below his chin. Very carefully he gave his attention to the other piece of clinging flesh partially hidden in Steve's throat. It came away with a suction sound like a vacuum, covered with blood and sputum. Giovanni and Tripp turned away repulsed by the sight of it.

"What the hell is it?"

Looking directly into Tripp's eyes, Stanley said, "It would take too long to explain. I'm not sure you'd ever understand." The two rangers exchanged glances.

"Did it work?" Giovanni wanted to know.

Rechecking for pulse, respirations and any sound at all Stanley let his head droop, "This man is dead, I'm sorry. Help me lift him we need to get him inside." With Stanley holding Steve's shoulders and the rangers carrying his legs they made their way back through the seething mass.

CHAPTER THIRTY-SIX

Amidst the clamouring and whooping, Spirit of the Wind was pulled away from his mother and hoisted onto the shoulders of the villagers, the power knife still in his hand and carried around the encampment. Clayton, Ross, Bobby and the warrior elite excitedly followed behind as the rowdy crowd quickly joined them. Jonathan Sparkling Eyes climbed down from Falling Eagle's pony; he'd sat behind the older man all the way home. He approached Talulah and Nonie. Her attention on her son, Nonie didn't hear him coming.

"Nonie, look at me."

Nonie turned quickly and stared at him in shock, her brain trying to register who actually stood before her. "Jonathan? Jonathan. You're supposed to be dead."

Not quite so surprised was Talulah Bearhead. Clasping his arm, she lifted her face to kiss her son-in-law's cheek her eyes shining with affection. "You have returned, my son."

"Mother, it is good to see you." He took his mother-in-law into his arms.

When she had recovered, Nonie's anger boiled over though tears hung in her eyes. "You'd better have a damn good explanation for turning up here eighteen years too late. Where have you been? Last year I told your son you were dead and now you're here as if nothing ever happened. I want to know why you left us alone and your son without a father. Do you have any idea how hard it's been for us? You should have contacted us let us know you were alive. Spirit of the Wind had a right to know." She was crying from deep in her heart. "I hate you."

Reaching for her Jonathan Sparkling Eyes crushed her to his chest, stroking the top of her head. "Come inside, Nonie. There is much I want to tell you, much you need to know." Lifting the flap of Talulah's lodge

Jonathan ducked inside pulling Nonie with him.

Rona looked on in shock and amazement; she was stupefied. Trying to get her head around Jonathan's exact likeness to his son was proving difficult, not to mention that he'd suddenly re-appeared after eighteen years. She looked at Talulah Bearhead. "When Nonie showed me Jonathan's photo, I hadn't realised to what extent he and Deacon matched each other. But now seeing him in the flesh is nothing short of a miracle. Usually incidents like this are connected way back in centuries past when you suddenly notice that one of your ancestors is an exact replica of you or member of your family. I'm flabbergasted." Rona had long since ceased trying to understand Deacon's family, very little actually surprised her... until now.

Smiling affectionately Talulah nodded. "This is so. Jonathan was born in 1732. When he reached eighteen years of age it was still only 1750. When he met Damien, he was given life everlasting—until he defied the demon when Spirit of the Wind was born and immortality was taken from him. Three months ago, Spirit of the Wind destroyed the demon but not the legacy. So yes, your assumption that incidents like this are connected to the past is quite correct."

"Of course they are," Rona replied slapping her own cheeks. "I should have remembered. Why do you think he's here, Talulah? There's must be an urgent reason for it. Would you like me to keep Spirit of the Wind here until Nonie and Jonathan have had a chance to talk?"

"I would be grateful, Rona. When the people have finished with my grandson and Clayton, bring them over to Red Crow's lodge. I shall be there."

Her anger still smouldering Nonie glared at Jonathan. "Why did you wait until after I told your son who his real parents were and how they died, before showing yourself. You're obviously very much alive, Spirit of the Wind should have been told. I could have done with your help. Have you any idea how hard it is to raise a native child in a white society and still keep him in touch with his own people and his culture? Do you?"

"If we are asking questions why did you go against my wishes and remove him from his family? You gave me your word that you would keep him always within the sacred hoop. I trusted you, Nonie. I trusted you with my beloved son."

"And I kept my promise, until he was six years old. I did everything Talulah asked of me. I didn't speak English, I didn't talk about my own childhood, about my family or my past. I didn't even mention Maskek or the people living there. He knew nothing about it. I learned to be a Native mother and I think I did a pretty good job of it. Can you say the same?"

Jonathan reeled as if hit by a lightning bolt, his pride taking a severe tumble. Used to having his own way Nonie's sharp words wounded him deeply.

"In those first six years in this village I saw the children seized and taken away by the officials and the so-called religious bodies that owned and governed the residential schools and I saw what the survivors had become. Many of the children died there; beaten, abused and starving. That was not going to happen to your son. I was willing to do anything to save him from the same fate as thousands of other Native children. Was that wrong? You gave him to me and begged me to take care of him. He became my son. I was not prepared to lose him." Tears spilled from her eyes. "By legally adopting him and moving him from here I believed he would be safe. I spoke with Talulah, Eagle Hawk and Nedipah and also with the tribal elders. After much deliberation the elders agreed and his grandparents reluctantly accepted that it would be the best and safest thing for him. We moved to the house by the lake, one of the cabins you built. I changed his name to Deacon but I kept his true name and I sent him to the white man's school. In all that time I encouraged him to keep coming back to his village, to continue learning the ways of his ancestors. I tried to give him the best of both worlds. I stand by that."

"I guess I've been well and truly chastised." The beautiful and disarming smile he gave Nonie lit up his stunning features. "Am I forgiven?"

She gazed up into Jonathan's sparkling eyes as black as coal. He'd been well named by his mother Shadow of the Moon. For a moment, she was the besotted seventeen-year-old girl from England, who had fallen in love with him all those years ago.

"You're forgiven." Pulling him close she stood on tiptoe and kissed him. "Why have you come to us now? How are you still alive? The longhouse burned to the ground, there was nothing left standing. Spirit of the Wind and I only just made it out."

"I could not have come to you before this time, it wouldn't have been safe for Spirit of the Wind or for you either. Now that he has destroyed the evil that has haunted us for centuries, we no longer need live in fear. Come to me Nonie." He held out his hand, "Let me tell you how I was found and my life saved."

~ * ~

In the forest the wolves were gathering. Restless and on edge the animals prowled, all their senses alert to an important event due to take place imminently. The black female Deacon encountered on two occasions appeared to be the leader. Her presence dominated the other members of the pack. Whatever was about to erupt was not far off.

CHAPTER THIRTY-SEVEN

Unable to leave the motel Emily paced the floor, biting her nails willing the phone to ring and praying that Steve would be spared. Twelve years of life with him flashed by in seconds. In spite of everything that had happened between them, even down to his suspicions of her having an affair with Deacon, she still loved him.

"I shouldn't have let him go. I should have made him stay."

The shrill trilling of the telephone cut through the air, startling her. "Yes? Is that you Captain McNally? Have you found Steve, is he alright?" She listened in devastated silence as Virgil McNally gave her the grave news.

"I'm sorry Mrs. Simpson we were too late." There was silence on the other end of the line. "Mrs. Simpson, are you alright? I'm sending Giovanni and Stanley Cuthand to bring you here. You'll need to identify your husband. Sergeant Hibbett and Constable Haynes will want to speak to you."

"Yes, Captain McNally I'll wait for them," her voice barely audible Emily collapsed onto the bed her stomach twisting and churning like a roller coaster. "Steve's dead?" Her brain refused to believe it, she could not conceive of it happening "Captain McNally must have made a mistake. It's that thing out there it's confusing them." But when she looked through the window the fog was gone.

~ * ~

Even as Stanley, Giovanni and Tripp were placing Steve Simpson's body on the table
in the RCMP's office until it could be taken to the clinic, there came a bellow of rage like nothing they had ever heard, as if all the gods

of thunder were crying out in fury. The town of Maskek fell si lent, all heads turned toward the Wapiti Hills. Stanley Cuthand sank to his knees. "Spirit of the Wind has destroyed the unthinkable and our ancient prophesy is fulfilled. We are free. The Great Mysterious has come through for us." Raising his head to the sky Stanley began to pray, a task he had not tackled in many years. In his desire to be accepted as an enterprising business man Stanley had neglected his roots and beliefs. But the young chief's belief in the Great Spirit had saved a great many lives.

As if sucked in by a huge fan the voluminous grey cloud began to dissipate, fading and fading until nothing but the noxious fumes remained. Then they also faded. The sky once again was bright with the brilliance of the winter sun.

Across the road Graph threw open the shutters and the patrons streamed from the coffee house. If Stanley spoke the truth the biggest and deadliest secret that held the town of Maskek in its malevolent grip for centuries had been extinguished. For the first time in memory the town felt clean and pure.

~ * ~

By his grandmother's side Spirit of the Wind waited patiently for his mother and father to appear to tell him that Sparkling Eyes was going to stay. Outside Red Crow's lodge preparations for the victory dance and powwow were taking place.

"You should be helping with the preparations. I will send Stands Alone to bring you when they are here. Go and join your friends."

"I will wait, grandmother."

"Talulah's right," Clayton told him, "you can't do anything sitting here. Let's go give them a hand."

"I will see my mother then I will come."

The sun kissed the moon before Nonie and Jonathan entered Red Crow's lodge. Nonie went directly to her son and hugged him. Bestowing a gentle kiss upon his face she said, "For a time your father will stay. Later he will return to his father's family."

Staggered by his mother's words, the young chief locked accusing eyes upon his father, "You have chosen not to stay. Why do you not wish to be with us?"

Tensing, Clayton moved to stand beside Deacon, ready to diffuse any situation that might arise. "Perhaps it is the better way, brother."

Glancing at Clayton he said, "How can I know it is the better way if we are not given the chance to find out?"

"Spirit of the Wind," Jonathan said, "I do this because of you, because I am afraid that my presence here might intrude upon your relationship with your mother. Nonie and I have discussed it at length and believe it to be the best way. But if you think you can handle it, I will stay."

"I can handle it."

"Then we'll give it a try. You and Clayton make ready for the victory dance I will join you directly. Nonie, go with them I'd like to talk to Talulah and Red Crow."

Darkness had painted the forest by the time Clayton and Spirit of the Wind joined the victory dance. Around the blazing fire sat the warrior elite, Red Crow, Grey Owl, Black Elk and the remaining members of the tribal council. Red Crow gestured to the boys to sit.

"Spirit of the Wind we are waiting for you to tell us of you victory."

The young chief sat down, Clayton at his side. The old, wise one, Moon Woman came and stood beside him and patted his arm. No words were required her pride in the young chief said it all.

While Deacon related the story of the conflict and their vaporous adversary, the villagers moved closer eager to hear the tale of victory. The people had not seen a battle such as this for over a century. Engrossed in the story telling Spirit of the Wind did not hear his father, Nonie or Talulah approaching.

"Are you proud of your son, Jonathan?"

"He is also your son Nonie, for I gave him into your safe keeping and now you have adopted him. I am indeed proud of him. He will be a fine chief just as his grandfather and great grandfather before him. The day he was born Lupin whispered to me that she had looked into the future and saw him just as he is now. It is a good omen."

Unable to keep her curiosity to herself, Nonie asked, "How long has Lyle known about your meetings with Damien in the basement of the Longhouse?"

For a second Jonathan's eyes flashed with indignation. Catching himself he let it wane. "Since he first bought Eliza to work for me. Lyle and Buffalo Bear were friends. Eliza was unaware we thought it better not to tell her..."

"Or me or Victoria, even Lupin? Didn't you trust us to keep your secret? I was certain I'd told Spirit of the Wind everything about you. Now I find out that there is much more you refused to tell me. Does he know?"

"I told him about Buffalo Bear and Eliza's husband Lyle. Lyle joined Damien before he came to me. I was as surprised as anyone."

"Is that all?" she asked reproachfully taking him aside, "or are there other skeletons you haven't told me about. I loved you Jonathan. I trusted you. I believed every single thing you told me. I would have sworn on my life that you were not implicated in the occult movement taking place in the Wapiti Hills or in the Longhouse. I read the newspaper articles, I even kept them. I could never accept that you were part of it until I saw that creature in your basement. Lupin wasn't aware of it was she?"

"Lupin knew only that which I considered important. Anything else would have put her in more danger."

"The demon took her anyway and her not knowing accomplished nothing. Perhaps if she'd been made aware of your involvement, she would have..."

"It would not have saved her. Only if she had stayed within the sacred hoop would she have lived. I begged her not to leave the safety of the village, she wouldn't listen. Talulah tried to make her see sense, even Eagle Hawk tried. She chose to ignore it. She was the most stubborn woman I have ever known. I loved her more than anything in the world."

"Did she know about your past?"

"Not all of it."

Nonie wanted to hold him close and make it all go away. She wanted to end the sadness in his tumultuous life. But as distressing as it was her priority was to her son. She could do nothing to alleviate Jonathan's suffering. "If there is more please tell me, Spirit of the Wind has a right to know."

Jonathan turned his face away indicating the conversation was finished. She'd forgotten how obstinate and determined he could be. Not surprisingly his son displayed the same traits.

~ * ~

The night was alive with the beating of the drum, the chanting singers and the pounding feet of the dancers.

During a pause in the dancing, Spirit of the Wind sought out his father and found him alone beyond the fringe of the encampment. Sparkling Eyes was staring across the lake, his mind festooned with memories of the past. "I shouldn't have come. I should have left the past buried in the past, let everyone think I died in the fire. It would be so much easier." But he couldn't. He longed to touch his son and hold him close to his heart. Yearned to be with him, to feel him in the flesh and in his arms as it had been when Spirit of the Wind was a baby. He'd kept the secret for nigh on twenty years he could wait no longer. Spirit of the Wind's fatal blow had released him and stolen away the terrible legacy that had stalked his family for two centuries.

"Are your thoughts with my mother?" Spirit of the Wind asked gently.

Tears still lingering in his eyes Jonathan faced his son, "Beautiful is she to me and will always be. I wish you could have known her."

"I felt the warmth and softness of her touch as I lay in her arms those memories can never be lost."

Peering into his son's eyes he saw himself as he had once been. Was it really two hundred years since he met Damien Drew and left behind the life he knew? So many years since the death of his beloved mother Shadow of the Moon. He'd been the same age as Spirit of the Wind was now and for what, to wander the earth forever, forever alone?

"There were many other women and four other wives. Not one of them touched me as your mother has done. She made every day wondrous and filled it with her love. You are much like her, you share the same special qualities. I hope they will remain always. I remember the day I found her sitting by the river surrounded by the wolves. She was completely at ease with them. A wild girl and a wild pack of wolves they understood each other completely. Lupin was as much as part of their lives as they were of hers, as they are a part of yours."

Spirit of the Wind said nothing, he pondered over his father's words hearing Jonathan's thoughts. For a long time, he listened to the crackling of the water lapping against the shore, the part of the lake which never froze and the whispering of the wind through the gently swaying pines. As the music and dancing ceased, he listened to the silence of the forest broken only by the eerie howling of the wolves, the hooting of an owl and the shuffling, snuffling creatures of the night. Without looking at his father he said, "Before the battle I had a vision. You were holding a human heart in your hands. Did you kill him?"

"I killed him. He was not a good man. It was necessary for him to die."

"I saw you and Damien standing over the altar on which a man lay bound with rawhide to his wrists and ankles, exactly as I was bound. Was he a sacrifice for the demon Arcus?" (Told in Child of the Heathen)

"He murdered a fellow disciple and Damien chose to make an example of him."

"Why did this man kill another of his kind?"

"You do not need to know the reason, only that it happened."

"You were their prince," Deacon insisted, "they looked up to you, worshipped you. The Prince of Darkness, that's what Reverend Solomon once called me, but he was not seeing me he was seeing you. Since we are exactly alike, he could be forgiven for thinking that. What of you, father," his tone was challenging, "you took a life and I cannot understand why. It was not a conflict or the need to protect yourself and others..."

"Spirit of the Wind, you need to understand that the lives I took were those of our enemies, the enemies of our people. In 1750 the only law was that of the white eyes and the black robes who were the Jesuit priests; self-administered and with no direction or purpose other than to eradicate our people. In the years I walked upon the earth with Damien we saw death and destruction at every turn. Nation after nation of Indians died under their hands. You are well aware of this you have been taught the true history of your people. What did you see in the grey shroud when the unthinkable was at its mightiest?"

"Our people murdered. I saw sickness which carried them to the place beyond the stars, the animals hunted to extinction..."

"So it was. That which you were seeing was the very thing we were trying to eradicate."

"Did you need Damien to do that? Did you need the demon? You were a warrior father, you could have fought with your own hands and with weapons, for that is the way of the warrior."

"I was too embroiled within it I enjoyed the power it gave me. You are now the chief you are responsible not only for your family but for everyone here. Decisions will stand or fall on your word. You will have the ultimate say. Only the council of elders can challenge your decision. That says power to me. I have spoken with your grandmother and Red Crow, they say you have taken to becoming the chief like a raven to the rocks, even before the ceremony. The warrior elite look up to you, the people look up to you. You are the only grandson of Talulah Bearhead and Chief Eagle Hawk. You are the prince and you like it."

Exhaling in frustration the young chief told his father, "I am not a prince. I am Spirit of the Wind."

"And Spirit of the Wind is chief. You could have refused and turned your back on all that you have been taught, denied your birth right, ignored your bloodline but you did not. Isn't there a small part of you that embraces the challenge and wants to be the one whom everyone looks up to?"

"Perhaps a little but I would not kill a human enemy. That which we destroyed today was not human."

"You are also a ranger sworn to uphold the law but given the right circumstances even a ranger will kill. When a member of our people is harmed by one who is not of native blood you will take him and deal with him in the manner of our ancestors. You say you will not kill, but if you release him in to the forest will he survive? Death is not just a bullet from a rifle or an arrow fired from a bow. Death is caused in many ways."

Gazing at his feet the young Indian considered his father's words. He thought about the promise he'd made to Thundercloud; if you harm my family, I will kill you.

"I will do whatever is necessary within the law to punish those who bring us harm. If that means losing them in the forest so it will be."

"Do you still think we are not alike?"

"No," he whispered solemnly, "I do this also for grandmother, she is growing tired and needs my help. I am proud to be chief."

"I told your mother you would make a fine chief and so you will. The women in this village adore you. Just as women fell at my feet so they will for you—if you let them. Nonie told me how it was at school. Those who did not like you found ways to antagonise you. Those who did were all over you. Or should I say you won them over."

"I am not like that father; my thoughts are only for Thorn Rose. I have no desire to have women eating out of my hand or swooning at my feet. In that respect we are not alike."

"Perhaps this is so." Sparkling Eyes exhaled tiredly, "Come, it is late your mother will be searching for you." He touched the red and white beaded necklace around his son's throat. "I am pleased that you still wear your great grandmother's necklace."

"Thundercloud came to me."

Jonathan stopped abruptly as if blocked by a stone wall, "Thundercloud? What does he want with you?"

"He wants to take over from you, to take your place. He was sent to bring me to Damien so that I may lead the disciples the way you once did. Thundercloud has great admiration for you. He told me I would never be the leader you were and he's determined that I won't be. He'll do whatever is necessary to prevent it from happening. He believes he will become the new prince. As your son I am expected to follow."

"Did you fight with him; did you challenge him?"

"I did not fight. I told him I would kill him if he came near my family."

"You should have taken his life there and then. Thundercloud is a demon child the offspring off a demon and a human. He is without feeling, without soul and you have made an enemy of him."

Reluctantly Spirit of the Wind followed his father back to the encampment. He wanted to talk longer, to know this man who was his father. Sparkling Eyes made it clear their discussion was over. Feeling less than satisfied he returned to his grandmother's lodge where his family waited.

Talulah told him, "Clayton has taken your friends to Little Beaver's lodge. It is too late for them to return to Maskek tonight. How are you, my child?" Her grandson's eyes were troubled, he seemed anxious and uncertain. "You have many questions Spirit of the Wind, they must wait until tomorrow. You have not completely recovered from your vision quest and you have today conquered the Unthinkable. You are exhausted you will sleep. Clayton White Hawk will join you directly."

~ * ~

"When do we take him Thundercloud, you said the son of Sparkling Eyes would die tonight?"

"This is not the right time Cody, there are too many surrounding him we cannot take them all. A better opportunity will present itself and I will not miss. When the time comes, I will end his life suddenly and painfully. He will never know his slayer."

CHAPTER THIRTY-EIGHT

While Spirit of the Wind recovered in his grandmother's lodge with Clayton forever at his side, Ross and Bobby returned to Maskek, filled with tales of a battle they could barely conceive of even though they had fought in it.

"Did it really happen or were we hallucinating?" Bobby enquired.

"Well if we were hallucinating it was damn good stuff we were given."

Bobby stared at him puzzled, "We weren't given any stuff."

"Then it must've really happened."

Approaching Stanley Cuthand's coffee house they were molested almost immediately by Leona and Melissa demanding a blow by blow account of the encounter with the mysterious enemy and if Deacon and Clayton were safe. Before either of them could speak Emily Simpson called them over to the opposite side of the street. Her face was pale and drawn and her eyes red from weeping. Ross thought she seemed a little unsteady on her feet.

"Are you okay, Mrs. Simpson?"

"Actually, I'm not. Steve is dead," she told him bluntly.

Struck by her plain-spoken words, he asked, "What're you talking about? What happened?" The two young men swapped troubled glances.

"That thing that attacked the town killed him. Choked and suffocated him in his own car."

"It was here? The Unthinkable was here?"

"Yes, that's what Tyrell called it. Why would it attack my husband?"

"We didn't know anything about it, we've only just come back from the village. I'm real sorry Mrs. Simpson. It won't harm anyone else because Spirit of the Wind destroyed it. It's over."

Leona and Melissa suddenly lost all interest in the fighting. Their immediate concern was for their favourite teacher. Putting her arms around Emily, Leona asked, "What will you do now. Will you stay here with us? Is there anyone you can stay with? You shouldn't be alone right now."

"I'm staying with Jeremy at the moment. I'll obviously have to go back to Edmonton for the funeral, but right now I can't even think about that. Thank you for caring."

"We've always cared about you Mrs. Simpson. You know how much we all think of you."

"I know Leona. Why aren't Deacon and Clayton with you?"

"It's a long story ma'am," Bobby said, "and this probably isn't the best time to tell it. We were heading over to the coffee house. Would you care to join us?"

"Thank you, Bobby, I'd like that."

Leona and Melissa led Emily over to a corner booth. Bobby and Ross ordered coffee. Stanley was behind the bar. "Guess you haven't heard what happened yesterday?"

Ross shook his head, "We just got back. Maybe you'd better fill us in?"

"Did you see Lucan? How's Spirit of the Wind and Clayton?"

"Yeah we saw Lucan he was in the war party too. He's safe. We hardly ever see your nephew he's always gone someplace. Where does he go?"

Stanley grinned, "To speak with Cloud Walker the man-spirit. I don't ask what it's about. But he's okay, right? "

"He's fine, Stanley. Nobody got hurt I guess we were pretty lucky. When we left the village, they were still celebrating. Spirit of the Wind has been ordered to rest. His grandmother says he hasn't recovered from the vision quest. I guess it takes a while to catch up when you've gone without food, water or sleep for days. He daren't argue with her. Clayton's cool and by his side as always. I swear those two should get married."

"What, and ruin a perfectly good friendship," Bobby cracked.

Ross became serious. "What went on yesterday?"

They listened without interruption until Stanley finished telling them about yesterday's terrible tragedy. "Man!" Ross exclaimed, "I wouldn't wish that on anyone. Did Mrs. Simpson see her husband?"

"Not right away. By the time we'd taken her to identify him the rangers had cleaned him up and made him presentable. Sergeant Hibbett and Captain McNally are dealing with it there's nobody here to take over. The worst of it is that even if Mr. Simpson hadn't been attacked he wouldn't have made it out of town, the trail is snow blocked."

Staggered by what they'd just heard Ross took a tray of coffee over to Emily and the girls and he and Bobby joined them. Their mood was subdued but they did their best to make Emily feel less alone.

~ * ~

Deacon awoke to find he was alone, apart from Clayton. Gathering his senses, he asked, "Where's momma I thought she'd be here?"

"She's been here most of the time while you were sleeping. Right now, she's with your father, she said they won't be long and Talulah is over at the council lodge. Bobby and Ross came back with some bad news. While we were fighting that thing up their part of it came in to town. Stanley told them that the entire town heard it howling when you struck its heart. Then it was swept away like a vacuum."

"Was anyone hurt?"

"Mr. Simpson died. Apparently, it attacked his car and managed to get in even with the doors and windows closed. He tried to escape and according to Stanley they found him by the side of the car with tentacles down his throat. Looks like it choked him and suffocated him."

Deacon was silent shocked by Clayton's words. Finally, he said, "How is Mrs. Simpson?"

"She's pretty shaken up. She's staying with Doc Lodge for the time being. That's all I know. If you hadn't destroyed it a lot of other folks could've died, would've died. Got to tell you that your momma and Talulah don't want us visiting Mrs. Simpson right now and my mom agreed. Maybe hearing about Mr. Simpson might change things, but I doubt it. Talulah has plans for you to stay around here for a while. I got in touch with Captain McNally he said you ain't going back to work until you're fully recovered."

"I am recovered Clayton. I'm not sick." Finding his clothes, he dressed and was about to go outside when Clayton stopped him.

"Not today Deke, maybe tomorrow."

"I'm okay Clayton. I've been sleeping forever and right now I godda pee."

"Alright, but I'm coming with you. I've been told to watch you and that's what I'm gonna do. If I let you go tearing off into Maskek, Talulah will have my hide."

Despite his urgency Deacon grinned, "Damn right she will," and sprinted into the trees.

Determined to keep her grandson away from Emily Simpson, Talulah kept him busy around the village. His efforts to speak again about his father's past were thwarted by his grandmother's insistence that he apply himself to the business at hand.

"For the next few days you will not be a Wildlife Ranger, you will be the chief. There is much for you to learn. We will begin today."

~ * ~

Spirit of the Wind, Clayton, Talulah and Nedipah sat with Sparkling Eyes inside Talulah's lodge. Nonie and Rona were not present. He, Clayton and Sparkling Eyes were dressed in warm moose hide shirts and pants. Clayton still retained his cowboy boots, choosing not to wear mukluks. Talulah and Nedipah wore traditional regalia, as always.

"Tell me about Thundercloud, father."

"He'll be back for you, he won't give up. Thundercloud is the off spring of a Native demon and a white woman. The woman is a long standing member of the disciples. The day she joined us she was marked. Young women are chosen for pleasure but a mature woman is always chosen to bear an offspring. The white woman was only fourteen when Damien bought her to us. She was guarded and protected until she reached maturity. On her thirty fourth birthday she was given to the demon. She went willingly."

"Did she live?"

"She lived. An older woman is more likely to die in childbirth that's why they're chosen. No strings, no attachments, no record. Thundercloud was born bad; you must destroy him before he destroys you."

Spirit of the Wind stared at his father, "Why would you want to be part of something like that, how could you be? I don't think I'll ever understand."

"Who told you about Thundercloud?"

"Grandmother and Red Crow spoke about him. He's been seen close to here. The people are afraid of him."

"They should be. He's merciless."

"Are you afraid of Thundercloud?"

"He challenged my leadership. I won. From then on, he was always at my side, waiting for the chance to replace me. If he hasn't then it's because the disciples would not accept him. Buffalo Bear gave him a different name, he called him Death Hand."

CHAPTER THIRTY-NINE

For a time, there was harmony within Deacon's family. It felt good to have his father present, seeing his mother so happy with Sparkling Eyes made his heart swell. Nonie devoted her energy to the two men in her life, only this time she was calling the shots. Cracks began to appear when on some occasions Deacon returned home off duty and his mother was not there to greet him.

"Three times I have come home and she has not been here," he told his grandmother. "Is she with my father?"

Hugging him Talulah led him inside, "Yes, child. Come, food is prepared. Both of us will eat then we will look for your mother." Talulah observed him while he ate, a frown creasing her forehead. She had been afraid of this happening and as much as she loved Sparkling Eyes his presence was beginning to erode the family unity.

"Twice now my father and I have spoken. Twice now we have raised our voices in anger. Twice now we have dealt a blow to our hearts. This is not the way it was meant to be."

Talulah recalled how things had been with her daughter Lupin. How when Spirit of the Wind was a new born baby, Lupin allowed few people to hold him. Devoted and possessive she had shared her precious treasure only with those she truly trusted.

Now I feel my grandson is doing the same even though he is not aware of it.

In the midst of her thoughts Stands-in-Timber called from outside, "Spirit of the Wind someone wishes to speak with you."

Talulah peered through the flap and for a split second her heart ceased to beat. A familiar face stood next to Stands-in-Timber. He looked to be around thirty-five years of age, with nondescript blonde hair and eyes of chilling blue. At five feet eight he was as thin as the trunk of a spruce tree. His skin so pale it was almost translucent. His features as fine as bone china were slightly effeminate and might be described as pretty. Attired in a long jacket of heavy blue velvet and moleskin fabric trousers under a heavy, calf length coat, he looked strangely out of place and time.

"Who is there, grandmother?"

The young chief ducked out of the tipi with Clayton right behind him. Recognising the fellow's face, he stopped in his tracks, his left hand flashing to the bowie knife. "Damien."

"Spirit of the Wind," Damien acknowledged, "put away your knife. As you can see, I am unarmed." After two centuries he still retained his English accent. This was Damien Drew, his father's lover and mentor, whom in 1750 had first introduced a teenage Jonathan to the maleficent entity known only as Arcus, promising him eternal life. This atrocity had plagued Jonathan's family for over two hundred years.

"What do you want with me?" Spirit of the Wind asked, his hand hovering above the hilt of the knife. From out of nowhere the Cree police quickly appeared, ready for action if necessary. They were not a police force, as such they had no affiliation with the Royal Canadian Mounted Police or an office to work from. They were the most skilled of the men in the encampment and retained an allegiance to the chief. Patrolling the area in and around the encampment, shielding the women and defending the people were their main duties. These men were well respected by Sergeant Abel Cain Hibbett and Constable Ira Haynes and Captain McNally's rangers. They were often called upon to help search for hikers lost in the forest or to help enforce the law when the town of Maskek was rammed with visitors.

"I am here to make amends for the past and the present," Damien Drew replied.

"Come to finish the job, have you?" Clayton said. He had been present last year when Damien had threatened Deacon's life.

"I am not here to take anyone's life. I see you remain as loyal as ever. No doubt you are a perfect Segundo to Spirit of the Wind."

"Why do you come here?" the young chief asked.

"You have destroyed me. But you have also freed me from the darkness which I created."

Spirit of the Wind watched him cautiously his hand still hovering above the Bowie. He did not trust this man. Damien took one step forward and found himself staring into Deacon's knife.

In one swift movement before either of them could speak, Jonathan appeared and lunged at Damien bringing him to the ground, his own knife glinting in the winter sun, "You will not harm my son."

Startled by the appearance of his lover and one time best friend, Damien could only stare in disbelief. "Sparkling Eyes you were dead. How can this be?" Struggling to his feet the Englishman reached out to him, "It is good to see you, my friend."

Sheathing his knife when he realised Damien was unarmed, Jonathan pushed the offered hand away. "I was found by Eliza and Lyle, they brought Buffalo Bear to me and nursed me back to health. I have been living among the Blackfoot."

"You were dying of old age. How have you reversed it?"

Jonathan Sparkling Eyes sacrificed his eternal life to save his son, by refusing to hand him over to the demon. Day by day he began to age until he became unrecognisable as the handsome young man Damien had first bought to Arcus, two centuries before.

"I begged you to help me Damien, to stop Arcus from taking Lupin and later my life. You said you could not stop it. You didn't even try. You are not welcome here."

"I tried to help you, Jonathan. I pleaded with him..."

"You evoked him. Why couldn't you send him back?"

"He became too powerful."

"You could have made it happen," Jonathan insisted, "just as you could have saved my first born daughter Kiche from becoming his wife."

"I might have managed to save Kiche and possibly you as well, but only by relinquishing my own immortality. At the time I was not prepared to do so..."

"Why are you here, Damien?" Spirit of the Wind asked again, "I will know why you are here."

Nonie came running forward fear in her eyes. "Why is here? Send him away Spirit of the Wind."

"Go inside, momma," he told her, "it is not your place to interfere.

Go inside."

At times Nonie became more aware of the differences in their two cultures. Steeped in tradition Talulah's village was a backward step into the past. When Deacon was a child the dissimilarities were not so noticeable. Her son was now the chief and things were changing faster than she had ever imagined. She returned reluctantly to the lodge.

"Was immortality more important than my life?" Sparkling Eyes asked accusingly." I would have forsaken my life to save yours."

Before Damien could respond Spirit of the Wind spoke with authority, "Be silent father, I will hear his words."

"When you destroyed the demon, my eyes were opened as if awakening from a terrible nightmare. A deep feeling of anguish and emptiness entered my soul and the nights began to haunt me. I am not a religious man it has nothing to do with God. But within myself I was beginning to change. On Christmas Eve when you defeated the demon, I was leading a procession into the Wapiti Hills and about to offer another young man the pleasure of eternal life. When I looked towards the sky my thoughts returned to a young Cree Indian I had known and loved lifetimes ago. I found I no longer had the stomach to continue with my quest. I left the disciples behind and I have not returned to them. That part of my existence is over. I cannot change the past or vanquish the foul deeds I have committed, but I can change the present. I am here to do whatever it takes to accomplish that. I am at your mercy Spirit of the Wind and willing to be punished for my crimes and foolishness. When I captured you, I could have killed you, instead I allowed you to live..."

"Wasn't it enough you took my daughter," Jonathan broke in reproachfully. "What did you hope to gain by taking my son? I loved you. Why did you take from me all that I cared about, my mother, my wife, my children?"

"He took them, not I."

"Had I not been with you the night my mother died and in your bed when my father attacked her, she would have lived." Jonathan lunged at Damien pushing him to the ground, the blade of the knife barely missing his throat. He slid astride the Englishman's chest, the tip of the blade pressing against the side of Damien's neck. With his free hand he tore open Damien's shirt curled his fingers into a claw and reached for his heart.

"No father." In a movement so swift it was almost indiscernible Spirit of the Wind yanked Jonathan's wrist and twisted it backwards forcing him to release his fierce grip on Damien's heart. Kicking the knife aside he hauled his father to his feet. "There has been enough killing."

Enraged, two centuries of lies and grief boiling up inside him, Sparkling Eyes snatched the Bowie from the sheath on his son's hip and faced him threateningly.

Terrified they might seriously hurt one another Nonie rushed from the lodge, "Jonathan, he's your son. Jonathan. Talulah stop them, they'll listen to you."

"Momma, stay inside." Fending off his father's attack with his bare hands Deacon grabbed the knife Lone Wolf was holding out to him and faced Jonathan head on. He matched and deflected every cut and slash.

Ambling over Red Crow and Black Elk came to stand by Nonie's side. "Do not fear Nonie, Spirit of the Wind is in no danger."

"You know how skilled Jonathan is, Red Crow."

"Spirit of the Wind can handle him. Have you forgotten how he took on Grey Owl?"

"Grey Owl is much older."

"Sparkling Eyes' age is many years beyond that of Grey Owl. Do not forget that his youthful appearance masks his true age. Spirit of the Wind is more than capable of handling anyone who comes at him with a knife no matter what their age."

By now the inhabitants were closing in, circling the fighters like buzzards around a kill. Observing Jonathan and Deacon anxiously Clayton was uncertain as to whether he or the warrior elite should wade in and try to end the encounter.

Lone Wolf pulled him aside. "White Hawk do not interfere. Sparkling Eyes' anger is not aimed at his son but at all that has happened since he joined with Damien. Damien's presence tortures him with memories he'd sooner forget. Do you doubt your brother's ability to disarm him?"

Shaking his head, Clayton exhaled heavily.

Lone Wolf told him, "Clayton White Hawk they are not trying to kill each other, it will soon be over."

Clayton didn't feel as confident as Lone Wolf. Sparkling Eyes and Spirit of the Wind were well matched and determined, separating them would be foolhardy and dangerous. Lunging forward suddenly, Jonathan cut Deacon's right arm. Unfazed Deacon struck back striking his father's shoulder. With blood seeping heavily from both of their wounds they carried on fighting, neither one giving an inch.

Talulah watched them carefully. At the first sign of serious injury she would order the fight stopped. For now, she allowed them to continue. Perhaps it was the best way for both of them to vent their emotions, anger and frustration.

"I cannot be the cause of father against son," Damien said, "it must be stopped."

The hostile encounter ended abruptly when Spirit of the Wind forced his father to the ground and knocked the knife from his hand. Throwing aside his own weapon he pulled Jonathan into his arms, tears spilling from his eyes, "No more father, please the killing has to stop."

There was no resistance from Jonathan as he leaned against his son. He was shaking, his chest heaving, sobbing from the depths of his soul. Nonie and Talulah held them close rocking them gently. "Hush now," Talulah whispered, "it is done."

CHAPTER FORTY

The majority of the able-bodied population of Maskek were clustered around Loon Lake, watching curiously as Emily Simpson's home went up in flames. For those old enough to remember it was like stepping back in time to 1950 when once before, the town's inhabitants stood and watched the Longhouse that Jonathan owned, burn into the night.

"Why'd she do it?" Ross wanted to know.

"Mrs. Simpson did this?" Clayton asked uneasily. He and Deacon were on duty today. Hoping they might finally get a chance to talk to Emily they planned on visiting her house.

"She didn't do it Clayton she wanted it," Bobby told them. "At first she was gonna let them bulldoze it until she figured fire might be a better way."

"Why?"

"Maybe because she hopes to kill whatever is living there," Bobby said.

"It's over," Deacon told them, "it's ended. The demon and all that it stood for is destroyed. It cannot live again, not even here."

"It's in the ground isn't it?"

"It can no longer exist, Bobby. It's gone."

Pushing their way through the excited throng, Deacon and Clayton sought Emily. She stood with Sergeant Hibbett, Constable Haynes, and two men in blue coveralls, strangers to the town of Maskek.

"Mrs. Simpson, are you okay? Captain McNally told us about your husband. We're real sorry to hear it."

Emily turned quickly toward them her face lighting up. "Clayton, Deacon, it's lovely to see you. I'm so pleased you didn't say 'sorry for your loss.' I couldn't stand to hear it one more time. How are you both?"

"We're fine. We were concerned about you."

"Oh, this," she gestured toward the flaming house, "this is wonderful. You can't imagine what a relief it is to know that nothing in that awful basement will ever hurt anyone again."

"There was no need for this, it is dead," Deacon told her. "It died two weeks ago. It will not return."

"Yes, there was need, there was plenty of need. Since we moved into the house it has bought us nothing but grief and debt. I'm glad it's destroyed. It murdered Steve didn't it? It caused the deaths of all those people last year. It tried to kill you."

"Where will you go?"

"I'm not going anywhere. I'm buying Ravens Lodge near the ranger station."

"Ravens Lodge," Clayton echoed, shaking his curly red head, "do you know the legend behind Raven's Lodge?"

"If by that you mean the mythology of it, yes I do and I like it. I'm sure the ravens will be glad of my company. Could anything be worse than what we had? Don't worry Clayton, this is one mythological tale I'm happy to believe in. My belongings are being moved in even as we speak. I sold everything from the house and purchased all new items. When I'm settled in, I'd like you all to come over and visit. I'd love to see you and I want to hear all about your battle, the town is abuzz with it. You're both heroes."

"I don't think Deacon will agree with you, it was a concerted effort between us, the warrior elite, the other me from the village and Lucan, Ross and Bobby,"

"That's very commendable. Deacon I heard that you struck the fatal blow. You should blow your own trumpet."

Deacon was looking at her with a strange expression on his face. It was obvious he'd hadn't heard that saying before.

"Wallow in your own triumph," Ross told him. "Still not getting it? Explain Clayt in a language he can understand."

"Not too many trumpets among the Cree," he grinned, "but I'll try."

"Got it?" Bobby asked when Clayton had finished explaining.

He broke into a smile, "Why didn't you say that?"

"Jeez, Deke, thirteen years among us white eyes even if you did keep going back to your grandmother's village, and you're still having problems with our language. Not much hope for you is there?"

"Nope, none at all I guess."

Emily noticed the sling on Deacon's right arm. "What happened to your arm?"

"Nothing to worry about, it'll heal."

"Battle scar," Clayton grinned.

"Stanley said nobody got hurt during the fighting?"

"Wasn't that fight."

"You should see the other guy," Clayton cracked, "he's sporting an injured shoulder." Inclining her head to one side Emily looked directly at him, "You're not going to tell me are you."

~ * ~

True to his word, still haunted by his dreams Damien championed the cause for good. Gradually he alerted the rangers to the whereabouts of his former disciples, all but one last group who were the mainstay of his inner circle, including Buffalo Bear the Blackfoot Medicine man who had saved the life of Jonathan Sparkling Eyes.

"Why don't you join us, Spirit of the Wind?" Buffalo Bear asked. "Now that Sparkling Eyes no longer wishes to be a part of us, we are in need of a prince who will bring us more members, who will join us together once more." He indicated a group of women huddled together away from the men, ranging from eighteen to seventy. "The women have expressed a desire to serve you as they served your father. By winning the battle you have proved yourself more than capable. With the help of your blood brother Clayton White Hawk we could be great again."

Gathered in the depths of the forest the last group of disciples clustered around the new chief. Reunited, Damien and Jonathan watched from the sidelines. Despite Jonathan's previous misgivings they had talked long into the night, night after night. He and Damien were the only two who could enlighten the people about their ancient past, the truth as they saw it happening in other lifetimes, events the historians could not relate. The two of them were bound by their previous existence.

Deacon spoke in the tongue of the Blackfoot, "I have no wish to join you Buffalo Bear or to become your prince. I have no interest in your followers. I'm grateful you saved my father's life. If you are to remain alive you should not practise here anymore. You will take your people and go from here forever."

Outnumbered by the warrior elite, Buffalo Bear bowed to Spirit of the Wind's command. To disobey would be foolish. Members of the disciples betrayed by Damien had been apprehended by Sergeant Hibbett and McNally's rangers. This remaining group was given a reprieve because Spirit of the Wind had discovered them hiding in the forest. Leading the small band of men and women, Buffalo Bear vanished into the Wapiti Hills. The medicine man would keep his word, they would not return.

Damien did not offer any help with regard to Thundercloud, nor did any member of the disciples volunteer information as to the whereabouts of Death Hand. In spite of Clayton and Deacon's extensive search for the half demon, Thundercloud remained elusive.

CHAPTER FORTY-ONE

Gradually accepting that the Unthinkable would never again hold the town hostage with its poisonous tongues, the people of Maskek agreed that a winter fair to celebrate their newly won freedom was in order. Stalls selling anything and everything were set up among the overindulgence of bunting in the high school classroom and the hall was procured for the purpose of dancing and merry making in the evening. Harry Mackenzie the town mayor, managed to obtain the services of the local disc jockey DJ Zee to open and preside over the ceremonies throughout the day and to provide the music before, in between and after the bands, ranging from rock to traditional Native songs, from country to black blues.

"I think we've just about covered all the music styles this town can handle. Hopefully that will keep everybody happy. Can you do it?"

"No problem. I could use s little help setting up. Hey Bobby, wanna give me a hand here?"

"Sure. Tell me what to do and point me in the right direction."

While Bobby was helping out, Leona and Melissa turned up. Melissa did a double take and Leona stopped dead in her tracks. "Isn't that the DJ from the radio station? Oh wow! I didn't know he was going to be here." Beckoning Bobby over, Leona asked, "How do you know DJ Zee? You never said anything."

"I've known him for five years. He's got a place near my uncle."

"And you didn't think to tell us important facts like that?"

"You weren't listening. If you could've taken your mind off Deacon once in a while you might have heard what I was saying."

"Where are they anyway?"

"If you mean Deacon and Clayton, they're over by the cake stall, along with most of the village. You'd think they'd never eaten cake before."

Leaving Bobby to finish setting up, the girls wandered over to the homemade cake stall. Deacon's entire family were present; as were the warrior elite, Thorn Rose, Shell Woman, Ross, and the disgraced Billy Joel Kramer. Billy Joel had tried to redeem himself after his attack on the wolves. In aid of the ceremony all of them were wearing traditional dress and they looked fabulous. Ross, Bobby and Billy Joel seemed out of place in their jeans and modern parkas.

"Ooh, I like what I see," Leona said wistfully.

"So does Thorn Rose," Melissa muttered, "You'd better keep your eyes off."

The high school was filled to the breaking point with merry makers. Winters were long and harsh here so any respite in the monotony of the snow capped days was greeted with great enthusiasm. Today was no exception.

DJ Zee stepped onto the stage in the school hall, bringing a sigh of adoration from many of the town's teenagers. At five feet five inches of lean build he was a handsome young man with dark brown eyes and even darker hair. His high cheekbones hinted at Native ancestry. Since taking over the local radio station broadcast from an old barn at the back of the ranger station, Zee had amassed a large following of mixed age groups.

"I've been asked to speak today to welcome you all to Maskek's winter dance and snow fair but this is no ordinary fair. Today we're celebrating the end of the terrifying and toxic phenomenon our Cree brothers and sisters call the Unthinkable. Two weeks ago armed only with knives, bows and arrows, the new chief, Spirit of the Wind led a war party of first class warriors—the warrior elite; you know them better as the Cree police, to seek out and destroy the supernatural force that has haunted our town for hundreds of years. In a fierce battle this small band single handedly took on the most frightening spectacle Maskek has ever witnessed. Fighting mostly in the dark the war party eventually disabled the entity, with Spirit of the Wind striking the final and fatal blow with the sacred Bone Knife of Power. The Bone Knife of Power is said to belong to the greatest of all warriors, Protector of the Wind, from whom Spirit of the Wind is descended..." The rest of his words were drowned out amidst the massive applause and whooping and war cries of the Indians.

Glancing at Deacon where he stood with Nonie and his grandmother, Clayton said, "They're gonna want you to make a speech."

"No chance," the young chief replied moving behind his mother and Talulah.

"Thought you'd stopped hiding behind your momma's skirts a long time ago, Deke," Ross cracked.

Grinning sheepishly, Deacon said, "Safest place right now."

"What do ya say folks," Zee continued after the applause died, "shall we bring Spirit of the Wind up here? Do you want him to speak?" A second roar of approval even louder than the first arose from the waiting crowd, "I guess that means yes. Come on up here Spirit of the Wind, bring the warriors with you."

Can't you speak to them, Clayton?"

"They wanna hear you let's go." When he hesitated Clayton said, "I'm here, my brother we'll do it together."

"Can't believe he's still so shy," Leona whispered to Melissa, "you'd think now he's chief he'd have conquered it."

The warrior elite had no such qualms and coaxing their young chief they managed to get him onto the stage. He whispered to Lone Wolf who immediately called Ross, Bobby and Lucan to join them. "You also fought with us," Lone Wolf told them as they stepped onto the stage. "Spirit of the Wind wishes your part in the battle to be recognised."

"Awesome!" Bobby said.

When everyone stood on the raised platform Zee took the microphone over to Deacon who stepped deftly behind Clayton. "My brother will speak."

"I think the folks would like to hear you speak. You're the Chief and the leader, without you the battle wouldn't have taken place. The town of Maskek and the people in your village owe their lives and the lives of the next generation to you. This celebration is in aid of that."

"I don't wanna speak Clayton."

"Alright I'll do the talking if you come out of hiding. Better still you talk and I'll translate, that a deal?" Clayton understood that Deacon would feel more comfortable speaking in his own tongue. At school he'd become so flustered and nervous about speaking in front of the class that he often forgot the English words.

"Deal."

Miles Broderick the editor of the local newspaper, the Northern Light and his one full time journalist and photographer Casey, pushed their way through the crowd until they were standing at the foot of the stage. This was one event they definitely wanted to capture in all its glory. Wasn't often the Northern Light was handed such a fantastic scoop way above the usual calibre of neighbourhood fiascos and the church women's news. This headline would even infiltrate the scattering of villages in this rural area.

"For those of you who don't know," Clayton told the spectators, "when Spirit of the Wind was at school he hated speaking out in front of the class. He got away with it most of the time because he melted the teacher with his big black eyes. Well, he still hates speaking in public, but seeing as there ain't no teacher around this time he's got no other choice." Clayton's comment produced a good natured response from the crowd and Deacon's sheepish grin melted many a heart.

Watching the proceedings with disgust Billy Joel rounded on Melissa, "How does Clayton get away with saying those things? If I or anyone of us said anything like that Deke would go ape."

"Because Clayton is his best friend and blood brother, that's how."

"Yeah, but even Clayton can only go so far," Leona told them wisely, "he knows when to stop."

The young chief waved the bothersome microphone away and nervously began to speak in the beautiful tongue of the woodlands Cree. Taking the microphone Clayton translated.

"Spirit of the Wind wishes us to know that he could not have destroyed the 'enemy' without the help of every member of the war party." He paused glancing at Deacon and nodding, "He hopes never again will the white man and the Cree draw weapons against each other, whether it is with words or guns or with what we have recently overthrown, and that we can now live in peace. The evil that has transcended centuries is now ended. That's all he has to say. Now as you know or maybe you don't, Indians only speak when they have something of importance to say and that was a mighty long speech for our Chief. If you want to ask us anything and I know you do 'cos I've heard you whispering, you can find us somewhere in this maze of classrooms, but be warned Spirit of the Wind is notoriously shy with those he don't know so you may not always receive the answer you're looking for. That's all folks."

Three cheers filled the room and the citizens in the town on the edge of civilisation applauded once more. DJ Zee took the mike, but before he could speak snap happy Casey jumped onto the stage, his camera flashing frantically.

"Enough." Spirit of the Wind commanded. He turned to Lone Wolf. Instantly Lone Wolf and Stands-in-Timber converged on Casey and lifting him gently lowered him to the floor.

"He doesn't much like cameras," Clayton explained. "Sorry about that, Casey."

"Could have been worse," his editor told him, "you could have lost your camera."

Checking to see that he was all in one piece, a startled Casey glared at Lone Wolf, "You didn't have to manhandle me, you could just have asked me to stop."

"We didn't mean any harm," Lone Wolf said, "but he is the Chief."

Mumbling under his breath Casey wandered over to Captain Virgil McNally where he stood with the ranger troop, watching the proceedings. He smiled as Casey accosted him.

"Don't feel bad, Casey he never has liked cameras. There are too many tourists prowling around with them all summer, snapping shot after shot especially when they realise he's a 'real' Indian. It gets to you after a while."

"I am not a tourist!" he answered, affronted.

"If you really want to take photographs do it discreetly, don't flaunt your camera in his face."

"And if he finds out or sees me taking them?"

"Discreetly, Casey, okay?"

Billy Joel told Bobby, "Deke sure can be miserable sometimes. I don't remember him ever being like that at school."

Beaming all over his face DJ Zee took up the microphone. "Never a dull moment in this town is there? Like I said it's a special day. I just want to thank you for talking to us, Spirit of the Wind even if it was through Clayton and to let you and your people know that we share the same hopes for the future. Whatever the world outside decides, it has nothing to do with us. Here in Maskek we are united."

Relieved to be out of the limelight Deacon led the warriors from the stage. While the elite were still basking in the glory, Deacon returned to his mother to be greeted by tribal elder Red Crow and Grey Owl.

Red Crow touched his shoulder, "Those were fine words, Spirit of the Wind. Let us hope that the white man's desire for peace and harmony is as strong as ours."

"The white eye will soon break his word," Grey Owl responded bitterly, "even as he broke the treaties. Our lives and the lives of many nations are full of the white man's treachery and broken promises. They are not to be trusted. Have we not yet learned?"

"In the past we have never broken a treaty or broken our word," Spirit of the Wind told him, "of that we can be proud." He was troubled by Grey Owl's distrust and anger. "If the white man chooses to break his word he has to live with his failures, we do not. You should not allow the past to intrude upon the present, uncle. You also must learn to forgive. We are not at war."

"My grandson speaks for most of us, Grey Owl," Talulah said. "Discretions of the past must remain there if we are to live happily among our white neighbours; this was my husband Eagle Hawk's greatest wish. His grandson is now carrying out that wish. It is not just about the way it was but how it is now and will be in the future and the hope that the badness, which has lived among our people and the people of this town will never return. Surely peace must be the answer."

"Don't forget folks, the dance begins at eight and ends when nobody is left standing," DJ Zee was saying. "The Watering Hole is kindly providing the bar and for those of you who don't drink, our friend Stanley Cuthand is donating gallons of coffee. If you ask nicely you might even get a piece of his legendary blueberry pie. Just don't eat too much this afternoon as there will be an unending supply of food throughout the night very kindly prepared by the ladies of the church and the ladies quilting bee. Have a good day and an even better evening. I will continue to play your requests as long as y'all want to listen, until the first band arrives at two thirty. This is DJ Zee signing off for now."

"Let's go talk to him," Melissa said excitedly, "before he gets lost in the crowd. If we tell him we're friends of Bobby's we might get special attention."

Ross pulled Deacon aside, "What's with Grey Owl, why's he so bitter?"

"He has good reason. Many years ago, he was fishing while his wife Blue Feather and his daughter Wild Rose picked berries. They were alone when four hunters spotted them. The hunters figured there was more to gain by hunting women instead of moose. Blue Feather and Wild Rose tried to run from them, the hunters were too fast and too strong. Grey Owl said he heard the women screaming as they were dragged into the trees. When he found them, they had been beaten and violated. Wild Rose was eleven years old."

"Eleven years old?" Ross was stunned, "that's sick. Were they ever caught?"

"My grandfather killed them."

~ * ~

Outside the school hall the wind howled and screeched as if despatched from the grave, tossing the falling snow across the frozen landscape, reminding the townsfolk that winter was not yet over. However hot the mood inside was the spirit of winter would have its way.

Amidst the lamenting of the wind and flurries of heavy snow, a skeletal figure skulked. Barely leaving a footprint he encroached upon the school. Only his black eyes were visible beneath the head of the wolverine. He was alert but in no hurry, he had all night.

~ * ~

Running the fair inside the building rather than outside, did not deter the citizens of Maskek from erecting as many outdoor games as they could fit into the empty classrooms. Deacon was about to toss is horseshoe when he was approached by an elderly, grey haired man of eighty years. A younger, chestnut haired woman of fifty-five walked at his side.

"Spirit of the Wind."

"Mr. Reynard, good to see you. How are you?"

"Thanks to you and Clayton I'm alive and happy. If you guys hadn't found me when you did, I wouldn't be here now. Your cousin Mo-he-ya told me I was very close to shuffling off my mortal coil. I want to thank you both from the bottom of my heart. No, don't stop I've been waiting weeks to tell you, but Mo-he-ya insisted I remained a guest in the clinic until I was well enough to go home." He bought forward the woman by his side. "This is Kathy Morgan, she's my live-in carer and let me tell you she's absolutely wonderful. After you asked Mo-he-ya if I could have someone to help me in the house, she got right on it. Kathy's an ex nurse. She has been a carer for many years. Good thing she knows how to handle a disgruntled old rogue like me. What's more important she loves my dog. Alamo has really taken to her."

Flashing back to his fear of Mr. Reynard's huge dog, Deacon smiled, "I'm real pleased to hear that."

"Graph told me about your issue with dogs so I do apologise for Alamo's behaviour. He's boisterous, but he wouldn't have hurt you."

"I've never seen a dog that big before. Hope I don't see another."

Abe Reynard laughed, "Yeah, I heard how you roped him like he was a steer."

"I'm sorry about that Mr. Reynard, I didn't know what else to do."

"No harm done, I might try it myself one day. I'd also like to say thanks for fixing up the house and the outbuildings. The place looks as good as it did when my wife and I first moved in. I really appreciate it. Will you tell the other rangers?"

"I'll do that."

"Well come along Kathy, there's lots to see and I want to see it all. Had my wife Peggy still been alive she would have embraced every minute of it. She was always one for social gatherings, especially those involving a dance or two. How are you at dancing my dear?"

Deacon and Clayton watched him steer Kathy in the direction of the dance floor.

"I'm glad he pulled through," Clayton said, "it sure didn't look good when we found him on the bedroom floor. It's episodes like this that make being a ranger worthwhile."

Tyrell McAllister wandered over to Deacon and Clayton, his eyes on the woman with Abe Reynard. "Who's the lady with Abe?"

"Her name is Kathy Morgan, she's Mr. Reynard's carer." Deacon grinned at him, "Why, you got designs on her?"

For most of the night Melissa and Leona divided their time between flirting with the DJ and making up to the warrior elite; Stands-in-Timber and Lone Wolf being their chosen favourites, leaving Deacon and Clayton free to dance with Thorn Rose, Shell Woman and each of their mothers.

Jonathan Sparkling Eyes and Damien Drew reluctantly stayed on the sidelines out of public view.

"It has to be this way my friend," Damien told an unhappy Jonathan. "You cannot show yourself after all this time. The townsfolk believe you to be dead and it must stay that way. How could you begin to explain the last eighteen years?"

Despite his misgivings Jonathan had to admit Damien had a point. To reveal the truth could have untold repercussions that could indirectly affect his son. "Almost twenty year and I still cannot stand by my son's side and show everyone how proud I am of him."

"I think he knows how you feel Sparkling Eyes. Be patient my friend, things have a way of working out."

~ * ~

Later in the evening whilst Deacon and Thorn Rose, Clayton and Shell Woman were smooching to Elvis singing, 'The Thrill of your

Love," the band having taken a well-earned break. Clayton spotted Tyrell dancing up close with Kathy. Glancing around the school hall he searched for Abe Reynard. The old man sat in the corner talking excitedly to Mayor Mackenzie his aged eyes sparkling with new life.

"Way to go, Tyrell," Clayton whispered as they passed each other on the dance floor.

Tyrell gave him the thumbs up. Moving closer to Deacon and Thorn Rose he said, "Guess Mr. Reynard must've got tired. First time I've ever seen Tyrell dancing."

Smiling wickedly Deacon said, "Looks to be more than dancing."

By the way Tyrell and Kathy were moving up close and intimate Clayton had to admit Deacon had a point.

Catching up to Iris Mayall and her husband, he heard Iris say, "Doesn't that woman realise how young Tyrell is? Why, it's practically cradle snatching. Kathy is employed to take care of Mr. Reynard, not to flaunt herself on the dance floor. We ladies of the church need to have serious words with her. It's scandalous."

"It's none of your business, Iris," her husband Ron told her. "Miss Morgan is entitled to follow her own life when she's not working. It obviously isn't bothering Abe."

"There has been far too much disreputable behaviour in Maskek lately, this town does not need anymore. Tomorrow Rita and I will pay her a visit..."

"They're only dancing, ma'am," Clayton said.

"She must be in her in her fifties much too old for Tyrell. I can't imagine what his mother is thinking. Not to mention Captain McNally."

"Tyrell's old enough to make up his own mind, it's not your concern." Shaking his head Clayton led Shell Woman across the room. "The trouble with small towns is that they're too damn small. Everyone knows your business."

Gazing up at Clayton with open adoration Shell Woman said, "You wouldn't live anywhere else. You love it here. I wouldn't let you live anywhere else, I'd never see you."

Kissing her Clayton whispered, "Shell Woman I will always be here for you."

~ * ~

Leaning against the makeshift bar late in the evening Deacon scanned the room for his mother and Rona Rykker.

"You seen momma, Clayton?"

"Nope, haven't seen my mom either come to think of it. Maybe they just stepped out for a minute."

"Yeah, maybe that's it."

When neither of them had returned in thirty minutes Deacon began to worry. "We should go look for them."

"They could just be talking, Deke."

"You don't really believe that do you?"

The way his best friend was looking at him Clayton knew better than to argue. Deacon's expression said a thousand words. They questioned everyone they knew. Nobody had seen Nonie or Rona for a while or noticed them leaving. Eliza entered the hall carrying a tray of glasses, she placed them next to the punchbowl. Perhaps Eliza had seen them. Deacon strode over to her.

"Hello Spirit of the Wind," she said, kissing him before he could speak. "Have you had a good time tonight?"

"Yeah, it's been a real good night. The Cree police love the attention, they've never been so popular. They'll want to be doing it all over again. Have you seen momma or Aunt Rona?"

Eliza looked into Deacon's black eyes and saw fear there. "Whatever's the matter love?"

"Did you see them?"

"Yes, about an hour ago they were heading for the washroom. Haven't they come back?"

"They haven't."

"I'm sure it's nothing to worry about." Eliza squeezed his hand and felt him trembling "They've probably run into some old friends."

"Something's wrong."

All senses on red alert Deacon bolted for the door, "Thundercloud."

CHAPTER FORTY-TWO

"As much as I enjoy living in the encampment, I do miss spending time with our friends, it's been marvellous to catch up with all the news," Rona said as she and Nonie walked back towards the hall.

The washrooms were housed in a separate building at the back of the main school. Surrounded by pine trees and dark shadows it was a popular haunt for students with extra curriculum plans on their minds that had nothing to do with books or learning.

"I've been thinking about that, Rona. Deacon and Clayton come into town all the time. I know they have to for their job, but you and I are expected to wait until one of the warriors can escort us here. That doesn't seem very fair does it?"

"That's one of the drawbacks of having a son who is the chief, we've got to do as we're told. Never mind though, tonight has been wonderful. We might even be able to persuade them to bring us again very soon, what do you think?"

Before Nonie could answer she was grabbed from behind and dragged backwards into the trees, a strong arm around her throat.

"Nonie," Rona cried running after Nonie's abductor, "leave her alone!" She tried to kick him in the shins but Nonie's body was shielding her attacker. Rona couldn't reach him.

Spurred on by fear and anger Nonie bent her arms and jabbed her elbows backwards into her assailant caching him in his midriff. Winded, his arm slipped away from her throat. Jumping onto his back Rona grabbed him around his neck and hung on with all her might. Incensed, his skeletal features forming into an animal-like snarl, he forced Rona's hands apart and threw her from his back. She landed heavily on the hard ground. Nonie was by her side in an instant realising too late that she had turned her back on the enemy. Deacon had told her so many times, drilled it into her and now she'd forgotten the most basic of safety precautions.

"Who are you? What do you want with us?"

"I will have Spirit of the Wind. But first, I will have the white woman who is his mother."

"Run, Rona, bring help."

"I won't leave you with him."

"Wise words white woman." Hauling Nonie away from Rona he pushed her up against a tree, drew his knife and slashed her buckskin dress. "It will only take a moment."

He sheathed the knife and with one hand held her arms above her head. With his free hand he loosened the lacings on his pants and pulled out his penis. Stunned, Nonie could only stare at the size of his engorged testicles and the width and length of his hard cock. They were the size of a horse's genitals.

"Like what you see?" His smile was heinous. He ripped her underwear and forced himself between her legs.

Rona's terrified scream shattered the frosty night.

CHAPTER FORTY-THREE

Inside the main hall loud boisterous music wore a hole in the night. The dance floor was overflowing into the corner of the room, forcing the bystanders to move further and further back. Tables and chairs had been removed to allow extra space for the pounding feet of the square dancers. Outside the snow continued to fall, the area surrounding the school deserted. Most had stayed within the warmth and welcoming light of the main hall.

Heading toward the washroom in search of their parents, Deacon and Clayton pulled up abruptly chilled by a piercing cry that split the night.

"Go," Deacon ordered. Pulling ahead of Clayton he was running as though his life depended on it. His heart was pounding fit to shatter his ribs not from exertion but from the sheer terror in the woman's cry and from a frigid strangling fear that was crushing his chest. Let them be safe. Close behind Deacon, Clayton tried to close off his thoughts, dare not think what might lie in store for them.

~ * ~

Rona dragged herself to her feet her legs like sticks of pasta. She was quivering so much she could barely stand. With determination born of dread she attacked the man a second time, grinding her nails down his back with such force that she drew blood.

He half turned, raised his foot and kicked her in the stomach knocking the breath from her body, doubling her over in pain.

"Rona!" Nonie screamed. Twisting and turning she fought against her assailant, he was too strong for her. She was helpless.

With Rona monetarily out of the picture Nonie's captor plunged forward, his penis strung out like a battering ram focused completely on its target.

Deacon dived through the trees the bowie knife already in his hand. Without hesitation, he sent the eleven-inch blade hissing threw the air. The man screamed and collapsed, the knife imbedded in the centre of his back.

"Momma," Deacon caught his mother as she fell. His hands were shaking so badly he had trouble holding her. He cradled her to his chest, holding her so tightly she was imprisoned in his arms. Clayton was by Rona's side instantly. He lifted her from the frozen ground and held her as if she were a child. From shock, pain, relief or all three the tears came in torrents of uncontrolled, hysterical sobs. Nonie gripped her son until her knuckles turned white, afraid that if she let go Thundercloud might rise again and finish the job. Deacon was gentle and reassuring stroking her corn coloured hair, his words spoken in the Cree tongue. Rona leaned against Clayton her head on his chest, her warm tears saturating the moose hide shirt inside his parka. "I tried to help her, Clayton but he was too strong for me."

"Hush now, mom. He's gone."

When Nonie could speak, she asked, "Who is he?"

"My father calls him Death Hand. I know him as Thundercloud."

On the ground Thundercloud was stirring. He clawed at the snow attempting to crawl away, his colossal genitals ploughing through the snow leaving furrows deep enough to plant trees.

Releasing his mother, Deacon grasped Thundercloud tightly and retrieved the knife. He watched the blood seeping from the wound in Thundercloud's back pooling and staining the newly fallen snow. "I told you if you hurt my family, I would kill you."

Thundercloud tried to focus, tried to speak. The world grew darker, fading from his vision. The feral light in his dark eyes died and he lay still.

Nonie and Rona looked on in shock. Clayton couldn't speak.

"It's finished," Deacon said. Grabbing Thundercloud's arms, he dragged the body well into the trees where it would be hidden from prying eyes.

"What are you doing?" Clayton asked when he'd recovered, "You can't just leave him there."

"We need to take your momma and my momma away from here. I'll come back and bury him. We'll stay at the house tonight. Tomorrow we'll return to the...." Deacon paused in mid-sentence. He sensed rather than saw Thundercloud move.

Thundercloud is a demon child.

Jonathan's words hit him with the force of a juggernaut. Pivoting with speed and grace that would do credit to a ballerina, Deacon knelt and slashed Thundercloud's shirt.

"No, Deacon!" Clayton yelled realising with horror what his brother was about to do. Acting swiftly, he tried to pull Deacon off the man's fallen body. Pushing his best friend aside, Deacon curled his hand into a vicious claw, grabbed Thundercloud's chest and tore out his heart.

"He's half demon. There's no other way to kill him."

Clayton had seen dead bodies before. Last year he and Deacon had discovered the mutilated body of a woman tourist hidden in the reeds in a remote corner of Loon Lake. What they had seen was horrific. Compared with what he'd just witnessed it had been a walk in the park. He bent double and vomited.

Rona stood ashen faced by Nonie's side unable to respond to her son. Nonie said nothing her mind on the awful events in Jonathan's past...and Deacon was his son.

Even as they stood paralysed by what had taken place over the last few minutes Thundercloud's form was changing. The demon was emerging. Already dying, the transformation could not be completed. While the lower half of Thundercloud's body took on the appearance of a cloven hoofed animal the top half was that of a man.

Deacon found the wolverine skin and laid it over Thundercloud's face. "He had to die, Clayton."

CHAPTER FORTY-FOUR

"Where'd Deke and Clayt go?" Ross asked when he couldn't locate either of them. "I thought they'd have stayed all night, nothing they like better than a good dance."

"I asked around, nobody has seen them, the warriors have disappeared too," Bobby replied. "Come to think of it, I haven't seen Mrs. Pierce or Mrs. Rykker either. Maybe they took them home."

"Thorn Rose and Shell Woman weren't too happy with Clayton and Deacon leaving them alone, but now they've gone presumably with the warriors."

"Yeah, well the women can't remain alone in town without an escort, those are Deke's orders."

By the end of the night everyone who was not asleep had heard about Abe Reynard's carer dancing with Tyrell and the tongues were wagging loud and strong. To avoid any possibility of repercussions between Iris Mayall and the ladies of the church and Tyrell and Kathy, DJ Zee called time.

"How'd you enjoy that, folks? I'm sorry to disappoint you all, but Mayor Mackenzie says it's time to go. I'm going to play one more smoochy number so grab your partners, lovers, husbands or someone else's husband and hit the floor for, 'Save the Last Dance for Me.' Hope you've all enjoyed yourselves, I know I have. Shake hands with the bands and don't forget you can hear me every day on your local swamp radio. Where else can you hear the news and the blues? Tune in for the latest on the scandals and the vandals. Anytime you want to romp in the swamp give me a call. This is DJ Zee signing off. Thank you and good night."

Somewhere along the way Maskek had become muskeg or swamp land and the swamp covered a large area around the town. Thus, swamp radio was born.

CHAPTER FORTY-FIVE

Concerned there might be some internal injury from the blow to his mother's stomach Clayton wanted to take her to the clinic. Rona refused. Reluctantly he bowed to her request. Wrapping Nonie in the moose hide robe she'd worn over her dress, Deacon carried her to the dogsled they'd used to bring them from the village into Maskek. With both women snuggled under the warm furs he set the dogsled moving. Clayton rode by his side pacing the buckskin mare with the dogs' stride.

When the boys didn't return, Lone Wolf told the warriors to collect the women and follow after them. They reached them just as Deacon was settling Nonie and Rona into the dogsled. Summoned by Deacon the warrior elite rode behind.

~ * ~

When he was satisfied that his mother and Rona were warm, safe and sleeping he and Clayton returned on horseback to the place where Thundercloud's body was hidden.

The warriors—the Indian police—stayed behind to protect the women.

"You killed him Deacon. You ripped out his heart!"

"Grandmother told us that the only way to kill the Wendigo was to destroy his heart. You were by my side when she said it. You told Doctor Lodge last year...."

"Thundercloud wasn't a Wendigo he was half human."

"He was half demon."

"The Wendigo is a bad spirit."

"And a bad spirit is also a demon."

Unable to restrain himself any longer, Clayton asked, "How does it feel to kill? You said all life was sacred and yet he's dead. You told your father the killing had to stop. How does it feel to kill?"

The new chief stared ahead his beautiful black eyes troubled. "Death Hand would have killed both of them. He'd have had his way with my mother and then with yours. He would not have let them live. Could you live with that?"

Clayton gave a long drawn out exhalation, "Of course I couldn't. But you tore out his heart! While we were fighting the Unthinkable you had a vision of your father doing the same thing. You were stunned. But here you are doing exactly as he did. It scares me. Why?"

Deacon gazed intently into Clayton's green eyes, "What would you have me say? I did what was necessary, don't mean I liked it. I'm a warrior, Clayton that's how I was raised and I will do whatever it takes to protect my family, your family and my people." Once more the dissimilarity between their two cultures raised its head. "I'm sorry you had to see it. I'm not sorry for what I did."

"I'll bring the shovels."

His vision blurred by tears Deacon tugged Thundercloud's frozen corpse to a sitting position. "We won't need the shovels."

"Aren't you going to bury him?"

"I'll burn him."

"To be sure he's dead?" Claytons said sarcastically. "You sent a knife into his back, you ripped his heart out. Do you think he's going to get up and walk away?"

"The flesh will burn, but his human spirit will look out forever across the land."

Working in the darkness with the aid of Clayton's flashlight, well away from the school, Deacon struggled to find enough wood to burn despite the acres of trees. Without hammer or nails he built a makeshift pyre and laid the body of Thundercloud Death Hand on it in a sitting position. Taking a handful of sparse grass and pine needles he set it alight. When it was burning strongly, he pushed it between the wooden stakes and added more pine needles, the pitch from the needles helped to fan the flames. The pyre was soon blazing and crackling around the body of the demon child.

"He is silenced for all eternity," Deacon said softly, turning away.

~ * ~

Returning to the village Rona watched Clayton closely, her heart troubled. In thirteen years, she had never known such a rift between her son and his best friend.

"Clayton, sit with me we need to talk."

They were alone in the lodge, Talulah, Nonie and Nedipah having gone to speak with Black Shawl. Deacon, Spirit of the Wind, was sitting in the council lodge with his father, Red Crow and Black Elk.

"What is it you fear, Spirit of the Wind?" Sparkling Eyes asked, "Are you afraid it might happen again, that you might come to enjoy the killing? You did what was necessary to save your mother and Rona."

"I wanted to kill Thundercloud. If I hadn't done it then it would have happened at another time. I feel no remorse, father."

"Not even for ripping the heart from his body?"

"There was no other way. He had to die."

"And so he has. It is done, my son. Too much of your mother Lupin lives within you, you do not have the heart to become a killer."

"You are worried about your brother," Red Crow stated, "he'll come around. Clayton White Hawk will follow you and support you as he has for thirteen winters. But he is not a warrior at heart. He needs time to absorb all that has happened. Be patient."

~ * ~

Clayton joined Rona and sat cross legged by the fire. He knew what was coming, his mother had been working up to it all day.

"Deacon saved our lives. Without his swift response Thundercloud would have killed us. If you had been in front of Deacon you would have done the same, wouldn't you? Perhaps not with a knife in his back but you'd have found a way. He just got there first. As shocking as it seems, there wasn't anything else he could have done. He's a warrior, like most of the men here. He'll do whatever he's trained to do.

He'll fight to defend and support his people, I can find no fault in that." Squeezing Clayton's hands, she planted a kiss on his cheek. "When you were adopted into this tribe, when you became Deacon's right hand, you agreed to share with him to always be at his side no matter what. He believes in you and cares for you. He loves you. He'll always be there for you. Please don't let this incident tear you apart. I don't think I could handle it."

"You don't think it was wrong to steal a man's heart?"

"If it keeps others alive it was the right thing to do. That's what's really bothering you isn't it, not the fact that he killed a demon but that he destroyed its' heart? Let it go, Clayton. Please let it go." Rona pulled her only son into her arms.

~ * ~

"Spirit of the Wind can I come in?" Clayton ducked through the flap, his head bowed in shame. "I was wrong my brother. Will you forgive me?"

Spirit of the Wind's response was to jump at Clayton and throw his arms around his back. "There is nothing to forgive."

With an arm around each other's shoulders they ducked out of Red Crow's lodge.

"In true happiness," Red Crow said.

CHAPTER FORTY-SIX

Deacon and Clayton next saw Melissa wrapped in Stands-in-Timber's arms and clearly enjoying it.

"Looks like your troubles are over, brother," Clayton grinned.

"Not just yet," Deacon said seeing Thorn Rose approaching.

"Are you avoiding me, Spirit of the Wind? When I look for you, you are gone; funny how an entire village has not seen you when I ask your whereabouts. Don't tell me you've been busy because I will not believe you."

"Thorn Rose," his smile was intoxicating. "I have not been avoiding you. I am here." He stood before her, his whole demeanour sexually charged and electrifying. After meeting his father Sparkling Eyes, Thorn Rose finally understood the extent of his son's appeal.

Her eyes were drawn to the zipper on Deacon's black jeans where they snuggled against him, hinting at the pleasures that lay beneath the tightly stretched denim. Tearing her gaze away from his crotch Thorn Rose lifted her head seeking his deep black eyes. He was looking directly at her, his dark eyes intense and displaying his own powerful need of her. Placing his hand gently at the back of her neck he pulled her to him, "I am here."

"Your father's legacy is ended," she told him, "the Unthinkable is dead. You are now free to make me your wife. How soon will it be?"

Waiting anxiously Clayton knew that Deacon's next words could change their lives.

"Thorn Rose you are already my woman. I do not need a wife, I need a woman, you are she."

Those were the words Clayton hoped to hear him say.

"All will be well," Shell Woman said sensing Clayton's concern.

"Then how long will it be before we become one. You promised me once the legacy was ended, we would be together. Why do you still evade me?"

"We are still only eighteen, I have not long left school and Clayton and I have recently become rangers. The people have made me chief and there is much I must learn. I have the responsibility of our people and of our village. Right now, I can't handle any more responsibility, especially that of a wife. Give me time Thorn Rose. If we were married, I could not devote as much time to you as I would want to. We have years yet..."

"How many years, I will be an old woman before you come to me."

Grinning at her Deacon replied, "And I will be an old man. Give it time. Be patient it will happen."

"It's her isn't it?" Thorn Rose spat at him, "the white woman who went to school with you. Do you think I have not seen the way she looks at you, the way she touches you, I have ears and I have eyes. She loves you, she will not let you go nor give you up. Your grandmother has spoken with her and still she will not accept that you and I are together. Do you love her?"

Deacon reeled taken aback by her accusation. "You know that is not the truth. I love you. From the time we were children I have cared about you. Have I not proved it to you? What else would you have me do, Thorn Rose? Look at Melissa," he pointed to Melissa, she stood close to Stands-in-Timber her body rubbing up against his. "How could she be with

Stands-in-Timber in that manner and still want me?"

"To make you jealous, that is how we women are."

"Your thorns are showing put them away. I am here."

Shaking his head woefully Clayton turned to Shell Woman. "What will it take to prove to her Spirit of the Wind loves her?"

"She already knows that, she is just being a woman."

Without warning, Thorn Rose stopped talking and grabbed Deacon around his waist pulling him tightly against her. "If I am to wait even longer until you are ready to become my husband, then I shall want proof of your devotion to me that I may show the other women. They will then be certain that you are mine: perhaps a similar token to that which our white brothers and sisters expect when they are in love."

"Then you shall have whatever you desire."

Stunned, Thorn Rose stared hard at him. "I will?"

"Wouldn't say it if I didn't mean it."

"Spirit of the Wind," she cried flinging her arms around his neck her eyes shining with happiness. "Thank you."

"Guess that's our cue to go," Clayton chuckled.

"Stay brother."

"What about Melissa?"

Melissa appeared to be completely enraptured with her new romance. "She seems to be handling things okay," he replied suggestively.

"Where did Leona go?"

"Last time I saw her she was headed over to Lone Wolf."

"Leona likes him," Thorn Rose explained, "She calls him your 'cute cousin'."

"It figures."

"Sure didn't take Stands-in-Timber long to get over you Thorn Rose," Clayton responded.

"I was already a lost cause and he's enjoying the attention."

"It won't sit too well with Grey Owl if he finds out. You know how he feels about mixed relationships."

"I've been meaning to talk to him about that," Spirit of the Wind said.

CHAPTER FORTY-SEVEN

In the month of April, Clayton and Deacon stood in the cabin of Aaron Gentle Horse. Gentle Horse worked with his father designing and crafting Native American jewellery. He specialised in silver and turquoise.

"Have you always lived up here Gentle Horse?" Clayton asked as they waited for him to complete the silver and turquoise ring Deacon had requested for Thorn Rose. "It's kinda isolated."

"We like quiet. My parents have not lived in the village for many years."

"I guess it don't suit everyone. Man, that is really something, Thorn Rose is gonna love it."

"It is done," Gentle Horse announced, displaying the delicate ring on a cloth of black velvet covering a quarter of his working bench. "Is it all you desire, Spirit of the Wind?"

"Wow."

"I guess that says it all," Clayton laughed.

Deacon held the silver ring up to the light, watching it sparkle in the sun streaming through the unshuttered window. The turquoise stone was fashioned in the shape of a rose, its silver thorns clearly visible beneath the heart of the flower. It was exquisite.

"It is strange to look upon you as the chief and not the child in your mother's arms as you were when you first came here," Gentle Horse told him.

Deacon and Clayton spent the rest of the day with Gentle Horse and his parents. They were eager to hear of the events in the village before and since Spirit of the Wind was officially made Chief. Caught up with the news, the boys waved goodbye promising to visit soon. They set out for the encampment both of them bearing gifts.

~ * ~

The snow was almost gone, the spring melt was well on its way and the sun was beginning to throw out some heat except in the parts of the Wapiti Hills and where Gentle Horse's family home stood. Farther down the valley where the altitude took a wondrous leap to the bottom, spring flowers were starting to push up through the softening earth. Stopping to relieve themselves, the boys took time to sit and admire the beauty of their magnificent country.

"We're real lucky to live out here," Clayton said gesturing to the majestic scenery enveloping them.

"That's not what you said when we were digging out of the snow."

"That was different." Glancing at his brother Clayton watched the light breeze toying with Deacon's waist-long hair and ruffling the fringes on his moose hide shirt.

"What?"

"I was thinking about the first day you came to school. We'd known each other for three months by then. You sure weren't happy about the idea of attending school."

"Would you be? I didn't speak or understand English. I didn't know what to expect. I'd never seen a school let alone attended one. Hell, I hadn't even had time to adjust to living in a house. I was afraid."

"I didn't speak Cree at the time either. We learned to communicate by sign language. After Mr. Reynolds locked you in the washroom I figured it was time I learned your tongue."

~ * ~

Maskek School March, 1957

"I'm going to teach you a lesson once and for all, boy," Harmon Reynolds hissed in Deacon's ear. "Why in hell's name don't you ask to use the bathroom? Or maybe your mother didn't bother to show you how." Hauling him from the desk, Reynolds dragged the struggling six-year-old boy toward the door.

"He doesn't speak English Mr. Reynolds," Clayton told the teacher. "He can't ask. He doesn't understand. If you hadn't got between us, he'd have signed me."

Ignoring Clayton, the irate teacher forced Deacon through the classroom door and marched him over to an old, disused washroom. Shoving him into the dark, dank, mildewed building he locked the door. "That'll be the last time you wet your pants in my class. Damned Indians don't know any better."

Deacon had tried to communicate his needs to Clayton but Harmon Reynolds deliberately got in the way. Frightened and unable to ask, he'd sat at the desk with tears in his eyes, trembling. Within minutes Harmon Reynolds noticed the puddle on the floor and seized him. While most of the children sat in shocked silence, afraid of Mr. Reynolds, Clayton ran after them. Before he reached the outside the teacher had vanished.

Inside the dark, dank windowless room Deacon cried out in fear. He couldn't find the door he couldn't see it. Shivering with cold he huddled against the wall, tears burning his eyes. Maybe someone would come? Kicking and banging he called out again and again. Nobody heard him. He remained trapped and alone. Claustrophobia seized him in its terrifying grip, he couldn't breathe and the walls were closing in on him...

~ * ~

"Mrs. Cartwright you godda come quick!"

"Whatever is the matter Clayton?" Elaine Cartwright looked up in alarm as Clayton burst into her classroom, breathless and agitated. Placing her arm around the boy's shoulders she listened attentively while he explained. "We'll go and look for him right now." Telling her class to sit tight until Miss Carter arrived to watch them, she took Clayton's hand and went in search of Deacon. They had just about given up when they were alerted by banging and shouting. The rusty key sat in the lock outside the door. Forcing it to turn Elaine gasped as the door creaked open. Deacon leaned against the wall he was wet, shivering and crying. Taking the exhausted, frightened child in her arms she carried him back inside the school. In the warmth of the classroom she removed his wet clothes and wrapped him in a blanket borrowed from the nurse's room, sat him on her lap and hugged him. Shaking, he clung to her desperately. Harmon Reynolds was not in attendance.

"Clayton, go ask the secretary to call Deacon's mother. Tell her to come and fetch him right away. She has the number."

Following the incident in the washroom Nonie at first refused to send him back to school. For months afterwards he suffered terrible nightmares. Afraid to be alone he'd slept in his mother's bed every night. Now and then after thirteen years the nightmares still resurfaced.

~ * ~

1969

"Your mom sure laid into Mr. Reynolds when she found out. She, Mrs. Cartwright and my mom tried to get him banned from teaching altogether."

"Didn't do any good, he's still teaching."

"That's because the school has a shortage of teachers. Nobody wants to move out here they think it's uncivilised."

"Damn right it is. Hope it stays that way."

"That's not very nice," Clayton quipped.

"That's what you said when I went after Ryan Hoffman. If you hadn't wanted to go sneaking around Mr. Gibson's garden Ryan Hoffman wouldn't have heard you talking about it and he wouldn't have gone and told Mr. Gibson. We spent three hours in a goddamn tree until he went back inside."

"You could've been a little gentler," Clayton grinned "you scared the hell outta him. But I guess not as much as the time you let the lab animals loose...and scared the hell outta everybody else. You said nothing should be caged, so we sneaked in one lunch time when Gibson was out and set 'em free. We had rats and mice running all over the school."

"He knew damn well who'd done it and he came looking for me..."

"We were sixteen and you just stood there defiantly while he tried to whip your ass. Me, Ross and Bobby had to pull him off you in the end."

"He didn't like Indians much. He got what was coming to him."

"Yeah when you laid into him one morning and knocked him cold." Clayton suddenly chuckled, "Sure was funny watching the whole class scurrying after the rats. Not to mention all those screaming women. It was awesome. Was it worth the beating?"

"Sure was, I could've watched that all day." Deacon was quiet for a moment then he said, "If you had not learned to speak our tongue I'd have been stuck. You saved my life many times, I owe you a lot, man."

"That's what friends are supposed to do. You helped me out plenty of times. Anyhow I got to learn the Cree tongue, which is what I wanted. It's a beautiful language. More folks should take the time to learn it. Hey, do you remember your first Halloween? What a night that was."

~ * ~

October 31, 1957

Deacon's first experience of Halloween was one he would remember for a long time. Spending the first six years of his life in his grandmother's village he was unfamiliar with the All Hallows Eve festival. Clayton, Ross, Bobby, Leona and Melissa were determined to make it a good one for him.

Answering the door to the five of them Deacon stepped back abruptly more surprised than frightened. "What is this, Momma?"

While Nonie attempted to explain the reason for dressing up in costume and the origin of the Halloween festival, she invited them all inside. Having dropped Clayton off at Ross Porter's house before she drove to see Nonie and Deacon, Rona waited to welcome them and take them trick or treating. Try as she might Nonie could not make Deacon understand what Halloween was all about.

"Perhaps it would be better if we just take them all into town and let him see for himself," Rona suggested.

"Yeah, that be best," Clayton said from underneath his werewolf mask, "he'll really flip."

Hearing his best friend's voice, Deacon pulled Clayton's mask off and smiled at him, "Werewolf."

"Well, you learned that much anyway."

"Werewolves are known among my people," Deacon told him as Nonie translated, sometimes they are also called Wendigo." Moving over to Bobby he pointed at his costume "We usually eat pumpkins."

"Bobby was staring at him aghast, "I didn't think you'd know about pumpkins."

"Native tribes were growing pumpkins and squash long before the white man came here but we don't usually wear them on our bodies."

"Okay, so you don't like my pumpkin. What do you think of Ross's costume?"

Looking to his mother for the closest translation of Bobby's question, Deacon said, "We have another name for vampires. To explain the origin of the Native vampire would take time."

Now his friends were staring at him in disbelief. "Clayton, you said he wouldn't understand, you lied, you spoilt our fun."

"I said he didn't understand Halloween not that he didn't understand werewolves and vampires. Anyway, Bobby you're neither, you're a pumpkin."

"What's the matter with a pumpkin? It's better than dressing up like a stupid witch."

"I am not a stupid witch!" seven-year-old Leona bristled, "I'm a sorceress. Can't you tell by my outfit? Do you see a witch's hat?"

"No, but I see a witch's cat." He was looking at Melissa.

Settling into a slinky pose she would later perfect, Melissa purred, "Why would I want to be a common cat when I can be a beautiful black cougar?"

"Alright, kids come on," Rona said hustling them outside and into her old Pontiac station wagon. "We're short on room so you'll have to sit on each other's knees."

When all the children were cloistered in the back, Nonie got into the front seat and lifted Deacon onto her lap. In Maskek they parked the car up by the holding corral. Rona handed them each a pumpkin shaped bag and they headed toward Main Street. The snow clad road was heavy with trick or treating children accompanied by their parents. Holding his mother's hand Deacon kept back heedful of so many people in one place. He watched, perplexed as the white people from the wooden lodges filled the children's bags with tiny paper packages.

"What do they place in their baskets, momma?"

"It's candy. In England where I come from, we call them sweeties. You can eat them."

"Can I taste them?"

"You may taste them but not too many or they'll make you poorly."

Bringing his half-filled bag of goodies Clayton offered it to Deacon. Sinking his hand into the bag he withdrew something pink, soft and squashy and placed it gingerly into his mouth.

"Hasn't he ever tasted candy, Aunt Nonie?"

"This will be his first time. Do you like it?" Her son's beaming smile said it all.

Since they became friends Clayton always referred to Deacon's mother as Auntie Nonie.

"How come Deacon's not dressed up?" Billy Joel asked when he caught up to Clayton. Billy Joel was all gangling limbs and messy hair, barely any meat on him at all. Seemed as if the wind blew too hard the force of it would bowl him over.

"Because this is all new to him, next year he will be, won't you Deacon?"

After the trick or treating, the children were taken to the high school for the start of annual Halloween party the town mayor organised every year. He watched curiously from the sidelines, never straying far from his mother's side until, fascinated by the apple bobbing and encouraged by his friends he agreed to join in.

"He's obviously enjoying it," Rona told Nonie, "I'm pleased he's taking part."

By the end of the evening while the adults stayed for the Halloween Ball, Rona and Nonie collected the kids and deposited them with their respective parents. On the way back to their house by Loon

Lake, Deacon vomited up all the sweets and candy he'd consumed.

"Oh boy, were you sick," Clayton told him, "took you almost a week to get over it. Your momma told you to go easy on them candies."

"It was the first time I'd eaten anything like that. I liked them."

"You may have liked them but you haven't eaten any since."

"I learned my lesson."

For the most part the population of Maskek treated Deacon no differently than the other children, his troubles began when he started high school. Some of the students didn't quite know how to take him or what to expect of him. Others were afraid of him, a fear instilled in them by their grandparents. Few members of staff knew how to teach a child from a different culture especially one who didn't speak English.

CHAPTER FORTY-EIGHT

Over the intervening years the friendship shared between the two boys continued to grow, so did Deacon's altercations with the establishment. With a deep rooted pride in his heritage he defied all the efforts of certain teachers to mould him into a 'white Indian', telling them via Clayton translating, "Grandfather taught me to hold my head up and be of proud of my culture and my heritage."

On the day these same teachers approached him with scissors in their hands, determined to shear his long hair. "You will not cut my hair; our strength is in our hair. It is part of my culture you will not take that from me."

Backed up by Clayton, Ross, Bobby, Leona and Melissa's threats to involve the school principal the teachers backed down, the possibility of losing their jobs bought home to them rather astutely. The school Principal Barnstable Emett believed Deacon should be given the right to choose.

In his first year of school he ran away at least once a week. After Nonie or Rona had dropped them off at the gate, he lit out for the river refusing to come back until his mother arrived to pick him up at the end of the day. Clayton often found him staring into the water. Using sign language Deacon told him, "You should not follow me, friend-brother you will be in trouble."

To which Clayton always replied, "I can handle it. My father tells me to be a man and to act like a man. That's what I'm doing."

Giving up in despair Nonie and Rona began to turn a blind eye to their sons' misadventures. Elaine Cartwright and a younger teacher, Lena Carter, spent many hours smoothing over the rough patches and calming the angry waters of Deacon's discontent. Married to a Cree Indian, Elaine Cartwright understood the trauma he was going through, attempting to straddle two cultures. She could sympathise with the boy's fears.

~ * ~

Despite his mother's teachings and Clayton's attempts to help him, by the age of fifteen Deacon had still not completely mastered the English language. He relied heavily on Clayton to help him understand what the teachers were saying and to explain the work that was expected of him. Clayton happily obliged and when they were talking between themselves conversed only in the Cree tongue. Because the majority of the school staff were ill-equipped to deal with the situation, they left Clayton to show Deacon the ropes.

In the residential schools run by a number of different churches, Deacon would not have been allowed to get away with such behaviour. The reason he'd been admitted to the local school was because his adopted mother was white and the government wanted native children to be adopted by white families.

From the 1960s to the 1980s thousands of aboriginal children were taken from their homes by child-welfare services and placed with non-aboriginal families. It was called the Adopt Indian/ Métis programme. Today it is referred to as the Sixties Scoop.

~ * ~

Come here, Deacon," Nonie said, patting the couch.

"My name is Spirit of the Wind," he replied stubbornly sitting beside her.

"While you are at school you will be called Deacon. I will call you Spirit of the Wind when you are with me. Why are you refusing to learn the tongue of the white man? Explain to me in English why you are so resentful."

"I will not speak it."

"Sometimes you can be so infuriating. Is it fair to expect Clayton to speak for you all the time? Eight years you have lived among the people here and still you are struggling with our language..." Nonie was beginning to lose patience. Talking to him in English had not produced the desired results. Unable to understand completely what his mother was saying he either ignored her words and answered her in his native tongue or looked on helplessly.

"Why, Deacon? Tell me why."

"You will not like what you hear."

"Try me."

Taking a deep breath Deacon faced his mother, "When you bought me here you took me from my family and my friends, from my people and everything I knew. You sent me to the white man's school, gave me a white man's name and asked me to live in the white man's house. You did not ask me what I desired. My language is the one thing you cannot take from me."

Stunned by his abrupt but honest answer, with tears stabbing the corner of her eyes and a knife gutting her heart Nonie took him into her arms. "Oh love, I had no idea you felt that way. I thought you were happy here now that you have made friends."

"How can I know true happiness when this is not my home?"

Nonie recalled numerous times he'd slipped off to his grandmother's village without her consent, taking Clayton with him. Thinking about it he had tried to tell her, she just wasn't listening. In her mind she heard him saying, "White men do not listen."

And neither, it seemed, did white women.

CHAPTER FORTY-NINE

Upset and hurting following her discussion with Deacon's reluctance to learn his mother's first language, Nonie resolved never to mention it again. When he was ready, he would make the choice. A choice that came sooner than expected when his grandmother Talulah, arrived at school one day, held him close and speaking softly, said, "Today you will begin to learn the tongue of your mother."

With Elaine Cartwright's permission Talulah took him to the back of the room and slowly and patiently began to teach him the basic words of the English language. A practise she continued for months until her grandson started to speak and understand the tongue he'd ignored for eight years.

For centuries the Cree and the French trappers had run trap lines and traded furs with the Hudson's Bay Company's representatives and Spanish business men who had travelled up river from Mexico, with the intention of claiming a stake in the lucrative fur trade. Constantly interacting they learned each other's language. French was still spoken among certain Cree nations and the Métis. Deacon was as fluent in French as he was in Spanish, but he found the English language extremely hard to master. In time his written English became a thing of beauty, but after three years he still struggled with the spoken word.

~ * ~

"Talulah spent months helping you to learn English. Since you returned to the village you've started slipping again," Clayton told him.

"Noticed that, did ya?"

Grinning all over his face Clayton threw up his hands. "Don't know what the hell I'm gonna do with you, everyone in your village can speak English and they do when they're away from there." He sighed with exasperation. "Deke, you're a problem. It wasn't long after that when we realised that our feelings for each other were much deeper than friendship." With longing in his eyes, he reached for his blood brother.

~ * ~

Content, Deacon lay back recalling the time he and Clayton had first become acquainted in Maskek's Wilderness Park in the summer of Fifty-seven. It wasn't so much Clayton's struggle to make a bow and arrows that intrigued Deacon but his flame coloured curly hair, the whiteness of his skin and his green eyes as deep as the emerald waters of Lake Louise. He was a sight to behold. Other than his mother, Deacon had seen no other white people. His first glance at the pale faced boy was staggering.

"What're you thinking, my brother?" Clayton asked.

"How we met."

"That was really something, man. I couldn't take my eyes off you, standing there n nothing but a breechclout and moccasins. Your hair was long even then, the sun was shining on it slick as a thoroughbred's coat and your body gleamed. I remember thinking wow I wish I looked like that. You kept touching my hair I couldn't figure out why."

"It was the same colour as fire. I wondered if it would burn my hand. I asked momma, 'Who made you?' She did not answer she just kinda smiled. Whoever made you forgot to colour you in."

"Wouldn't do for us all to look alike now would it? Something happened to both of us that day, it wasn't just coincidence it was meant to happen. Your grandmother told us it had been prophesised and it's still happening."

CHAPTER FIFTY

Word spread quickly through the village that the young chief had returned with the long awaited gift for Thorn Rose and now the women and girls waited, hoping to catch a glimpse of this treasure. They hoped to see him present it to her.

"Just like in town," Clayton muttered, "folks know what you're gonna say before you say it."

Staring at Leona as if she'd gone mad, Bobby said, "Deke's getting engaged? I don't believe it. He is seriously gonna break so many hearts including Clayton's. I never thought I'd see the day."

"It's not an engagement," Leona said, "Indians don't get engaged...do they?"

"Times have changed, Leona. What would you call it?"

"I suppose," she said with a shrug.

"D'you figure he's gonna go down on his knees and present it to her?"

"We're talking Spirit of the Wind here, Bobby," Ross said, "not just any guy. He does things different."

Talulah took her grandson's hand, "Do you wish this to be private? I can send them away."

"No, grandmother it's fine. Better they know." As he was speaking Thorn Rose resplendent in the dress she had made for his inauguration, came towards him. He took her into his arms. Removing the tiny doeskin pouch from his neck he handed it to her.

Excitedly Thorn Rose took the pouch from him. "This is for me, what is it?"

Wearing the necklace and earrings her son had purchased for her as he had for his grandmother and Nedipah, Nonie stood with Talulah, Nedipah and Rona. Rona wore the turquoise and silver bracelet and ring

Clayton had also bought from Gentle Horse. Nonie's smile was warm and tender, tears glistening in the corner of her lavender blue eyes. "My baby boy is growing up."

Thorn Rose opened the pouch and withdrew the delicate ring, the look on her face was indescribable. "It is my namesake. It's so beautiful." She held it up to the sun. "Look how it shines."

Sneaking up behind him, Lone Wolf said, "You're supposed to place it on her finger."

"I'm getting there. Give me a minute..."

"Where does that leave you, Clayt?" Ross asked.

"Same place it did before. Nothing's changed between us."

Taking the ring from Thorn Rose, Spirit of the Wind slipped it on her finger. "Now they will know you belong to me. You are my heart song. You have always been. You will always be."

"I wish someone would say that to me, it's so sweet," Leona whispered wiping a tear from her eye, "and it's so moving."

"When it is time," Deacon told Thorn Rose, "you will become my wife in the traditional manner of our people."

Melissa gasped as if kicked in the stomach by an ornery mule. She could pass it off while he was still free, but the ring meant he was bound to Thorn Rose forever. Despite the talk she'd shared with Deacon's grandmother and the fact that she was now interested in Stands-in-Timber, her love for Deacon had not diminished. It still hurt to see him with Thorn Rose.

Grasping her young warrior gently by the ears Thorn Rose kissed him passionately, her lips lingering on his.

"They godda come up for air sometime," Stalking Moon cracked.

While Thorn Rose flashed her ring around the women of the village, Melissa turned away with tears in her eyes. Taking her friend aside, Leona said, "You didn't really believe it could happen to you? He's an Indian Melissa, taking a white girl for his woman was never in his plans, we've been through this. You're not the only one who's hurt, how do you think I feel. I care about him too, you know."

"I lived in hopes. We all have dreams. If we didn't have dreams what would we have? Dreams help us to carry on."

"Look around you Melissa, this village is a monument to the past, living here wouldn't be any picnic. It's a hard life steeped in tradition with many laws and rules that need to be followed. It's no place for people like us. Your head is filled with romanticism and tales of majestic warriors and war chiefs of the plains. It's not real. It's a fantasy."

"Are you saying that if Lone Wolf asked for your hand, you'd turn him down?"

"Of course not," she replied affronted, "He'd have to live with me though not the other way around. When Spirit of the Wind lived in the house by the lake, it was different, he was one of us. Now he's the chief he lives in Talulah's encampment and he has to toe the line. He isn't free to do whatever he pleases, we still have choices. He has the responsibility of his extended family, his people and this village. I'm sure living on a reserve would be totally different than this camp, this is a one off. You can't predict where your heart will go any more than you can choose your parents. All we can do is stay friends with him and never lose that. I thought you'd found solace in Stands-in-Timber, anyway?"

"I like him, but he isn't Deacon; we're just friends."

"Deacon is gone his life and future are changed forever it'll never be the same as it was when we were at school. You have to accept it."

"I don't have to like it."

"But we have to make the most of it. Eventually all our lives will go in different directions. We may not see each other for years but we'll be friends until we die...and that's what really matters."

CHAPTER FIFTY-ONE

"What's happening with your father, Spirit of the Wind?" Captain McNally enquired. He sat in the office at the ranger headquarters with Clayton and Deacon. "Is he going to stay with your mother? I'd sure like the chance to spend time with him, been a while since I last saw him. We were real good friends and don't even get my started on those parties he used to host."

"He's not leaving for a few days."

"Will he be back?"

"I don't know, captain. He figures to go away for a while with Damien and then return here doesn't mean he will."

"He says it isn't safe for him to stay around here, sooner or later people will start to notice. He's concerned that his presence in Maskek could indirectly affect Deacon," Clayton said.

"I guess there are a few scores to settle," Virgil McNally said. "He was a popular guy but not without enemies."

"He'll return to his father's people, the Blackfoot. We will go there to see him," the young Indian replied.

"You tell him I'm coming after him when I get my next vacation. Now while you pair were having the time of your lives up in the village and shirking your duties, I've been interviewing possible recruits." Reaching into the right hand drawer of his desk he pulled out three letters, "One for Ross one for Bobby and the third for Billy Joel. They're waiting on these papers so go on down to the school and hand 'em out. And you can tell Leona and Melissa to give me a call it's important. Oh, and Spirit of the Wind don't forget your hat. One other thing..." Deacon turned with his hand on the door, "congratulations on your engagement."

"I'm not engaged," he showed Virgil his hand, "See, no ring."

"He forgot to mention the necklace Thorn Rose made him with

the symbol of the wind emblazoned on it," Clayton said, "and the bracelet on his wrist, that's as good as any ring."

Virgil glanced at the intricately woven band on Deacon's left wrist, "That's mighty fancy. You better take care of it."

Pulling a face Deacon pushed his brother through the door.

"Go on git outta here," Virgil laughed.

~ * ~

News of Deacon and Thorn Rose's 'engagement' leaked through the school like a broken water pipe. Many of his ex-classmates held mixed feelings about it, not least Billy Joel. "Why'd you do that?"

"Why would you?"

"All the girls you could have and you go and choose one of your own. It beats me."

"Why shouldn't he choose one of his own?" Leona piped up, "you'd have done the same."

"Nah," Bobby said, "in order to win Billy Joel's affection she'd have to be a choir girl or something. His folks wouldn't accept anything else them being religious 'n all."

Mr. and Mrs. Kramer were more than just stalwart members of the church, obsessively religious they lived their lives according to the 'good book.' A fact that did not sit well with Billy Joel.

"Can we forget about Deke's love life for a minute," Clayton butted in, "we got something for you."

"Spirit of the Wind," they said in unison. "Remember?"

Clayton grinned sheepishly. "I stand corrected. We got some letters here for you from Cap'n McNally."

"What's in 'em?" Billy Joel asked.

"That's for you to know." Producing the letters from the top pocket of his uniform, Clayton handed them out.

There was silence while the boys ripped open the envelopes and quickly read the contents of the letters. Ross was first to holler. "I've been accepted. Far out! Captain McNally says we godda go see him. Me, a ranger, I can't believe it." Pushing his chair away from the desk Ross stood up and pointed his finger at a non-existent figure. "Who was that masked man? That was the Lone Ranger."

Next to shout was Bobby as excited as a child with a new puppy. "They want me too. Right on, man!" Springing from his chair he did a nifty little dance and sat back down. "D'you think the reason we've been accepted might have something to do with us fighting those dead things?"

"Won't be anything to do with that," Ross answered. "How about you, Billy Joel?"

Shaking his head sadly, he said, "I've been turned down."

Silence filled the classroom and Ross laid his hand on Billy's arm. "I'm sorry, man."

"Maybe you can try again at a later time," Leona suggested hoping to make him feel better.

"Yeah, maybe," he replied despondently.

"Does he say why?" Clayton wanted to know.

"Something about me not having the right attitude and the wrong idea about the rangers? Guess I'm just not good enough."

"I'm sure it isn't that," Leona replied. "Why don't you ask to speak to him?"

"Captain McNally wants you and Melissa to call him," Clayton told them. "He said it was important."

"Do you know what it's about?"

Clayton shook his head. "Nope he just said to give him a call. Maybe you should give Captain McNally a call, Billy Joel..."

A sudden commotion in the school ground grabbing his attention, Deacon darted from the classroom. Panicked teachers and students were running all over the place shouting, screaming and pointing.

"What the hell's going on?" Clayton demanded coming up behind him.

"Horses got loose," someone yelled, "they're running riot."

"Which horses?"

"Those horses."

As he was speaking a dozen head of horses came careering across the yard, with a magnificent black stallion in lead.

"That's Diablero," Deacon said, "better get everyone inside."

Before Clayton could stop him, he was off and running. Dodging the speeding animals, he vaulted onto the piebald closest to him and galloped on ahead until he was level with the stallion and leapt onto the horse's back. Whipping the reins from the ground he pulled on them halting the animal's progress. The other horses stopped and waited. Clayton's buckskin mare trotted up behind. After a few choice words to Diablero, Deacon glanced at the reins.

"Did he just swear?" Bobby asked. They'd lit out after Deacon on hearing the commotion.

"Close," Clayton told him. He glanced at Deacon, "What's up?"

"Leather's been cut." He showed him the severed edge of the reins.

"That's how Diablero broke away?"

"I don't think so. He could've unfastened the reins with his teeth and still not wandered off."

"Well whoever it was, he or they must've turned the other horses loose from the holding corral, hoping they'd follow him."

"Why would they follow Diablero?" Melissa asked

"They're mustangs—wild horses and Diablero used to lead a herd of mustangs before Spirit of the Wind caught him. Instinct I guess. "

"You caught 'em," horse rancher Stove Colton called, limping over to the boys. He was red faced and breathless. "Sure do appreciate it fellers. Some wise guy left the corral gate open."

"Did you get a look at who it was?" Clayton asked.

"I believe it was your friend Hoffman and those two deadbeats he hangs around with. He'd know your horse, Spirit of the Wind. Who could miss it?"

Fellow student and ex classmate Ryan Hoffman had been a pain in their butt all through school. A replica of his arrogant, aggressive father, Ryan Hoffman's hatred of Deacon was well known.

"It figures. Got any idea where they went?"

"Saw 'em running over to the coffee house, like the devil was after 'em. They were cacklin' like a bunch of witches. Anybody hurt here?"

"Not as far as we know."

"Was there any damage done to the school buildings?"

"I don't think so. Folks were more scared than anything. Are these the horses Pakito and Reno bought in?"

"Sure are," the old man replied, "first class stock too. They'd bring top dollar if I wanted to sell 'em. A pair of fine wranglers in the making I'd say, Reno and Pakito. I could sure use a couple of wranglers. They need a job?"

Spirit of the Wind smiled, "You'd have to speak with them."

"I might just do that. Where do you guys find these animals?"

"They run free in the forest."

Clayton chuckled, "They gather in the clearing. Good grazing, clean water, no predators. In the winter his people feed them and they breed. All good stock and free as the wind... a bit like my brother here."

His black eyes twinkling Deacon smiled at him, "Liked that did ya?"

Principal Barnstable Emett and Elaine Cartwright came running over. "Is everyone alright, Deacon?"

"As far as I can tell."

"Thank goodness for that. That's your horse isn't it?"

"Yes ma'am. He doesn't usually take off unless I tell him to. Seems he had some help this time. Let's go, Clayton."

"Are we going after Hoffman?" There was a delightfully evil glint in Clayton's eyes.

"You bet."

~ * ~

Cackling like a lunatic, Ryan Hoffman pushed his companions further into the red leather booth. "Man did ya see 'em running? I ain't never seen a teacher run before. I'd say we gave 'em a taste of their own medicine." He turned to Stanley. "Hey Injun we're waiting to be served. Get your red hide over here right now."

Ignoring their ignorance Stanley Cuthand stayed behind the bar. Familiar with the attitude of the three youths and others like them, he learned early in his career to avoid any confrontations providing there was no chance of danger. In his experience it only made matters worse. Whatever business a person was in he or she had to learn to ride the wind. When you were running a Native owned business in a town with a mostly white population you stayed on your toes.

Stanley's nineteen-year-old nephew Lucan (Loo-can) chose a different path. He'd fought with his cousin Spirit of the Wind against the Unthinkable and he wasn't easily intimidated. Close to Deacon in height Lucan, wore his hair long and loose. Attired in blue denim jeans and a cowhide vest worn over a red shirt, and moccasins, Lucan approache d the booth. His right hand stroked the knife sheathed at his hip. "I sometimes find it helps to have manners," he told Hoffman. His words were amiable enough though is tone wasn't.

"When you learn a little respect, my uncle might choose to serve you."

Stanley watched the hot-headed Lucan closely. While he'd tolerate so much from Hoffman and the two meatheads with him, he wasn't about to allow his nephew to raise a ruckus while he had customers in attendance, particularly when those customers were the ladie s from the church.

"Who'd you think you're talking to?" Hoffman growled. "Git over here and pour us coffee before I tear your sorry ass apart!"

"Oh dear sweet Jesus," Iris Mayall said, "I hope there isn't going to be any trouble."

Ready to pounce on his nephew if necessary... Lucan's fingers were already hovering above his knife... Stanley was relieved when Spirit of the Wind and Clayton walked through the door.

"Leave it, Lucan," Spirit of the Wind told him, "they ain't worth it." Reluctantly Lucan withdrew his hand and went to join his uncle behind the bar.

"What the hell?"

"Howdy Hoffman," Clayton said.

Hoffman's companions tried to move quickly out of the booth and out of harm's way. Releasing the horses was one thing, facing ex classmate Deacon who was now the new Chief and a ranger to boot was another. "You guys going someplace?"

"N-no, Deke, we were just..."

"Sit down."

Having experienced Deacon's wrath before while they were still at school, Hoffman's companions said, "Yeah okay, whatever you say. It wasn't our idea it was Hoffman. He made us do it."

Shaking his head in dismay Clayton threw them a look of contempt. "He made you do it, huh? Well now seems to me like it's two against one. Folks could've been hurt if those horses had made it into Main Street and a lot of property damaged. It was stupid and senseless. When are you guys gonna grew up and start taking some responsibility?"

"You guy things really think you're something else don't ya?" Hoffman sneered, "Since you got to be rangers you think you're so smart. Well you ain't nothin'."

Deacon mumbled something in his own tongue and by his tone it was less than complimentary.

"Amen to that, my brother," Clayton concurred.

"What'd he say?"

"You don't need to know. We're gonna take a little walk right on down the street."

"I ain't going no place with you, you red belly lover," Hoffman spat, barring his teeth.

In one swift movement Deacon hauled Hoffman from the booth and punched him hard on the jaw. He went down as if he'd been pole axed. "I don't like that, Hoffman. I never have and I never will. Get up, we're gonna go see Sergeant Hibbett."

"Better do like my brother says."

Hoffman scrambled to his feet holding his jaw, wavering uncertainly.

"Get moving." Clayton addressed the group of five church women, "You ladies alright?"

"Why, yes thank you Clayton. It's about time somebody did something about the riff raff in this town. People like that give Maskek a bad name," Iris told him. "I hope Sergeant Hibbett will keep them locked up for a long time."

"I'm sure he will, ma'am."

"He ought to do something about that young ranger and Kathy Morgan too," Rita added. "That's almost as bad as those hooligans."

Lucan strode over to the door and touched Deacon's arm, "Why didn't you let me take him?"

"Because you would have been the one in trouble for pulling a knife on an unarmed man, wouldn't you?"

Blowing air through his lips, Lucan said, "You'd have done it."

"Yeah, and I'd have been in deep water. No way we can win cousin you know that."

Iris directed her attention to Deacon, "Spirit of the Wind...that's what we have to call you now isn't it, how is your mother? I haven't seen her around town at all. We wondered if she and Mrs. Rykker might like to help with the church bazaar as they have in the past."

"They've been in here for the last two weeks asking about your mom," Stanley told him.

"Momma and Aunt Rona are fine, thank you. I don't know about the church bazaar you'd have to speak with them."

"I expect they're kept busy up there in the village, perhaps we'll catch them later. Give them both my regards."

"Yes ma'am."

"Oh, he's such a sweet boy. To think we once believed Mrs. Pierce wouldn't be able to handle him. It's no easy job raising an Indian child, you know. Do you remember the first time Mrs. Pierce bought him to town? He was so cute and so shy and completely wild. I thought she would never be able to raise him properly."

"He's still completely wild. In fact, I think he's worse now than he was then. Now Stanley, he's a real gentleman. He could teach our men folk a thing or too... What are we going to do about Kathy and Tyrell?"

Waving at Stanley and Lucan as they left the coffee shop, pushing Ryan Hoffman and companions before them, Deacon mouthed, "Church bazaar?"

"What about that? Better hope they don't rope us in too."

CHAPTER FIFTY-TWO

"What did you do with Hoffman?" Ross asked as they caught up with Clayton and Deacon in Stanley's coffee house, after school.

"Handed them over to Abel Cain," Deacon told them. "They're gonna be his guests for awhile."

"Hoffman's in the hoosegow?" Bobby said with a look of glee in his grey eyes, "best place for him. At least it'll keep him and those idiot friends of his off the street for awhile. I figured by now that he'd have got over his dislike of you, it's not like you're at school anymore. Hardly a day went by when he didn't have a go at you, one way or the other. Got a question for you Spirit of the Wind, been meaning to ask you before. Do any of the warriors have first names, apart from Pakito and Reno?"

"You mean like white man's name? Yeah, but they don't use them. Why?"

"Just curious is all. "

"You guys still on duty?" Ross wanted to know.

"Nope, we just finished," Clayton told him. "We're waiting for my mom and Deke's momma so we can escort them back to the village. May as well stay awhile we won't be leaving yet."

Pulling up two chairs Ross and Bobby joined them around the last empty table. All the booths were taken. "Sure is busy here," Ross said glancing around the crowded coffee house. "Stanley must be making a mint. I see Night Horse is working today. What does his wife Yellow Hair get up to while he's in town?"

"Probably stays in the tipi and waits for him to come home like any good Indian wife should," Melissa replied acidly as she and Leona walked through the door.

"What the hell, Melissa," Bobby said angrily, "there's no call for that."

Spirit of the Wind chose to ignore her vehemence. He knew she was still hurting. It would take time for her to adjust and to accept that he and Thorn Rose were together.

"Your momma's on the way." Leona told him, "we just saw her with Mrs. Rykker."

While she was speaking Nonie and Rona came through the door, spied their sons and joined them at the table. Deacon pulled up a chair for both of them.

"Are we having coffee before we go?" Nonie asked.

"Sure, we got time."

"I already got it brewing," Stanley Cuthand said before his cousin could ask, "and choke cherry pie. I'm all out of blueberry."

"That'll do nicely, Stanley, thank you," Nonie replied.

"I godda pee I'll be right back," Deacon told her.

"Do they still go everywhere together, Mrs. Pierce?" Leona asked as Clayton disappeared along with Deacon.

She smiled, "All the time. Don't you know they're joined at the hip?"

"And at the heart," Rona responded.

"We really miss them at school it's just not the same. In fact it's boring. No cute guys to slather over..."

"You know why it's busy don't you," Bobby said in answer to Ross's earlier comment, "it's because Deacon is here. Haven't you noticed how every time he comes the place fills up with women like they've got a sixth sense or something?"

"Nothing new there then."

"It's charisma. Don't you remember what Mrs. Simpson told Doctor Lodge while we were at her party? She said Deacon was a charismatic enigma."

"Perhaps they're just curious," Leona dared suggest.

The look they threw her knocked that suggestion right on its head.

From out of nowhere four ladies of varying age descended upon the table and with beaming smiles clustered around Nonie. "Nonie Pierce. We've finally pinned you down."

Glancing over her shoulder in surprise, Nonie saw a familiar, expensively dressed brunette in her early fifties, accompanied by three younger women. Despite the intervening years Nonie recognised her immediately. A few of the local women looked the newcomers up and down with a mixture of curiosity and disdain, some making waspish remarks.

"Ilona, I haven't seen you for a long time. What brings you back to Maskek? This is my friend, Rona." Turning to Clayton's mother she said, "Ilona was a regular visitor to Jonathan's home, she used to attend all his parties. She couldn't stay away from him."

"Pleased to meet you, Rona," Ilona replied offering a well-manicured hand. "It's been nineteen years since we last spoke Nonie and almost nineteen years since we lost Jonathan. We're here on a trip down memory lane. I was hoping to look you up until I remembered I had no idea where you lived. I asked around until I found someone who knew you, she said you might be in here. You haven't met my niece, Carolina." She bought forward a very bored looking girl in her early twenties, the youngest of the three ladies. Unlike her elegantly dressed aunt, Carolina was built on the biggish side and wearing garishly pink jeans and a flowing floral blouse of green silk, her expression said she would rather be anywhere than here. "You remember Corrina and Melody, don't you?" The two remaining women clustered forward and threw their arms around Nonie's neck.

Along with Ilona and the late Victoria, Jonathan's live in girlfriend these women were the forerunners of Jonathan's 'fan club'; scratching, clawing and squabbling as they vied for his attention.

"Guess that calls for more drinks," Stanley said placing the coffee and pie on the table.

Nonie introduced Stanley. "Ilona, I'd like you to meet Stanley Cuthand. He owns the coffee shop."

"Pleased to make your acquaintance, ma'am," Cut hand replied politely.

"Oh, you're cute, Stanley. Why don't you come a little closer?" With a quick glance in Nonie's direction Stanley high tailed it back to the kitchen.

"Let him alone, Ilona he's already spoken for."

"That's a shame. Can we join you, we've got so much to catch up on?"

Bobby and Ross managed to locate the last four empty chairs and fitted them snugly around the already bulging table.

"Am I gonna need a pack mule or a dog sleigh to carry your stuff home?" Deacon asked when he and Clayton reappeared.

Startled by a familiar accent last heard years before and a face etched forever in her memory, Ilona turned to Deacon her heart drumming furiously. "Is it really you Jonathan? We heard you were killed in the fire. Surely you can't be alive. I should be shocked but I'm not at least, I don't think I am. If a thing is too good to be true then it probably isn't. I'm wittering, aren't I? I don't know what to say..."

Stunned into silence Corrina and Melody stared right at him, unable to comprehend. All these years they believed Jonathan to be deceased. The second shockwave hit even harder when Nonie said, "He's not Jonathan, Ilona."

Mouth open like a dead fish, Ilona finally managed to gather her shattered wits. "Oh my goodness, you must be Spirit of the Wind, Jonathan's baby son. You have his face."

Speechless for the moment Deacon stared back at her.

"Yes, ma'am he is," Clayton answered when it became clear his friend wasn't about to.

"Jonathan's baby son, are you sure?" Corrina asked doubtfully. "The last time we saw him he was only six months old."

"That was eighteen years ago, Corrina," Nonie replied. "After Jonathan died, I took Spirit of the Wind back to his grandmother's village. When he was six years old, I adopted him. He's my son now."

Her jaw sagging like an empty purse Ilona shifted her gaze to the women who accompanied her and saw the same shock and confusion registered in their eyes, except for her niece. Carolina's bored expression had grown into a full scale assault on the young man named Spirit of the Wind. Her eyes were roaming his body as diligently as an eagle scours the earth. "He's some baby."

Deacon had not yet sat down and Carolina's prying eyes were devouring every inch, every muscle, and every bulge inside his ranger's uniform pants. Even down to where he had not completely closed his zipper.

"Seen enough?" Deacon asked, grinning.

Carolina pointed to his partially open zipper. "You were showing."

"You were looking."

"I guess I was," her face broke into a pretty smile.

"She couldn't help it," Corrina mumbled feeling weak at the knees, "How could she not look? We were always looking at Jonathan. Just because we're older it doesn't mean we have to stop looking." While she was speaking, Corrina crept behind Spirit of the Wind and took his long hair in her hands. "Your hair is so beautiful just like your father's was."

"That'll do it every time," Clayton chuckled, "touch his hair and he'll be yours forever."

Breaking into a devastating smile, Deacon said, "You'd know, of course."

"I can vouch for it," Clayton grinned.

"Spirit of the Wind this is Ilona. I told you about her last year when we were talking about your father. The lady with her hands in your hair is called Corrina and the young girl mesmerised by your body is Carolina. Ilona this is Rona's son, Clayton."

"And I'm Melody," the third woman replied not wishing to be left out.

Deacon studied the three older women, he didn't know much about fashion or clothing but the lady called Ilona was wearing an expensive outfit of pale blue silk, with shoes to match—not the kind of outfit you would expect to find in Lola's Trading Post. Her hair was immaculate her face heavy with too much make up. The two women with her were dressed stylishly though more conservatively, definitely not the type of thing you'd find in a small backwater town like Maskek. Shaking her head Nonie studied the faces of the women who had once been her friends more to be around Jonathan than anything. In less than five minutes they'd singled out his son and were converging on him the way they had his father. Turning to Rona in despair, Nonie caught a glimpse of Eliza emerging through the doorway.

"I thought you might need some help, Nonie," Eliza said when she reached the table. "Lola told me Ilona was looking for you. They came over to the trading post asking questions." Going directly to Deacon, Eliza took his face between her fingers and kissed him just as she had when he was a baby.

"Eliza."

Glaring at Eliza with suspicion, Ilona asked "How long have you known he was Jonathan's son?"

"I was there, remember? I prepared all those scintillating meals for Jonathan's dinner parties. But I was only domestic staff. Unlike Lupin, you considered yourself to be above me. Jonathan and Lupin saw me as an equal just as his son does now." Holding her arms out to Deacon she said, "Come and give me a big hug, love." Glancing at Ilona over Deacon's shoulder Eliza said, "He's the Chief of the Native village now."

"He's a chief?" Melody and Corrina chorused, "how fantastic."

"Wow! A real life Indian chief," Carolina cried her eyes bulging, "I didn't think there was any such thing in this day and age. That's amazing, I'd like to hear more about you."

Watching him hugging Eliza, Ilona felt the first stab of jealousy as she had when other women, including Lupin, had kissed Jonathan. "Well I suppose we should be grateful you're not Victoria."

"She died along with Jonathan."

"I know that, Nonie and I'm delighted, selfish bitch she was. Even before Lupin died, Victoria set her sights on Jonathan. She told me all along she had plans for their future together. Our parents were friends so we were expected to be friends. I hated Victoria, I'm delighted she's dead. It wouldn't surprise me if she had a hand in Lupin's death..."

Not liking the way the situation was turning, Deacon waved to Stanley.

"Hold off on the coffee Night Horse, I think they're leaving," Stanley said.

"Momma, we will go now." It was not a question.

Rising from the chair Nonie told her, "It's time for us to leave, Ilona. If you're staying in town, I'll catch up with you."

"We're staying at the Tamarack Motel. Why are you going so soon, we've got such a lot to talk about?"

Rounding on her aunt, Carolina said, "It might have something to do with what you said about Victoria and Lupin. Didn't you see Spirit of the Wind's face? I don't think he was very happy."

"Why should it bother him he didn't know Victoria."

"No, but you told me Lupin was his mother."

Ignoring her niece, Ilona directed the next question to Deacon, "Why does Nonie have to go?"

"This is no time to open old wounds."

"In other words, auntie, keep a civil tongue in your head."

"Mind your manners, girl. Where are you living, Nonie?"

"We're living in Talulah's village. Next time Spirit of the Wind or one of the other young men can bring me in I'll meet you and we'll go to our old house. We can talk there."

"Can't he go home on his own, he's a big boy?" Ilona said, aware that the patrons of the coffee house were watching them curiously.

"He can but we can't. He's forbidden any of the women to come here unescorted it, isn't safe. He's the Chief and that's that. I will be in touch."

"Well!" Ilona snorted disgustedly.

CHAPTER FIFTY-THREE

"Is it wise for you to show yourself in town, Jonathan?" Damien asked as they sat their ponies by the holding corral on the edge of Maskek. "You said it could have repercussions for your son."

"I know what I said, Damien. I've waited eighteen years for the chance to walk by my son's side I'll wait no longer."

Letting their ponies into the corral, Jonathan and Damien made their way into town.

Not only was the corral used to keep horses or any other livestock out of harm's way avoiding incidents like the one at the high school recently, it was also a meeting place for the town's youth away from the prying eyes of their parents and a dance floor during the social events of the summer. It was also used when the annual rodeo came to town.

"There they are," Jonathan said pointing to Clayton and Spirit of the Wind, along with four members of the Cree police. They were just leaving Sergeant Hibbett's office.

"You're even dressed the same," Damien remarked appraising Jonathan from head to toe. Both he and Spirit of the Wind were wearing black jeans and almost identical shirts of turquoise. "How will they tell you apart?"

Grinning, Jonathan said, "Spirit of the Wind hardly ever fastens his shirt up. Clayton told me it became his trade mark at school much to the teachers' discontent. It's not a problem."

"He's far too much Indian for today. If he'd been born one hundred and fifty years ago, he'd be a war chief by now. He's out of time."

"He's in perfect harmony with his grandmother. They work well together. And he's exactly as Lupin and I wanted him to be."

Today was Saturday and the main street was busy with early

vacationers making the most of a quiet time. In June the town would be heaving with campers, hikers and day tripping visitors attracted by the splendour of the forest and the serenity of the lake and rivers.

Stepping up behind him Jonathan touched his son on the shoulder. Deacon spun around, knife in hand.

"Whoa!" Jonathan said, "you're fast I'll give you that."

"Need to be. Why are you here? Thought you didn't wanna be seen with me?"

"You're my son I want to show you off as I did when you were a child.

"You said it wouldn't be safe for you to come into Maskek."

"Maybe not, but I'm willing to take the chance. Are you?"

"I am."

Further talk was suspended as Leona and Melissa came running over. Leona was the first to speak. "Spirit of the Wind, we were talking to Captain McNally earlier today..."

Almost identical, father and son turned to face the girls. Leona's mouth flapped open as if her jaw had suddenly become unhinged. Stands-in-Timber caught Melissa as she swayed with shock. When Leona had fully recovered, she said, "There are two of you. Which one is Spirit of the Wind?"

Melissa appeared to be on the verge of a nervous breakdown.

"Leona, this is my father, Sparkling Eyes."

Regaining her sanity for the second time Leona said, "Your father? He's dead, isn't he?"

"For someone who supposed to be dead he's looking pretty good."

"Leona," Jonathan acknowledged. He nodded toward Melissa.

Despite the initial shock of seeing two 'Deacons,' Leona's wicked eyes betrayed her drawing her gaze to and below Jonathan's belt buckle. Feeling Spirit of the Wind grinning knowingly at her she quickly shifted her gaze to Jonathan's face. God he was gorgeous. Everything about him shouted sex." Wow! I'm not even going to ask how this miracle came about."

"That's good," Clayton answered, "because it's too damn complicated."

"You knew and you didn't tell us?" she asked accusingly.

"I only recently found out, I..."

"Don't. Don't say another word."

Stands-in-Timber lowered Melissa to the sidewalk. She was staring directly at Jonathan Sparkling Eyes. "If I can't have Deacon, can I have him?"

"Clayton, Spirit of the Wind," Graph called from across the street, "You'd better come quick there's a posse of vigilantes meeting in the church...."

Clayton stared at an agitated Graph in disbelief, "Vigilantes?

"Yeah, all hell's gonna break loose any minute. I tried to reach Captain McNally but no one's answering the radio or the phone. Iris Mayall, Rita Brewster and the women of the church are firing up a crowd to seek out Kathy Morgan and Tyrell McAllister. They're head hunting."

With a swift glance in Clayton's direction, Spirit of the Wind headed across the street. The Cree police, Jonathan and Damien followed them.

"Maybe we should get Sergeant Hibbett," Clayton suggested.

"We should go see."

Inside the church Rita and Iris were inciting a riot demanding that something be done about Ranger Tyrell McAllister and Kathy Morgan. Waving placards proclaiming 'cradle snatcher' and 'scarlet woman', the ladies of the church were marching up and down the aisle as if they were soldiers on a drilling squad.

"Jesus," Clayton said. He could hear the noise at the end of the street. "Guess we'd better take a look."

The moment Spirit of the Wind opened the door Iris and Rita flew at him. "Just the person we want. Where is Tyrell?"

Backing off slightly, he replied, "On duty as far as we know."

"And Captain McNally, where is he?" Iris demanded.

"I don't know, ma'am."

"Then you will have to do. Kathy Morgan is far too mature to be courting Tyrell McAllister, it's nothing short of cradle snatching. Why, she's old enough to be his mother. Maskek is a good, clean living town we will not tolerate scandal of this kind. Tyrell is a ranger—Captain

McNally's second in command or whatever you call him, working in a professional capacity. His behaviour is most unprofessional. And to think we trust our lives and the lives of our children to such a man? Well it's just not acceptable."

The hyped-up crowd of pious men and women nodded in agreement, muttering between themselves.

"Why hasn't Captain McNally brought this matter to Tyrell's attention?" Rita asked.

"Shouldn't you be speaking to Tyrell?" Deacon said.

"And tell him what? That the townsfolk don't approve of his love life?

"Captain McNally already knows that, ma'am. What Tyrell does with his personal life has nothing to do with anyone else. Think you'll find the Captain feels the same way."

The Cree police watched with amusement and wonder. The ladies of the church and the citizens of Maskek never failed to entertain them with their petty quarrels and high morals, which they believed placed them above the citizens of other towns.

"She's no better than a whore," Rita Brewster said acidly.

Deacon stared at her incredulously. When he spoke, there was a hard edge to his voice. "There's no call for that, Mrs. Brewster." He turned to Clayton, "Better see if you can get a hold of Tyrell and Captain McNally before these women start a war."

"Rita's right," a bald headed, bespectacled man piped up, "we've got to keep our town free from the temptations of the flesh."

Deacon looked directly at the fellow who was speaking. "Didn't stop you chasing Aurelia Bright Water did it, Riff?" the young Chief pointed out, "and she's half your age."

Caught with his pants down Riff felt his face burning with embarrassment, wishing he could slither under the door. "That was three years ago. How-how did you know about it? She wasn't supposed to say anything."

"Bright Water told grandmother she came to church to see you and you hit on her. When she returned to the encampment her dress was torn and her face and legs were badly bruised. You hurt her. Good thing my grandfather dealt with it, if it had been me you would not now be walking."

"Cool it, Deke," Clayton warned.

"Now just a minute, Spirit of the Wind," Iris argued, "you might be the new Chief but that doesn't give you the right to falsely accuse Riff of improper conduct. Every now and then a man makes mistake for which he asks God's forgiveness. It's in a man's nature to... "

"That what you told your husband when you saw him walking out with Jovielle Brasselet?"

"How dare you!" Iris flew at him, her nails ready to rip his cheek.

Instantly alert, Clayton and the Indian police were at his side.

As Iris went for the young Chief's face, he grabbed her wrist and pushed it away. "Don't."

"Let he who is without sin cast the first stone," Clayton quoted.

"Yeah?" Spirit of the Wind asked.

"Don't you ever read the Bible?"

"Not if I can help it."

"It figures. Let's all calm down and deal with this problem accordingly."

The church door was forced open and three men staggered in, half walking half carrying Kathy Morgan. Struggling against them she was making their lives difficult.

"Let her go," Spirit of the Wind ordered, silencing them immediately.

Shaking his head, Clayton reached for Kathy, "Did they hurt you?"

"Nothing serious, Clayton, thank you. Did you send these morons round to me, Iris? They broke into Mr. Reynard's house as if it were a den of iniquity and scared the poor man half to death." She turned to the three men standing shame faced by the door. "If anything happens to Mr. Reynard after this incident you'll have to answer for it. Three strong men for a little woman like me. What are you afraid of Iris, or is it that I'm an easy target for the bitterness you feel toward your husband? Everybody in town knows about him and that French Canadian girl Jovielle. It's been going on under your nose for months."

Speechless, her face flaming, Iris Mayall fell to her knees. Spirit of the Wind helped her to a pew.

"And you, Mrs. Brewster, you pious cow, hiding under a mantle of respectability. I saw you sneaking into the Wapiti Hills on many occasions, dressed in a black robe."

Now it was the new Chief's turn to be surprised. "You knew she was a disciple of Damien?" He exchanged glances with his father. Deacon found out last year that Rita Brewster was indeed a member of Damien's disciples. He was amazed that anyone else knew of her nocturnal activities. She had kept it quiet for many years. The women of the church turned startled eyes on her staggered by Kathy Morgan's accusation.

"Indeed, I do. Rita threw caution to the wind when she tripped off to join in the debauchery that followed those gatherings. Before you ask me, I'll tell you how I know. About thirty-five years ago Rita disappeared. Her husband claimed she was visiting sick relatives over in Edmonton. Not long after Rita disappeared, I left Maskek and went to work at a private clinic. I was nursing there when Mrs. Brewster came to us. She was three months pregnant but she looked to be about seven months. She was having a tough time of it and kept having to be admitted for rest and special care. The thing in her uterus was living off her, killing her. It was growing far too rapidly..."

Rita looked on horror stricken it would be pointless to deny it. "My husband sent me away so nobody would find out. I couldn't stay here a woman of the church, pregnant with another man's child. My age alone would have aroused suspicion. But I didn't join in the debauchery, I was chosen. That's what they do..."

Kathy continued with her story. "On the night the child was born, Rita went into labour lasting thirty-six hours. We managed to save her but the child, if that's what it was, didn't survive."

"A demon child," Jonathan said, "and it did survive."

"It couldn't have. We threw it out, it was dead."

"Or was it that you left him for dead? His father's his name was Spotted Elk."

"A native demon, are there such things?"

"Demons come from all walks of life and all nations. They are everywhere. Most human mothers die in childbirth, particularly the older ones, that is why a woman of mature years is chosen. If the demon child lives, he will never know his mother and will not be tempted to turn from that which he is destined for."

Shocked to the core the congregation in the little church focused on Jonathan and what he had just revealed. So was it true? Many of them immediately identified him, their thoughts racing back to the speculation and accusations that in the past he had been involved with the occult. In the quietude that followed a leaf could be heard to fall.

"My son survived?" Rita asked her eyes accusing. "He was my child born of my flesh why did you let him die?" Her eyes clouding with tears Rita stumbled. Deacon caught her and held her against his chest.

"He was an abomination not even human," Kathy told her. Appalled though she was with Jonathan Sparkling Eyes' revelation, Kathy went on with her story. "The demon Rita had sex with, for it was nothing more than that, was a young man of twenty-five around the same age as Tyrell McAllister. Rita told me that after the consummation he wanted nothing more to do with her. A scorned and rejected woman can become very bitter. Did you think I'd forgotten, Rita? Anything as hideous as that creature could never be forgotten."

"He was my child you had no right."

"The demon child did not die immediately it was cast aside and left for dead," Jonathan explained. "His father Spotted Elk sensed his cries, felt his pain. He was found and returned to us and lived. Children of demons grow very quickly. He became a strong and compelling force among the disciples."

"Thundercloud," Deacon said. He knew it without being told.

Jonathan nodded, "Thundercloud—death hand. You killed him."

Not a sound escaped anybody's lips. The room was silent except for Rita Brewster weeping against Deacon's chest.

Jonathan spoke again. "There were many off springs born to the disciples. Some of them were human, most were not. The human ones live among you, they appear to be no different than anyone else. You would not know...

Everybody turned to look as the church door was thrown open a second time. Tyrell McAllister, Sergeant Hibbett and Constable Hayes stood in the doorway.

"I've just had a very distressed gentleman in my office," Hibbett told the assembled congregation, "Something about three men grabbing Miss Morgan against her will?"

"Are you alright, Kathy?" Tyrell asked striding quickly over to her. "They didn't harm you? Sergeant Hibbett managed to get hold of me."

"I don't think that was their intention. Rita and Iris are the guilty parties here along with the other Christian women of the church," Kathy replied scathingly.

Sergeant Hibbett scoured the congregation, his seething gaze coming to rest on the discarded placards thrown to the floor.

"Well, I guess I'm just going to have to charge you ladies with inciting a riot. Tyrell, take Miss Morgan out of here. Spirit of the Wind, Clayton and the elite give me a hand. Round up all the men and anyone else who saw fit to take part in this ridiculous charade. Burn those placards. Start walking, ladies."

"I guess this means that Tyrell and Kathy are still on," Clayton said as Tyrell took her hand and led her outside.

Rita Brewster turned to Deacon a look of despair upon her face. "You killed my son?"

"I had no choice he was attacking my mother. When he'd finished with her, he'd have done the same to Clayton's mother. There was nothing else I could do. I didn't know he was your son. You were in the coffee house when he appeared. He was speaking through you. I told him then if he harmed my family, I would kill him."

"I don't remember coming in here..."

"It is better that you don't remember."

CHAPTER FIFTY-FOUR

On the opposite sidewalk three men in late middle age stood in the doorway of the Trading Post each holding a rifle, watching the exchange with deep interest. The attention of the ever curious population of Mas kek was drawn toward the Cree police hanging around the RCMP's office, after depositing a large number of the town's most respectable citizens in the cell block at the back of building.

All heads turned as Virgil McNally pulled up in the land rover. Rolling down the window he smiled with recognition. "Jonathan. Goddamn it's a long time since I saw you."

"It's good to see you, Virgil," Jonathan replied taking the ranger's extended hand. "You made captain, I see."

"Someone's godda keep these unruly rangers in check."

"That's him. That's Jonathan Hare. He's the one that turned my wife against me," the eldest of the three men sneered. "Got an invite to one of his parties. Next thing I know my wife's all over him and he's taking up with her..."

"Hold on, Isaac that's the new Chief," his companion said.

"I don't mean the new Chief. The other one is Jonathan, the boy's father. He's the one took her. They might look alike but once you've met Jonathan you never forget him." The more he thought about it and the longer Jonathan stood talking to Virgil, the more enraged he was becoming. "I'm going to kill him Gene I swear..."

"Simmer down, Isaac you can't just go around threatening folk. They're right outside Hibbett's office, anyhow you'd never get away with it. I know you lost your wife and you're still grieving but is it worth screwing up your life? Did Marsha really go off with him or was there another reason? The two of you hadn't been getting along for a while you sure it wasn't anything to do with that?"

"It wasn't that at all. Marsha kept going over to the Longhouse, telling me she was visiting Eliza. One night she didn't come home, folks said they'd been seen together, my wife and Jonathan."

"You shouldn't believe everything you hear, not in this town, they all have poisonous tongues. Did you actually see them together? That was a long time ago, Isaac. It's dead and buried let it lie." Nodding to the third fellow standing with them Gene crossed over the street.

"I won't be cheated," Isaac hissed to anyone listening. No one was. They were all much too interested in what was happening at Sergeant Hibbett's office. Bringing up the rifle he cocked it.

Always alert especially when he was in town, Spirit of the Wind caught a glimpse of sun light on Isaac's rifle, it was trained directly on his father's back. Before Isaac eased back the trigger, he felt the wind cast by the new Chief's bowie knife as it whistled passed his head, ending its flight in the wooden door. The young Chief was on him instantly. Snatching the rifle from Isaac's hands he threw it aside. The look in his eyes was enough to calm the hardest of men. "There will be no shooting."

Jonathan spun round just as Deacon's knife pierced the door. He recognised Isaac immediately. "Guess you're still mad at me, huh."

Having followed them from the coffee house, Leona was astonished by how much like Deacon he sounded

"You want I should kiss your ass? You stole my wife you damned savage."

Spirit of the Wind's searing glance silenced further racial outbursts. Retrieving his knife from the wounded door he replaced it in its sheath and waited.

"You ruined my life, Jonathan," Isaac protested, "and that kid of yours is set to do the same. I've seen the way my granddaughter looks at him, she's been dewy eyed over him all through high school. I deserve to know why my wife turned against me, before my granddaughter does the same."

"Then I will tell you. When Marsha came to my house, I was alone. She told me she was looking for a way to leave you but in the style to which she had become accustomed. She believed that I could provide her with that lifestyle. She told me that if she had walked out on you, she would have lost everything."

"That was part of our arrangement."

"We talked for many hours, I agreed to let her stay for what was left of the night. She was to have returned to you in the morning. I tried to make it clear to her that I was not interested in a relationship with her but that she was welcome in my home when others came to visit."

"What did you talk about?"

"Mostly how dissatisfied she was with the 'arrangement' and how she didn't love you anymore."

"That wasn't any of your damn business."

"She needed to talk and I was happy to listen..."

"You didn't want any commitment yet you were real happy to listen to her and accept her favours. I'll bet she heaped them on you every time she claimed to be visiting Eliza, like they were the best of friends. I knew how Marsha felt about you. She talked about you all the time. She couldn't wait for the next invitation. She was smitten like so many other women. Goddamn it, Jonathan, even men wanted to be around you. I guess your lover Damien would've seen them off. Never could understand why an Indian attracted so much attention from so many women or what it was about you that compelled them. What did you do to my wife the night she didn't come home? Did you take her to bed, help her to realise her fantasies, promise her you'd love her forever? Whatever it was it must have been pretty fantastic."

Spirit of the Wind anxiously awaited his father's response. Although they had spoken about his past, they still had a long route to travel. Every time he thought he was getting closer to the truth Jonathan ended their discussion. What seemed like the entire town although it probably wasn't, were standing around listening to the two men as if they were discussing a summer picnic.

"I took her to bed and left her there, but not without a fight. She was a determined woman. She took some subduing."

"Did you hurt her?"

"Of course I didn't hurt her. Goddamn it, Isaac, I don't rough up women."

Startled, Clayton stared at Jonathan. He remembered hearing

Deacon use those exact words when the recently demoted Sergeant McCready had accused him of hitting a female guest at Emily Simpson's party last year, to which he, Deacon and four other students had been invited. Apart from the obvious in the looks department it was uncanny how much alike they were.

"I'm well aware of how she felt about me, Isaac."

"You've had dozens of women, Jonathan that's one thing you can't deny."

"I'm not denying it. None of them were married, Marsha was. I drove her to your place later in the day then I returned home. I believed she was coming back to you. If she did not then..." he gestured helplessly, "I don't know..."

"You expect me to believe that?" If Isaac had fur it would be standing on end.

Exhaling exasperatedly, Jonathan said, "That's up to you. I have spoken the truth."

"Hold on, Jonathan. How did she find the money to get away from me? Did you give it to her?"

"I have no idea, Isaac." Turning to his son he asked, "Where is your mother?"

"Where'd you get your money from, Jonathan?" Isaac snarled. "How'd you come by all the land you own? Never come across an Indian yet had a dollar to his name. Steal it did you, kill innocent folks then steal it?"

"If I did steal it, I was only doing to your people what your people have been doing to mine for three hundred years. How I acquired it is my business. I've told you what happened with Marsha there's nothing more to say."

"Still can't figure out what is it captivates women around him," Deacon told Clayton.

Peering at his best friend, Clayton said, "Oh no? Taken a look at yourself lately Deacon? You oughta look in the mirror once in a while."

"Spirit of the Wind, where is your mother?" Jonathan repeated.

"In the coffee house she's meeting us there."

Inclining his head Jonathan waved the Indians forward. "We'll go there. Catch you later, Virgil."

"Sure, Jonathan, look forward to it." Nudging Isaac he said, "Pick up your rifle, Isaac go on home and forget about it. Thirty years is a long time to hold a grudge." Virgil pushed him in the direction of his home.

Open mouthed, Melissa and Leona watched them leave. "He can take me to bed anytime," Leona said.

"He is Spirit of the Wind's father."

"Don't sound so shocked. I saw you eyeing him up and down and more down than up."

"Like you weren't doing the same?" Melissa said leaning into her friend's face. "I saw him first."

"I was the one," Leona insisted, stabbing her finger into her chest, "He spoke to me."

Waiting until Jonathan and Isaac were out of earshot, Vigil approached Damien, "I think you know what happened to Marsha."

"Are you certain of that?" the Englishman asked.

"I'm dead certain. Where is she, did you kill her?"

CHAPTER FIFTY-FIVE

"Your momma left about half an hour ago," Stanley Cuthand told Spirit of the Wind. "They were heading for your house." He shook his head woefully, "All those women together it's asking for trouble."

"Ain't that a fact," Clayton drawled.

"Who went with them? They shouldn't be going anywhere without one of us to escort them."

"Lame Deer took her, he took all of them. I think you've drilled it into her that she shouldn't be alone. Sparkling Eyes, it's good to see you. Lucan told me he'd spoken to you."

"It's been awhile, Stanley. The last time I saw you, you were sixteen. You have done well for yourself."

"It was a lot of hard work but it was worth it in the end. Why should the white guys have all the fun? Guess you won't be staying for coffee, then."

~ * ~

Retrieving their ponies, Jonathan minus Damien, joined Spirit of the Wind, Clayton and Lone Wolf who were also on horseback and rode slowly along the main street. The other three members of the Indian Police remained in town.

The ever inquisitive and now extremely astonished population of Maskek, watched their progress. Staggered by Jonathan Hare's re-appearance those who remembered him from two decades ago, were intrigued as to how he'd returned from the dead. They had long since adjusted to the shock of seeing Deacon's likeness to his father, as he was growing up and the realisation of whom he was. Jonathan's presence was another matter entirely.

"Could be something in that occult stuff," one of them said with an air of nonchalance.

"And just maybe he never died at all," his neighbour replied, "just needed to hide away while everything died down." The townsfolk watched the riders until they turned off Main Street and on to Loon Lake trail.

~ * ~

Nearing the lake where Rona and Clayton's previous house still stood, the small band of riders continued onward until they reached Nonie and Deacon's former home.

"Got visitors," Clayton commented noticing the car rental sitting outside the porch, "and it ain't the ladies from the church. Guess your momma must've finalised the arrangements for the bazaar."

"As long it doesn't include us," Deacon said.

Inside the house, Carolina asked Nonie, "Why are there so many horses. I've never seen so many horses in one town, it's like something out of the movies."

"Because this area is so heavily forested, the lake and the rivers are difficult to reach by any other means. Beyond this house Loon Lake trail becomes a dirt track and fades out altogether. It's unsuitable and far too narrow for any kind of vehicle. Much of the land here is muskeg, it can only be negotiated by surefooted horses, hence the name Maskek."

Deacon was first onto the porch and through the door.

"We came home when the trouble in the church started," Nonie told him. "Lame Deer came with us." Lounging at the back of the room away from the lady visitors, Lame Deer respectfully lowered his head.

"What brings you back so soon?" Nonie asked suspiciously.

"Somebody wishes to see you." When he looked up four pairs of adoring eyes stared at him. "Whoa." Turning to warn his father he was too late as Jonathan stepped into the room and four pairs of eyes darted toward him. A shattering silence descended on the house until Ilona cried out excitedly, "Jonathan, oh my God, Jonathan! Why didn't you tell us Nonie?"

310

Within seconds he was surrounded by Ilona, Corrina and Melody, "Darling Jonathan." So enraptured were they, they failed to notice his youthful looks. It hadn't occurred to them they had aged and he had not.

Totally confused, Carolina looked to Nonie for an explanation.

"He's the man they all came to mourn."

Untangling himself from the three hungry women Jonathan grinned boyishly, "Nice to see you ladies."

"What is going on?" Melody asked, "we were told you were dead."

"All I can say is don't believe everything you hear." He tried to reach Nonie and was promptly ambushed a second time by his onetime admirers, who flung themselves at him outrageously.

"Oka-a-y," Deacon said as his father was forced into a chair by thee rampant, middle aged women, "I guess that explains it. You've seen this before, Lone Wolf?"

"Too many times to recall," Lone Wolf replied beaming all over his face, "I was much younger then."

"My mother, how did she feel about it?"

"Lupin knew how deeply he loved her she didn't see other women as a threat. Your grandmother said he was never unfaithful to her in spite of all the women. Before he met her..." Lone Wolf spread his hands and shrugged, "I couldn't say."

Leaning over the back of the couch his arms resting on his mother's shoulders, Clayton said, "I had to see it to believe it."

"Jonathan is still quite a catch," Rona answered. "Not surprising that Deacon turned out the way he did."

"Yeah, but Deke's not a womaniser. I can't imagine Thorn Rose allowing it anyway. I don't know, mom it's crazy."

"Spirit of the Wind, will you please pull them off your father."

"Hell, momma, it don't seem to be bothering him any." The look Nonie gave him urged him to reconsider.

"Enough!" he commanded. Amazingly his authoritative tone had the desired effect as one by one the women released Jonathan and composed themselves.

"Way to go, Spirit of the Wind," Clayton whispered.

"Thank you," Nonie kissed Deacon and gave her attention to Jonathan. "I want to talk to you."

"Yes ma'am," he smiled disarmingly following her into the kitchen. He looked like a little boy who'd been caught stealing the neighbour's cat.

Shutting the door Nonie pushed him up against the sink. "What's the idea of showing up in town, you were supposed to remain anonymous? Now that Ilona has seen you the entire world will know of your presence. How is that going to help your son?"

"I was wrong Nonie, I believe everything will work out. I want to spend time with my son. Give me one good reason why I should continue to deny him?"

"Ilona."

"I didn't know she was here. I'll handle Ilona."

"Didn't you notice the rented car? Surely that should have got you thinking."

"Clayton mentioned it. I didn't think it was of any importance."

"You didn't think at all."

"Maybe I didn't. But I'm here now and I'm gonna stay awhile."

"Jonathan..." Nonie started to protest.

"Nonie..." Closing in he pulled her into his arms. His lips urgently seeking hers Jonathan walked her over to the kitchen door, leaned his back against it and moved his body up against hers. She was a little shocked but delighted to feel his solid erection. Ever since he'd appeared out of the blue after the destruction of the Unthinkable, she wanted to touch him, to taste him just as she had before the incident at the Longhouse. While he slept, she wanted desperately to crawl into his blanket and lie beside him. She wanted to hold him in her arms and caress his body, as strong and muscular as it had been before the onset of old age induced by the demon had debilitated him. For her son's sake she'd resisted. Now it didn't matter, Jonathan was here she desired him and she would have him. The fact that Ilona, Melody and Corrina were sitting just beyond the door enhanced her feelings and excited her more. Right under their noses she allowed him to take her.

Intending to see to the horses Deacon paused, his hand on the door handle. He and his mother were so close that as she surrendered to Jonathan, he didn't need any visions to explain the piercing pain in his heart.

Lone Wolf saw and comforted him. "It is to be expected. I'm surprised it took so long, for she has always loved your father. This does not mean she loves you any less."

"I know Lone Wolf, I just didn't expect it at, least not yet. I don't know what made me think it would be any different, it was me who wanted them to be together. I..." he exhaled slowly, "I'll go tend the horses."

"I warned him," Clayton told Lone Wolf.

"He needs time to adjust he'll be alright. He isn't the first teenager to resent his mother's interest in another man...even if that man does happen to be his father."

"Yeah, father in name only."

Lone Wolf peered into Clayton's eyes, "Not completely, Clayton White Hawk they are trying."

Shuffling his feet Clayton stared at the floor. "I guess you're right. Just 'cos my pa and I can't get along, doesn't mean they won't. I'll go give him a hand with the horses."

"You're not leaving me alone with these feuding women I'm coming with you."

"What are Jonathan and Nonie doing in the kitchen?" Ilona wanted to know. "They're taking a long time. Perhaps we should see if everything is alright."

Rona was about to speak when Ilona's niece Carolina butted in, "It's nothing to do with you, auntie, or with Corrina or Melody. They'll come out eventually. This is Mrs. Pierce's house. Sit and talk among yourselves until she comes back." Carolina stood and headed for the door.

"Where do you think you're going?"

"To talk to Spirit of the Wind, I prefer his company and I want to ask him about that magnificent black horse I saw him riding."

"Did you know Nonie had adopted Jonathan's son?" Corrina asked Eliza.

In the hope of keeping the peace between the three women and

Nonie, Eliza drove out to the house with them. She parked her car at the back of the house as she always did. Now she waited expectantly. "I lost touch with Nonie after the fire. I had no idea whether she and Spirit of the Wind survived and we had no way of finding out. They escaped and she took him back to his grandmother's village. I didn't see her again until six years later when she bought him to live in one of Jonathan's cabins right next to the lake. She turned up on my door step one day with Spirit of the Wind. I was so pleased to see them. Since then we've stayed in touch."

"He seems very fond of you."

Smiling affectionately Eliza replied, "He is. I love him to pieces just as I did when he was a baby."

"If you ask me, you're far too affectionate with him," Ilona said waspishly.

"Nobody asked you. What makes you so special? You're just another of Jonathan's ridiculously wealthy and empty headed admirers."

"How dare you!"

Eliza's hopes of peace were soon dashed when Ilona slapped her hard across her face. "Don't ever talk to me like that, you bitch! You were nothing more than a common cook."

"You haven't changed, Ilona. I thought you might have mellowed with age."

"I'm no older than you are. But I at least I know how to make the most of myself." She eyed Eliza's knee length gingham dress contemptuously. "That style went out with the arc."

"That's not nice, Ilona," Melody piped up, "Not everyone has your money and not everyone wants to look like a walking mannequin from Macy's. You're so made up you can't tell where the makeup ends and you begin. If you smile, you'll crack your face."

Spinning toward Melody, Ilona lashed out at her face, scratching it. She tugged Melody's hair and pulled her downwards, toppling one of the chairs. When Corrina and Rona attempted to separate them, Ilona kicked Corrina in the shin and Melody fell into Eliza knocking her against the sewing table, sending the machine flying. It hit the picture window and landed on the floor. Fortunately, the window remained undamaged.

Temper flaring, Corrina latched onto Ilona punching her in the chest and stomach. Winded and fuming Ilona tackled Corrina. She ripped her nails down Corrina's face and pulled her short hair, yanking her head backwards. Corrina's piercing scream and the sound of toppling furniture sent Deacon sprinting into the house, Lone Wolf, Clayton, Lame Deer who'd followed them outside and Carolina right behind him. Busting through the front door he stopped abruptly appalled by what he was seeing. There was something degenerate and feral about a group of middle-aged women wrestling with each other on the floor, like a bunch of teenagers. At the same moment, Jonathan tucking his shirt into his jeans and Nonie buttoning her dress barged through the kitchen door.

Looking directly at his father Deacon said, "These are you women father, you sort it."

Hanging back while the other women were arguing Rona moved to stand by Nonie's side.

"What happened?" Nonie asked her.

"I'm not sure but I think Ilona started it by insulting Eliza." While she gave Nonie the gist of it, Jonathan tried to calm the battling women. They completely ignored him.

"Jesus Christ," Deacon growled impatiently. He waded into the midst of them and hauled every one of them to one side. "Stop it, now." As if struck by a lightning bolt they turned instantly toward him their previous actions forgotten.

"A lot of help you were," he told Jonathan. Righting the furniture, he lifted the sewing machine and put it back on the table. Next, he gathered up all of their coats and bags and heaped them onto the couch. "Go."

Feeling compelled to speak in their defence, Corrina said, "We're sorry, Spirit of the Wind. Things got a little out of hand. I'm sure we can sort it out if you give us a chance..."

"You will go now."

"We promise to behave if you let us stay."

"I have spoken."

Geared into action by the tone of Deacon's voice Clayton and Lone Wolf assisted the very apologetic ladies with their coats and ushered them outside.

"Come along, Carolina," Ilona called.

Carolina didn't come along. She was staring dreamily into Deacon's face, "You can tell you're the Chief."

"You'd better go, Carolina," Rona told her, "we've had enough trouble for one day."

"I hope to see you soon," she whispered blowing Deacon a kiss.

Deacon turned to his father, "If that's what happens when women fall at your feet, you're welcome to it."

"What can I say?

"Don't say anything."

"I can handle Ilona you said," Nonie told Jonathan glaring at him, "is that what you call handling her? You must be losing your touch, Jonathan."

"Am I to go as well?" Eliza asked.

"You can stay," Deacon said "What was that all about?"

"Just another moment in the lives of women with nothing better to do. They're still fighting yesterday's war. Every time Jonathan held a party certain of his guests almost always came to blows."

"It's crazy, man. Where's Damien?"

"Stayed in town," Clayton responded, "Cap'n McNally had something to say to him."

Taking her son's arm Nonie pulled him aside. "There's something I want to tell you."

"No need to, momma."

"You don't know what I'm going to say."

His black eyes warm with affection he spoke in his own tongue, "You have been with my father. You have touched. It's good."

Peering into her son's eyes she smiled. She knew exactly what he meant. "Now we are a family again."

~ * ~

"I want the truth, Damien...did you kill Isaac's wife?" McNally asked.

"The woman was very persistent. Marsha wanted more than Jonathan was willing to give. She wanted him and his money. It was her intention to have both, by fair means or foul. She wasn't aware his money was tied up in the land. If she'd known that it could have been a different story. After Jonathan dropped her off, I followed her to the house. Isaac wasn't home. I asked her if she would like to take a walk in the forest with me and that Jonathan would be meeting us later. Marsha readily agreed. It was a foul deed. If there ever was a body it was never found."

Virgil tried to read the truth behind Damien's veiled eyes. Marsha may have returned to her home in Lac La Biche but he very much doubted it.

"You sure jealousy wasn't the cause of it, Damien?"

He didn't reply.

Little evidence had been found regarding 'occult related' incidents in the Wapiti Hills over the last two centuries and now it seemed that what had transpired in the depths of the forest thirty years ago, would never be known.

CHAPTER FIFTY-SIX

In the Native encampment Nonie and Jonathan Sparkling Eyes were getting along as if they'd never been apart. Unable to say how long it would be before his wander lust claimed the better of him and he moved on Nonie began to relax, telling herself that after eighteen years she was finally sharing the life she'd dreamed of after Lupin's untimely death.

"Are you happy, Jonathan?"

"How could I not be happy when I have you and I have my son? Lupin still holds my heart but there is much space for you. This is what she wanted."

"I don't expect you ever to forget her. She was my best friend and I loved her. I can live with that."

"One question Nonie, how long is Ilona staying?"

"What, you don't like the attention? That's got to be a first for you."

"She's the past along with all the others. We have a new life now."

"Damien doesn't think so. He wants your relationship to continue the way it always has."

"This is what he told you?"

"He tells me every day. He may have turned over a new leaf, but not every branch bears one."

"Spirit of the Wind and Clayton share their love with each other and with Thorn Rose and Shell Woman. Damien will have to share mine with you just as he did with my wives."

"I suppose if he did before he can again as long as he doesn't hurt you anymore."

"He will not. He and our son seem to have found a mutual respect for one another, therefore he is no longer in any danger from Damien. I will stay with you."

~ * ~

"It's time we went home, Ilona," Melody insisted. "We've hardly seen Nonie or Jonathan." They were idling away the hours in Cuthand's coffee house, "I don't think she wants to see us."

"Can you blame her?" Carolina remarked, "your behaviour at her home was despicable. I'm surprised that Spirit of the Wind didn't force us all to leave town." Her expression became dreamy. "He might have given us an escort all the way home. How exciting is that? Does he have a girlfriend?"

"How would I know," her aunt stated, "he hasn't been particularly welcoming has he? Not at a bit like his father. Jonathan was always a gentleman. No, we are not leaving we're staying for the time being, unless you want to go Melody or you Corrina? I'm quite prepared to wait alone."

"No way am I going," Carolina said, "I want to see Jonathan's son again. I need to know if he has a girlfriend. Clayton might tell me."

~ * ~

Tyrell McAlister sat with his arm around Kathy Morgan, their faces almost touching.

"I never thought I'd meet anybody in Maskek. Nothing happens during the winter and in the summer we're so busy we don't have time to talk to anybody let alone meet them. I can't believe my luck. Why didn't you stay in Edmonton you had a good job there?"

"I'm still a country girl at heart. Maskek is my home, I had to go away to realise it. You either love it or you hate it. I love it."

Tyrell moved in for a kiss. "Do you love me?"

Taking his face between her fingers, she said, "Do you have to ask?" She kissed him full on the lips.

Certain patrons of the coffee house gasped in horror while others smiled knowingly. Stanley Cuthand grinned and nodded, "Go for it, Tyrell."

Released from Sergeant Hibbett's custody with a caution, Iris

Mayall and Rita Brewster watched the fervent exchange between Tyrell and Kathy. "Not a word, Iris we've been warned. I for one do not want to spend another night in Sergeant Hibbett's jail. It was so humiliating being marched through town like a common criminal. I certainly didn't expect to be treated in such a manner."

"If Sergeant McCready had still been in charge, we would have received worse than that. He was always so forceful and aggressive. At least Sergeant Hibbett is a little more respectful toward our maturity. We'll put it all behind us now and start preparing for the church bazaar. Mrs. Pierce and Mrs. Rykker have kindly offered to help us again this year. If those friends of hers are staying I'll rope them in as well." Rita glanced over to Tyrell again, "I hope he's not planning to marry her."

~ * ~

From the garden swing on the porch of Ravens Lodge, her new home, Emily Simpson stared out across the eternal forest. Loon Lake was so vast it appeared to be drawing the entire pine wood into it shimmering depths. Somewhere out there Deacon had realised his dream of reuniting his mother and father. It was wonderful news so it was with some guilt she found herself missing him and Clayton. Prowling the streets of the tiny hamlet of Maskek had not produced any results, she'd even drawn a blank at Stanley Cuthand's coffee house.

"I'd like to meet Deacon's father but I don't suppose it'll happen yet. Perhaps one day."

Closing her eyes Emily let her mind wander over the past two years from the day she first arrived in Maskek to teach at the high school, to her first meeting with Deacon, the only Indian student she'd ever seen or had the pleasure to teach. To the terrifying events surrounding the demon Arcus and how her life had become inexplicably entangled with the young Indian and the evil forces that affected him and his family, inadvertently leading to the death of her husband.

"I'm so glad it's over. I can breathe now and relax." She smiled dreamily. "It wasn't all bad, Deacon did come to me that night, oh such a night. Well, not to worry," she patted her stomach, "I'll soon have something just as wonderful."

Overhead a pair of ravens landed on the roof. "Hello, nice to see you back."

Inside her uterus the baby kicked.

CHAPTER FIFTY-SEVEN

Again, Captain Virgil McNally stared out across the lake his head ringing with the sound of the wolves.

~ * ~

Something was stirring inside Deacon, he seemed distracted, wary but fully alert. His nostrils twitched, his black eyes piercing. Glancing to the left, to the right, ahead and behind him he stopped abruptly.

"You sure are jumpy. What's up?" Clayton asked.

"I don't know. I feel kinda strange, pulled someplace, like a longing for something. I haven't felt this way before...it's weird."

"Aw jeez, I hope this isn't any indication of another demon this way comes."

Grinning at his best friend Deacon said, "I figure we can tackle anything now. What could be worse than the Unthinkable?"

"Give me a minute I'll think of something."

"Maybe it's the wolves..."

"They're starting to get to me, why don't you go talk to them. I swear you're half wolf anyway."

Deacon didn't answer instead he lifted his face to the Wapiti Hills. His mother Lupin understood the wolves as if she were one of them, compelled to follow them whenever they appeared. He shared the same ability, the same compulsion, the need to be among them in their commanding and noble presence. When Deacon was a child, his grandfather the late Chief Eagle Hawk, had told him the tale of the wolf woman.

Voicing his thoughts, he said, "Grandfather didn't say if she was completely human."

"What's that?"

"Nothing, I was just thinking out loud."

The eerie and haunting howl of the wolves came again, beautiful in its lamenting. Deacon could feel his heart drumming madly against his ribs, his stomach twisting and tumbling. He shivered almost with desire. Tears filled his eyes for no reason he could think of. He brushed them away with a trembling hand. The power of the wolf was strong.

Observing Deacon closely Clayton remained quiet. He was certain he could anticipate each of Deacon's moods and emotions and usually he presumed correctly. In the thirteen years they'd known each other they had hardly left each other's side. Today was different. He was completely baffled, bereft of any explanation. Concern soon replaced his confusion. Observing the warriors riding with them he saw nothing out of the ordinary that might explain his best friend's behaviour.

~ * ~

With the day of the church bazaar looming, Emily Simpson devoted her time to baking cakes and preparing food for the event.

"If I'd still been teaching, I wouldn't have had time for this. To think I didn't want to be a lady of leisure, I'm actually quite enjoying it."

Country music playing loudly on Emily's stereo drowned out the incessant howling of the wolves so she wasn't aware that it had increased significantly since first thing this morning.

Knocking on the door startled her out of her reverie. "If that's Rita wanting my cakes she'll have to wait. She's so impatient." Wiping floury hands on her apron, Emily strode over to the front door and pulled it open. "Come back later Rita I haven't finished baking yet...Oh my goodness, Deacon, Clayton this is a surprise. What brings you here?" Behind them she saw the warrior elite. Emily stood back to let them in. "Has something happened?"

"Ma'am," Clayton said, "you asked us to visit when you got settled so here we are."

"But the warriors why are they here? Is there trouble?"

"No ma'am," Deacon replied, "they're with me."

"Now he's Chief he's not supposed to go anywhere without them," Clayton explained "not that he always does as he's told."

"I wouldn't have thought he needed protecting."

"He's the Chief, Mrs. Simpson he's a target for every Tom, Dick or Harry that wants to start a war. His grandfather Eagle Hawk thwarted numerous attempts on his person over the years. The warriors always ride with the Chief, they won't be any trouble."

"I'm sure they won't. Come in, all of you and see what I've done with the place. It's so much easier to manage than that big house we had. I don't think Steve would have liked it he was a bit of a show off. He always wanted bigger and better. I love it here. The ravens and I have become close friends. They seem to be bringing me good luck." Emily unconsciously touched her stomach.

Deacon immediately noticed and glanced at Clayton.

"Sure hope it belongs to Steve," Clayton whispered catching the expression in his best friend's eyes.

"Something smells good," Deacon said.

"Oh, that's my cake it's for the bazaar."

"Mrs. Brewster roped you in too, huh."

"Yes, and almost everyone in town who can mix flour."

"Clayton's pretty good at that," Deacon grinned, "he used to do it all the time when he was at home. How are you Mrs. Simpson?"

"I'm absolutely fine and even better for seeing you both. You haven't been around for a while."

"Cap'n McNally keeps us pretty busy," Clayton said.

Outside Ravens Lodge the wolves crept stealthily towards the house. Approaching the building from behind they fanned out until all four corners and the front and back doors were covered by members of the pack. Patiently they waited.

~ * ~

"I heard some terrible rumours about Rita Brewster," Emily said, cutting them all a slice of cake, "Are they true?"

"Depends on what you heard," Deacon replied picking up the

cake. "Thank you."

"She had an affair with another man while she was still married to her husband?"

"He wasn't a man, he was a demon..."

The sharp knife clattered to the floor. Emily stared at Deacon, stunned "A demon? It wasn't just me who was targeted, then?"

"When you had us do a paper on mythology at school," Clayton said, "I told you then this town was steeped in dark secrets. Mrs. Brewster wasn't targeted, she chose to go with Damien."

"Are you telling me she was one of Damien's disciples? How could she be; she was a stalwart member of the church, Reverend Solomon's right hand woman..."

"Yeah and we all know what happened to the reverend."

Deacon placed the slice of cake back on the plate.

"Don't you like it?" Clayton asked.

Distracted, Deacon didn't reply. His skin was prickling as if thousands of ants were crawling across it, his legs felt heavy and his heart rate was rapidly increasing.

"Deke, what is it?"

Wordlessly he stepped into Emily's lounge and removed the needle from the record on Emily's stereo. The howling had stopped and the explosive silence was deafening. Unnerved by the sudden quiet, Emily grabbed Clayton's arm. "Why have they stopped?"

Clayton moved over to the window of the lounge, he counted six wolves strung out around the lodge their bodies tense and expectant, their yellow eyes focused on the front door, which was open to the forest. His breathe stuck in his throat. Deacon strode over to the door and came face to face with a beautiful, black wolf. Locking eyes with the bold and majestic creature he moved toward her.

He said she knew him.

Leaving their posts, the smaller grey wolves fell in behind the young Chief, circling as if to protect him. Dropping to his knees and then onto his hands he felt the weirdest sensation as if looking at the world through the eyes of a wolf. The black female was licking him affectionately.

Recovering from the initial shock of seeing so many wolves outside the lodge, Clayton shook his head, "What the hell?" He counted six wolves. When he looked again there were seven. A black wolf walked by the side of the big female. Deacon was nowhere to be seen.

"Deacon," Clayton called sprinting through the door. "Where are you?"

As the magnificent beasts loped away the second black wolf turned his head and looked directly at Clayton. He stepped back, startled. The wolf's eyes were human.

"Deacon?" Clayton's heart was thundering alarmingly inside his chest. "His mother's name was Lupin. Lupin means wolf."

To be continued in book three.

Talulah Bearhead's village exists only in the author's imagination the encampment in no way represents any actual Native village or reserve.

With respect for Native American culture and mythology, I have tried to convey a way of life taken from different aspects of the First Nations culture especially the Cree, to fit the story they are the author's thoughts and ideas and not necessarily those of the people themselves.

There are many true facts within the story but some events have been fictionalised.

Lucia Carter Keates

About the Author

I was born in the market town of Leek, North Staffordshire, UK. Presently living in Derbyshire, UK. With two corn snakes, a leopard gecko and a very smart and cocky cockatiel. I lived and worked in Alberta and Saskatchewan, Canada for many years, part of that time with the Cree Indians, some of whom became my friends. From here I was able to continue my love of and interest in the people of First Nations and their culture.

Among my other interests are gothic weekends in Whitby, the local theatre of which I am a member, dancing and most types of music. I have two grown sons who are very supportive of my writing. This is my second novel to be published by Rogue Phoenix Press. The first book in the trilogy is *Child of the Heathen.* The third is underway.

Child of the Heathen

People are dying inexplicably in Maskek and the local police are divided as to the cause. It's been happening for centuries.

For Deacon Pierce who has grown up with the legends and mythology of the First Nations Cree, a visit to his teacher's home unlocks the door to his father's tortured past.

In 1750 Jonathan Sparkling Eyes Hare signed away his mortal soul and those of his unborn children, for life eternal: a deal with a demon or a creature of ancient Cree legend?

When nightmares and darker visions begin to affect Deacon's health and sanity, his white, adopted mother is forced to reveal the truth about his bloodline and the sinister events surrounding his father Jonathan and his lover Damien Drew.

Can past and present combine to prevent Deacon's death?

Preface

Thomas Mason proudly dusted off the last of the shelved books for the final time. He was nearing the time when the Guardian of the Souls would be just another anguished spirit trapped forever in the twilight between two worlds. He looked forward to his release with morbid expectation.

The years weighed heavily on his sagging shoulders, the strain of hiding his secret for countless lifetimes, taking its toll. This day he would impart the crushing burden upon the shoulders of another. She came towards him now stepping out bravely to take from him the responsibility of centuries.

Chapter One

The Wapiti Hills, Alberta, Canada 1968

Sergeant McCready of the Royal Canadian Mounted Police hauled the body of a young hiker from the chilling waters of Bittern Creek. McCready glanced at his partner, Constable Abel Cain Hibbett, an expression of distaste on his weathered countenance,

"This is the second body we've found in as many weeks, with the heart missing. I want to know why. Find out who he is, where he's from and if he has any relatives."

"No driving licence," Constable Hibbett said as he searched through the sodden pockets of the young man's shirt and jeans, "but I did find this card in his wallet. Think it says his name is Jerry Marsden, date of birth January 1945 or '46. He has or had an appointment with what looks like a Doctor Eldon or Alston, in Fort McMurray. Can't read the date or time, the creek took care of that."

He handed McCready the water smudged handwritten card. Inside the young man's shirt Constable Hibbett found a folded paper map, "I'm guessing this a route map, probably the reason he was in the hills but I can't find an address for him."

"It's a helluva way to end a hiking trip. Until we've got more information keep this one under wraps."

~ * ~

Maskek High School, Alberta 1968

"I saw the cops heading into the Wapiti hills on my way here," Bobby announced to his fellow students in the senior class at Maskek High, "They got a report of something bad happening up there. They were going hell bent for leather. They've been twice already this month. I'd sure like to know what brought it on this time." He glanced at the teacher, "Whose paper is she reading now?"

"It's Deacon's. Can't you tell?" Ross said. "He hates it when she reads his work in class."

"Yeah, that's why he's keeping quiet," Deacon's best friend, Clayton Rykker, remarked. "He's hoping if he stays silent, she'll forget he's here." Clayton turned to face the young Cree Indian sitting next to him "You're lucky she isn't asking you to read it out loud."

"No way am I standing out in front of the class."

"Not much chance of that, Clayt, he's teacher's pet."

Grinning broadly, Deacon said, "You godda problem with that, Ross?"

"Not me, man. I was just wondering if you'd bought her an apple today." He ducked as Deacon hurled a book at him.

"Indians don't do apples, "Clayton quipped. "Horses are more his style and plenty of 'em."

"Deacon, behave yourself, I'm trying to read your essay," Emily Simpson told him, glancing over the top of the paper, "and pick up your book."

Lowering his eyes, the young Indian turned away, "Yes ma'am." Amidst good natured catcalls he retrieved the book and returned to his desk.

"What you've written is quite impressive, Deacon. When I asked you all to do a class study on mythology, I never expected anything so in depth. This is by far the best paper I've read up to now..."

"Told you he was teacher's pet," Ross mouthed to Melissa and Leona where they sat to his left.

"If I was a teacher, he'd sure be *my* pet..." Melissa responded dreamily.

Rolling his eyes Ross gave his attention to his teacher as she directed another question to the young Cree. "You mentioned something called a misi...misiski...how is it pronounced? "

"*Msikinepikwa.* It means great horned serpent. It's common to most Algonquin nations, to which my people the Cree belong," Deacon told her. "*Msikinepikwa* lives in the lake. It is said that he eats humans..."

"You mean it lives in *Loon* Lake?" Bobby asked his eyes wide with wonderment.

"He lives in many lakes."

"Wow, no kidding?"

"You truly believe this, Deacon?"

"Yes ma'am."

"Boy, are you stupid," Ryan Hoffman scoffed. "I can't believe you've been living among us white folks for twelve years and you've learned nothin.' I figured all that superstitious nonsense went out with the caveman."

"That will do, Ryan." Emily told him sternly before he started a war. "Everybody is entitled to their own beliefs, even you. Deacon, you've mentioned another creature here called a *Wendigo* but you haven't written anything about it. What is it?"

The young Cree's face fell, alarm showed in his black eyes. "The *Wendigo* is a demon spirit." He glanced toward the distant hills and for a fleeting moment a cold, inexplicable fear assaulted him "I don't wanna talk about it."

"You scared, momma's boy?" Ryan asked, "You talk tough, carry a knife like some great Indian warrior, but you run to your momma when things don't go your way. Too bad she's not here to hold your hand—"

Deacon spun in his chair, his eyes riveted on Ryan's face "You wanna get home tonight?"

Ryan recoiled, apparently startled by the threat in Deacon's tone.

"Back off, Deke." Clayton told him. "The guy's not worth it."

Turning to Ryan he said, "Ain't you learned yet, Hoffman? Don't ever mess with my brother. Cool it, Deke."

It was evident Ryan's unkind remark annoyed Leona as she piped up, "Just because you don't get along with your folks doesn't mean everyone is the same. They used to call Elvis 'momma's boy' when he was at school, but it didn't stop him becoming successful, did it? You should keep your mouth shut, Ryan."

"What's Elvis got to do with it?" Ross asked.

"Ryan made it sound dirty as if it's a bad thing to be close to your mom. I think it's lovely. More of us should feel that way."

Clayton attempted to diffuse the hostility between Deacon and Ryan. "That didn't accomplish much, did it?"

"Made *me* feel better," but the haunted look in his eyes remained.

To distract him, Clayton said, "Deke, do you know you have an accent?"

"I have an accent?"

"Sure. It signifies your Native heritage."

"You mean it gives me away; not the colour of my skin or my hair, huh, just my accent?"

"Aw hush up. I was merely stating a fact. I'm surprised Mrs. Simpson didn't notice. She notices everything else about you."

Feeling Melissa's eyes on the back of his head Deacon knew any minute now her hands would be in his waist-long black hair.

"He is so sexy. He can come to my bed anytime," Melissa whispered to Leona.

"Mine first. You'll have to wait in line."

"If there *is* a serpent in Loon Lake, Mrs. Simpson," Ross chuckled, "you'd better watch out, it's awful close to your house."

"Near to my house, do you know where I live?"

"Everybody knows where you live, Mrs. Simpson," Deacon told her. "We all watched it being built."

"I realise this is a small town, but have you nothing better to do?"

"Nope," Clayton said. "Anything that happens here is big news especially when it involves chopping down the trees all the way back to the Wapiti Hills. That was unnecessary."

Glancing through the classroom window, Emily's gaze was inadvertently drawn beyond the school boundaries to the grass and pine covered hills that back dropped the serene and beautiful Loon Lake. Wherever you lived in Maskek, the lake and the hills were always in sight, as if this town sprung from the water.

"We were hoping the land would be reclaimed by the earth," Deacon replied, "I guess some people had other ideas."

"Well it's a lovely house and it does make the most of the spectacular views. It's a lot of house for what we paid for it. It should have been priced much higher. My husband is in real estate, so he's very much aware of the cost of housing. One of the reasons we moved to Maskek was because property is much cheaper out here but ours was a steal."

"What was the other reason?" Ross asked.

"It's a bit personal so I'd rather keep it a secret."

"Know what the biggest secret in Maskek is, ma'am...why people bother to live here at all."

Deacon jumped, startled as Melissa clamped onto his hair.

"Whoa, Deke," Clayton chortled, "did ya think the monsters got ya?"

Grinning sheepishly Deacon recovered his composure and gave his attention to his teacher.

"Can we forget about my house for now and get on with the lesson? We were talking about the monster in the lake..."

"Here also in the rivers are the *memekwesiw,* the water spirits. They're called the little people," Deacon said.

"Do *they* eat humans?" Bobby wanted to know.

"They're mischievous but not dangerous as long as you treat them with respect. If you don't, the spirits will capsize your canoe," Deacon grinned.

"Wow, no kidding?"

"We've got to entertain ourselves somehow," Leona explained "Maskek is hardly a metropolis. In one year, we have a strawberry social and barn dance, that's coming up soon and a church bazaar everyone gets roped into. Maskek Indian Daze is a big event. That's when we really get to see our Native brothers and sisters in traditional regalia. There is a parade and traditional dancing, native handicraft workshops, and feats of endurance, among other things. There's much more to it than that, but you have to be present to enjoy it. It's our favourite event. We have a summer ball held here at school, and once a year the rodeo comes to town. That's the extent of our annual calendar. Easy to see why a new house being built is such a big deal."

"Don't forget the Saturday night dance once a month in the school hall," Clayton reminded her. "That's the town's one contribution to its youth."

"How did we get from water spirits to social events?" Emily asked.

"Because listening to tales of Indian folklore is entertainment for us," Leona said.

"Are you seriously interested in this subject or is just because I asked you to write a paper about it?

"Sure, we are," Ross assured her "living so close to the Indians it's hard not to be. You're the first teacher who's considered the supernatural as a subject."

"There's no such thing as the supernatural," Ryan scoffed, "they're just stories made up to scare us when we're kids so we'll behave. My folks were always threatening me and my sister with the bogeyman. It's bullshit."

Turning to Clayton, a puzzled expression on his face Deacon asked, "What's the bogey man? I never heard of him before."

"I guess you won't have been told about that. It's kinda what you'd call a bad spirit that comes to take you away when you've been naughty."

"Mrs. Simpson, Maskek is a very boring, backward town. You'd think it was 1868 not 1968," Melissa said. "If a girl shortens her dress by an inch, she's a shameless hussy and the whole town will know about it. It's really pathetic."

Rubbing her chin with a perfectly manicured finger, Emily said, "That's all the more reason for us to seek out the unknown, to stretch our horizons. To go beyond what our parents have been taught in the past."

For six months since moving into her spanking new six-bedroom house Emily taught at the local high school. Originally from the city of Edmonton, she found teaching in Maskek's only high school to be more rewarding than it had been in the city. The atmosphere was relaxed and the students and staff generally appeared to have a lot of support and a stronger rapport. On the surface Maskek was quiet, mundane, uncluttered giving her a sense of security but like any other town it bred its share of rebellious troublemakers.

As early as her first day on the job she had been stunned by Deacon Pierce's innocent charm and good looks. He respected his elders and authoritarian figures a characteristic unheard of in the majority of her teenage students. Deacon was also the first and only Native Canadian student she'd ever had the pleasure to teach, let alone actually meet. As far as she could tell, Deacon was the only Indian student in the school, which surprised her.

Emily was about to continue when there was a knock on the door and the school secretary entered the classroom. "I'm sorry to disturb you

Mrs, Simpson, but there's a phone call for Clayton. Would you mind if he came and took it? It's your father, Clayton."

"My pa, what does he want? I figured now my mom and dad are divorced he'd have returned to his folk's ranch in Montana..."

"Go ahead, Clayton," Emily told him.

"Where're you going, Clayt?" Deacon asked, glancing up.

"My pa's on the phone. I'll be right back."

As Clayton left with the secretary, Melissa slipped into the seat next to Deacon and kissed him on his cheek. Behind her black, pointed framed glasses her hazel flecked eyes twinkled with wickedness. "Would you like me to keep you company until Clayton comes back, honey? I know how much you two miss each other." Deacon threw her a smile that sent shivers spiralling down her back.

"Way to go, Melissa," Bobby said.

Having recovered from his earlier tussle with Deacon and with Clayton out of earshot Ryan Hoffman began to feel a little bolder "What the hell do you see in him, Melissa, you could have any guy in class...including me. I'll give you a good time."

Screwing up her face, Melissa said, "Geez, why would I want you? I'd probably wind up on my back in someone's barn with you slathering all over me." Her friends giggled conspiratorially.

"He's a goddamn Indian, for Christ's sake."

"I think he's cute, and it's none of your business who my friends are."

"Most folks don't have time for Indians," he sneered, "but I guess your mom did, huh, Deke? She's godda find a guy someplace, doesn't she?" His demeanour was pure evil.

The smile leaving his face instantly, a scalpel could not have sliced through the tension as Deacon rounded on Ryan, his eyes glittering, his voice dripping venom, "You got anything else to say about my mother, 'cos if you do, you'd better say it now while you still got your tongue."

Bobby jumped out of the way knocking his chair over in his haste as Deacon pounced on Ryan. A shattering, nervous silence descended over the entire class, their eyes on the Bowie knife strapped to Deacon's left hip. Time and time again he'd been asked to leave the weapon at home.

Horrified that he might actually use it, Emily shouted, "Stop it, Deacon."

"You don't hear the things he says about my mother, Mrs. Simpson. Nobody hears. If they did, they wouldn't care."

"That isn't true, Deacon. I care. Your friends care..."

Without releasing his hold on Ryan's neck, Deacon turned to face her...and she saw the hurt in his dark eyes, the tears he was trying so hard to hide, and felt a lump welling up in her throat.

"I can see you're upset," Emily told him gently, "but hurting Ryan won't help. We can talk about it if you want to."

"That's gonna fix it?"

"I'm not saying it will fix things, but it might help."

Ryan tried to back away, but Deacon had him against the wall. There was nowhere for him to run. Rigid in their seats the students waited apprehensively for the young Indian's next move. Bobby was unaware of how strongly he was gripping the edge of the desk until his fingers went numb. This was an explosive subject no one wanted to talk about.

Deacon leaned closer to Ryan until they were almost touching, but the knife remained in its beaded sheath.

Biting her nails, Melissa turned toward the door, hoping to see Clayton returning. He entered a few seconds later.

One glance was all Clayton needed. Speaking quietly, he addressed Deacon by his true name, "Spirit of the Wind, let him go." Striding over to him he, placed a hand on his best friend's shoulder.

For a moment, Deacon resisted then loosened his grip on Ryan's neck.

"Okay, that's good," Clayton said.

Shaking his head, he told Ryan, "You never learn, do you?"

His legs quivering, Ryan went back to his desk.

Grateful for Clayton's intervention, a relieved Emily Simpson sat down. "I don't know how you do it, Clayton, but thank you."

Her hands were trembling as she picked up Deacon's essay.

His arm still around Deacon's shoulder, Clayton escorted him back to his desk. In the Cree tongue he asked, "Tell me what happened, my brother."

www.ingramcontent.com/pod-product-compliance
Lightning Source LLC
Chambersburg PA
CBHW061928170626
46813CB00006B/2339